High Praise for **TAKEN**

" [AN] ENGROSSING THRILLER... A LYRICALLY WRITTEN AND FASCINATING TALE."—*Booklist*

"*Taken* is a tough and tender thriller by a writer who knows the world of the heart as well as the world of crime. Kathleen George takes the reader on an intense, suspenseful ride in which even evil has a human face. This is a moving, gripping, and multilayered story in which the search for love touches everything, even grief for a lost baby."
—Perri O'Shaughnessy, *New York Times* bestselling author of *Unfit to Practice*

"A thinking person's thriller, WRITTEN WITH SKILL, SELF-CONFIDENCE AND SENSITIVITY—A FINE PIECE OF WORK."—*The Washington Post*

"*Taken* is that rare thriller that gives as much weight to its characters and prose as it does to its ticking-time-bomb plot. The story drew me in, but it was the author's fallible, very human cast that kept me coming back for more. I look forward to reading anything that Kathleen George writes."—George P. Pelecanos, author of *Right As Rain*

"From the opening pages of *Taken* to the final, heart-stopping paragraphs, I was transported by Kathleen George's complex characters and masterful storytelling. IT'S A RARE PLEASURE TO READ A NOVEL SO BRILLIANTLY PLOTTED, SO RICHLY PEOPLED, AND SO ELEGANTLY WRITTEN."
—Margot Livesey, author of *Criminals*

"[An] offbeat thriller... *Taken* boasts three ingredients too often missing from the suspense genre: irony, humor, and plausibly flawed, cliché-free characters."
—*Entertainment Weekly*

"A GRIPPING THRILLER with real emotional power and remarkably subtle characterization."
— *Kirkus Reviews*

TAKEN

KATHLEEN GEORGE

A DELL BOOK

Published by
Dell Publishing
a division of
Random House, Inc.
1540 Broadway
New York, New York 10036

The characters and events in this novel are fictional and in no way intended to represent actual persons or events. The closing dates of Ralph's Discount City, bits of local geography, and the Pirates' playing schedule for 1998 have been altered, when necessary, to serve the story.

Library of Congress Catalog Card Number: 00-065706

ISBN: 0-385-33547-4

Reprinted by arrangement with Delacorte Press

Manufactured in the United States of America
Published simultaneously in Canada

For Hilary

For Hillary

ACKNOWLEDGMENTS

I would like to thank—for extraordinary generosity in sharing time and knowledge during the preparation of this work—Commander Ronald B. Freeman, Head, Major Crimes, Pittsburgh Police; Marc Silverman, librarian, University of Pittsburgh Barco Law Library; and the Pittsburgh Branch of the FBI.

I would also like to thank my agent, Ann Rittenberg, and my editor, Jackie Cantor, for their advocacy and superb guidance throughout the publication process.

TAKEN

1

IF RICHARD CHRISTIE HAD SEEN HER STANDING ON SIXTH, IF he'd been driving his dusty blue unmarked Taurus, headed for a crime scene on the hazy, humid morning of June 26, would he have noticed her? Or would she, if she'd stopped, turned, looked outward into the rows and rows of cars, looked through dirty or rolled-down windows, into faces, have seen him? *He* thinks, later, he would have. She, well, she wasn't looking outward, she knows that, hadn't been for a while.

If he had noticed her, he would have felt an automatic nudge of lust. And why? The hair, partly, she had long hair, which he liked. Abundant. Very large eyes, a dark gray-green he would call them, and not at all serene; unusual bone structure about the cheeks and mouth; a thin face with determined curved lines under the eyes. Most people would have described her hair as black, but as a policeman, he knew it was actually a dark brown. She had a look of summer, islands. Put her in a sarong, have her sell suntan lotion. That kind of thing.

Still. If he'd seen her then, he would have seen sadness in her and understood she was one of what nearly all of us are in his opinion—motherless children.

She, she blamed herself for not looking outward. A narcissistic blot, she had it. A constant soul-searching. She didn't think much about how she looked, although most people would have been surprised to hear that, since she dressed and walked with what passed for self-awareness, even self-love.

If she'd looked outward toward Christie, she would not have noticed him. Even closer up—if he'd popped on his blinkers, hopped out of the car, if someone had introduced them—she would have dismissed him. A detective, essentially a cop. A thickheaded flatfoot. Light-years away. Maybe even a Republican. Not somebody she could know or want to know.

SHE STOOD ON SIXTH WITH MICHAEL. HE HELD HIS BRIEFCASE stiffly. People walked around them. "I have to go, Marina," he said. "I'm supposed to be there by ten-fifteen."

"It's okay."

"I'd drive you, but it would make me late."

"I know."

He offered a new suggestion, dropping each word reluctantly. "You could take me and then pick me up. Then you'd have the car."

There was tightness around his eyes as if he fought a glare. She felt badly for him, wished she could embrace him, but that was the point, she couldn't, hadn't been able to get in for a long time now. The tense muscles of his face worked hard as he tried to stay calm.

There was a moment, before he turned and strode off, in which she might have undone everything—taken back what she'd just said upstairs in Dr. Caldwell's office. And she almost did, out of agony for the look on his face. But something stopped her words. The way he tightened his lips, maybe, the reminder of recent cruelties. From that point on, many things were decided.

Dr. Caldwell had asked her, "And do you still feel you ought to leave, be on your own?" The homework assignment had been to think this through, or more accurately, feel it through, Marina having lost her ability to act for herself instead of for Michael. "You keep saying what *he* wants," Dr. Caldwell had pointed out. This morning Marina caught Dr. Caldwell's almost imperceptible nod when she said she'd decided a separation might be better for both of them. "I think we're hurting each other too much." Him on the love seat, her on the matching sofa, the doctor in the high-backed chair, all of them on their sandy-colored islands. Again that nod. Or her imagination.

Michael made an exhalation of pretend affront, surprise.

Dr. Caldwell turned to Michael. "It's been going on for a long time," she reminded him.

"Whatever she wants. I don't care." He sank back with an arm around the shoulder of the sofa and looked toward his own crossed legs, unable to make eye contact.

Dr. Caldwell looked hard at him, but he didn't look up. "You don't care?" she asked finally.

"No. I've had it."

"What?"

He looked up. "Failure. I can't take any more failure."

"Separation—I know I've said this—has rules. You have to make them and keep to them. Decide exactly what you want out of it. You told me your wishes, your needs, didn't you, last week?" Here she turned to Marina.

Marina said, "It's hard to remember. Change. Peace. Peace is what I want."

"You told me last week, 'Self-knowledge. A chance to figure out what I feel.' " Dr. Caldwell seemed to be reading from her yellow legal pad. The room was a court, of sorts, judge, plaintiff, and accused.

Marina was exhausted with trying.

Dr. Caldwell had looked downward at her tablet and honored the seriousness of this about-to-happen parting with a long silence. For a long time, nobody said anything.

"I'm so sad," Marina said finally. "And yet it still feels the right thing to do."

Even the way Michael bristled, the little bit he moved, as soon as she showed the soft underbelly of her sadness, spoke of the violence in him. Marina's breath caught. If she needed a warning not to go soft now, this was it. He had not struck her except for that once. But the books, papers, dishes, he had thrown, broken. He had been on the *verge* of striking her a million times. The threat of it was almost worse, given her family history, than if he'd hit her.

Dr. Caldwell by now knew all about Marina's family history—a violent father who'd struck her mother repeatedly, her sister as well, and Marina sometimes, too, or began to, but somehow left off, mysteriously collapsed into himself. As a child of ten, Marina had yelled at her father, "Don't you ever hit my mother again!" And her father had stopped moving forward—chaos all around them, the table turned over, the pie makings on the floor. Her mother whimpering in a corner. After that, he waited till Marina was at school to go crazy. He was clearly afraid of her, a child. Twice she called the police about him. Dr. Caldwell puzzled over these stories, saying she thought there was something unusual, forceful in Marina even when there didn't seem to be.

And the blame, a few years later, on Marina for his illness and death. Can you kill someone with a look, with accusations? Her mother and sister seemed to imply she had.

She was afraid to look at Michael, today, upstairs . . . did not want to hurt him . . . did not want to hurt herself, either . . . could not understand how this was her drama, to be enacted over and over, being faced with violence and seeking to stop it. Why? Are people born into certain patterns?

She'd said, riding down the elevator, "I'll take the bus home. I don't mind."

He did not say, "Is it real, then? Are you leaving?"

She did not say, "I meant it, I'm leaving." The discussion was over, and now only the action to be done.

She watched him walk up the street until he was out of sight and felt grief that she had once loved him and didn't anymore. People who turned to look at her probably sensed her making a decision, saw her almost run after him, but in the end, *not*. And in that pause, she was shifting roles. Right there on Sixth Avenue, beneath Dr. Caldwell's office. Deciding to go it alone. Small steps forward, acting on her own interests for once, even if afraid.

"You are too accommodating," Dr. Caldwell said once. "People take advantage."

"She's too fucking saintly," Michael said. "Not a great turn-on!"

"No," Dr. Caldwell said seriously. "No, it's not."

After Marina watched Michael hurry up the street, head bent, she turned the other way and went toward Liberty Avenue. A tiny plan was forming. She and Michael were scheduled to see Dr. Caldwell next week to work out finances and rules: How would they separate? Would they see each other, call each other in that time? How often? Who would pay for what?

The fact was, they had hardly enough money for one household, definitely not enough for two. Michael had loans to pay off, they had a high mortgage, their bank account was a mess. One of their cars had broken down and they'd given it up—just told the guys at the station to sell it. They were down to one car, but Marina was going to need a car, on her own, in her own place.

They'd lived beyond their means, like so many in their generation, with their Cuisinarts and all-wool carpets and two cars. The dull facts emerged six months back, along with everything else, bigger things than money, when they first went to Dr. Caldwell, pretending to themselves they needed to figure out what to do *differently,* but really in the beginning stages of unwinding from each other.

Beside myself, Marina thought, feeling the truth of that expression. She was someone else walking along beside her body. Why, she couldn't even remember where the bus stop was! Finally remembered. After she did her one tiny bit of investigation, she would walk up past that newspaper box and take the bus home.

She headed toward the Clark Building.

All she wanted was truth and yet she kept up appearances, walking as if she could think, and people smiled back at her, one jaunty man, one old woman, as if this were some other time in her life when she was a woman of fashion, feeling good. Was this her way of not offending anyone with the dark wells of sadness in her?

Had she become an actress—Dr. Caldwell thought so—because she had a need to turn rage and grief into something acceptable? Make something good out of it.

Not bother anybody.

And so she wore a pink-and-orange-flowered sheath dress, classic cut, short. A small black shoulder bag, an old thing, of black leather, very un-summery, and black strapped sandals with small stacked heels. Her starburst earrings picked up and reflected the colors of the dress. A costume for an Italian comedy. And this on a day her life was falling apart. A director had told her once that she was like the Marina in Shakespeare's *Pericles;* she confused people; empathy and beauty together, he said, is a curse. Because people don't know what to do, aren't sure they like it. You seem to be flaunting something—*goodness*—he told her. And it makes them feel kind of shabby with their grubby inner lives.

She understood. Kindness in an unkind world seemed disingenuous. *Was* disingenuous. Even laughable. Well, she had changes to make. She was going to be *of* the world from now on, responsive to it, harsher, grabbing.

She crossed the street toward the Clark Building. There was a jewelry shop on the second floor where for years Michael had bought her gold and silver, sapphires and emeralds, adornments for the ears, neck, wrists, fingers. At first, the weight and beauty of the jewelry against her skin seemed a measure of her worth. Now these things felt like blackmail. How could she keep jewelry when she needed money so badly for an apartment, for food?

In the shop, she would be stepping over the line. Onstage to off. She had told only her best friend, Lizzie, that she and Michael were in trouble, not her mother or sister or anyone else. When she asked about selling the jewels back . . . Well, it would be obvious.

Even Lizzie didn't know how bad things really were.

Michael could be charming. People were not going to want to believe the level of his fury at himself, at life, at luck, the way he'd routinely taken it out on her. Her mother and sister would remember Michael teasing, joking with them, and they would think that was the whole of him, for he managed to be charming even when things were very bad between them. Ha. Who was the actor in the family?

The building's lobby was cool and dark, with patterned marble floors and walls. She didn't look around, didn't pay attention to anybody or anything, except the cool green walls with their deco brassy outlining bands. She wished she could rest her head against the smooth marble. A sob began to well up in her and she imagined death was a nice thing, cool, and preferable to living. After all, maybe the trouble was her fault. *Too fucking saintly.* Why did she not strike out for herself? Nobody liked weakness. "You're too nice," the receptionist at the casting agency had said soberly, a hint of instruction in her tone. Who wanted nice?

Suddenly Marina felt light-headed and unsteady. She leaned against the wall. "Better eat something," she heard someone say. She looked up to see the very old man who ran the concessions counter. He had been there every time she ever came in. He looked as if he had sold candy bars and sodas from that spot his whole life.

His counter was full of dusty goods. She wanted one of the chocolate bars, but didn't trust them—where was it she'd bought a Clark bar and opened it to find a tiny worm poking its head up at her? Irrationally, she felt the Granola bar, more newly invented, might be fresher; so she took a chance on it.

While she was paying for the candy bar, she heard the elevator open behind her. "Oh, I ought to get that." She watched the man take her change and begin counting it.

"You don't get it now, you get it a minute from now. Right? That's not so terrible."

"I know."

He looked closely at her. "What's the matter? Your boyfriend giving you a hard time?"

She shook her head.

The elevator doors closed and the thing went upward without her.

Unwrapping the candy bar, she watched a woman who'd evidently just come out of the elevator, leaning over a baby stroller. The woman was twenty-five, maybe less, and she was pretty in a wholesome way, all her features in line, nothing particularly outstanding. She wore a light blue, flower-patterned sundress, and she looked happy. The young mother looked up at Marina and back down to her baby, who waved arms and legs in a wobbly but energetic semaphore. The woman tucked a diaper into a plastic bag, looked around for a waste bin, thought better of it, and tucked the wrapped bag back in the star-spangled one.

Boy, Marina registered, because he wore little blue overalls and a T-shirt underneath that was a sea of small sailboats. Marina always looked at babies, always had, even when she was too young to be so desperate and full of longing as she was now. And that was one of the large strands in the undoing of her marriage, their failure to make a child. In her heart she felt an actual physical pain of longing.

Studying the baby, she was enchanted. He was ordinary enough, she supposed, but she loved the roundness of his blue eyes, the particular way his lips puckered as if he were working hard on a decision—whether to let his mother coo him into good humor or to let out his other complaints now that his diaper had been changed. And so unprivately.

She guessed what the baby's remaining frustrations might be. The heat. The discomfort with new places—dark interiors with marble floors and nobody talking and elevators taking forever and then thunking into place. Poor sweetie, she thought. You don't much like it here, in the dark, in the unfamiliar.

He made a sound. He seemed to hear her unvoiced sympathy. He seemed to like her smile.

All this time, the mother was going through the baby's

star-spangled diaper bag, as if inventorying its contents.
Marina broke off a small corner of the candy bar and ate it,
putting the rest in her purse. The baby watched her chew-
ing, which made her laugh. *You've cheered me up, you clever
fellow,* she thought. The baby laughed as if she'd said it out
loud.

"Hello, little one. Hello."

The baby's legs and arms stopped moving and he
looked at her with something that might be amazement.
Was it her eyes? Something about her voice that mesmer-
ized him? Or did he simply get the message that she liked
him?

Actually, it wasn't unusual. Babies often reacted this
way to her.

His mother stopped and looked up, smiled and looked
down again.

The elevator sank into position once more and its
doors opened. It was empty this time. Marina waved
good-bye to the little boy and he seemed to follow her
with his eyes. She hummed an ongoing prayer for a child
much like him. The elevator moved silently and mysteriously up one floor. Hardly a whisper of machinery working, even when it opened its doors.

In Joy's Antique Jewelry Shop, the owners greeted
Marina by name and said, "Oh, have we got something to
show you!" And before she knew it, before she could stop
them, they had carefully taken out and displayed on a
cloth an emerald ring.

"Oh, that's beautiful," she said, "but I can't. I couldn't."

The owlish young woman named Joy, who kept ebul-
lience in check, and the tall, sober, Greek-looking man
who was her husband nodded sadly.

"I don't know if it's possible, or how you work, but I've
been thinking I might sell a few things back. If you ever
do that."

They looked at her, surprised.

"I have too much," she said quickly. "I'm not wearing
things."

The couple seemed to shrug at the same time. The husband was taking the ring box out of the case and putting the emerald back into it. "Not impossible," he said, summoning a light tone. "This is one of the most beautiful rings we've ever had. We thought of you."

"I could remind you of what I have or just bring the things in."

"Wait and bring them in," Joy said.

Marina was struck by the thought that maybe Joy and her husband couldn't *afford* to buy her rings and bracelets back from her. Theirs was a small specialty shop. What if it threw them off for a month, two months?

But what was she to do? She needed money.

And what *did* people do with jewelry that stood for meanings that no longer existed?

She had only two hundred dollars in her account. Hadn't had an acting job in a year. Needed work. Needed an apartment, a car, furniture, phone service—all of that cost more money than she usually made typing briefs, teaching acting, selling clothing—her piecemeal income.

"Let us know when you're coming in. We'll look up your slips."

"We keep good records," Joy said, shifting position and looking downward for no good reason at all.

Yes, they understood. It made tears come to her eyes and she had to wave a farewell without actually looking back, but they understood that, too, she could tell, from the tone of the good-byes.

When she left Joy's she walked past the other shops, which sold new jewelry. The new glitter didn't appeal to her at all, never had, not compared to a ring or a necklace with history. The rings she wore carried a hundred years of feelings. And the company of other women who made decisions, felt love, got angry, struggled to put a life together.

Marina took the elevator back down to the lobby, thinking briefly of the child in the stroller, sorry to see that he and his mother were gone. She started across town toward the bus stop.

As she walked, she remembered something Michael had said that morning, something so sad she wanted to put it aside. "I tried to give her things I thought she wanted," he told Dr. Caldwell. "I knew I could never be enough for her. I thought she was above me."

Maybe this was a clue to her worst faults. Hers or his. She couldn't tell anymore.

She stopped and looked in Lerner's window, but only because she couldn't move anymore. Shorts, tank tops, a defeated-looking woman moving a mannequin that had been arranged to suggest a confident strut, ridiculous when being dragged at an angle with only the heels on the floor, the arms and knees upward, help-less. Finally, she made herself move. She headed up the street.

For a while she stood at the crowded bus stop, just thinking. At last, the 16A came along and she hopped on, dropped a dollar and a quarter into the box, and started for a seat. In the front of the bus, the scattered passengers were staking out territory with packages, or their arms and legs spread out to discourage anyone from taking the seat next to them. Their angry, sleepy faces told their own stories of unhappiness. Love and money in short supply, no doubt, just like in her life. Plays, comedies, turned on the moment of getting both, like a miracle. Marina headed for the back of the bus as it pulled out jerkily, throwing her off balance. After several quick, balancing steps, she caught on to a pole, swung in a circle, and plopped too hard into an empty row. Well, she was no Cyd Charisse. Clumsy.

In the row in front of her was a man and a baby.

If she hadn't looked. If she had sat in the front of the bus, so many things might have been different.

But she did look, as she always had (on planes, in doctors' waiting rooms, anywhere), toward the sound of a child. In the man's lap was a boy in blue overalls and a T-shirt that was a sea of sailboats. "Oh, hello!" she said. "There you are again!"

For a moment there was stillness.

It seemed the man would turn to her, but he moved his shoulder forward to shield the baby.

Marina's gut reacted long before her mind did. Her stomach dropped. A moment's vertigo seized her—space became fuzzy, the surfaces of things lost their hardness. She floated briefly, then suddenly she felt the surfaces again—windowpane, cold aluminum frame, wall of the bus. Cold air from the bus's air-conditioning hit her body. She was sweating, shivering.

Some other child, she told herself. The man is simply being protective. She looked again.

And the baby looked at her, studied her, making his little thoughtful faces. No, this was the same child, so almost certainly a father or uncle, wouldn't it be, taking the . . . ?

She rode for a while working out a theory that all was innocent. Perhaps a relative had taken over for the afternoon. Yet her stomach continued to register alarm. Why had the man turned away? When she stretched forward to look at the floor around his seat, she saw there was no stroller, no diaper bag, no bottle in sight. This kind of thing was on television all the time—a father in an estranged marriage snatching a child back, running to another city.

The man shifted again, but she still could not see him.

"Hello, little one," she said. "Hello!" Her voice was too high and light, betraying her. "What's his name?"

After a pause the man said, "Brian."

"Hello, Brian," Marina whispered, leaning forward. "Hello, Brian."

With a few sharp jabs of breath to get him going, the baby began to cry. The man muttered angrily and began a crude rocking motion.

"How old is he?"

"Two months."

Marina eased herself back in her seat. The man did not know what he was talking about. The baby was three or four months old. Four. Alert and thoughtful. The child who strained in front of her, trying to look back at her, was surely more than two months old.

The bus driver turned a corner badly, and began to lurch back and forth, cursing, as he tried to avoid hitting parked cars. Everyone watched.

"Bet he's sweating," someone said up front, laughing.

All this time, Marina, being jostled, looked at the child when the driver brought them into view of each other; always the child looked back.

When the bus began to make steady progress again, she made a decision. She got up and sat down in the space next to the man. She had to see more than the undistinguished brown-gray hair, conventionally cut, and the side of the man's cheek.

The man wore dark summer pants and a simple tan sport shirt. He had a large hawkish nose and a receding chin. He looked awkward, a little slow. His eyes, which bulged slightly, were blue—not bright blue like the child's, but a faded, tired color. A spectacles case poked up out of his shirt pocket. Black socks and hard shoes made him look old-fashioned, like a recent immigrant. He did not quite fit in. He was about fifty, possibly a little more, roughly a generation older than she was. He was not overweight, but not toned either. His body looked defeated.

No, the woman in the Clark Building would not have been married to him. . . . They didn't match at all.

The grandfather, possibly. The father's father come to snatch the grandchild home to the *right* side of the family? But he had not thought to bring anything with him, water, milk, juice, diapers. Perhaps on the other end of a brief trip was a grandma who knew what to do.

Perhaps.

She began to memorize. Gray pants, possibly of light wool, a tan shirt with a linen-cotton look. No labels that she could see. No rings on the man's fingers. Moles? Yes, a large one on the right eyebrow and a small one on the left chin. The moles are good, she thought. Remember the moles. His voice? If she had to describe it? She could remember no telling vocal characteristics.

She thought, What am I doing, my life is falling apart, why court someone else's trouble?

The boy she thought of as Brian began to cry again, at first almost tentatively, but then with increasing conviction until he was yowling. Good, she thought, hoping for allies, but the people in the front of the bus only focused more intently on whatever they carried—books, papers, shopping bags. One man went through a handful of change. Did they notice? Did they hear?

"Okay, okay." The man rocked the child crudely.

"He's miserable about something," Marina ventured. "Do you have a bottle somewhere? I'll get it out for you."

"It's okay. We're . . . almost home."

Almost home. General Robinson Street, Reedsdale Avenue. She looked out at the bus lane, the derelict housing off the road to the right, and wondered what "almost home" meant. The man shifted the baby in his arms, but not enough to stop the crying. She almost asked the man where he lived when he moved the child awkwardly to burping position. Now she could no longer see the man's face. Was this the intention?

The change of position had made the crying change tenor. Now it was aggrieved, puzzled, no longer outraged.

The baby's face was only inches away from Marina's.

"Hi. Hi, sweetie." Such dumb surprised faces people made for babies . . . Anything, somersaults, to keep a baby from crying. "Hi," she said in a soothing whisper. "Not so bad, huh? Whatever it was that was bothering you. Not so bad."

And he seemed to consider her truth.

She rode in silence for a while. Brian's wide eyes were brimming and his bottom lip trembled. She made faces and held silent encouraging conversations with him.

A rude jolt to her knee was the first sign the man was fighting back. He shifted in his seat and spread his legs wide so she would have no room. She felt his elbow hard against her upper arm. Wires of anger went through her. She felt her face flush. The rage she felt—something stored up from childhood?—filled her with dread. She withstood the pushing for several minutes, but finally couldn't bear it any longer and got up and went back again to the row behind him.

"... got the message," the man muttered bitterly. The baby's eyes found her again.

She'd seen the man. She could describe him. That was the main thing.

She could see where he got off the bus, and then she could file a report. Was that enough? If she went to the front of the bus, to the man counting change, the woman reading a paperback, to tell them she knew something terrible was happening ... She imagined dazed faces, heads shaking. And perhaps she was wrong. Perhaps the man could explain everything.

Very probably she was wrong. Missing some fact.

She told herself to let it all go. This affair was not her business. Leaning back in the seat, she closed her eyes and ordered herself to think of something else.

Images of Michael came to her. His face loomed up like a swimmer run out of air and pushing toward the surface, measuring endurance against time. She felt a pang of remorse for her part in hurting him. But they had hurt each other. How awful the downward slide is, when things get worse and worse, day by day, for three years.

The bus came to an abrupt stop. She opened her eyes. She leaned forward after all, and tried again. "I met Brian earlier today. Not too long ago."

"Beg pardon?"

"In the Clark Building. With his mother. He was in the Aprica, I think it's called, or a stroller that looked like an Aprica."

"Wrong kid."

"No, it was Brian, all right."

"I'm telling you, you got it wrong. I don't know who you are."

Again her heart pounded.

The man way up in the front had put his change away and was now gathering his things to exit the bus. Another man slept. The woman who read turned a page, yawned grotesquely.

Get off the bus, call the police, she told herself. But if she did, she would lose track of the man.

And what would persuade a police officer? "Don't babies all look alike at that age?" he might counter. "No hair, chubby cheeks. And isn't it possible these clothes you describe are sold in big lots? Same outfit on a thousand kids on any one day?"

She looked at the tiny blue tennis shoes on the baby. Had she seen them before?

MINUTES LATER SHE WAS OFF THE BUS, ON A STREET SHE didn't know at all, in a very run-down part of town, still miles from her own bus stop.

The street she hurried down was surprisingly empty, as streets often are in summer. It was almost ghostly quiet. Marina wanted to slow down, catch her breath, think more clearly, but something pushed her on. She made her way up and over broken sidewalks, almost running, so that when one car did pass her, the driver looked at her as if she might be in trouble. He slowed down, backed up, rolled down the passenger window to ask if she needed help. She shook her head and the man drove on. She could hardly breathe.

Do this one thing, she thought, and then you are free. Then you can take two good long hours to walk the four more miles home. This one thing was: get an address. Give the police something to go on.

The man had gotten off at the corner of the Ohio River Boulevard and Superior and she saw him look back at the bus and at her sitting there. She pretended to be caught up in something out the opposite window. This was a chance she took, letting him go. And as soon as the bus started out again, she rang the bell nonstop until the driver pulled over short of the next block. She lurched forward mumbling something about an emergency and he let her off. Now she was running back a block to where the man got off. She'd managed to keep him in sight, through the bus window, and even when she first got down off the bus to the street, but just after that he'd disappeared. He'd turned left, but she'd caught up to the spot where he did that and couldn't see him any longer.

At the corner of two dreary streets, she stood as still as possible, listening—if she could hear the baby's cry, she could follow it. She heard nothing. And she saw nothing, one or two cars moving, a person walking determinedly past her, but not the tan shirt, the dark pants, the baby in the blue overalls. The block was full of closely spaced buildings, some from the forties and shingled, others more than a hundred years old, all neglected. The grasses around them grew wild; cement steps were broken. She decided the houses to her left were almost completely derelict, but the ones to her right appeared more habitable. Given the man's clothing, not stylish or expensive, but clean and neat . . .

She turned right. Her strapped sandals bit into her feet as she ran. She gritted her teeth and pushed on. When one block produced nothing, she turned to the left, saw what looked like rows of large, better-kept houses, and kept going. A second look told her that many of these houses were run-down as well. One had been damaged by fire, some had windows boarded up. She began to think she'd made the wrong decision.

A teenage boy rode toward her on a bike. Even though it was hot, he wore a long-sleeve shirt with tails. The tails bagged out as he rode. She hesitated and then hailed him. At first she thought he hadn't seen her wave, but he circled once and weaved toward her.

"Did you see a man carrying a baby going down this street? A minute ago?" she asked, breathless.

The boy kept pedaling and circling, momentum being the main thing for him at his age, the feeling of movement, possibility. His figure eight turned him away from her when she asked her question but toward her when he answered.

"Yeah. I saw him."

"Do you know him?"

"No," he said, facing away.

"Do you know where he went?"

Back to her again. "One of those buildings, I think." He pointed to a row of three nearly identical houses, brick with brown wood trim.

"Did you ever see him around before?"

"Maybe. I think so. I'm not sure." He slowed down and stopped, curious now. He took a hard look at her.

"Which building?"

"Like maybe the middle one of those three brown ones."

"Thanks."

That should be enough, shouldn't it? she asked herself. Enough for the police.

Yet she, too, was possessed by a kind of momentum, and went toward the buildings to read the nameplates on the door. If she was going to give a report, it would be a complete report, with enough facts to be believable. She'd like nothing more than to be proved wrong, a meddler, a fool. That was preferable to the other—Brian, the boy she thought of as Brian, somewhere among strangers and unable to understand why his mother was no longer with him.

The middle brown building. She went up to it. From the mailboxes, it was clear there was one apartment on each floor. There were no name tags for any of the floors, but there was a scrap of paper left over for the second, a corner, which was blank.

This is enough, she thought. I should go.

But the momentum, or something like it, kept her moving. She reached out gingerly and tried the front door, expecting nothing. It opened, thrilling her. She found herself in an unlit hallway, which had once been lovely with gleaming dark wood. The oak wall panels were still unharmed by paint, but they were scratched and dusty. The floor was mainly covered in a worn green carpet.

Up the stairs. She couldn't help herself. The open door was the one, yes. For she could hear the baby, but more than that, she could hear the *hush*, which was the dead giveaway. There was no comforting adult voice trying to soothe the child. She stood in the hallway taking in her discovery.

A large, thickly built man came to the door. He was

bald, or so it looked in the dim hallway, and his clothes were dirty. He appeared not to notice her as he came out of the apartment door. He seemed to be looking hard at the dull, old, chipping wall.

It was a trick and she was unprepared for it.

She turned toward the stairway, moving not very fast (her trick) as if to pretend she'd made a small mistake, thought better of a visit she was about to make, got a wrong address.

In a moment a hand clapped over her mouth and the man's legs slammed into the back of her knees so that she lost her balance. "Aren't you a laugh a minute?" he said. "What the fuck do you think you're doing? You ain't going nowhere, baby." He pushed her the five, six, seven steps into the apartment and slammed the door shut.

■ ■

THE PATROL OFFICER WHO TOOK THE MISSING CHILD CALL parked right in the middle of construction on Fifth Avenue, in front of Ralph's Discount City, and ran into the store only three minutes after the call was placed to 911. Everything happened very quickly. He responded well and so did the other police, but the child was already on a bus going north.

The young officer took only five minutes to talk to the mother, Karen Graves, and the employees of Ralph's Discount before he made a quick assessment. This looked like a good snatch, a real kidnapping. He radioed immediately to East Liberty, to Investigation, for a supervisor from Major Crimes. He got Commander Christie, who asked the routine first question. "Where's the father?"

"Get this. Turns out he's a ballplayer. A new pitcher for the Pirates. Ryan Graves. He's out in L.A. with the team."

"How does she sound about him? Trouble there?"

"She wants to call him. No trouble that I can sniff."

Commander Christie told him to go ahead and set up a fast command post. He ordered all available cars to comb the downtown streets, doing a visual search. He took Artie Dolan and Janet Littlefield with him. Artie could get a confession out of a priest if it came to that and Janet could manage to comfort a madman with a gun at his head.

This was one of those cases in which Christie would say later that his people did everything right. To no avail. In minutes a second patrol car was there. The two policemen from that car got the store cordoned off; they took over the back offices, commandeered the phones, the works. Karen Graves was led into the stockroom and placed in an office chair covered in crumbling green vinyl upholstery.

Minutes later, and only minutes later, twelve by his count, Christie and a couple of other detectives arrived. The whole thing didn't take very long. The bus with the child on it was hardly clear of the downtown area.

Walking into Ralph's Discount City, Commander Christie asked for the first officer's notes and checked the situation from the front edges of the store. Behind and around him a crowd was gathering. The store manager and his employees were helping one of the officers keep people away.

Fine.

The mother was out of sight.

Good.

Christie had to deal with a woman who held on to his coat, asking what had happened. He took a good look at her, decided she was one of the street crazies, and freed himself gently, promising to get back to her. "Impound the stroller," he said to Phil Schultz, one of the three detectives with him. "Dust for prints. Check for the child's hair. Look for other hairs. All prints, all fibers, all hairs."

"Yes, sir."

"Careful with that stroller. Get it on a wagon to the crime lab as quick as you can. Is there a surveillance tape?" he asked the patrolman who'd first come to the crime scene.

"Yes, sir."

"Get it."

"I've got it."

"Where do we play it?"

"In my office," the manager called out.

Christie chose Artie Dolan, who was his best detective, to deal with the tape. "Let me know if it's sound. Let me know as soon as we're ready to roll it." Dolan hurried toward the manager's office. "Where's the mother?" he asked the third patrol officer on the scene.

"We have her back in the stockroom. Back here." The officer led him and Janet Littlefield back to the place with the green vinyl chair, beckoning as he moved.

"Stockroom?" Christie muttered to Janet, wondering what the child's mother felt like being shoved into the stockroom.

Janet said, "I'll move her if it's a mistake."

As Christie walked, he read the first officer's interview with the woman. He was by now so used to the spelling of some of the officers he almost didn't notice it.

... store wasn't crowded ... she was getting suplies, reading labels, getting shampoo, hair liteners, conditioners ... using the stroler baskett ... something was in the way, boxes or stock of something and she just thought it was safe to run around the corner to the next ile ... ten seconds, hardly more ... gets back empty stroler ... runs around to one ile and another ... finally finds the stroler but the baby is gone. ...

Justin is baby's name, the officer wrote.

"Justin," Christie said to himself, getting used to it. *Justin.*

At first the stockroom seemed to be only boxes and fluorescent lights. The place was cavernous and blank and seemed too large and frightening a place to put a woman who had lost her child. But then he saw the young blond woman in a flowered sundress in a corner of the large room, next to a desk. The corner was an island of domesticity in a sea of cardboard boxes, a little place, set out, separate and distinct. He could smell something chemical, either cleaning fluid or glue, strong, but bearable.

"It seemed cozier than the manager's office, sir. That guy's office is filthy. The lady who uses *this* desk—she's an accounts clerk—put that little rug under the desk and there was that lamp on the desk and that vase of real flowers. I thought it was better, sir." The young officer was from the second patrol car and he was not the man who couldn't spell. He looked promising.

"You did right," Christie told him.

"Thank you."

Karen Graves clutched the arms of the chair. "I want to go," she said to Christie when he and Littlefield came up to her. "I have to look for him. He could be just around the corner."

Christie took out a card and gave it to her. He introduced Janet Littlefield. Then he said, "Mrs. Graves. Look at me. I want you to stay here and help us. We've got men canvassing the whole downtown area. They have a description of Justin, his clothes, his age, everything. Now I need for you to keep talking to us. Okay? Can you do that?" He looked up at a startled-looking bald man with dirty glasses. "You work here? Want to make yourself useful? Get me a clean cup and some water.

"Would you happen to have any pictures of Justin with you? I'll copy them and get them right back to you."

When Karen Graves went to lift her purse off the desk and put it on her lap, she dropped it. Her hands were like fluttery birds. She retrieved the purse and managed to open her wallet, but the smaller movements defeated her. She couldn't get the pictures out of the pockets and plastic sleeves.

"Let Detective Littlefield help you." Christie nodded to Janet, who was already taking over.

Christie was a well-built man, forty-three years old, with plainly cut dark brown hair, paling with gray, a once-broken nose. He might have been a retired middleweight with a sense of style and a college degree. There was something contradictory in him, plain and not plain. He wore a taupe linen jacket and chinos. His tie was muted—somewhere between dark blue and charcoal. His shirt was a soft slate-blue. He had a sensual face, brown eyes with a considerable depth to them, suntanned skin, and large,

slender hands which he placed palms down on the desk
that belonged to the assistant to the manager of Ralph's
Discount City. "I'm going to ask you a couple of questions," he said. "Then after you're tired of me, we're going
to let you talk to Detective Littlefield here."

Karen Graves couldn't stop shaking. She touched her
face repeatedly in that way people do, with both hands
spread over the mouth, movement and speech both arrested.

He took four photos from Littlefield and studied
them. "These two are more recent?" he asked the mother.

"Yes."

He handed the two he wanted to use to the bright young
officer, who had materialized behind him. "Make lots of
copies."

The bald clerk from Ralph's Discount City appeared
with a couple of large bottles of springwater and a plastic
bag full of plastic cups. Detective Littlefield took the of-
ferings and began to open them.

"Thanks," Christie said to both of them. "We're getting
you some water," he said to Karen Graves. "You want to
call your husband, right, and talk to him about what happened? That's exactly what we want, too. Let's do that
now." He lifted the office phone and placed it next to her.

Her hands were still shaking so badly she could not
hold the receiver. He felt terrible for her.

The way she talked to her husband would be *part* of
what they watched. When Commander Christie started
out in this job, he hadn't assumed first-off the parents
were the culprits, but now you had to consider that as one
of the major possibilities. Susan Smith, supposedly distraught about her missing boys, made cynics of everyone when she faced the cameras, lying and fabricating.
Desperate people, parents among them, could weave and
invent until they half believed their own lies, at least part of
the time.

Christie put two open notebooks on the desk—the one
with his officer's notes and his own, in which he was beginning to write.

He wanted to reach over to Karen Graves' shaking hands and calm her, but she was not ready to be touched by him. He nodded to Janet, who had put a glass of water down on the desk and now crouched near Karen with a hand on her knee.

Littlefield said, "Please. Have some water. Hold on to the table. Do you need help dialing?" Karen Graves shook her head and unfolded a piece of paper that was on her lap.

"Who got you the number?" Christie asked gently.

"The first policeman."

"Good. Excellent work. We want you to try to dial it now."

She pressed the numbers carefully and waited. "I need to talk to Ryan Graves," she said into the phone in a hoarse and whispery voice. "It's an emergency." Then, a moment later, "I'm his wife." Saying those words, she began to cry. She listened to the man on the other end of the line and turned to Richard Christie, explaining, "They think he's out to breakfast."

Christie nodded, took the phone from her, got the name of the hotel clerk. "Have him call this number as soon as you locate him." He gave the number of Ralph's Discount City. "Thanks. It's important, yes."

He could hear more noise than usual out in the store itself, which meant the news media had arrived in force. There would be at least four cameras, at least four television reporters with them, probably two print reporters. And this was just the beginning. When the news got out, even if he was able to solve this in the next hour—and wouldn't that be sweet?—there would be national coverage, for the baby's father was celebrity material. Not exactly a celebrity yet, a rookie most of the country had never heard of, but now the limelight would find him. Overnight fame.

"They're finished with the stand in L.A., right?" He knew they were, having watched the game last night and cheered on as the rookie relief pitcher struck out three in a row. He knew it, but he wanted to get her to focus on plain facts. "And where do they go next?"

She'd nodded to his first question, but she couldn't hold on to the second. She tried to look out the office door to the store where her son was taken. "Maybe they've got Justin in an alley or maybe another shop."

Before he could ask why she said "they," Dolan knocked, came in, saying, "The tape is good."

"Mrs. Graves? I have to leave you for a moment. Detective Littlefield will take care of you for a couple of minutes."

Christie and his colleagues gathered in the very dirty office to watch the tape.

It began with a general clatter of noises, voices saying indistinguishable things, bottles and boxes being plunked down on counters and in carts. There was an even rhythm of movement in the place. Seven customers, to be exact. Karen had a foot on the stroller while she looked at things on the shelves. In the store five other customers walked around, but one, some twelve feet away from her, was still and not very visible behind boxes of merchandise that blocked the aisle. Commander Christie watched Karen Graves closely. She did not look over her shoulder or around her, but seemed intent on the packages she was reading. She put something back on a shelf, steered the stroller to a spot a few inches from the boxes waiting to be shelved, and scooted around the corner. So far, so good. She stayed—he counted this—twelve or thirteen seconds in the aisle, where she put two boxes back, took another box off the shelves. One of the young detectives whistled and said, "Man, that's a long time." The tape was grainy, so that he couldn't tell what product she was handling. But while she stood in the other aisle for those twelve or thirteen seconds, a man in dark pants and a light shirt came from behind the boxes. He wheeled the stroller as easily as if it belonged to him over to an aisle where no one else was around. He managed the straps quickly, then lifted Justin up and walked toward the camera, out the door. Karen came back, looked confused, ran in the wrong direction, opposite where the stroller was. On the tape her voice started to come through. She was calling for her son, more and more frantically, and when she found the stroller, she kept calling his name. All the other people in the shop seemed to come alert at once. They began to move toward her. She cried out, "Help, help, help me!" She ran toward the camera and off the tape.

"What do you see?" Christie asked Dolan.

"She looks honest to me."

"The man?" He was a couple of streaks on the tape, not very clear.

"Not much. Doesn't look particularly young. Ordinary clothes, not too casual. Looks to be Caucasian. That's all I'm getting."

"Before you take it away, I'm going to ask her to look at the tape."

Dolan nodded.

Christie had to ask if she recognized the man, the shadowy, difficult-to-see figure on the tape. In a case like this, there was always a fair chance she'd turn out to know him. If not, perhaps there was something she could add to the bare facts of age and clothing suggested by the video.

Commander Christie had two children, a six-year-old boy, a four-year-old girl. It was almost inhuman to ask her to watch this tape and to study her face while she did. But he had to. Then he'd send the tape off to the experts to see what they could do. There were a few seconds in which the man's face was partly visible. Perhaps there was enough to make a police sketch.

He went back himself to get her and Detective Littlefield. He ushered them into the manager's office, warning Littlefield with a look that this was going to be rough. "Mrs. Graves?" he said. "Karen? I know it's hard, but what will help us the most is you remembering and talking us through it. Can you concentrate? Tell us what was happening?"

"Yes."

He asked her to sit at the manager's desk. She held on

to the desk edge so hard her fingers looked like an old woman's.

What Christie remembered most about her after he showed her the tape were the sounds she made, horrible sounds. Her voice chilled him. "It was my fault," she cried, "my fault. Who is that man? How did he know?"

"You never saw this man before?"

"No!"

Christie told one of the promising young policemen to run the tape to the photo lab they used in the Strip District and get multiple copies made—for them, for the television news, all that. And hard copies of the picture of the man, the best they could do, for the newspapers and other police zones.

Detective Littlefield and Commander Christie together took Karen Graves back to the stockroom, soothing her, telling her having this on tape would help them in the long run.

"You listen to Commander Christie." Janet Littlefield smiled. "He's a good guy. You're in the best hands."

Was he a good guy? He wanted to be, that was for sure. But he fell far short in a million ways.

He tried to be very steady with the distraught mother. "Tell me again every place you went today. From the start. From waking up."

"We're staying at Gateway Towers. We can't really afford it. It's a loan. Kind of a sublet."

"You're where at the Towers?"

"Tenth floor, apartment C, belongs to Kularik, the hockey player."

"Do you have a baby-sitter, a nanny?"

"No, nothing like that. We're new here. We just got to town."

"You're doing well. Keep going. You woke up in your apartment. What time?"

"Late. Nine o'clock this morning. I never get up that late, but I got Justin to go back to sleep at six. I was up late watching the game. . . ."

"I'll bet," he added lightly.

"I couldn't leave it. Ryan did so well I wanted to stay up to talk to him. I knew he'd call. And then once he did, I really couldn't sleep. I was all wired up."

"Tell me the part about this morning."

"I got up about nine and dressed Justin in a hurry and took him out in the stroller. I had an appointment with a financial adviser in the Park Building at one o'clock, but I don't know my way around yet— Do you need all this?"

"Yes."

"I . . . don't know where I am here, all the bridges and ramps. I come from a tiny town. So I started out real early, thought I should try to get to know the city."

"Keep going. Everything that happened downtown."

"I stopped in one office building—a couple of blocks away from here—to look for a bathroom. I usually look for a McDonald's to change his diaper, but I couldn't find one so I just used a hallway on the third floor in that other building."

Christie's notes from the first officer said, *Clark Building??? something on Liberty, probably Clark.* "Later," Christie told her, "I'll drive you by to find the place. Keep going."

"Then I kept walking. I found the Park Building where my appointment is—" She looked at a wall clock. "I don't care about money. People on the team told Ryan one of us should go right away and get our finances in order. . . . I was early and I had time to kill; I needed some things, so I came in here. Don't you think we should—"

"You had Justin with you the whole time until—?"

"Of course! Oh, how can you ask that?"

"I have to ask. I'm sorry. Believe me, people do . . . funny things." Strollers left at parking meters, babies left in cars, strange things indeed. People courting the theft of their children. And did she, this nice woman, maybe even inadvertently, court it, too?

"I kept thinking, He's here in the store somewhere— and I ran around calling him and then people started helping me and then the store manager called the police. That's everything. We're losing time."

"We've got men working on it. Somebody will remember seeing something."

"How could it happen? How can people be so asleep? How could they let it happen? I don't come from a place like this."

Christie looked at her. He saw a woman to whom nothing very startling had ever happened. Pretty. Reasonably popular. Probably religious. And now . . . this ugly thing, this jolt.

"Mrs. Graves, I'm not prying without good cause. What I'm about to ask you . . . could be very important. Here's what we need to know . . . how have you and your husband been getting along lately? Agreeing on things?"

"The other cop asked me that! What are you saying? We get along fine. If you're thinking like that, you're never going to find Justin. You're holding me here and you're never going to find him." Her hands began to thrash around. This time, Richard Christie couldn't overcome his sympathetic nature and he reached over and grabbed her hands and clasped them in his, saying, "I'm sorry. I'm sorry. We have to know these things. There are all kinds of situations out there, all kinds of motives. Did you notice anyone in the store, anyone at all?"

"No," she wailed. "There were people there, but I wasn't looking. I wasn't seeing them. There was a stock boy somewhere, but that's all I know. I'd never be able to tell you anything about him. I was thinking about Ryan. How I wanted to look nice when he got home. Things like that. Dumb things like that. Please, you've got to help me. We can't just sit here while they're driving away."

"Why do you say 'they'? You said it before."

"I don't know. I picture something organized. Otherwise . . . how could so many people have missed it?"

It was strange, very strange. A snatch like this right downtown, middle of the day, people all around. He couldn't find the sense of it. "Now I have to ask you one or two more things: Have you felt anybody was following you around?"

"No. I never felt anything like that."

"Have you received any threats? Any odd mail?"

"No, nothing. Nothing."

Commander Christie looked to the notes his young not-literate cop had written: *watch for the ranson call. Father is Ball Player.*

But would the youngest member of the poorest-paid team in baseball have a salary that inspired thoughts of ransom? Not to anybody who knew what these guys got paid. He turned the question over. The *organization* had a lot of money. But who would hold up an organization? Who would think that way?

No. Something was definitely odd. He would assume nothing in the way of motive.

He asked her to close her eyes and remember. Had she seen a car following her? Any kind of suspicious driver? Did anybody hang around her anywhere? Did she remember any strangers?

She shook her head at first. Then she remembered a woman—beautiful, really beautiful in a movie-star way, maybe her age, she thought, all dressed up—who seemed to look at Justin for a long time in the first office building she stopped in. "That's all," she said. "That's all. The woman didn't seem creepy, though."

■ ■

IF MICHAEL COULD HAVE ADMITTED THAT HE *LIKED* BEING IN HIS car for part of the day, doing the people-to-people work of the law, it would have been easier on him. If Michael had been a cement pourer or a salesman, that tight spot on his chest might have lifted. Instead he was an attorney, the most junior member at the firm, who worried about being given the drudge jobs: *Drive and talk and type up reports and kowtow.* His wife was out of love with him—and he couldn't do his part to make a baby. He felt useless.

He was a sturdily built, athletic thirty-five-year-old, not

quite six feet tall and already balding on top—it happened early in his family. The rest of his brown hair was curly, so he had to keep it trimmed or he could look clownlike. He thought so, anyway. He had tawny skin, blue eyes, wore glasses most of the time because he didn't tolerate lenses well. He had refined features. So women had told him. Maybe not stellar genes. Decent genes. But no hope of handing them on, so he'd been told.

In his car, he tuned in to WQED. He leaned toward classical music in almost any setting. He even put it on when cutting the lawn! Swelling orchestras fighting the grind of machinery. For entertainment, he chose live concerts where he was able to erase everything and really listen. Music filled him up and calmed him.

People had considered him shy as a child, a wuss in high school, a sensitive intellect in college, a quiet team-player in law school, and now, what? A reliable, somewhat intellectual, old-fashioned drudge. Well, good, so much for that, what did people know anyway? He didn't have to be a star.

He didn't have to stay married or have a kid. He could change. Change was possible. He could begin to go out drinking with the guys and stay out late, pick up women, come to work with a hangover. Why not? Why did people believe they had to stick with what they were? He had never had a long reckless youth. One and a half years of callow living at best. Why not grab some more now?

He drove toward Monroeville, trying not to curse about the road construction. He tried on other lives as he steered around striped barrels and orange construction cones. He worked on falling in love with other women—like Kendall at the office, who thought him interesting. Well, the word she had used at the office party was "cute." Kendall flirted with him all the time. Why couldn't he fall in love with her? Or why couldn't he be the breezy young man he once had hoped to be, the man who didn't fall in love right away but simply enjoyed himself?

He thought about what it would be like if he took

Kendall for a drink. Talk about the office at first, then no doubt other things. CD players, parents, whatever. Kendall arching her back the way she does, as if she doesn't know how that shows her full breasts. Drift into dinner. Listen, sympathize. One thing leads to another.

He and Marina had gone to see Marian Caldwell twenty times. It felt like handing their lives over to a stranger and it had cost a fortune, too. They'd told her just about everything. Summaries came pouring out, but were they truths? Things twisted and changed before his eyes until he didn't know what he thought anymore. Dr. Caldwell tried to be sympathetic to both of them, but she seemed to favor Marina's point of view on things. Michael did not want to be surprised anymore. If he had to say the thing he wanted most in his life, it would be that.

A workman flagged him to stop and a wire of fear went through him as if he'd done something wrong and the man in orange was a policeman and not a sunburned, sweaty laborer standing in the middle of traffic. Couldn't Marina see he was on the edge? Couldn't she sympathize, pay some attention to him? How much more disappointment could he take? After the baby thing. His fault. That, too.

Marina was going to move out "for a while." Fine. She'd do it, too. That's how she was, always full of determination about something. The therapist didn't discourage her, either. Just the opposite. He thought so. There you had it, two women's opinions that Marina ought to go. Fine.

"And where would you go? Do you have somewhere in mind?" the good doctor had asked in that whispery voice.

Marina shook her head sadly and talked about the simple necessity to get away from arguments and what she called his violence, although he wouldn't call it anything like violence. She said she didn't know where she'd go, but she needed to get her *self* back. Said she'd been numb for a couple of years, unfeeling. Well, it sure felt that way to him.

Couple of years. It made him furious. And he knew what had started it, too.

Michael passed the Swissvale exit and moved over a

lane, turning down the radio, which was suddenly over-whelmingly loud. Shubert. Souping it out. Marina was going to leave him. Fine. Let her.

He reached over with his right hand to his car phone and dialed the office. When he had passed through a par-ticularly fluid throng of traffic, he pressed the SEND but-ton and turned the radio off. Kendall's cheery voice lifted him. "Hey, fella, so you're on the road today?"

"I was thinking, I haven't properly thanked you for all your help rescheduling all those interviews. Would you like to go for a drink later? How bad is your workload?" he stumbled, his three opening lines vying for first place.

"What do you mean by later?"

"After work if you're not going overtime . . ."

"After work it is, then. I'll brush my hair."

Kendall wore her hair in that messy, tangled way that looked so good on blondes with almost straight hair. That went-swimming, got-fucked, took-a-nap-and-got-up-and-this-is-how-I-look look. There must have been much more of a sense of pounding at the fortifications back in the fifties when hair was so stiff and hard-edged. Movies. Elizabeth Taylor with a pouf. There was really much more need of *conquest* then. You had to be a really tough sperm to get through all that hair-sprayed feminin-ity to the soft, ragged center. Now the hairdos said, "The soft ragged center is for the taking, my darling, if I decide you are the one." So why weren't women getting pregnant these days? There was something to it, something wrong with the world. Russian potions in the drinking water. No, not Russian. Iraqi, maybe.

He'd get home when he got home. Kendall would brush her hair for him. He wasn't in any hurry to get home tonight.

■   ■

AT FIRST THERE IS NO VIOLENCE.

The sound of the door locking. The large man pushing her into a chair, the baby crying across the room on a

sagging brown tweed sofa, the sounds of two voices—
questions, interrogation, inquisition?—from the other
room. The large man tells her not to move and she does
not move from the sagging armchair, which matches the
couch; after a while, quieter questions and answers from
the other room; finally, the three men sit across from
her, two on the drooping couch, discolored with age and
wear, the other man on a green brocade armchair with
dark green fringe at the bottom. And the baby. From the
center of the awful sofa, the baby cries with a desperation
that breaks her heart.

No violence. Unless you count the feel, the print, of the
large man's hand over her mouth, his body pushing at her
knees and back, propelling her into the room. The acrid
sweat and sour-breath smell of him. And the baby crying
unattended.

There is the promise of violence in the way they sit
across from her, the gap filled by a threadbare carpet. She
can't see a gun, yet she has no doubt there is at least one
here, and if not, other things that these men might use to
hurt her.

The large man, who caught her and pushed her into
the room, looks bald at first glance, but now she sees
he has thin hair, almost invisible hair, plastered close to
his head. Flesh-colored hair. The man's nose is too small
for his face; that and his large bony forehead make him
look primitive. He is a drawing in an anthropology text-
book. Comic in another setting, but not now, not now. He
is tall and heavy, uncomfortable in his body, in his
clothes. Marina is memorizing him. She can hardly
breathe, but she has set herself tasks, and one of them is
the memory game. For years now, she has taught acting
students to pay attention, remember, and she must do it,
too, in this time and place cut out from the rest of her life.
She has been plopped into someone else's story. A seedy
story, a terrible story. The large man is dressed in jeans
and a dingy white T-shirt and he is sweating profusely.
Wheezing. After he slammed shut the door of the apartment and pushed her into the chair, he said, in a low

breathy voice with aspirated consonants (there, she can remember voices, too), "We already heard, you've been following Joe, here, all day."

So *Joe* is the tidy man from the bus. He sits almost primly on one end of the sofa, while the big man spreads out over the other end. Joe doesn't move much. She can see his face clearly now. Joe cannot hold a glance with anyone, not the large man, not her, nor the other man, the third man, who is younger, neater, than the other two, and different, handsome.

This third man is clearly the leader. He commandeers the other room in the apartment, she saw that. Nobody goes in without knocking. He is bristling with anger and that keeps the other two nervous. Because of her, Joe is the victim here, guilty of having been followed.

The third man knows his moves. He sits, enthroned, on the *different* chair, the green brocade. He wears a summerweight suit with the tie loosened. He leans back with one leg crossed over the other and watches her. She was not able to hear his voice clearly from the other room, but she can report what he looks like. This is what she tells herself in a wish to believe she will someday be telling someone about this. The man is fine-skinned. His black hair is not quite straight. Marina realizes she half expects him to have an accent when he speaks. As if he's an actor onstage, giving preparatory signals for what he's about. Spanish, Slavic, maybe Italian or Greek. He's around her age. Not so slick as he wants to appear. After a while he begins to thread the fingernail of his trigger finger through his front teeth. He looks disgustedly at the baby, who is now crying hard. The look chills her. She is afraid he will do just about anything to stop the crying.

"Let me hold the baby," Marina says. "Let me at least do that."

This is that trick her mind does, maybe not such an unusual thing among people who've been traumatized as children. When something terrible happens (a car rearends her, she hears of a death), she behaves with utter calmness at the very first. As if it's nothing. As if it's almost nothing. A switch is thrown to shut off the shaking and stuttering—so that she seems ordinary, normal, while her mind works to catch up. Later, when she realizes what she's kept at bay, everything collapses, all of it is there at once, feelings tumbling over other feelings, almost more than she can bear.

"Let her." It's the man who was rough with her. "She followed them all the way here. She's fixated on the kid. Let her shut him up, before I do it."

The third man nods.

Then the large man lifts the baby and starts across the room. "Here. Do something."

She reaches quickly to support Brian's head and to let him feel the firmness of her touch, but the crying doesn't stop even though she can hear in its tones and pauses some change. The small red face stretches into a tragic mask. Hungry. Hungry and scared. Terrified. She can feel the sweat of the baby's body, the full diaper. Sweetheart, sweetheart, she thinks, but doesn't say aloud. Let me help you. She lifts him to her shoulder, and after a few moments, the wailing gives way to hiccoughing intermittent sobs.

"Some touch you have," the large man says.

"He's hungry, he's thirsty. His diaper needs to be changed."

"So you're the expert."

"You steal a baby and you don't have any way to care for him? Babies need to be fed, for one thing."

"She's mouthy, this girlfriend of yours," he mutters to Joe.

The third man laughs, a small, mean sound.

Encouraged, the large one adds, "This skinny girl. Joe picked one up. Finally!"

Marina decides to ignore the man and keep her focus on the baby. She rubs Brian's back and murmurs, "It's going to be all right, sweetie. You're going to be fine."

"Sure he is," the big guy says. "No thanks to you."

She looks up then at each one in turn—the frightened Joe, who can't return her glance. The big one, who wants to insult her. And the smaller, almost elegant man, who hangs on to his silence. Now it begins to hit her. Now she begins to feel things. Her body is in seeming control, but her heart, now she feels it, is pounding so hard she feels it will give out. Her mind is full of racing thoughts. The numbness begins to recede and the thoughts sail by like paper airplanes, losing flow, falling bluntly. She is outside herself trying to reenter and yet she is taking things in, sailing paper airplanes of possibility. One of them is a desperate, hopeful thought, thrumming with the blood in her ears: Maybe if she can help them out of this, they will let her go. She says in a shaking voice, "Whatever you're doing, there's time to stop it. Let it go. I'll help you get the baby back to his mother."

The quiet man surveys her, the large man chuckles. "She is one stupid bitch, isn't she?"

She pats the baby's back and allows her body to sway.

Now her surroundings start to surface more clearly. She widens her circle of concentration to take in more of the place.

Outside the sun shines brilliantly, flooding the dusty room with light. The windows have not been cleaned for a long time, but this dirt makes the light hazy, dreamy. She's seen worse. When she and Michael were looking at houses to buy, they visited some HUD derelict buildings, thinking to put all the loan money they could get into renovation. Finally, they couldn't bring themselves to do it. Years of garbage on the floors of those places, rotten carpets, broken furniture. Places that supposedly had been empty for four years had pizza cartons on the floors with bits of food that the rats hadn't gotten to yet. Which meant someone had squatted there, lived there in the rot. So, yes, she's seen worse. This place is dreary, depressing, not particularly clean, but it *looks* like a living room. It's recognizable. And she takes a small hope from that, that somewhere in this group of men there is some ache toward the normal. She rocks her body softly to calm the baby, all the while noticing, remembering. Scratched mahogany tables on either side of the sofa, with unmatched lamps and ashtrays on them. The floor is covered in brown wall-to-wall carpeting, threadbare and stained, but all of a piece still. There's a card table under the window with a deck of cards on it, and a small reading lamp. Her purse is on the floor next to the couch, where the big man threw it when he snatched it away from her. Suddenly she wants it back. Suddenly it feels like a part of her, cut off.

She forces herself to speak. She pretends to make conversational connections as if what she said minutes ago is linked to what she says now. "You're not related to this child, are you?"

"Whew, she wants to know everything! Want me to shut her up?" The big man directs this question to the elegant man. He raises a beefy hand, shows it off. "You give the word," he adds when he gets no answer. He paces a few steps and then finally turns to Joe, who looks lost and hapless in the corner of the sofa. "She asked you a lot of questions on the bus, right?"

"She asked a couple questions. I couldn't shake her."

There is a long silence. In it, she feels the two men waiting for their boss to do something, say something. He uses the old tricks. Stillness, silence. Apartness. The air of superiority that makes the others defer to him. She forces herself to turn and look at him, knowing what she will see. He stares at her with a hatred that makes her want to gasp, but she holds on.

"Man, she's trouble," the large man whispers.

Suddenly, Marina realizes the baby has fallen asleep. The relaxation of his small body against hers throws her off balance. She finds herself saying, "He's . . . he's not going to sleep long. Pretty soon he's going to be . . . crying again."

Her voice has betrayed her, letting them know how uncertain of everything she really is, how sure she is that she will not live through this day. She presses herself to sound strong. "You have to get him to his mother. And, look, if you're stealing him for his father—Are you?—he still has to eat. Don't you know anything? You have to take care of him. It's hot. People get dehydrated in this weather. Babies especially."

"Yeah. Babies left in cars in the heat," the large man says dryly. He gestures around him. "This isn't so bad."

But she continues, hoping to scare them. "If this baby dies, where are you going to be?"

"Maybe we should go buy some supplies for the car trip," the man named Joe suggests quietly. "She's right. I couldn't grab the other stuff. What's the use if we can't present him in decent condition?"

Present him in decent condition. She must remember this phrase.

Marina goes still long enough to be able to feel the baby breathing against her chest, a small whisper of air on her neck. "Look, you mustn't do this, whatever it is. Let's get him back to his mother."

"It's going to be hours yet," Joe advises his boss. "We ought to get whatever we're going to need."

She is trying to remember how long a baby can go without food or water. Pretty long, she's almost certain, but she doesn't want these guys thinking so. "You can't do this," Marina cries. "You aren't capable of taking care of this baby. You have no right to. . . . And a car trip, too? If he gets sick, if he dies . . ."

The quiet one motions his head slightly toward her purse on the floor and the large fellow understands the command and hurries to bring it to him. For a wild moment, Marina tries to remember how much cash she has—would that do it? If they take her money, will they let her go?

But the man in the green brocade chair is not interested in her money, although he does note it in a detached way. It's her cards, her pictures and identity cards, that occupy him.

Finally he speaks. "What is SAG?"

She almost laughs at the irrelevance of the question. "Screen Actors Guild."

"AFTRA?"

"Association of Film, Television, and Radio Actors."

If he has an accent, it is so slight she cannot catch it. He appears to mull over this information about her.

"You're an actress," he says after a while and with a smirk.

"Yes."

"How did you get into this?" He points toward Brian.

"I recognized Brian on the bus."

"You know his mother."

She is about to say, "No. I saw him. I remembered him, that's all," but she stops herself. Would they be more ready to give him up if they thought she knew the mother?

"You know his mother?"

This is a strange thing, how she can't lie. She is an actress, but she can't bring herself to lie. She can play a fiction that is written, that's different. Otherwise, even now, with thugs, even in this sun-drenched surreal place, she will veer away from the lie. She shakes her head.

"How do you know his name?"

She points to Joe. "He told me. On the bus."

The other two look at the small man sitting daintily at the end of the sofa, as if to say, "His name is Brian?"

Joe looks downward, embarrassed.

So. They don't know anything about this baby.

Plain theft, then.

Joe scans the ceiling.

They don't know the child at all. It's not a family squabble but something much, much worse. She holds the baby tighter and pleads, "Let me take him. I'll take him to the police and make up something. I'll blame myself. Let me get him to someplace safe."

For a moment they don't answer. The air is full of dust motes in the sunlight. Pretty. Swimming fast.

"She has enough cash," the elegant man says. "She wants to buy supplies, let her buy supplies."

"ARE YOU BROTHERS?" SHE ASKS.

They are in a car. She couldn't see the license plate when

she got in, but she knows it's a black car, compact, and she searches the dash for more information. Chevrolet. Joe drives and the large man sits behind her, but so close through the gap in the seats, she can smell his sweat again and the rank, sour breath. He holds a gun to the base of her skull. Before they left the house, the large man tucked a gun into his belt, and pulled his T-shirt out over his jeans. Joe must have a gun, too, because he did the same with his sport shirt. They told her to behave calmly as they put her into the car.

It is ninety degrees. Five minutes to get to a Rite Aid, they've said. Stay calm and everything is all right. Twitch, and they shoot her.

It's broad daylight out. Do they mean it? She is not sure what they would do.

"She is one stupid broad," the large man tells Joe. "This girlie of yours."

She feels the large man lean closer to her. He is easy with the gun and seemingly unworried about being seen. She knows he's found a way to block the view with his own body, his left shoulder forward. She smells onions on his breath. "You'd be surprised how people don't notice things. People pass this car, they think you're asleep or pissed off. You see, right now it just looks like I'm talking to you. People might think you're my girl."

Guns make noise, she thinks, but they don't seem to care.

"You run," Joe says, "and it's worse."

The man behind her pushes the gun harder against her neck. The metal is no longer cool, but now heated with her blood. "Put the radio on really loud," he tells Joe. And Joe does, finding in two tries a large, pounding rock sound.

They are stupid, crazy. She wonders if they know what they're doing. Any of them. Even the boss. That he would let her go, let her out of the apartment, only because he couldn't bear to look at her any longer. She knows that. Can picture him back there, making phone calls, pulling himself together.

"Nobody will hear anything," the large one says, "if that's what you're thinking."

This car trip is the end of capture, imprisonment. She will run. She will get out of the car, something will happen, she will see her opportunity, and one way or another she will be free.

"Do I look like this jerk?" the large one asks with a laugh. "Look at his big ugly nose and his little squatty body. Why would you think we're brothers? Or you just feel like talking, any dumb thing to move your trap."

She can see the Rite Aid, a block away.

Once inside, she will find the stockroom, make a run for it. Or get herself behind the counter, crouch there, lie flat against it. The men who are not brothers will think better of shooting her there in public in the store and they will get out fast; if they are too stupid to save themselves and they do try to shoot her, perhaps someone will grab hold of them. Maybe an obstacle—a box, a crate, a counter—will shield her.

She will do *something*. She fully believes at this point that if she gets out of the car, she will not get in it again. No place could be less safe than a passenger seat with a gun pointed at the base of her skull. She can feel the round circle of metal, just behind her ear. Every time she moves, it moves.

Michael's face keeps coming to her. She keeps imagining he knows about this and will do something to help her. This was the best of Michael, his wanting to rescue her from hurt. She remembers him with something of her dreamer's mind, so the feeling is of longing. A simple wish to be in his arms.

DIAPERS, BABY WIPES, POWDER; THESE THINGS SHE PUTS INTO the cart. Two bottles, a bottle scrubber. Some of her friends have had babies. But who notices details? Has he been breast-fed? Bottled formula may be completely unfamiliar. Rows and rows of cans with babies' faces in Warholian repetition, happy no matter what. Normal or soy, which is better? She stands at the shelves, uncertain.

Behind her, so close she can feel them, are the men who are not brothers. It's the way they move in sync that made her ask that question. As well as her own aim to provoke reactions from them, anything that might yield more information.

"Hurry up," Joe says.

"I need to read this label. Do you have a pot at home that—" People don't sterilize bottles anymore. What is she thinking?

"Hurry up," the big one says again. "You know he'll cut our ears off."

She pretends to read the label, trying to work out how to get more information from these men before she makes her run. If only there were other customers in the store . . .

She can feel the large man tense up behind her. "Come on."

"I only want to figure out what the baby needs."

"We don't get back, that baby don't have long for this world. And I'm not talking starvation."

"Vol, shut your yap. Motormouth," Joe whispers behind her. "Just try to be quiet."

Vol? Vol?

"Listen to you. I shoulda never let you alone, you stupid fuckup. Whoever told you to—"

"Shut your trap."

Marina puts back the bottles she has chosen. Joe can speak when he's provoked. But he's the one who made the mistake. In what way was taking Brian a mistake? If only they would talk more. She will remember everything they say, forget not one word.

"What's going on?" Vol, if that's his name, asks.

"These. These are what you need." She gets two packages of disposable bottles off the shelves, eight altogether.

"We're not going to live with the kid."

"What if there's a delay?"

"What are you talking about?"

"Wherever you're taking him." She goes still, hoping for an answer. After some moments have gone by, she stacks eight cans of Enfamil in the cart. When she raises her head from the bent-over position, the glaring lights of the store hit her. Dizziness grips her, she loses her balance slightly, tips toward the cart, so that it skitters forward a few feet. The men are at her side in an instant.

"What was that all about?"

"I feel faint."

"Let's get moving."

If she is going to go behind the counter it must happen now. She tries to get a burst of energy, but is stunned by how hard it is to breathe. And if she does faint here where there are people around her—? But she is carried along by her companions, their hands on her elbows. She wonders where they are taking Brian, and wishes she could know that before she makes her break. . . .

The counter is seven feet away from her. One customer is finishing up. The thought that flies by, whizzing as she approaches the counter, is of her preparing formula, eight bottles of it, and giving instructions to the third man. A part of her is thinking about caring for Brian and another part of her is planning to do something sudden, even reckless—run down the street, calling for help, enter the first public building she comes to, hide.

In this same divided mind, she behaves at the cash register with a combination of calculation and resignation. She is both very awake and asleep at once. "Excuse me, do you know anything about children . . . formulas?" she asks the checkout woman. She wills the woman to look up, to notice her phrasing. "Is this a pretty safe choice for formula? Regular Enfamil? Oh, and are these disposable bottles really safe?"

The woman doesn't look up. Answers "Yep," or "Should be," to each of the questions. When the clerk gives her the total, Marina says, "Joe? Do you have the money?"

"Me?"

"Who's paying for this?" she asks him.

"You are, honey," Vol says. He is right up against her,

and she can feel the gun in the small of her back. "Reach in your purse, honey," he says, "and get out the dough."

The small, wiry woman at the counter only half looks up at the three of them now and shakes her head. Her mouth goes to one side in a look of utter contempt and she sighs while Joe gets the money out of Marina's purse.

The trio steers its way out of the store.

Marina feels the gun in her back the whole time. She wonders why nobody notices her now. Three people walk past them into the store. All are preoccupied. She is just a dumb woman who got herself a very possessive and not very attractive man who runs errands with a friend along for the ride. A woman who made a bad deal. She lifts outside herself, leaves herself, as she gets into the passenger seat once again.

■ ■

AFTER A HALF HOUR, FORTY-FIVE MINUTES AT MOST, AND THE men drifting back with no sightings downtown, Christie clasps his hands and brings them to his mouth in a motion like prayer. At the end of this brief interlude, he heaves a sigh and calls the FBI. He asks for help with helicopters, downtown car checks, dogs, airport checks. There is no way he can do all of this on his own. He doesn't have the resources, and a missing child is a priority.

Pete Horner of the FBI jumps at the thing in big leaps. In an hour he'll have a court order for tapping the parents' phone. He'll have fifty men on the spot. Portable copy machines. "We're in charge, then?"

"I am," Christie answers quickly. "I'm setting up a task force. Three of us and three of you on the inside. Your fifty and another twenty-five at least of mine in the field. I'll coordinate."

He waits out the pause. Horner says, "We can use Rapid-Start. We have the goods."

"Right. I want it. Everything you can bring to bear."

"That case in West Virginia," Horner says, "we did in

forty-eight hours. Everything dovetailed. It was like running a touchdown. It was like—"

Christie knew what was coming. It was, to say the least, an ironic comment, under the circumstances.

"Like hitting a home run."

"I know. Let's hope for that."

He hangs up. Sure. In the West Virginia case, they had a witness and a suspect. This one is not starting out like a touchdown pass. This one does not have the feel of a fast ball in the strike zone.

He is still at Ralph's Discount City, standing at the front of the store. Four of his men are looking at him. They look like little boys trying to figure out how grown-ups do things. Who knows how? In a flawed manner. Humanly. He could have called Pete Horner twenty-five minutes ago, but he'd wanted to see what he could see first. He'd wanted control.

He whispers to Littlefield to take Karen Graves over to Allegheny General and get her seen to. A sedative seems to be in order, sounds mighty good to him, too, but he's going in the opposite direction completely. He feels it, he knows it. Nerves, caffeine highs, the pace of a sprinter sustained for hours, days. Heading up a task force where half to three-quarters of the guys were trained to feel they should be in charge instead of him.

He is mature. He will delegate when he can.

AT FIRST SHE STARTS TOWARD THE KITCHEN, WHICH IS A BARE thing except for two water glasses, a large garbage pail, and a sloppily folded bedsheet on the small portion of counter near the sink. "Making yourself at home?" Vol asks. He grabs her by the back of her dress until she feels the neckline seam up against her neck, choking her. Moments later, she is flying back to the chair, the brown tweed chair again. Vol's aim is bad, though, and her tailbone hits the arm of the chair where the padding is worn off. She cries out in pain. He pulls her up and sits her down hard.

The third man comes out of the other room, saying, "Shut her up." He carries a cellular phone, hand clasped over the speaker section. He has a readiness and comfort with the small instrument in his hand, the look of a person who proposes and argues and deals by phone. She sees then that the baby has been on the couch this whole time, unattended, only a sheet stuffed around him.

Vol brings her the bags from the Rite Aid, which landed on the kitchen floor when he grabbed her out of there. He says, "This what you wanted to work on?"

"Bring me the baby."

He doesn't move, only looks at her with contempt.

Joe brings the baby over and puts him on the floor in front of her. She slides off the chair and kneels close to him. Trembling, she takes off the old diaper, which is soaked and smells sharply of urine. She remembers his mother in the Clark Building searching for a place to deposit a dirty diaper and thinks how the woman must be frantic now. Then she sets about wiping and powdering. The fresh artificial smells fill the air while Vol keeps up a running verbal torment.

"What a mouth on her. Giving the orders, huh? She doesn't seem to understand that this is it for her. Curtain call. End of the show. What a dummy."

She looks up finally, but avoids Vol. Joe is watching her from the other end of the room, at the window.

She goes back to the baby, who seems to search her face. For a moment there is only the two of them, an intense communion that keeps her from falling apart. If she looks up, she will lose herself.

With shaking hands, she opens the first can of formula and pours the contents into one of the disposable bottles, holding the bottle in front of her. Some of the formula spills to the floor. She lets out an inadvertent sound.

"What's the matter?" Joe asks.

"I didn't want to waste any of it."

" 'Are you brothers?' " Vol says, imitating her. "As if we were trying to pick her up at a bar. Chitchat."

She takes the child up off the floor and begins to feed

him. The baby seems surprised at the taste of the formula. Her heart sinks. If he's been breast-fed only, his body might struggle with the new stuff. "Oh, please," she says to him. After a gasp and another, he appears to consider trying what she offers; he swallows twice, carefully, and then he drinks greedily, filling himself up. She can see it, feel his stomach expanding. He is in her arms. "That's it, darling, that's it." Babies are strong. She can't slow him down. He gulps the formula, the whole thing in little more than seconds, and begins to cry for more.

She lifts him and burps him, saying, "Okay. There's more, there's more."

Joe paces on his end of the room. "Why didn't she run?" he asks Vol in a whisper.

"Why didn't you run?" Vol laughs. "Dumber than you look, huh?"

She gets up and kneels by the chair, putting Brian on its seat. He cries questioningly now, in stops and starts. Marina hates it that they can hear what she says to the baby, but she has no choice. It's important that he hear her voice. She removes the blue overalls she has just put back on him. "We're going to fix you up. Take care of everything. We'll make you all fresh and clean and then—"

"You just did that."

"He needs it again."

"Shit this time. The kid's shitting himself. Not her. She don't shit."

Tilting her arm, Marina catches a quick look at her watch. It's after three o'clock in the afternoon. She must have gotten here somewhere around noon. Is anyone looking for the baby yet? Is that what the third man is talking about on the phone? Although she can hear his voice rising up and pausing, she can't make out anything else. The voice continues through the closed door. At one point a light laugh.

The smell of the baby's diaper almost overwhelms her. She uses a clean end of it to wipe at the yellowish streaks, hoping this is not a violent reaction to the bottle she just gave him. She directs her comments to Joe as she reaches for the box of wipes. "Whoever's going to take care of him—you need to use these and powder him. I'll put these things back in the bag." She tries to work slowly. "If he tolerates the formula, I'm going to give him another bottle in ten minutes. Then I'll make the rest up."

"Is that so? You're calling the shots, huh?" Vol asks.

"Somebody has to."

"Maybe you figured out you don't get to move around anymore when you're done feeding the brat. Maybe you think you're buying time."

His words reactivate the wires of panic in her, making her feel suddenly weak. She has fleeting, crazy thoughts. Grab her purse. Stuff the candy bar into her mouth. Drink the formula. Feed herself. She lifts and holds the baby again. Holds him tight. The realness of his small body gives her temporary strength. "I have other things to get ready," she whispers. To him? To them? While holding the baby she manages to open the other cans of formula, filling the bottles, packing them all back in their boxes to keep them upright, and while she does this, the two men watch her.

"She's getting the picture. Her hands are shaking."

Joe doesn't appear to take as much pleasure from her suffering as Vol does, even though he looks angry and restless. She wonders if she could appeal to him somehow. What would she say? "Just let me go. I'll never tell anyone. Let me go." Although she's an actress, the lie would be apparent. She is clearly someone who will tell what she knows. She can't pretend to be otherwise.

Sweat is pouring down her forehead. It's very hot in here. Ninety degrees, she thinks. After a month of rain and terrible storms, today is a beautiful day, fluffy clouds, bright skies, but hot and humid, too. In the apartment, the windows are all shut, and the place is stuffy and dirty. Will anyone on the street notice the windows are locked shut? No one will notice.

"I haven't had anything to eat." She eyes her purse, which the men have placed on the card table. "I have half a candy bar in there. It might help."

Vol is incredulous. "What kind of a hotel do you think this is?" he asks.

She gets up from the floor and sits in the chair, putting the baby squarely on her lap. She reaches for a bottle from the bag at her feet.

Suddenly the large man snatches Brian from her, saying, "We can take it the rest of the way with the kid. This is where you get off, bitch."

She reaches toward the baby squirming in his arms. The bottle in her hand drops to the floor. Vol is quick, though. He holds the baby in one arm and keeps a gun on her with the other as he steps around the bottle. "We're going to stop this shit," he tells her, coming at her with the gun to the side of her face. She ducks and he curses. "Hurry up," he tells Joe. "Do it now."

Before she knows Joe is about to yank her, she is out of the chair, on the floor, her face pressing into the rug, her arms being pinned behind her back, a knee in her back where it already hurts horribly. "No," she begs, "no. Let me go! Let me go! I haven't done anything to you."

"Unbelievable," Vol says. "What a movie star!" He puts the baby down on the sofa and claps a hand over the baby's mouth.

"Don't do that. I'll take care of him. I can quiet him."

She can feel something thin being lashed to her wrists. Joe is working fast. She tries to get to her knees, but Joe pushes her down again. She feels him unclasp her watch, pull her rings off her fingers.

Vol lets the baby alone long enough to pull the upholstered cushion off the chair. Under it is a hard plywood bottom.

Joe lifts her up by her dress, which cuts into her underarms.

She lands in the chair, hitting hard. Pain sears through her lower back.

Vol comes close and holds the gun to her face. He holds it just on her left eye. The feel of it there is so terrifying she goes completely still.

And then her feet are tight together, tied by some of the same rope or cord that lashes her arms. She can't see the cord, only a knife flashing. She feels the movement of the rope being cut. The gun remains against her left eye; she has to fight to keep her right eye open. From the kitchen, Joe grabs and unfolds the grimy-looking bedsheet she saw on the counter. "Stay still," he orders her. He pulls her head back and gathers the sheet in rough pleats along the hemline. When he guides this bulk of material toward her mouth, she pleads, "Please no, please, please, tell me what to do, please no."

He places the thick folds in her mouth and ties the sheet behind the chair, jerking and pulling tighter and tighter. Brian watches. Her legs scramble trying to get up onto the chair.

Vol says, "She's squirming like a worm. We should do it now. Put on loud music and just—"

"Shut up." Joe presses her legs back to the chair. He takes the bottom of the sheet and wraps it tight around her now still legs, winding the fabric to the back of the chair, where he jerks the pieces tight.

"Hate the bitch."

"She didn't think—"

She didn't think it would come to this.

At first thoughts come to her, simple, isolated thoughts: I am tied up. One is named Vol and the other is Joe. I will get out somehow. My hands and feet are swelling, my mouth hurts. I will figure something out. The baby is crying again. The baby is going to die. Only I can help.

It is a good ten minutes before the shock wears off and she understands this is the end of her life.

■ ■

HE HAS CHOSEN HOULIHAN'S BECAUSE IT'S BIG ENOUGH TO have some quiet booths in the corner. He drinks plain beer, IC they said it was, on tap. Kendall (this is her first name, she has to keep explaining to people, her mother's maiden name, which her mother so much hated giving up, she gave it to her daughter) is on her second frozen margarita.

"Are they very strong here?" he asks.

"Strong enough." She laughs. She slides her glass over for him to take a taste. He doesn't particularly want to mix the salt and lime with his beer, but he figures she might be insulted if he refuses to sip from her glass, so he does it. "I love these things," she says.

"I don't order mixed drinks much. Beer, wine. That's about it."

"So, do you have a wine cellar?" Kendall asks.

Michael looks up to see a couple of other lawyers at the bar, people he knows peripherally, and he has the distinct impression they are giving him a nod of approval. How easy to come up two notches in the view of the world. He just needs to show that Kendall, who is pretty and bright-eyed with anticipation, likes him. Michael answers, "About eight bottles. And they're in the cellar. If that counts."

"I want to have a wine cellar one day. French and Italian wines."

"No California?"

"No. Well, maybe a few to take to parties." She makes a long, comical face. "So what went wrong with the depositions?"

"Nothing. Why?"

"I thought somebody gave you a hard time. You seem down."

"I'm just tired."

"You know, people didn't used to work our kind of hours. There used to be more time for everything. That's what my mother says. People read for hours in the evenings. And went out a couple of nights a week. And they weren't exhausted. She says it was all different."

"We can't go back. We are where we are," Michael says, more to encourage himself than to philosophize with her.

"You are down."

"Am I?" He rouses himself. "Talk to me about your mother, your family. I always wondered about you."

"You did?"

"Yeah," he says thoughtfully, "I really did. What are you, twenty-five?"

"More. And in agony. The big threes are coming up."

"Tell me about it! They already came for me."

"Yeah. And every year I say I'm going back to school and every year I don't. I keep needing the money for my car and my apartment, and then I want to go on vacations, and then I think, no, I'll wait another year."

She tells him about the one and a half years she needs to finish her degree in social work, and about how close she is with her mother and her two sisters. Marina did it the other way—school and ambition, lots of trying, no closeness with mother and sister, and now she was floating. Life can fall apart either way. Either direction. He thinks Kendall might be luckier, with her natural good humor and an upbeat fantasy of the future to keep her going. Fantasy, he figures, is one of the necessary ingredients.

He sits back and with his eyes open allows his own fantasies to creep in while Kendall sketches in her life story. She wears some kind of lip gloss that makes her lips light and delicious looking and she arches her back, showing off her very full breasts. He works on his new role, a new free life with women like Kendall, who like him without wanting to know everything about him. "So then I broke up with *him,* and after that I came to work at the firm. Which I like. I'm good at it. I could probably get into law school if I really decided to do it." She finishes her margarita and licks the rim of the glass. "I don't want to shock you, but I want another one. Don't worry. I'm not a lightweight. I can drink."

Michael has contradictory impulses. He wants to go home and see Marina doing whatever she's doing. It used to be rehearsing a scene or working on a dialect. Now it's reading or chopping mushrooms. Meals have improved since she's had so much bad luck in the theatre. She's calmer, even sweeter, but her sense of self has declined. On the other hand, he wants *not* to go home.

Kendall is so sexual, the way she stretches back, the way she drinks. Not too thin. Reminds him of the women he used to get involved with, before Marina, in college, women who got pregnant if you blinked at them. He doesn't care what the fucking doctors say, it's not his fault.

"Want another right away?"

An hour later the waitress asks them if they're going to want to eat and Michael says, "Certainly. Absolutely." Then he gives a "Can you?" look to Kendall and they order.

Kendall's eyes are alight with the effort to read Michael's cues. He is having dinner out and he does not go to a pay phone. He is down in the dumps. Michael sees her seeing these things about him. He watches her determined walk when she gets up, partway through dinner, to go to the bathroom.

On the four televisions, he keeps seeing the same blond woman crying in front of the cameras. And always after the clips of her, there is a guy in a coat and tie at a table, answering questions into a microphone and then Gene Lamont and a couple of baseball players come on. Then they do a clip of a Pirates' game—last night's game. He can't hear the sound. Nobody could, unless the crowd was quieted down and the volume raised. It's only picture-news. Not even closed captions here. He wonders what it's about—some scandal with one of the players, or maybe somebody got hurt, or it could be the blond woman is bringing suit against one of the Pirates. The customers standing near the bar and closer to the television seem riveted. Before Kendall comes back, one of the stations shows the same clips, but this time with a starburst of a caption in the corner that says, "Kidnapping."

Jeez, Michael thinks, and he sighs with a full heart. He knows nothing, but he feels immediate large welling emotions for the blond woman and the ballplayer. Yes, they've had their Armageddon, their asteroid in the middle of their lives. He waves down a stranger. "This just happen?"

"Earlier today. Right downtown. Nobody saw anything. Can you believe it? They're waiting for the ransom notes."

Michael nods. The channel he's decided to watch now has photos of a baby—two of them, side by side at first, then each blown up. After that, a run of a dull, almost impossible-to-see surveillance tape. And the police phone number people are supposed to call if they know anything.

Kendall returns, sliding into the seat a little arrhythmically. "I'm so glad you had time for dinner," she says.

He reaches over and touches her hair. It has a slightly stiff feel. He had thought it was going to be soft and rippling. He squeezes.

"That's exactly what my hairdresser does," she says. "Scrunching, it's called." She looks as if she might cry.

■ ■

NO SOUNDS COME FROM OUTDOORS. ONLY THE CONTINUING murmur from the other room. The quiet is eerie. She cannot see the baby, whom she wants to talk to, soothe. She can't see him because she can't turn her head. Vol carried him to her right, toward the windows, and talked about putting him on the floor. There is room on the floor, beside or under the card table, she remembers. At first Brian cried, but then he stopped. Now she would welcome the sound of his crying.

The quiet has stretched out long through the afternoon. The ropes around her wrists and legs, the binding sheet, all are tied so tight, any movement hurts. She has been still. She has watched the men and made it her business to be able to describe them. She has closed her eyes and fixed in her mind every detail of this place. *Observation.* She could draw it, in ground plan or rendering. The wall directly across from her reads, right to left, backward from the windows: wall, fireplace with mantel, long wall with nothing on it, but couch and two end tables in front of it. Although she can't move her head, she knows everything about the room. The couch is the only part she can see right now.

She keeps her eyes closed and works on her breathing, getting it as steady as possible. It is still ragged, but she keeps working on it. She has to strain to breathe with the cloth of the sheet pushing up against her nose. She breathes, works on her memory, prays. She tries to imagine someone coming to rescue her. But no one in the world knows where she is. No one in the whole world could ever guess where she is. She tries to think where there is something in the room that she might use to cut through the sheet. But she can think of nothing except the broken glass of a lamp or a window and she cannot imagine how she will be able to move the chair to break anything. Still, she tries to imagine an escape and she hangs on to the fact that her will is strong enough to try.

How much time goes by is hard to measure.

She keeps her eyes closed and works, works. Finally there is a hushed conversation between Joe and Vol, so low she can catch only a part of it. It sounds for all the world like they are saying, "tango, tango." She hears "a hundred at least" and wonders if they mean thousands, if they mean ransom amounts. She hears a lot of sound that won't become words and she manages to hear "tomorrow" and at another point, "over in Ohio."

"Why are we whispering?" Vol says at one point, laughing. "She's listening anyway. You can bet the bitch is listening." She does not open her eyes because she knows he's looking at her. Then she smells him. "Maybe she croaked. The little mother." When he shakes her knee her eyes come open in spite of herself.

Not long after that, Vol knocks on the hollow-core door and she hears him say, as if it's a joke, "Sorry, if you were sleeping in there or something. We're sending out for food." Vol's gun sits in the middle of the sofa. He says, "Hoagies. Huh? What? You're right. Fuck, why didn't I think of that? I'll send Joe." Vol's voice disappears for a minute—it seems he enters the other room and comes back with cash, which he hands to Joe. "Food, yeah, I'm supposed to get it and you're supposed to bring back a TV that works. Used, he says. Like a resale shop. He says don't try to fucking lift one, not today."

"Shit."

"That's what he said. And hurry."

"Shit." Joe leaves, closing the front door quietly. Vol takes a hard look at her, murmurs something to the one in the other room, and leaves. She hears a key turning in the lock.

Time goes by.

Vol returns with food. The first thing he does is take some to the third man, who stays in the other room. Vol tears paper off his sandwich and eats right in front of her. He takes huge bites, chews elaborately, making sure she sees. A smell of fried onions drifts over. The smell goes up her nose, down her throat, toward her belly. Her stomach jumps up and devours itself. A whiff of yeasty soft bread comes next. A wave of dizziness sweeps over her.

After about ten minutes, there are awkward thumping sounds, and Vol goes to the door and unlocks it. "Does this thing work?" he asks. "You better hope it works." She hears the hushed thump as the large man drops the TV on the card table near the window. Through her sideways glance, she sees Joe wander over to the window.

"Almost show time," Vol says. "We're gonna find out just how good or bad you did."

"If you'd been here with the car this morning—"

"This one is all yours. Don't fucking put it on me."

"What were you going to do, let it go?"

"Put on the tube. And you better get some kind of reception."

Vol taps on the wooden-core door with the butt of his gun. "Boss," he says. "Show time, like you said."

Marina can hear the third man come into the room and she can see him in her peripheral vision in his special chair. The three men turn to the TV.

The news is full of it. How did they think it wouldn't be? Joe and the others are up out of their seats and Vol is crazy, pacing back and forth, but sticking close to his boss and as much away from Joe as he can. The third man is muttering, cursing. She knows what it means that she is left there to witness all of this. They have hidden very little from her. She knows what it means.

Vol explodes. "This is way bigger than I thought. Did you—"

"This has probably been on all afternoon!" the third man mutters.

Marina tries to hear past them to the news of the baby taken from his stroller in Ralph's Discount City downtown. The mother of the baby is pleading for his return in a choked, crying voice. The father is a Pittsburgh Pirate, the newest one, a pitcher just brought in. He says the same things his wife is saying, simple, humble things, "Anything, we'll do anything. Please don't harm him. Please return Justin to us."

Justin.

After a long pause, Vol whistles. "Jesus Christ," he says. "We maybe ought to figure the angles better than what we were doing. Huh, couldn't we? Maybe we should—"

"You couldn't do us any favors?" the third one says in a low, mean voice, and Joe stares back at him, unable to look away. "You had to get us into this—"

Joe says, "I was told, do something, fix it." Vol overlaps with, "We should rethink this. There's a lot more to be had if we can figure how to play it without—"

"You really are an idiot," the third man says. "I don't know what I'm doing with either of you. Just shut up."

The third man switches back and forth between the channels, trying to get the whole of the story.

"—partially seen on this surveillance camera."

They freeze.

"What the fuck? And you got your picture taken, too!"

"Can't see him," Vol says. "Can't see anything except the dumb top of his head."

"A store like that—" the third man sputters. "Are you trying to ruin all of us, you son of a bitch?"

"I have a feel," Joe says. "You know I do. I have timing. I knew I could do it."

"—police sketch from the surveillance tape."

The three men stare, slack-jawed.

"Don't look like him at all. It don't. They got him wrong."

"Shit," Joe says. "Is that supposed to be me?" He stares with terrified eyes at the television.

"Unbelievable," the third man says. "Fucking unbelievable."

After an uncomfortable pause, Vol laughs. "It don't look like you. Not ugly enough."

"At least there's that. It doesn't look like him yet." The third man watches for a while in silence. There are moments, but only moments, when he moves and she can see the back of his head. He says, "They're looking for witnesses. That sketch is going to get better and better."

"And we're going to be out of town, right?" Vol says tensely.

The third man answers levelly, "You're going to need to be out of the country."

"I hope you got a good story who this kid is," the big man says. "Because people are going to be aware now about this one missing."

"No kidding. We're burning his clothes, let me tell you that. That's your job." He points to Joe. "I'll wrap him in the other sheet. Shit. She could have left something here to use."

She.

Joe gestures toward Marina. She can just see him. "You might want to watch—"

"Jerk-off," the third man says. "What do you think you got yourself into? Huh? You got a lot of cleaning up to do. Now, you think, who saw you? Her, all right, we know she did. A bus full of people, right? People who are going to help with that sketch. Right? You dumb fuck. Right now, you go check the building. See if there's anybody at all hanging about. *Any*body. Anywhere. Get a look out the front door. Report anything you see, you hear? Anything."

Joe nods and quietly opens the front door.

The people on television are talking, somehow they are talking about the weather being unpredictable and how the Pirates are due back in town to face the Tigers.

"Is he gone?"

Vol goes to the door to look. She can feel him behind her. He says, "He's checking downstairs. I don't think there's anybody around. This place don't even have mice."

No one in the other apartments, then. Nausea fills her when she realizes the building is empty. Derelict. Otherwise why was it so easy for her to get in? The courage she felt goes out of her. She had been so sure someone would see, somewhere. The Rite Aid. She tried to be notice-able in the Rite Aid. Even though the clerk barely looked up, maybe she will remember.

"You know what you have to do?" the man in charge says to Vol. "You understand me?"

"I know."

"Take him some other direction. Take him north, east, I don't care. Make some excuse. Lose no time. You under-stand? No ID left whatsoever."

"Nothing."

"Take no time. You understand?"

"Yep."

"Someplace else, a different place, take care of the kid's clothes. So they'll never be found, ever. Burn 'em."

"Okay."

"Don't contact me for at least two weeks. Don't come back here to this place ever. I'll have it taken care of. Understand?"

"Got it."

"Christ. Get the clothes off that kid. Pack up my car. Use shopping bags, grocery bags, stuff that looks ordi-nary. Check in the kitchen cabinet for bags. Put in all that stuff in case I need it."

"The baby bottles? Okay."

"And put this bitch in the other room."

"Why?"

" 'Cause I hate her eyes. And I got things to do."

Marina tries to tell them to take off the sheet that gags her. She can hardly breathe. She wants to say, "I won't talk or scream, I'll just leave," but this is a lie, maybe even apparent before it is spoken, because Vol slaps her hard, gets her right at the cheek and forehead, and tells her to "shut it." Her face hurts, all the way to her eye socket.

"Take the chair and all, just get her out of here."

Vol jerks the chair as he tries to slide it forward. He has to go backwards first, then turn. While he does this, Joe comes back in.

"There's nobody," Joe says. "But it's bright out there. . . ."

"Yeah. Longest day. Close enough."

The chair slides backwards. Marina's eyes almost close with resignation. She remembers for a moment the appendix surgery she had when she was seven, or rather, remembers the gurney rolling backwards, backwards as she left the faces she knew and went with no will of her own toward nothingness.

"You know what you have to do?" the other one is saying to Joe. "She's your guest, your little problem. You've got the cleanup. You understand?"

"Yeah."

"You get me?"

"Yeah."

"No messing up this time. Show me what you can do."

So this is it. This is how she will end. In a filthy bedroom with a stripped bed and plywood over the only window. The hot and the dark are almost welcome, sedatives in their way. She feels herself giving up, being pulled toward resignation. It's not so awful to say good-bye, to leave the struggling behind and just let it be. Sleep is sweetest when you stumble toward it, unable to help yourself. She is light-headed. The door closes and she is hardly able to see a thing, just a small glow of light around the rectangular window.

BABY CRYING HARD. SOUNDS OF MOVEMENT. TELEVISION OFF. Voices. Something about "get rid of the TV," and "sure." Baby crying and crying. Oh, little one. So unhappy, so hot and terrible among strangers. It will be better, it will be better. Give up. Give in. Pray. There is nothing you can do. Nothing. The crying suddenly stops.

Light around the windows expands and grows. It's only her eyes becoming used to the dark. She can see a little. The bed out of the right side of her glance. The door straight ahead. If only she could tip toward the bed, lie down. If only her legs and hands had some feeling in them. If only she could speak. Prayer is silent. Prayer.

Voices. Sounds. The closing of a door. Voices again. "Ready." And "in a minute . . . this other thing I have to do." And "the bitch."

All of it comes alive again, everything in her, and she twists hopelessly in the chair, the only thing she can move being her middle section, where the sheet does not bind her. She squirms and moans. Please, please no, she thinks. It's not possible to let go of it after all. She can't stop moving, no matter how it hurts. She's pleading when the door opens. Joe and Vol in the picture frame of the door, but then Vol and the other one hurrying things toward the outside door, moving out of her vision. She can hear Vol's "Hurry up, then," but she can only see Joe, her eyes meet his, she prays to him over and over, please no. He raises the gun, breaks her gaze, meets it again, breaks it again.

The sound is not so loud. There is fire in her side at the end of her life, lightning in her head, and then blackness.

■ ■ ■

COMMANDER RICHARD CHRISTIE PUNCHED IN HIS HOME NUMber on his desk phone. "I'll be here most of the night," he told his wife. "You saw the news? I've got to be here."

He was about to hang up, but she said, "I know tonight's different, but I wish you worked construction."

He very consciously decided to give her fifteen seconds, fifteen seconds out of the case, to keep a connection going. He'd already told her many times before, "Right. Then I'd be out drinking with my buddies. Now I just work."

He tried to pull up Rapid-Start on his computer while she said, "Some husbands and wives are together all the time. They own shops together. They choose that."

"Very few." There is no time for an argument. "Baseball players go on the road. Lawyers work late. I gotta hang up."

"According to you nobody's having any fun," she'd said once.

"That's what I'm seeing," he'd told her. It was true. In his line of work, he didn't often see people having any fun.

"So you'll be out all night."

The Rapid-Start connections began to come up. "Midnight or after if nothing new happens. I have to go. I have phone calls to screen. I need to visit Karen Graves again. Her husband's on his way in. I question him around eleven. Then I see what's new."

"Maybe you could get the kids an autograph."

"I hope that was a joke." He hung up without trying any longer.

Christie sat for a moment with his head in his hands, wondering why Catherine, who'd seemed so normal when he met her, had come to have no ordinary human feelings. She didn't *think*. She didn't *feel*. Or she did feel, but only one thing: neglect, his neglect of her. That was the filter for everything she took in.

He went outside his office and talked to the ten who were reporting on the seventy-five out in the field. He listened to reports of nothing found yet by dogs, helicopters, and nodded approval that there were now copies of the videotape, and the first printout from Rapid-Start was put in front of him. He waved to junior detectives McGranahan and Coleson, who were waiting for his attention. "I faxed an order for the 911 tape. Did it come in?"

McGranahan brandished it.

He waved them into his office. "What do we have?"

"Calls. About forty of them so far. About fifteen of them on 911—so those you can hear. We took the rest on the hotline. We transcribed them. Shitheads talk about the reward right off. Depressing."

Bill Coleson assured him. "Schultz is out there covering the phones now."

"Summarize."

"Various people saying they saw a man and a baby in a car alone, no woman in the car. We've been asking what else, where, what car, was there a car seat, behavior of the man, rate of driving, relationship of man and baby," Coleson explained. "We're checking out three of them where the ages seem right. There's nothing definite in most of the calls. Could be any man and any baby up to this point."

"One guy actually said, after we took all his information, 'Lottery. Ding. Maybe I hit it, maybe I didn't,'" McGranahan interrupted.

Christie tucked away the thought that McGranahan might be having money problems, the way he kept bringing up the money-grubbers. "Don't get cynical," he said. McGranahan pursed his lips and nodded. Christie often gave his men orders about their emotions. They were used to his directions on their feelings. They actually, he noticed, seemed to like it—his work on their inner lives.

"Find my tape player. It's under those boxes of files. Let's go." While they unearthed the tape player, Christie read their written transcripts of phone calls. He got a sudden searing pain in his head and a sensation in his stomach. He'd forgotten to eat.

He dialed the front desk. "Do you have anyone you could send for food? Anything! Yeah. Primanti's would be fine." He looked up at Coleson and McGranahan and asked quickly, "You guys eat? Want anything?"

"We sent out a couple of hours ago," Coleson said.

Into the phone he said, "Okay. Corned beef. Fine. And a milk shake." And he looked up at them again, reading their demure looks, and added, "Make that three milk shakes." He pushed the speaker button on the phone and nodded toward them. "Chocolate or vanilla, she's asking. Make it quick."

"Strawberry, unless it's broken, otherwise vanilla," McGranahan said toward the phone.

"Chocolate," Coleson muttered.

"Chocolate for you, Commander?" the crackly voice came back.

"Chocolate for me, too."

Christie put the phone back and checked the connections on the old boom box they handed him. It was an ancient silver thing. On a day like today, he worried the old machine might get crotchety and eat the tape. He put the copy of the 911 audiotape in, hoping he could hear it without trouble. "And what else about these?" He brandished the written transcripts.

"Somebody saw a guy and a little kid check into a motel in Breezewood, but it turned out the kid was about two years old. He was running around the motel parking lot on his own steam. So, wrong kid there for sure. No pattern so far. We couldn't find one."

"How the hell could a kid disappear in the middle of the day?" Christie asked.

The tape began to play. Smooth enough. He listened and made notes: *corner of . . . guy acting kind of funny . . . shopping in the Ames store just ten minutes ago.* Christie pressed the rewind at times and skipped ahead when he'd heard enough. "Um, some guy carrying this baby and then some woman came a couple minutes later looking for him and asked me what house and I told her which one and she was in a big hurry. I saw the guy later, too. I was riding my bike past and he was putting things in a car." Christie took a note, paused, moved ahead. "In my Giant Eagle, and he was buying diapers." "That police sketch looks just like this guy who lives one street over, and he's a weirdo."

McGranahan said, consulting a notebook, "On the anonymous line, here's something really odd. One woman said, 'I think I saw the guy. I was waiting at the bus stop and I saw him get on a bus with a baby. I remember thinking something about him seemed funny, but I couldn't figure what. It was just him and the baby. Nobody else. Nothing else.'"

"Bus?" Christie asked.

"A PAT bus, she had to mean. She sounded pretty steady, but it's unlikely, isn't it—kidnapper using a city bus?" Coleson ventured.

Christie's face said, "Check everything."

McGranahan hastened to say, "We'll check it out."

The 911 tape went on and on in the background. Christie called in two more officers and four eagerly waiting Special Agents and gave them assignments to check out the guy who said his neighbor looked like the police sketch and the calls that fixed a person in a place. The rest—shadowy figures shopping at various times—he determined to try to remember in case some pattern emerged.

The boy who saw the woman following a man with a baby had given no name and no number and no location. He stopped the tape, rewound, and played the section again, but there was nothing more to go on.

"It's a kid," McGranahan said.

After he gave the officers their assignments, Christie went to the outer office and bumped Schultz aside. "Let me take them for a while," he said. Reading over Schultz's shoulder, he said, "You go follow up on this one and this one. Let me know immediately if you come up with anything. In an hour or so, come and relieve me."

Schultz looked surprised that Commander Christie was going to man the phones, but he nodded and went off. The fact was, Christie always felt jittery after a press conference, and he could command as well while listening to phone calls as not. He could at least listen while he ate, before he visited the Graves' apartment and then made a trip to the airport to catch up with Ryan Graves when the plane from L.A. came in.

He managed to eat the whole of his sandwich from Primanti's. The sandwich was an indulgence he allowed himself about once a year—a Dagwood of a thing, piled almost a foot high, probably nearly a pound of corned beef on it and the French fries *on*, not beside, the sandwich, a signature of the shop. The milk shake was a little plastic-tasting. It was from the McDonald's next door.

He took calls until nearly nine o'clock at night. All the while, he kept dispatching men and taking reports. He knew he was good at it, juggling twenty things at once, and it thrilled him to keep all the balls in the air. He asked questions that blew the stuffing out of most of the calls. "Was the little kid you're telling me about walking? Talking? How old was the guy?" he'd challenge. "What did the guy have on? What did the kid have on? What did the guy have with him?" He pressed on, hoping for some luck. He tried to believe in luck, that something would come through. The case had not begun well. And it was a very public case.

The whole dinner, if it could be called by such a fine name, sat in his stomach like wet dough. His guts ached. The men always vowed to stock the department freezer with Lean Cuisine for the microwave and to keep vegetables and fruits around. Some of them made a point of bringing in healthy leftovers from home.

At nine o'clock he headed for the Graves' apartment. He thought Karen Graves was a pretty nice woman and wondered what her husband would be like up close. And what he would learn about them as a couple.

Sometimes Christie stayed out, worked overtime when the cases were routine. Tonight was different, extraordinary. Sometimes he just stayed away from home. When his wife accused him of liking work better than his home life, he didn't deny it, but talked around it, told her what specific tasks he had to do that day. It was the commonest form of lying, the indirect answer.

He started up his car. He kept the police radio on and his phone beside him and used Baum Boulevard, driving very fast toward Bigelow. The sky was still full of light. He liked this time in the summer when the days were long and people moved easily, unburdened by winter clothes. Things didn't shut down. Dairy Queen was open. He liked that. Knew perfectly well most cops liked the opposite, everybody tucked away, no interference in the picture.

He was very much out of love and he figured there wasn't a thing he could do about it except pour himself into work. He was Catholic and responsible. He wasn't about to dump his wife, and so he practiced avoidance. Catherine's voice bothered him; in the last couple of years, it had become abrupt and higher-pitched. She was often negative about things—well, about *him*—and half her utterances compared the two of them, as a couple, to others.

Everybody in the world was better off, she thought. Once she envied aloud the welfare couple down the street who sat together and drank all day. He said, "You are one ungrateful woman." He slowed down his anger and pointed out that he and she somehow had produced two wonderful kids. He turned to practical matters: they had enough to eat, medical benefits; she had occasional work as a secretary at the university. He joked grimly: Excellent death benefits came with his job! But deep down he was lying, because he, too, thought love was the most important thing, and if the welfare couple had it, if they did, well, maybe that was better than anything else.

The constant bickering made his head ache. All the while, he knew he didn't love her anymore.

Once he confided to his best detective, his best friend, Artie Dolan.

"Leave," Artie said. And Artie wasn't a careless guy, either. He was even religious, Christie suspected, in a quiet way. "You only have one life. In this business, maybe not even that. Leave."

Leave. He couldn't do it. The kids, for one thing. The kids, mainly. He saw abandonment every day and nothing pretty about it.

The disappearance of the Graves child now—he'd grabbed the case, took over, and what did he think he could do?

GATEWAY TOWERS WAS A PRETTY FANCY PLACE, FANCIER THAN a rookie pitcher could generally afford. A hockey player who *could* afford the place, but who was away for months, had offered it to the Pirates management for a minimal rent. It had seemed just the thing for Graves and his wife while they were looking for a place to live.

He parked outside and left his flashers on so he would not have to take the time to go below to the parking lot. Sometimes he got tickets, and he had to pay them, too, for moves like this. What a joke. Policemen didn't get any breaks anymore. Why do it, why do it? In moments he was up the elevator and in the apartment.

There were six FBI agents there doing the work of tapping the phones. One was finishing up the wiring. Two were sitting at a table in the living room, making notes, testing the receiver. Three were in the kitchen doing he didn't know what, but they emerged when he began to speak. He had a good relationship with these guys, and so for a moment all seven stood in the living room, talking over the case, while Christie waited for Karen to come out of the bedroom where she'd been lying down. The men from the Bureau deferred to him, going against the cliché of the relationship between city police and the FBI. They deferred partly because he was officially in charge of the task force, even though they had more means and more reach, but partly because of his personality.

He stood behind one of the trendy overstuffed chairs and looked at the snippets of wire on the floor. He told the agents to go ahead and finish their work.

He paced around and looked at things. On the tables and bookcases were framed photos of Ryan, Karen, and Justin.

Ryan and Karen sitting at the side of a swimming pool, toes stretched out into a deep aqua blue, arms around each other. With relatives at some sort of formal gathering, maybe a reunion, arms around each other. At their wedding, stiff in clothing they probably paid a fortune for, looking into each other's eyes.

Christie felt an uncomfortable longing for his old self, young and hopeful.

He remembered a rough, unsentimental sort of a guy he'd seen on the news once, being interviewed. He thought of the story often. Terrible flood, everything destroyed, and the guy risked his life paddling back for his wife's wedding dress. Christie envied him that feeling.

Karen emerged from the bedroom in a different dress. She had probably showered. Her hair was limper and she had no makeup on. She'd been given some pills late in the afternoon, he knew that. She seemed different, slowed down, but she kept asking, "Can't I do something?"

"Waiting is the hardest. The hardest thing. We're working very hard. You're doing well. We're proud of you."

She nodded, looking absently at the wires on the carpet. "Can I get you something? A beer or a Coke or something?"

"Coke," he said.

He studied the pictures. People did all kinds of terrible things, faked love and terror and innocence. He studied pictures of Justin alone and the parents with Justin.

"You and your husband look to be very close," he said when she returned with the Coke. He could feel the agents listening behind him.

"I can't bear to be without him. It's hard, him being a baseball player."

Christie looked at his watch. "He'll be here soon. I have men meeting him at the airport."

"I'll go with you," she said.

"No. You'll have to stay here. We need you here to answer the phone. I'm going to go out there and talk with him; then, as soon as I can, I'll bring him to you."

Her lip trembled. "You don't think we're like those other people, do you? You don't think we had anything to do with this? I thought you were looking for who did this."

He saw the hysteria beginning to rise. "I don't expect you to understand everything now," he said. "Someday, when this is all over, and you've had lots of time, maybe you'll understand everything I've done. Someday. I hope so. Right now you can go into another room and be mad at me. Throw something. I'll understand."

He'd said this speech many times over the years.

Learned it from Bogart, and needed it often when he talked to the families of victims.

Her face continued to fight tears. He was reminded suddenly of his four-year-old daughter when she was trying to be brave.

"I'll try to have him back to you by eleven."

■ * ■

WHEN MICHAEL GOT HOME AT TEN-THIRTY, HE WAS FEELING something between abject apology and elation. He had had a lot to drink and he was rolling with it. He had every expectation of a scene; he looked forward to it. Yelling! In his head, he was already yelling to defend himself. Marina would be amazed to see him walk in, drunk and cocky. Her jaw would drop with uncertainty, puzzlement. Then she would tell him how worried she'd been, calling his office and a few of his friends, how frightened she'd been, thinking maybe he'd had a car accident or something. On the table would be a plate set for him and on the stove would be food that was now dried out and sad-looking. Maybe pasta tubes with sausages. He would tell her he'd eaten. Otherwise he wouldn't say much. Silence, he told himself, was power.

So when he realized she was not home, his assurance wavered. He tried to guess where she might have gone. No note. Not on the kitchen table at least, where he would expect to find one. He sat for a moment in the living room, thinking and getting nowhere because he was so muddleheaded. A movie with a friend was a possibility. Maybe she and her friend Lizzie were sitting in some bar trashing him. Probably. That was probably it. And since she was angry, she left no note.

He needed coffee. The real thing, too, no decaf, he decided, as he rummaged around in the refrigerator, reading the labels of various bags of coffee. He cursed himself for having had so much to drink. While he gathered the coffee and filter and scoop, he looked around the kitchen for the remains of the dinner she'd made, but he saw no evidence of it. So she ate out, too! There were cereal bowls in the sink from when both of them had rushed out in the morning to Dr. Caldwell. He couldn't find evidence of Marina in the house. It was as if she'd come in, packed a bag, and left.

A terrible feeling went through him. While the coffee brewed, he went into the bedroom and looked for any piece of paper that might . . . Nothing. He checked their closet to see if any of her clothes seemed to be missing, but he couldn't tell for sure. It looked normal enough. The small overnight bag was not on the shelf in the cabinet above the closet. He made his way to the bathroom and noted her toothbrush was still there, but she had several, so maybe that didn't mean anything. He checked the extra bedroom. Nothing. The coffee was still brewing, so he went down to the basement, stepping carefully since he felt so unsteady. There it was. The evidence. The suitcases were gone. Man. There was the answer. Suitcases gone and not even a note. He went back upstairs.

Pouring himself a huge mug of coffee, he absently read the calendar in the kitchen. The appointment with the marriage therapist was penned in. There was nothing for the week coming up except Marina's dentist appointment. Then "dinner with Liz and Doug?" for ten days hence.

Once he had finished one cup of coffee, he realized how out of sync he was. The first thing he generally did when he came into an empty house was listen to the phone answering machine on the kitchen counter. Now it had to blink rapidly at him to make him notice it. He counted. Five messages.

The messages went back to earlier in the day. Four o'clock and onward. So she had come in before midafternoon, packed, and not come back. Two messages were for him, one from his uncle, wanting advice on how to handle a real estate sale, one from his bank, asking about an overdraft. One message was from the dentist, reminding Marina of her upcoming appointment on Monday. Two messages were from her friend Lizzie, saying, "Jeez, what a day I'm having. I need a dose of sanity. Call me," and "Liz again. Call me."

So she was not with Liz. He turned the machine off. It was blank now, no flashing lights.

He had another cup of coffee. He picked up a book he'd been dabbling in, a history of legal thought, and he tried to read it. His own thoughts, not particularly legal ones, swam in and out through the sentences so that he didn't register meanings.

At eleven-forty, he threw the book across the room and grabbed at his jacket, which was thrown over the couch. Fumbling, he found the piece of paper he was looking for. He reached over and used the living room phone to dial Kendall.

"Did I wake you?"

"No. I can't sleep. I don't think I'll get any sleep tonight."

"I don't know what I'm doing."

"I know. I don't want to hurt anyone, like I said. I've been there."

"I wish I hadn't left. I should have just stayed with you. It was sweet. But I figured, if I stayed, we were in for it. We would have been in bed in two more minutes."

He was answered with a long silence. He said, finally, "I don't want to do anything to hurt you, either. I'm"—he looked around at his empty house—"trying to figure things out. It wouldn't take a genius to figure out my wife and I are having a shaky time."

"I thought so."

"You probably don't believe me. Every guy says that."

"Maybe sometimes it's true."

"I was starting to feel really comfortable with you to-night. Then I pushed myself to leave. I wish I hadn't."

She answered him with another long silence.

"I'm coming over," he said.

It felt like the end of his life, this thing other men did all the time. It felt weird and scary, something he could not possibly survive.

■　　■

THERE IS NOTHING BUT DARKNESS. THIS MUST BE PART OF waiting, a stage on the way to dying. Her head is wet, there is something in her eye, and she would like to wipe it.

Hands don't move, nothing moves, only pain when she tries. She is sitting. Is she sitting or lying down with legs bent? Her head feels wet. It is hot. The sheet is soaked. It's so dark, she cannot wake up, and yet she wants to, to see something before she dies. She remembers the man who was on the bus and the same man skulking in corners and then the way he looked at her, then the shots.

She remembers him and the other two. She reaches out for their names, but they slip away.

She is sitting maybe.

Her breathing is making a noise. She tries to quiet it so she can hear something else. Nothing. Nothing. Utter silence. A car. Coming and going. A rattly-sounding engine. Gone. She *is* breathing. She is alive. What if the men have left her here forever in an empty building? In an empty neighborhood. No one will ever find her.

She can make out a little of her surroundings. Some of it is memory. The window with its plywood is hopeless, no way to break that down. There is now only the faintest light coming through at the edges. But behind her is the door. If she can rock her body, make the chair move backwards to the door, then hit it *against* the door. She has to contract her stomach to try to move the chair. Pain shoots through her body. She contracts and pushes, again and again. The chair will not move on the carpet, but she keeps trying. Seven times, eight times, nine times, and she senses a little movement finally. She has to lift her whole body up in its sack to move at all, and she moves, if at all, maybe a quarter of an inch. Something to do while dying, a goal. She tries again, moaning, and again, but then she stops, thinks. She will use all her available energy if she keeps this up, and the usefulness is uncertain. No, she will wait, think, try something else.

She goes still, trying to bring her mind into focus, summoning energy. Suddenly she hears a sound. Someone is coming. She fills her lungs and cries out as loud as she can. The gag muffles her cries, so that they sound weak and much too quiet for anyone to hear. The effort exhausts her and she slips into blackness again.

The next time she comes to, she has very clear memories

of trying to back up the chair, of calling out. If someone came into the building once, she reasons, it could happen again. She must get some part of her free. She is able to rock and make a thumping noise on the floor, but it isn't very loud. If only she could get the gag out of her mouth. If she sinks back as hard as she can against the upholstery of the chair and pushes at the sheet with her tongue, maybe, maybe she will be able to free her mouth. She sets to work on this, with the realization that her mind is clearing even though her body feels stiff and weak. She understands that the wetness she feels on her forehead and over her left eye is blood. She understands that she will pass out again at some point. For a day she has had nothing to eat or drink and she is losing blood. It seems to her she must free her face, her mouth, to be able to do anything else. She presses against the chair, trying to get enough space to force out the dirty sheet that gags her. She works at this for a long time until it happens; it happens finally by pushing back and tilting her face to the side and forcing the gag out over her lower lip with her tongue. She waits for a moment and slides back upward in the chair. The wet sheet hugs her throat like a tight collar. She grabs for breath and begins calling for help. She calls loudly enough to be heard in a tiny auditorium, but not beyond the walls of a theatre. This is not her big voice, not her Greek tragedy voice, but she can't make that sound now for anything. She calls for the better part of an hour before passing out again.

■   ■

"AND THEN I RODE BY AGAIN AND THE SAME CARS THAT WERE there were gone. I told my friends about it and they said they'd go up with me. We went real late at night. We were hanging out at the pizza shop and we went over there. The cars weren't back, but we took baseball bats anyway. We listened at a couple of doorways and we heard the baby crying on the second floor. I called before. Only on the 911 number. My number is 555-8207."

Two hours at home and no gift of sleep. It was a little before five in the morning and Christie froze when he played this part of the tape. "What did you do with this?" he asked the two young cops who had taken over from Schultz.

"Nothing yet. We got a whole list to get to first. Sounds like some teenager's thinking about the reward."

"He called before. This one. I know this voice."

"We thought that." One officer looked at the other. "Clearly a kid."

"You're only about three years older than he is," Christie muttered. "I like the sound of this kid. He left me his phone number."

He wrote the number down and headed back to his office.

He and two of his detectives had gone to meet Ryan Graves at the airport. Airport security had lent them an interview room that they could use for the first phase, the initial interrogation, the debriefing, the idea being that if Graves seemed clean, they would take him to East Liberty only long enough to watch the surveillance tape, then get him home.

What Christie saw last night was a pale and terrified young man getting off the plane. The way his new teammates rallied around him, that was something to see. They were a phalanx, supporting him. Christie had had to dismiss them in order to conduct the interview, but some of them stayed at the airport for a while, just to let Ryan know they were there. Christie was impressed, as he always was, when he saw affection, unselfishness.

In the Airport Security offices, Graves sure came off like the clean-cut American boy who just wanted to play ball. He didn't even understand the questions about whether he or his wife might be having an affair. When he did get it, he seemed shocked. Boyish, that's what he was. "Did he smoke dope?" they asked. "Abuse any kind of medication? Had he been gambling, maybe?" They had to ask these things. The kid came off like a poster boy for goodness. They got gentler with him, put him in a car, and took him to the Investigative Branch.

At the office in East Liberty, right out in the main room, where the men were still monitoring phone calls, Graves studied the tape hard and told them in a shaken voice that to the best of his knowledge he'd never seen the guy before. He broke down crying, and Christie felt jaded standing there with the kid holding up two hands to his eyes and big fat drops squeezing through anyway. Then he explained to Ryan that when he got back to the apartment he shared with his wife, he'd find a couple of Special Agents and a lot of equipment there.

He'd run the case from his post at Investigations until one-thirty or so, gone home. Got into bed with the cell phone beside him. Not slept. Come back in.

Now he went to dial the boy who'd called twice. He sighed. He hesitated, looked at the clock, then punched in the number. Almost five A.M.

Probably the guys were right. It was just a kid hoping for reward money. But he was impressed by the kid's attempt to do detective work, the persistence. Something called to him.

Maybe he was just feeling desperate. The idea of handing that baby back to his destroyed parents was pushing at him. It came to him as an image, an icon. One of the guys had a little statuette on his desk of a cop carrying a child. Every policeman's fantasy—to save the child. To be worth it.

The phone rang for a long time before a very angry woman answered it. "What?!" she asked right away, and then when she partway heard Christie's question, "What kind of a son of a bitch would call in the middle of the night? *What* about my son? What did he do now?"

"Wake him up and keep him there. I'll be there to talk to him in ten minutes."

He took a young detective, Jerrod Davidson, with him. He told Davidson to drive.

"You must think you have something," Davidson said,

pulling out of the precinct with a questioning look on his face.

"I'm not holding out any big hopes. But there was something about this kid that made me remember him from the first time. See, I heard his voice on the 911 tape. He's into reporting facts. I guess he wants to be a cop."

"Maybe he's just playing out some TV script."

"Maybe."

"Any contact between the kidnapper and the parents?"

"Nothing. Not a thing."

"Too soon, probably."

A fierce-looking, heavyset woman was trying to bar the door when Davidson pulled the car up. Davidson and Christie got out slowly, so she could look at them and the badges they displayed, but she kept her arms spread out. "What did Darnell do? You bastards don't care it's the middle of the night?"

He refrained from pointing out that, for many people, it was morning. The boy appeared behind her. "I got to tell them, Mom, about something I saw yesterday."

"He might be of help to us," Christie said levelly. "If he did anything wrong, we sure don't know about it at this point. Give us a couple of minutes of your time."

"Mom! It's maybe important!"

She let her arms down and moved aside. "I don't even want to know what you been up to."

"I think maybe I saw the guy," Darnell told Christie. "Should I start at the beginning?"

"We got some of it on the phone tape. The man with the baby, a woman running after, then you went back and heard a baby crying, is that right? You're the guy who called?"

"Yeah," Darnell said. "The woman looked really worried. That's what made me remember her. Then when I saw it on the news, I thought the guy could have been, you know, the guy on the sketch. So I started watching the house. I saw the guy again—he come out the front door and I think it *was* him. The cars hit me because they're not always there. Two of them. My friends didn't remember ever seeing those cars, but I did. Couple of months ago and a long time before that. Both cars are gone now. I didn't see them actually leave because I went way around a couple of blocks. I didn't want to seem obvious. But somebody maybe stayed behind, because I took my friends in there and we heard a baby crying."

"Why did you make that face just now?"

"What face?"

"When you said there was a baby crying."

"It was a weird cry. . . ."

"In what way?"

"I don't know."

"What's your full name, son?"

"Darnell Flowers," he said uncomfortably.

Hates his last name, Christie thought. "Your age?"

"Fifteen."

"You live here every day?"

"Yeah!"

"You want to show us where you heard the sounds of crying?"

"Yeah." Darnell Flowers bounced on the balls of his feet like a basketball player. "Now?"

"You can't just take him like that, can you?"

"I'll be back, Mom."

Christie asked, "It's how far?"

"Two blocks."

"Let's go." He turned to the boy's mother. "Davidson will drive him back. Darnell doesn't go in the building again, Mrs. Flowers. Davidson will bring him right back."

"And I'm supposed to believe you?"

Christie didn't answer her. She was angry. The fact was, she looked pretty crazy; his gut told him she was damaged in some permanent way, and he wasn't sure why the boy seemed to be rising above that, but he didn't want to lose momentum with the kid. And he was in a hurry. Afraid of what he would find, sick with the dread of it.

Of course, Darnell Flowers didn't want to be driven back home.

"You aren't going in without me, too, sir, are you?"

Davidson asked when Christie got out of the car and waved them back toward Flowers' house.

The commander shook his head. "I'll wait."

"How much backup?"

After a hesitation, Christie said, "Nothing yet. No noise. No lights."

Davidson let out a long stream of breath.

Commander Christie watched Davidson drive off and he looked at his watch. Three minutes or so, it would take. He hurried to the side of the house where he could stand in darkness. There he shrugged his shoulders up as high as he could and then stretched them downward to relax them. His stomach was in chaos and his hands were shaking. Probably it would turn out to be nothing, but if he did have to do something, the adrenaline shot was going to be more useful than not, probably. Waiting, expecting, felt awful and exhilarating at the same time, getting this pumped, a reminder every time how close he was to junkies and repeat offenders.

The building, so far as he could see, was one of those great old turn-of-the-century houses that nobody had the money to keep up. Two blocks away, where Darnell Flowers lived, everything looked occupied, but not so here. Across the street there was lots of darkness and not a little plywood at the windows. Just about when he was getting restless enough to go up to the door on his own, Davidson returned, dousing the lights the last fifty yards and coming as quietly as possible to a stop. The sun was just beginning to crest over the hill, and in the moments in which they nodded to each other and began to move, the darkness switched to light.

They both moved quickly and quietly to meet at the front door, hands on their guns. Christie looked out at the street and Davidson looked in through the glass.

"Nothing," Davidson said. "No activity whatsoever."

He tried the door and it opened easily. Both men stood in the front hall. They slammed up against the wall and tried the door on the first floor, even though Christie thought from his canvassing outside the house that the apartment there looked empty. The door was locked.

"What now?" Davidson asked.

It was then that they heard sound. Thumping and then some sort of crying.

They started up the stairs fast and stood outside the second-floor door. Christie nodded once. Davidson tried the door, but this one was locked, too. The cries came clearer.

"That's no baby," Davidson said. "We got some other whole thing here."

Christie tapped on the door. Nobody answered. The voice stopped for a minute and then began again calling for help. "We're going in," Christie said. "Get another car here."

Davidson made the call.

The apartment door was an old heavy one that didn't want to move, so after a couple of hits, Christie shot the lock, careful to aim downward, and shaking the whole time. He finally rocked the door open.

He made his way easily in the direction of the cries. The hollow-core door between rooms opened without trouble.

He stepped into a room so dark he couldn't see anything clearly. As he fumbled for a light switch, Davidson's flashlight caught a form, a woman, a woman's face, bloody. Then Christie got the ceiling light on and he saw sheets stretched over a chair, bloody, and the woman's face again, with matted blood on one side. There was no one else in the room. Davidson guarded the door. Christie moved forward.

Gunshot wounds; she'd been shot.

"Easy, lady, easy, you're going to be okay, I'm going to cut this off you. Don't move."

Davidson called an ambulance. After that, Christie gave him orders to call Forensics for prints, fibers, the whole shebang.

"Another whole thing here," Christie remembered Davidson saying outside the door. Certainly true. "We have an ambulance coming," he told the woman. "Can you talk to us? Can you tell us who did this?"

"Three men . . . gone now . . ."

Three men had shot her?

"The baby. They have the baby."

"The Graves baby?"

"On television. They saw it. Then they knew."

"They shot you?"

"One man." She pointed toward the door.

He couldn't figure her part in this. "You know the mother?" he asked.

"No, no." She twisted to try to see him as he cut the last of the ropes.

"I'm listening. Tell me."

Then she spoke more carefully, as if she thought the story she told too wild to be believed. She told him she had only seen the mother, she had followed a man who had the baby. There were three men altogether, but they had left while it was still light out, and one of them, she thought, took the baby. She had thought she heard one of them say Ohio.

He saw that the effort to tell him these things weakened her further. He hated to keep pressing, but her tale was very peculiar. "You just followed this man?"

He tried to understand her words about not meaning to go that far, only getting the feeling something was wrong. Then wanting an address, and then, after, wanting to see to the safety of the kid.

Foolhardy, maybe, but amazingly clearheaded, it seemed, oddly articulate, and yes, brave—yes, he thought so. He explained he would need a lot of information, as much as she could tell him, and that he would ride with her to the hospital. "Will you help us?" he asked.

She seemed very weak and her eyes kept closing. She said she wanted to help the mother and the baby. Christie thanked her, and after a while, she began to cry. She asked him to call her husband.

He tried the number she gave him, but there was no answer, so he asked her to repeat the number, thinking she might have said it wrong or he had heard it wrong. But no, it was the same. He smiled and tried again. "We can't rouse him," he said. "I'll send a man around." She did not seem to understand what he meant. He radioed the precinct and asked that an officer be sent to the address she'd given him. He asked the officer to run a search on the address and phone number in case she was too delirious to be giving it correctly.

When the medics arrived at the apartment, they tried to work very fast. "You know your blood type?" one asked while the other stayed on the phone to the hospital.

Christie watched them ask her questions, different from his. How much pain was she feeling in her head? Had she passed out? How often? Could she see out of her left eye?

Christie stayed close. She was officially a suspect, of course, had to be, although he didn't suspect her of anything but maybe reckless compassion. Her voice was fluty and warm. Weak as she was, she gave the impression of trying to help the paramedics. Certainly the ruined dress, the shoes that had to be pried off her swollen feet, something about the hair, the nail polish, suggested a life completely different from this room she'd ended up in.

She turned to him. "Three men. They saw it on television . . . in the other room . . . didn't know who they had, just a baby . . . called him Brian, but — The mother wore a flowered dress. The baby wore a blue—"

"She's going to have to be still," the medic said. "We don't know where the bullets hit."

Christie told her, "As soon as you've seen the doctors, I'm going to see if you can talk some more to me. We have to make sure you're going to be okay first."

She shook her head. It was okay. She wanted to help.

2

AT FOUR IN THE MORNING ON THAT SATURDAY, JUST ABOUT when Commander Christie sat on the side of his bed in Pittsburgh, put a hand on his wife's hip and announced he was going back to the Investigative Branch, Manny LaPaglia lurched into his law office in Cleveland. To get to the Cleveland office, Manny had had to start out from Pittsburgh, where he lived, two hours earlier, smack dab in the middle of the night. A mountain of a man—he was used to being called that—who had to wear specially tailored suits, Manny never much liked having to armor himself in fine fabric on a Saturday, although he'd done it; he preferred to stay in his pajamas on the weekend. Bile rose in him. Mountain Manny was volcanic. He worked toward calm, placing himself behind his desk, hands— paws—on the table, stilling himself, a sphinx, while he was momentarily alone.

Manny's face was not only large-boned, but jowly, almost twice the size of other faces. He'd been born that way, large-boned, and then he went ahead and added weight to nature's gifts, as if collaborating to take up more and more space. He knew how he looked, might have whimsically called himself a new kind of sphinx, with a bulldog's face and the outsized body of a man. He knew he hunched forward when he sat, when he didn't want to be asked questions, which enhanced his canine look.

In the solo law practice he'd made, Manny LaPaglia had the reputation of being a hard worker, at least so far as his secretary was concerned. He came in early, was often there when she wasn't there, talked to her little, and that was the gist of the making of the reputation. He told her he generally came in at six-thirty, which she thought was fairly astonishing, but then she'd been chosen for her sleepy-headedness and easy astonishment. Actually, he often came in as early as four or five in the morning, and he did so on the Saturday in June that was the day of all the activity surrounding the Graves baby.

Bile was rising in him because Anton Vradek was there now, outside his door. When he'd driven into his parking space beside the building at four o'clock—minutes ago—he was furious to see Anton sitting in a car across the street. He had ordered Anton to *phone* him, *not* to visit, and that at exactly four-thirty. He'd intended to name a place Vradek should go to, in this case a motel they'd never used before, to meet the couple that was driving in from Pennsylvania. If Manny didn't find the couple steady, he'd make some excuse, put off the deal, never mention the motel to them.

So when Manny saw Anton sitting in the car, anger began at the tips of his fingers and crept inward. He'd watched Anton bound out of the white Buick with a shopping bag in each hand. Manny held up one hand, then two, warning that the other man should *stay back, stay away*. But Anton hurried over to him as if he hadn't seen a thing, and together the two men entered the small, yellow-brick, three-story building at the back door, Manny fuming. Manny had forced himself not to scan the empty Cleveland streets. If anyone was watching, or if a patrol car should appear, making its rounds, the very act of looking would be more suspicious than sticking to his own business.

The galling thing was, Anton had taken it into his head to call the shots and to treat Manny like the lackey.

A key summoned the elevator, which clicked, groaned, and finally hummed into position. Both men got in and stood in an almost breathless silence while the elevator lifted them. Manny heard a clicky hiccoughy sound coming from one of the shopping bags. The bag was stretched and bulky. He felt sick. He let out a breath and began gulping air. This was far from the first time he had dealt with Anton, but things were not happening in their usual way. He seethed. "Wait here. I have something I have to do." Anton snorted a laugh. That's when he went into his office alone and tried to work out how to handle the next two hours. He cursed his sister for bringing Anton Vradek into their lives. The first time he met him he'd called him a *slick dickie,* and she'd laughed and shrugged. But that was years ago and now there were patterns and he couldn't figure out how to undo them.

So. Manny LaPaglia entered his inner office at about the same time Richard Christie stood up, strapped on his gun, gathered his pager and phone, and tried to ignore his wife's sighing groan. Middle-of-the-night work for both men, "the dawn watch," Manny called it, when he made certain transactions that needed to be hidden from the light.

Christie closed the bedroom door, went downstairs and out into the night.

Manny squeezed into the seat behind his desk, taking his bulldog pose, his laughable riddling sphinx pose.

Even before it happened, Manny knew Anton would defy him by coming into the office before he was called in. The doorknob made a small click, the door scraped across the rug, and there he was.

Anton left the door open and stood between the two rooms. He still held the ridiculous shopping bags. They stared at each other for a moment. Anton turned and closed the door.

"Is he all right in there?" Manny asked finally, nodding toward the bowed and misshapen bag. "A boy? Is he all right?"

"He cried a lot last night. I did the number with the thimble of whiskey."

"You better hope it was a thimble. Take him out of the

bag, for Christ's sake. We're inside. You sure he's all right?"

"He could play football." Anton reached in and scooped out the baby. He pulled off the sheet, a fitted bottom bedsheet that made an awkward wrap, and moved forward to hand the child over the desk.

Manny was horrified when he saw the size of the baby. He had said "newborn" to the couple from Sewickley, and then he'd had to say, problems, problems, this and that, and finally told them, "two months old." Now that was going to turn out to be wrong.

"What's in the other bag?"

"Bottles. Diapers."

Manny could see the child was sweating terribly.

"Here he is. Like I said on the phone, we didn't have time to go buy clothes, so the diaper will have to be it in this case. You can do your 'We give him to you as God made him' kind of thing. I'm sure you're good at that." Anton let out a dry laugh. "Emelia has a way with words, you got to admit."

Manny looked up sharply. He decided not to answer. As he collected himself, he found himself swaying to rock the baby, who was still knocked out on whiskey.

"You look real natural. Go ahead. Examine him. I would."

Manny looked at the round, round cheeks, closed eyes, long lashes. The lack of any movement from the baby made him nervous. He put a hand on the small abdomen. Yes, the child was breathing. He supposed the boy was all right. But Manny was no natural, which Anton knew very well, had hardly ever handled the babies himself. He shifted this baby to the crook of his arm. His arm resting against his belly made a large balloony cushion.

"What—you what? Drove around all night?" He checked the clock on his desk, his watch. He hoped the couple would not be early; he needed to get Anton out of here—

"Secondary roads, dirt roads. Back-and-forth shit. Man, I wanted to check into a motel pretty bad, but I didn't, I didn't. I found a tiny road, if it was that, pulled off long enough to feed the kid. Fell asleep for an hour. That scared the shit out of me. Then a couple of hours ago, the little bastard got very crazy, so I gave him the whiskey."

Manny raised his eyebrows.

"Small amount."

Manny felt the baby's stomach again, the even breathing, trying to think how he would present him. He inwardly rehearsed what he would say to the new parents even while he resisted the idea of doing the thing in his office. "I'd feel better if we did something closer to the usual routine—" Manny began, but Anton cut him off in that way he did when he'd been drinking heavily.

"I know, I know. But I don't have the brilliant Emelia with me. I don't have my guys. My backup. Me alone, handing over the kid? I don't think so. You're the best bet and you know it. Do your lawyer thing." Anton opened his coat jacket to show his gun, and then opened his hands in a gesture of helpful innocence. "I'll back you up if you want. I can be in the hall." He seemed suddenly unsteady on his feet.

Manny, still holding the baby in his arms, thought, no, better to get him out of there, then, if that's how it was. One cross word and he might use that thing, and then what? He opened a desk drawer and took out a nine-by-twelve manila envelope. He took cash from it, and performed the counting for Anton to witness. He stood awkwardly because he had only one arm to support him, the other still making a cushiony cradle for the baby.

"I brought this cash from home," he explained. "Ten thousand. Given the circumstances, it's all I have. Emelia told me to pay you up front and get you on the road. Obviously, I like it better when we stick to procedure. If they take the kid, I'll have another ten for you."

"They better take the kid."

Manny sat down, this done awkwardly, too, and looked with a lowered head upward at Anton. He didn't want to work with Anton ever again. He wondered how he could make an end of it. This baby was evidence of a rash act, several rash acts, and although Manny didn't know what they were exactly, he wanted out of it, for good. Yet everything he thought of doing endangered him or his sister. He felt light-headed with failure. And Anton knew that. The man stood there reading his face.

"Emelia needs you to fix this one," Anton said almost kindly. "It won't happen like this again. I've seen to that."

"How?"

"Got rid of Joe. That was crucial."

Blood. Blood had been shed, then. Manny had known something like this would happen sooner or later. Joe, a pathetic creature. He had met him once. One of Emelia's finds. He felt nauseated.

The child slept quietly in the crook of his arm. Go through with it, cover all bases, and think later, he told himself.

He tried to steady his breathing as Anton recounted the money. The Emmonses were due to arrive at five o'clock. The couple was told yesterday at noon that their adoption had not come through, then at three in the afternoon that surprisingly it had come through after all, and then at four that they would be going to a motel in Cleveland at five the next morning to meet the representatives of the young Russian girl who had given up her child. This Russian girl had made a last-ditch try for a contact with the father of the child, Manny told them on the phone, but that hadn't been realistic at all, and she had finally decided to go ahead and give her two-month-old baby up for adoption. She'll change her mind again, then, the man said. Manny assured him it had only been false hopes that had held up the process this little while, but the baby was a beautiful, healthy baby and they'd be foolish not to take it. And only two months old. Two months was hardly time for the child to become aware of anything. No language problems or anything like that, he had said. And if you went the usual route, going to Russia—so long as the Russians were still allowing it—you got a kid who was over a year old. There was language confusion at that age, disorientation.

The couple said the mother might have an attachment to the baby that would play havoc with her decision at the last moment.

Manny guaranteed them the baby was in the hands of his associates from the New York office, and the girl herself was already on a plane.

All the while, he thought the colossal mess behind it all was apparent—the excuses, the age of the kid changing. Now when they finally saw the baby, they would see the age he gave them was plain wrong. . . .

The baby stirred in his arms. Manny felt relief at this. He tried to compose a speech. He knew his sister usually said something like, "You'll be taking him from poverty and giving him a good life." If she had a way with words, it was more in the performing of them. But she would have had a hefty challenge, selling this baby as poor, even naked in a diaper. "Strapping kid" came to mind.

Yesterday everything had gone wrong. He could still hear his sister's harried voice on the phone. There had been a baby—a tiny newborn, very small, born prematurely, it turned out, but Emelia didn't tell him at first. Instead she instructed him to call the couple and fix the meeting, begin the process, business as usual. And then a series of phone calls from Anton, the cancellations, the changed stories, Joe supposedly holding the fort in Pittsburgh, Emelia running off to New York again, and then mutterings about *another* baby, a better baby, he was told, suddenly available, and Manny left to guess what had gone on.

He guessed now that Joe had done something way out of routine to get this baby. He would learn the details from Emelia eventually, but he didn't want to be known to know them, not by Anton, whom he trusted as he would an adder. The more innocence he could preserve, the better he could protect himself if he was ever questioned: He took a baby from a man named Anton. Anton got it from a Russian girl who gave it up. He knew no more.

Every time Anton seemed about to divulge the hows and wheres of this new baby, Manny headed him off. It was what he was good at—diverting, pushing aside, keeping at a distance. It was the message his body gave to the world.

Of the "mysteries" of his adoption operation, Manny was philosophical. He was transferring precious goods, balancing nature's mistakes, for why was it these unloved, undernourished, always dirt-poor foreign women—the population he usually dealt with—could breed like crazy when well-fed American women with money couldn't. It was as if despair and poverty, victimization and bad food made the body's machinery work better. Nature's mistake or nature's joke.

When you're poor and wanting, everything is for sale, he figured, everything. I'm doing a service. Everybody wins.

Anton leafed through the money efficiently. He might have been a croupier, pretty and dandyish, hired for just this swaggering look, on a cruise ship.

Manny's mouth filled with saliva; he couldn't swallow.

What all of them now thought of as "procedure" had once seemed outrageous to Manny, but he had gotten used to it. People get used to things. Amazing how that happens. You do a thing once, it's easier to do it again, that's what they say. Adultery. Stealing. He'd come to accept the idea of newborns carried by Anton and Emelia to some motel or patch of ground, at the dawn watch, yes, as part of his business. Sometimes his sister and Anton pretended to be a couple who had decided to give up a child; mostly they pretended to be legal representatives for a single woman who was still recovering from the delivery. Vol and Joe often booked into the motel room behind them, ready with guns in case they had to get Anton and Emelia out of there fast. Sometimes one of them hung out behind the motel room or near a Dumpster. But miraculously, there hadn't been trouble, ever. Manny had chosen his customers brilliantly, people of desperation and means. Anton and Emelia delivered more than acceptable performances. The babies played their part, too, costumed humbly by Emelia in something simple, wrapped in a blanket.

The baby in Manny's arms, wearing only a diaper, was maybe four months old. Fairer than usual. Fatter than usual. And Manny was no award-winning actor. His nerves showed. But he would play stupid and say "two months."

How smart or dumb did his buyers intend to be? Everyone was pretending. As all of them knew, by the time the kid was six years old, the two months wouldn't matter at all.

He pointed to the crumpled Kaufmann's bag. "Take that with you," he said. "Give me the other." Anton handed it over. Manny took one diaper and one bottle and handed it back. "Get rid of everything you brought in here except the kid. You made a clean break from the apartment?" He stretched out his hands to say, "Answer only what I ask."

Anton nodded.

"Go away somewhere. Find one of your honeys. Stay away from me for a long, long time. And stay away from Emelia. She'll be in touch with us both."

"I'll be in Detroit by—"

"I don't want to know."

Anton laughed. "You don't want to know anything. Clean Manny, according to you. But you're in it deepest of all."

Manny pressed down his fury. "You've got to get going. For your own safety. Don't be stupid. I'll keep in touch with Emelia." Manny went to the door and opened it. "You weren't supposed to ever come here."

"We ought to have two more babies in about two months."

"Good. We don't have contact with each other until then."

Manny watched Anton leave. He saw him open a door

and take the stairway down. He looked out the window.
He watched him go to his car. Manny still held the baby in
his arms. The baby kicked once, which gave Manny great
relief, but then he thought, Why am I still holding the
kid? He put the baby down in the middle of his desk and
ran his hands through his hair. There was no getting out
of this thing he was in unless he took all his money out of
the bank and the house, flew to some other country, and
never came back.

If he got through the next hour and a half, he would go
eat a big breakfast and then figure out some way to turn
a page. Go on vacation, go volunteer at the church.
Something to clean out his mind. Tell Emelia he was out
of the business, once and for all. He looked at the baby lying on his desk with nothing to cover him. "You and me,
kid," he said. "In an hour, we start fresh."

At the back of the locked files in his office he found
something to wrap the baby in, an embroidered thing
Emelia had left once, from one of her trips, an odd material, the weight of a dish towel, but large enough to make
an envelope for a four-month-old. She'd told Manny she
stole it from a hotel room in Italy, oh, years and years ago,
and that it was a towel. She just *liked* it, so she took it. He
lifted and tucked. The baby slept through the movement.
"Jesus, you're practically snoring," he said to the baby. He
chose a name. Billy. He talked to the sleeping child. "The
creep turned you into a lush, Billy, just like him."

He locked the bottle and diaper in the file cabinet.

After a long struggle with himself, Manny dialed his
sister, waking her up. She answered angrily, but softened
when she heard his voice. "Manny, just do it," she said,
sounding half-asleep still. "They'll want him. You know
they'll want him. Don't look back. Just pull it off. You can
do it."

"That's easy for you to say. You don't have to come up
with story number six with these people."

"Easy? Don't you ever say that. Yesterday, day before or
whatever, was absolute hell. I didn't tell Joe to do what he

did. But he's Joe. He likes to please me. He likes to please
people. He acted. He's a dummy, but we move on. Okay?
What are you going to do, turn the baby in for the reward?"

"What reward?"

"What *reward*?" There was a long silence. "What did
Anton tell you?"

"Nothing. What's going—?"

"You don't know about this, do you?"

"Reward? Maybe you should just—" He couldn't say
"tell me." Something stuck in him. He watched the hand
on the clock jumping forward. Even now he didn't want
to know. Even sensing the danger.

"Put your radio on, your TV. You didn't put it on last
night—"

"Something hit the news?"

"The kid is a little bit famous."

"Famous?" he said in a puzzled way. "How do you
mean?"

He waited for the minute hand to jump again. It was a
few minutes before five. Most couples arrived early for an
appointment, and Manny had come to expect it. He
reached out toward his radio, an old thing on the book-
case, but his hand shook. He looked out his office window and just at that moment the BMW pulled up. His
breath caught. "They're here."

"You are some piece of work, sweetie," she was saying,
but there was an edge of bitterness in her voice. "Sometimes
I wonder if we came from the same—"

"They're here."

"Do it," she said. "Finesse it. Get it over with. You hear
me? Keep it together for ten minutes. I'll come in. I'll
spend some time with you. I'll take care of you for a week.
Okay? I promise. Okay?"

"I'll call you back," he said, and hung up. He watched
Emmons get out of the car and open the door for his wife,
then hold her elbow as they crossed the street. There was
something fragile about her, but Manny didn't know what

it was. He'd met them twice and thought both times she was a very sad woman. The way the man treated her—maybe it was just their deal, their way of being romantic—as if she'd fall apart without one hundred percent attention. What did it mean? He didn't know about these things. He didn't have a life of his own, not that sort of thing. Manny scanned the street for patrol cars, for anything other than the occasional driver. Luck was with him; the street was absolutely quiet. He used his buzzer to open the front door for the couple as he'd told them he would. He heard the machinery of the elevator start up. Well and good.

In moments, they were in his office. Yes, he'd studied them before. Steve Emmons was about five-ten, nondescript, with short brown hair. He was slender, well dressed, with a lean, nervous face. The wife, Valerie, was almost as tall as he. Her face reminded Manny of tears. She was slender and shapely, elegant even, in her lineny pantsuit and all that jewelry, which she would have had to choose and put on at, what, two in the morning.

They took in the fact that he held a child.

"Oh, my God. What—what happened?" the man asked. They rushed toward him. "I thought we were supposed to meet the mother's representatives."

"He's ours? This is the one? Oh, my God, he's so beautiful," the woman said as Manny handed the bundle over to her. The baby, still sleeping heavily, fell like deadweight from one set of arms to the other.

"What happened?" the man repeated.

"Couple of things," Manny said calmly.

Before he could say anything more, the woman handed the child over to her husband and they looked at each other, clearly puzzled about the size of the baby.

Manny said, "Beautiful kid. You asked for fair. He's fair."

"You said two months, then—"

"The main thing is: The birth mother held on to him quite a bit longer than she intended to."

"She can't be reliable, then," Emmons said sternly. But he looked down at the child and the fight went out of him. "You told us it was a sure thing, but how can we get comfortable—"

"It is. You can." Manny watched them closely, the woman letting her husband hold the baby. Words flowed out of Manny, as they had in the past. "The mother lied to us here at the firm, telling us she would put up her kid as soon as the child was born, but the child had already *been* born. She'd heard a newborn was more desirable, so she lied. Poor kid was hoping to get back with the father the first month or two. She lied about dates, is all. But she's on a plane right now. Closer to Russia than she is to here. She's gone. Long gone."

How they looked at him, wanting to believe.

"Without her money?"

"I paid her. I paid her her price. Believe me, if you don't want to adopt this child, there are *many* other couples—" Manny tapped the top of a shiny new lateral file cabinet he kept behind his desk. "Thousands, if you want the awful truth. He's gorgeous. Perfect. Change your mind if you want. I won't hold it against you. I'd just take care of him for a day, day and a half, and . . ." Manny looked solemn.

The woman began crying. "I . . . he seems healthy. That's absolutely crucial."

"Look. Examine him."

The woman unwrapped the baby and examined him, but she was hesitant, afraid to touch him firmly. She and her husband turned him over partway, then turned him back again and opened his diaper. The baby stirred, but did not wake up.

Manny said, "And no colic, I'm told. He's sleeping like an angel."

"He sleeps hard," she whispered to her husband. Manny watched her fumble awkwardly to put the diaper back together. More nervous about herself than the baby, he thought.

Manny took a chance and moved forward. "The birth certificate will arrive by mail. Under a month probably, six weeks at most."

These people were educated. They knew perfectly well

there was a lot of paperwork involved in a legal adoption and that the amended birth certificate arrived only after a court hearing, but their reaction, the way they looked
downward, told Manny they were willing to skip the legal
steps. He knew, too, that he could probably get away with
never offering a birth certificate at all, but he took a certain pride in being able to get actual certificates, excel-
lently forged, to the people he got babies for. It eased the
way down the road for them and made them less likely to
make trouble. "I have good friends in the courts," he usually said at an early meeting. "Let me work my magic."

The woman looked at her husband, took the baby
from him, murmuring, "I can do it." Still tentative, she
touched the child's nose and chin, then his hands. "All so
perfect," she said.

"According to his mother, his American name is
William." Manny consulted a note. "You said if it was a boy
you would name him . . . Joshua? Does that still sound
good to you?"

"Joshua," the man said. "That's the name we want."

"I need all this for the birth certificate. Joshua what? A
middle name?"

"John," the man said. "Joshua John Emmons."

Manny's habit was to send certificates three to six weeks
after the exchange by Priority Mail. He always added a
Post-it saying the document had come to his office first
and he was forwarding it. Clearly irregular, but nobody
had complained.

He leaned over, made a note, gave a smile and a sigh.
The harried lawyer with a lot to think about, but the patience of a saint. Manny amazed himself—how he could
want nothing more than to get rid of these people, have
fear creeping up his throat, and yet say, "Take some time.
Get used to him. Sit down."

But Emmons paced a little and his wife just stood, too
nervous to sit.

"I'm going to take you to ball games, on canoe trips,"
the man was murmuring into the baby's ear.

Spare me, Manny thought. He remembered it was the man who most wanted to become a parent. The woman was afraid of something. "Mr. Emmons, you look perfect with him. Very natural."

The baby, who'd had four first names in under twenty-four hours, made a sound.

Emmons seemed grateful. "I think he's waking up."

But that was wrong. The baby's eyes opened, and closed again in dismissal.

The couple now looked toward the door. Good.

"You have everything you need for him?" Manny hurried to ask.

"We've had everything for a long time," Emmons answered sadly. "Like I told you, we've been through the mill. Several mills."

"We even bought more clothes yesterday," Valerie volunteered. "Probably too small, though."

Manny stood and pushed the chair out from behind him. "Joshua's a healthy fellow."

"Good," she said. "That's the important thing."

Emmons said, more to his wife than to Manny, "Car seat's in the car. We're ready."

"All in order, then." Manny started around the desk, then interrupted himself with what he hoped sounded like a spontaneous, thoughtful addition: "She was amazingly beautiful, the mother. Only seventeen years old. At first she was just a voice on the phone, but then, yesterday, before she went back to Russia, she was—When I finally met her, she was . . . gorgeous. Like one of those Russian skating stars. Perfect skin. Bright eyes."

"Did you go to New York to get him?" Valerie Emmons asked. "You called us from New York?"

"Yes," he said. "Yes, I did. The father was a musician, she told me. That was the connection. She was a violinist on some kind of youth scholarship."

Valerie Emmons' breath caught. She liked something about that particular lie.

Manny continued, riffling the papers on the corner of

his desk. "The man left her, of course, old story . . . she finally accepted it and decided to go back home."

"What kind of family does she have?"

"Oh, intelligent and talented, all mus—" He stopped
himself. "I won't say any more. With blind adoptions, it's
better not to. Not even the name of the village."

"Joshua might want to know someday."

Joshua? Billy? Would he have to make up the name of a
village, of a family?

Emmons reached into his inside pocket.

Manny folded his hands to show he was patient.

Emmons produced a thick envelope and handed it
over.

Manny forced himself not to open it. "I'm sure it's fine.
I've got another appointment in a half hour," Manny said,
starting toward the door. "And an hour's worth of work
to do before it. Teenage boy who's in trouble. Father is in
terrible shape about it. He feels *shamed*. Which isn't going
to help the kid, is it? Then he needs to catch a plane at
seven or something. Which isn't going to help the kid, either. I hate to rush you, but I'm going to need privacy. I've
got some police records to review before this father and
son get here. Are you all set?"

"Let's go," Emmons urged his wife.

"This part of my work makes me feel my life is worthwhile," Manny said, seeing them out the door, reaching out
to shake the man's hand, then the woman's. "Blessings."

When they left, he counted the money. He transferred
the envelope to his inside jacket pocket. Then he went to
the window and watched the couple walk to the white
BMW. It took the woman and man together fifteen minutes to work the car seat. Manny's body turned to jelly. He
felt sweat seep the whole way to his suit jacket, dampen-
ing the money in the jacket pocket. He wondered if the
baby had awakened yet from his night on the town. He
wondered if Emmons and his wife were doubting their decision. Finally they drove off.

Manny reached for the radio and stopped himself

again. He would go home and put on the news. He had pulled it off as his sister asked him to. Yes, but what had he pulled off?

He wondered in a detached way how a baby with a hangover acted.

After the BMW was two minutes gone, he ran to his office bathroom and threw up.

He heard the light, clicking sound of the door lock and looked up to see Anton behind him.

"I'll have that other ten now. I'm going to need it sooner rather than later."

With shaking hands, Manny counted out the money. He wondered where Anton's car was. Anton nodded and left without another word. He waited five more minutes until he thought he heard a motor start up somewhere. Then, still shaking, he slipped out of the building.

It was only five-thirty in the morning and just about the time the detectives were getting Darnell Flowers back home and thinking about checking out the building where the sounds of a baby crying had been heard on the second floor in the night.

The powers that cause these things, if there are such powers, were in a special mood to uproot and toss out, to force people out to find new homes, to sleep in new places.

■　　■

MARINA HAD WHAT FELT LIKE SOUND-DREAMS—THERE'D BE periods of sleep, blankness, and then the rising up out of it to hear bits of conversation. The conversation floated like three or four radio stations colliding, and sometimes the talk held still and then floated off. Or returned, replayed like certain programs on public radio.

A man saying, "She has two last names. Marina Graham sometimes, Marina Benedict other times. Her union cards were under Benedict, apparently, and she had a phone listing under that name. Her medical insurance was under her husband's name, that's Graham. Several charge cards had his last name. One had hers. All that is gone, though; I mean, the actual cards are apparently in the hands of the kidnappers."

They spoke of her as if she were dead. Was she? The room was cold enough to be a morgue and she felt wrapped in cotton.

Her purse. She'd asked for it before they carried her out of that place where they'd found her. Gone, Commander Christie had told her then. Nothing in the apartment at all.

And now they talked and talked, these men, the tape looping around forever, one saying the credit-card banks had been alerted in case someone tried to use her old cards. "Which we fervently hope for," the person was saying in the dream with the looped tape. "Let's hope they're that dumb."

"They're never dumb when you want them to be."

They seemed to think she was going to need new cards. That was a good sign. She remembered a play she was in once, very futuristic, with people being assigned numbers and gates and places to live. She heard Christie say, "We'll have them reissue with new numbers and send them to my office, soon as we figure out where we're putting her and what name she's going to have."

Yes, just like the play. She would be given a name.

"Can she talk?"

"She's a dandy. She told us a bundle." That was Christie again. "But we want more, soon as she's ready. She's a great witness. Wonderful observation."

"So we should get the mug shots over here? And what's-his-face?"

"Right. Let's."

"Profession is actress, did you say?"

"Yes. Husband says she hasn't been getting that sort of work lately. Had to take other kinds of work."

Does she dream things they've never said? She can't tell. She slips in and out of consciousness. In lower tones, they speak of not having been able to find her husband in the early-morning hours. For a moment she thinks she hasn't heard that at all, only dreamed it, but then she remembers all the fuss back at the North Side house when they asked for her phone number and address.

She hears someone say, "Tried up until eight, nine o'clock this morning."

"We checked him out."

"Properly?"

"Oh, yeah. Ran all the checks."

"What's his name again?"

"Michael Graham. He's clean, even does do-good law. We finally found him coming home at ten in the morning. Scared the pants off the guy. Took him in for questioning." The voices move a little away from her and soften, but she hears, "He's outside somewhere. He took one look at her and almost fainted. We sent him to get coffee and something to eat."

"Out on the town?"

"More or less. They're kind of on the rocks. He's the guy in the suit over there. See? Right there. Sick look. Goes to the desk every ten, fifteen minutes. He's a wreck, believe me."

"But he checks out?"

"He knows dipshit about any of this. He's loaded with guilt, but it's the usual sort. He's the one told me they've been having troubles."

A little later, she remembers, or dreams, Michael's face over hers, very distressed, crying. Have hours gone by? She tries to ask what time it is, but nobody hears her.

Michael whispers that she should try to rest and he asks if the painkillers they injected are working.

So that explains it, the clouds and clouds she has to climb through.

In her half sleep, she understands fully something she will carry with her up into the light. Michael had not known she was missing. He had not been home when the police called. Simple fact.

Then she hears Michael's voice. "A sister and her mother. They live in Virginia."

"Any good bets there for a place for the two of you to stay?"

"I can't go anywhere. I work here. I'll pay whatever I have to pay to get us our own place. That's what she's going to need."

"What's the matter with her family?"

"The caretaking goes the other way. That's all."

"Anything with your family? Or friends?"

"I don't have any family left. Friends, yes. Marina wouldn't want that. I know her. Look, she's coming to—"

She manages, "Take care of myself . . . be okay . . . don't scare them with this," and hopes the force of her trying will suffice.

She feels Michael touching her face, holding on to her hands. "See what I mean?" he says.

Then Marina understands they are deciding something about a hotel first, then an apartment. ". . . people in our office who arrange for such things," Christie is saying. "Hotels don't give you much space, but they have other advantages. Room service is one. . . . Basically, if I had my way, I'd keep her here at the hospital till she's really strong, but you know how hospitals are. I'll be surprised if they keep her four days."

"Because they're in bed with the damned insurance companies. I'll get the money for a couple more days if it seems we should go that way."

"You cook?" Christie asks.

"Not a lot," Michael says.

"You can buy takeout, then, when you get to an apartment. You're going to have to take care of her. She's not going to want to cook for a while."

When she awakens to what feels like the day world—consciousness, bedsheets, bandages, pain, water through a straw (it's ice water through a straw that does it), voices and faces in clear focus—Michael is there, holding on to her arm, his face naked with shame.

"Is this the same day?" she asks.

"As—?"

"Yesterday."

Michael almost smiles. "It's three in the afternoon, if that's what you mean," he says. "Same day as yesterday, in a sense."

She sees then that there's a doctor in the room, too. It's he who got her to drink the ice water. He's a portly young man. He stands there rattling the ice cubes against the plastic.

"How bad am I?" she asks.

"Very lucky. You have— It's like a miracle. This guy shot you twice, pretty close range, I'm told. He must have thought he—you know—you maybe passed out; he thought he'd killed you, but guess what?" The young doctor looks nervous, even amazed, himself, at the news he is delivering. "He didn't hit anything vital. That's the miracle."

Michael's face is so sad. He keeps saying. "That's my girl. You're going to be okay."

"In my head and in my side?" she asks the doctor, as if to test his credibility.

"The bullet that hit you in the head 'rode the bone.' It didn't go in at ninety degrees, so it made a big mess going in and coming out, but it didn't do any permanent damage. It just traveled along, biting the bone. The one in your side made flesh wounds. Same thing: point of entry, point of exit, but it missed the vital organs. You'll have a scar there, but you're going to be okay."

"Are you sure?" For Joe did come right into the room. She can see him, if she allows herself, again and again.

The doctor nods.

"Talk about bad aim," she jokes limply.

"Your detective said it's not the worst case he's seen. He told us about one woman who had eight bullets, some lodged in the brain, some passed through parts of the brain, all at close range, too, but she went back to work two weeks later."

"Eight?"

"Eight."

"So I don't win the prize, then."

"Guess not."

She reaches up to her head. She can feel bandages.

"Pain?"

"Some."

"Dressings. We have to keep changing them. That part isn't any fun. We had to shave a little bit of your nice hair. Sorry about that."

"Can you drink more water?" Michael asks. The rattling glass is now in his hands. She's not sure how it got there.

She feels weak. Will water help? "I'll try."

"I'm supposed to report that you're awake. To that detective, Christie."

WHEN CHRISTIE CAME TO TALK TO HER AGAIN, HE ASKED HER more questions about her trip to the Rite Aid, which she had been able to give only small bits of on the way to the hospital.

Michael didn't know this part. She could see he was trying to follow Christie's questions. She could see puzzlement, incredulity cross his face—blame for her going back.

Christie said, "Do you remember the time?"

"Two-forty-five, maybe."

"Good. Good."

ABOUT FOUR IN THE AFTERNOON, CHRISTIE CAME BACK WITH the police sketch artist. He explained there was a press conference in an hour and he hoped for Marina's revisions on the sketch of Joe, which had been on the six o'clock news the night before, a bad sketch, he knew, just a series of guesses from the image on the surveillance tape. And, if she had the energy, would she start from scratch to build sketches of the other two?

She studied the picture of Joe for a few minutes before she told them to add the moles, widen his forehead, enlarge his nose. She looked intently again, then instructed the slight bulge of his eyes, the pouchy droop of his cheeks, until she said, "Yes, yes, that looks like him now."

Commander Christie said, "You're a trouper!" It was a familiar compliment, because theatre people always used that phrase, but she was too tired to explain why it made her smile. "Can you keep going?" he asked. She nodded.

The man who did the sketches was very sketchable himself. He had a chaotic haircut that stuck out in every direction and a round, surprised face, so memorable. He turned a page of the pad and started with oval faces, square faces, round faces. Marina chose a large oval and pointed to eyebrows, eyes, ears, hair, until Vol's face was accurate, too, so far as she could remember. His size and the clothing he wore had been more startling than his face. She took a drink of water and forced herself to move on to a sketch of the third man, for whom she had no name.

The artist kept drawing and discarding. Nothing satisfied her. She'd have thought the handsome man was the easiest to draw, but she'd seen less of him; that was part of it. She was more frightened of him; that was part of it, too. "Good-looking man, about thirty" and "dark wavy hair, straight nose, good bone structure" made for only a vague sketch, generic, the newspaper drawing for a men's suit sale, no personality.

The work on the drawing of the man who had ordered her execution took a long time and it didn't go well. Michael, standing a few feet from her, leaning against the wall, said, "You've got to let her stop." Even Christie agreed. He instructed one of his men to call the station and set the time for the second major press conference.

The artist handed over the three best sketches.

Marina looked around her. Television, white sheets, window. She wanted nothing more than to stay here for a long time, safe, in the white sheets and the quiet. She wanted to snuggle under the thermal bedcover. Even though it was late June and hot outside, it was practically polar inside, unreal. She saw Commander Christie watching her. She liked his sympathetic face, large brown eyes, generally worried look. He touched her shoulder this time and told her she was a great help to them. When he spoke he took a little breath first and then his sentences had a strange, even, measured pace, as if he'd learned to recite in school as a boy and had never quite shaken the habit off.

He seemed to be saying something else underneath the even-paced sentence. That he felt badly for her. Pitied her, maybe.

A nurse came in and brandished a hypodermic, which she then stuck into the IV track. "This is a little bit more morphine," the nurse said. "Doc ordered it. So none of this stuff feels so bad."

"I'd rather be awake," Marina said, too late. Her voice came out slurry, a two-cocktail voice.

"Nah," the nurse said. "You just think so."

"Sleep," Christie said. "Sleep is the cure."

A line of Shakespeare's slipped close to Marina and disappeared on her before she could catch it. Something that meant sleep was the cure for just about everything.

The drug crept over her, but she fought it off, aware of things in the room—the way Michael said, "Maybe if I got a gun. Maybe if I worked at home a lot." And the way Commander Christie said, "Under no circumstances. Your address is known to the men who thought they left her for dead. As soon as these guys see the news, they're gonna know she's alive. And when they see these terrific sketches of themselves, they're going to hate the fact she's not only alive but *very* clever and functional and cooperating and ready to stand up in court against them."

"Can't we keep pictures of her out of the paper?"

"Not a chance. They'll find something. Might as well turn a few over."

"You got her consent to being a witness when she was completely out of it."

"We'll talk again. She certainly sounded like she knew what she wanted to do. We need her. Bottom line. And she's in trouble no matter what. She's the link that puts them away."

"I'm a lawyer. I get it," Michael said stiffly.

"I'm sending two officers with you to your house. I want you to pack bags for both of you, and I want this taken absolutely seriously. Better to pack a lot of clothes, anything she might want, and whatever you'll need. Don't skimp. I don't want you popping back to pick something up."

Michael let out a long breath. "Oh, man. What a mess."

"It's a complete disruption. The sooner you get the size of it in your head, the better off you'll be."

"I'm so sorry," Marina managed to say, but her apology was all breathy vowels, no consonants.

"I thought you were asleep," Michael said.

Christie turned to her. "Anything you want to request from the house?"

"Maybe . . . CD player . . . disks," she tried. Her voice was more slurry than ever. "Clothes, nightgowns. A purse. Michael?" she mumbled.

Michael had to edge around Christie to take her hand, and it miffed him, she could see.

"The suitcases are all down in the cedar closet," she managed.

"Oh. Oh!" His face blanched. "I wondered where they were."

Later she would recall this moment and understand what it meant, that he had *wondered*. That at some point when she was in danger, he had looked for the suitcases. Later all this would make sense.

And sleep again. Then an actual radio. Then Christie's voice saying, "Not to mention she's one hell of a human being." So Christie was there again. Or still there. Or had been there all along. Or she was remembering. She couldn't tell.

In the dark, in the middle of the night, by then Sunday, she woke and saw a uniformed policeman outside her door. She was a prisoner, of sorts. She watched him stand and move in the sliver of light.

She fell asleep again, and woke before morning, thinking,

An apartment. A blank place without personality. A new start. It appealed to her.

■   ■

COMMANDER CHRISTIE HAD CALLED IN THE LAB RIGHT AWAY on Friday to run fingerprint checks on the stroller, and he called them again early Saturday morning to cover the whole apartment where Marina had been found. The team on Saturday morning was a combination of local and federal experts in fibers and prints.

They had sketches of the three men that they ran through various systems for identification all through Saturday evening after the press conference. They tried the two short names, "Joe" and "Vol," but didn't get any matches that looked good.

A computer program coughed up the name of the owner of the building on the far reaches of the North Side where the three men were last seen. Her name was Anne Pinkus, but she was nowhere to be found. Christie had given the FBI the task of tracking her and they had guys running searches in other cities. Her prints were not filed with any police force. She had not filed a tax return. She had no identity at this point other than "absentee owner of a rotting building."

Christie's men had found a significant number of prints on the first and third floors of Anne Pinkus' property, and three sets matched up with known druggies in the area, but none of those guys matched the sketches of the men Marina had provided. Still, they were looking for the addicts in case they'd seen something useful. On the other hand, the kidnappers had done such a massive cleanup, Christie guessed ahead of time the prints found on the other floors were not going to be of much use. The people who took the Graves baby definitely knew how to remove evidence. Marina had said the men ate there, and there were a few crumbs, but no trace of food or cartons. She said they'd brought an old television in, but it was gone with them by the time the police got there. And outside the apartment, there was no garbage in the bins. What garbage they'd made, they'd taken with them.

Christie sat at his desk early Sunday morning and made notes on all of it. Making notes always helped him think. The clean sweep of the apartment, he wrote, told him the men were purposeful, practiced, the failed murder notwithstanding.

He liked the clicking, humming silence of an early Sunday morning. He could actually hear the department refrigerator going off and on. There was an army coming and going downstairs in the conference room, there was a typist to transcribe their notes, and there was a table full of bagels and donuts and coffee. But up here, it was almost normal for a crack-of-dawn Sunday morning.

He went over his officers' written reports. Every neighbor for four blocks had been asked about the cars and the license plates. Nobody had memorized any actual plates, not one person, not even Darnell Flowers. But there was a consensus that the two cars had Pennsylvania plates on them and that one was a light cream or white Buick Skylark and the other was an older black Chevrolet Corsica. No major dents or identifying marks on the cars, so far as anyone could remember. The Corsica was worn and scratched, apparently, but that was about it.

The woman who called in saying she'd seen the man in the television sketch board a bus had been right after all. The bus stop was not far from Ralph's Discount City, and the 16A bus route went past where the man known as Joe fled with the baby—everything as Marina had reported it. The bus driver, when found, confirmed that a man with an infant had gotten on and off his bus and that a woman had made him stop the bus in the middle of a block. He barely remembered either of them.

Christie had sent Dolan and one of the other detectives to find the Rite Aid and look for a surveillance tape. His hopes spiked—a second tape to play on every television in the country. Images to add to the police sketches.

Dolan had called him at the hospital to tell him the surveillance tape that they had fetched and attempted to run was a dud. The manager told them shamefacedly that he'd had trouble with the camera, but hadn't had time to get it fixed. The tape showed nothing but video snow.

When Dolan asked the store manager how long the camera had been conked out, the manager, a Mr. Bobbs, said he thought maybe about three days. The tape itself indicated more like three weeks. Mr. Bobbs pretended to be surprised.

In fact, Bobbs seemed barely able to figure out which clerk had been on duty the afternoon before. He finally did come up with a name. May Helmhurst. Detectives went to her house, but she was out, nobody knew where. They had to wait until three on Saturday when she came to work to have a word with her. She was over sixty-five and, Dolan said, a little the worse for wear.

She remembered the trio and their purchases; the register tapes corroborated everything Marina had said. "Not my kind of people," she told them bitterly. "Dirty looking, and the men hanging on the woman. She put up with it, too."

If only people really looked at things. Why didn't they? If only this Helmhurst woman had seen there was something odd going on.

Christie kept seeing Karen Graves' face as it was at the crime scene, then Ryan's as he came off the plane. Innocents, both of them. He pictured them in that temporary apartment of theirs, ruined, holding on to each other.

He felt sick with the mounting stack of paper, which detailed a lack of evidence.

The only prints on the stroller belonged to the parents.

No request for ransom had so far come by mail or phone to anyone.

Can a man with someone else's baby just disappear?

The search for Anne Pinkus continued, but it was as if she had never existed except as the owner of the house on the North Side.

An APB was out on the Chevy and the Buick. Neither had been found yet.

He got up and went to the little office kitchen and started a pot of his own coffee brewing.

There were few other people around upstairs, an officer here, a cleaning man there. Soon there'd be a lot of other people around and lots of media badgering.

What they had, Christie had said last night to his friend Pete Horner of the FBI, was a lot of activity and nothing you wanted to take to the media. Cripes, what a pain it was to have to go before the cameras when you were holding a bag with a couple of pretzel sticks in the bottom. Nothing big.

And no logic. They didn't have the logic of it.

Christie, two of his detectives, Horner, and two of his federal agents had spent most of their Saturday night in the downstairs conference room puzzling out motive, logic. Now he poured a cup of coffee before the whole pot was brewed and went back to his desk to study the notes from that meeting, hoping in the morning light to see or recall something new.

The men had tossed all guesses onto the conference table. They joked a lot. The worse the case, the more the jokes. A twenty-one-year-old street tough dies of a stab wound and nobody needs gallows humor. A girl is mutilated, a baby dies or goes missing, and you haul out the laughs.

One Special Agent and one detective thought it had to be an intended kidnapping of the Graves kid. For ransom money, plain and simple. They thought Marina had misheard or was delirious with fear.

"Those kidnappers have got to be the last people in America to know how poor the Pittsburgh Pirates are!" Christie said.

"Last time I went to a game," Horner added, "the crowd was yelling things like, 'Hey, you're due. Hit one. Earn your ten thou a year!' "

Poverty jokes always appealed to Christie, he didn't

know why. Maybe because he'd never had money and never would and what could you do about it but laugh?

"I don't know," he'd told the men, "I'm thinking, thinking, thinking about the credibility of the woman at the hospital. Listen, she tells a story—how can I put this—there are equal amounts of accident and pattern operating, the way she tells it, but if she's right, the Graves baby *was* the accident. There was some familiar procedure, but the Graves baby was the accident. A mistake. As if they've *been* taking babies and not hitting the news."

Dolan spoke everybody's worst fear, that this was a Ted Bundy kind of case—that is, arbitrary and without connections, therefore virtually impossible to solve. "When we've got an uncle, a rival, a business partner," he said, "we jump over eight hundred hurdles without even knowing we did it, but . . ."

"Any possibility it was all a performance for the Benedict woman?" Horner asked.

"Maybe." But Christie didn't think so.

"I want to make sure we check out a different sort of thing," the youngest federal agent said, "the kind of thing Tonya Harding did to Nancy Kerrigan. Violent, personal. Coming from inside the sport. We have to consider it."

Christie believed in considering all points of view and tried never to embarrass anyone, not even FBI, not even the young ones, and what was the use of alienating somebody on his task force, so he said musingly, "We've rooted around a little on that, but okay, okay, see if you can get the players to speculate about this. You want to go ahead with that?"

The agent said he did.

Wasted time, maybe, but all the pockets, all the corners . . . Marina Benedict thought one of the men had said *Ohio*. Which, when it came to a thing like this, was a big place.

The ratio, as always, was astoundingly wasteful, so many men working and so many dead ends. People didn't know how much pure grunt and dull labor went into an investigation, even of a major case like this. And when it broke, three-quarters of the time it was some guy in prison squawking to buy himself a better deal.

Another Special Agent on the task force was going to head up a unit looking for prisoners who might know something. Nice guy. Nice, perfect family man. Hopeful face. Collins. Brad Collins.

The phone rang and Christie answered it. It was some journalist for *USA Today*.

"We are checking all possibilities. Yes, of a vendetta within the sport. Of a baby for ransom. Yes, yes, of a ring. We're checking all possibilities, as I said."

The journalist went on, giving his theories. The big clock on the wall inched forward by minutes. Finally Christie got off the phone. The morning paper came. They were front-page news. Pictures of Marina, of the Graves parents and the baby, of the three men whose sketches Marina had helped with. The picture of Marina was very slick, since it was a theatrical glossy, meant to get her work. She was the picture of a woman whose life was plums and roses. She was very beautiful.

The phone rang again. He expected it to be his wife or kids, waking up and checking in with him as they often did. But it was the youngest FBI agent saying he wanted clearance for a couple of men to check baby stores in Pittsburgh and then within a five-hundred-mile radius, looking for sudden large purchases. Christie okayed it, saying, "Do Pennsylvania and Ohio first, then move to the tristate area, then fan out from there."

Last night how they'd figured it was: People who *buy* babies black market don't talk about it. But, okay, eventually they do have to buy *things*. So if the Graves baby is alive, somewhere, maybe in Ohio, maybe far from Pittsburgh—could be in Switzerland, for God's sake—it got handed over or is about to be handed over to someone who might buy a stroller or some health insurance.

Christie checked his watch and thought briefly of the beautiful woman sleeping in the hospital, her good-looking husband watching over her, maybe crying again. They were like movie stars, those two, and he felt he was an enchanted observer.

■   ■

VOL KNEW ENOUGH TO STAY OUT OF LOCAL MOTELS.

When they'd wiped the apartment clean on Friday evening and started down the front steps to the black Chevrolet, he told Joe to do the driving. Joe shrugged and Vol chose an easterly direction. He had an extra set of plates taped to the bottom of the car and he wanted to put those on as soon as it seemed safe. He knew a place outside of Johnstown, he told Joe, Mundy's Corner, to be specific, where he could get his car painted. Unfortunately it was going to take more than a couple of days to come up to some other color from black. Still, what choice did he have? He didn't know any place to trade it safely and he wasn't much up for stealing a new car.

"It's faster," Joe said of stealing.

Joe's talent was theft. He had a way of moving into a space and acting like he belonged there. He had a fretful but somehow normal face. Vol looked at Joe while he drove. The smaller man was now wearing jeans and a polo shirt and sneakers, which looked all wrong on him even though they were his clothes. Vol was used to Joe the other way, a guy who looked like he carried flowers up and down the stairs in some small-town funeral home. He looked goofy in jeans. Still, the unfamiliar clothes amounted to a disguise of sorts. At least now the two men looked as if they belonged together, on the same excursion.

By the time they got through bridge traffic and onto the parkway, Vol let himself understand they were on the run. He allowed his heart to thump and his breath to come in sharp jabs. He felt for the gun in his belt. What Vol hadn't figured out was what order he would do things in. He had many things to dispose of. A large garbage bag Anton had given him. A smaller bag with the baby's clothes and Marina's purse in it. And Joe.

He was working himself around to the idea of what he had to do, founding a belief in it, much as an actor tiptoes toward gouging out Gloucester's eyes in *King Lear*. Preparation work. The arm can't move until the mind allows it, shuts some thoughts down, opens others up.

In Vol's case it wasn't too hard, it wasn't as if he'd never killed anyone before. Vol only had to forget the chitchat in the car, eating dinner with the guy, small familiar things that might suggest more sameness than difference. Much easier if he could go away and come upon Joe suddenly after a week's break, but that wasn't in the script.

So he kept in mind what would happen to him if he didn't do it. He'd be on the run, on his own forever, never able to go back to Anton again. Unprotected. And then if Anton found him—A fly buzzed around in the car. He kept swatting at it. When he opened the window he thought it was gone, but it came back. The fly was attracted to his right ear. It was hard to think with the thing dive-bombing him. "Son of a bitch," he said, hitting at air. "Fucking son of a bitch of a bitch."

"Take it easy," Joe said. "I'm trying to drive."

He swatted at Joe's head, stopped himself. He needed Joe's cooperation and calm. There was work to do—burning and burying the trash Anton had given him. Anton had ordered him to let Joe do the digging and afterward to dispatch Joe to calmer waters. But wouldn't he be better off to get the Joe thing over with *before* something went wrong, before Joe did something strange, like disappear? He'd known as soon as Joe's mug popped up on the television the job was going to fall to him. It was the obvious conclusion, if you knew Anton, who wasn't going to hide or protect anyone who fucked up that bad.

Vol wondered why Joe didn't seem to have figured it out, or if he had, why he wasn't more nervous. If he, Vol, had been plastered over the TV, he would have bolted by now. But with Joe, you could never tell; he was almost always in stupidville. Now he leaned forward over the steering wheel like an old man out on a Sunday drive. "A sort of a retard," Anton called him. Anton had always told Vol to keep an eye on Joe. Which mainly he did. In all the three or four years of working jobs with Joe, of him getting the orders from Anton and telling Joe where to look and how to act, Joe's face never showed much of anything except occasional irritation.

"I still can't believe you thought going out and getting another kid was going to solve it," Vol spat out.

Joe's lower jaw dropped; his mouth was open; he looked simple.

Vol reached over and rapped his fingers along the side of Joe's skull. "Slow."

"I'm not the slow one. Anton is. He should have figured how to adjust."

"Oh, really?" Vol started to snort in spite of himself. "You are a laugh."

Joe sat back in the seat as if he'd now just learned to drive the car.

Vol looked at his watch. Seven o'clock. Mostly, as he sat in the passenger seat humming and humming, he tried to figure out the when and the how of his upcoming tasks. Joe was a good digger and they did need to wait until nightfall to do the digging. And he was hungry.

In Murraysville, Vol said, "Pull in over at that Shop 'n Save up there on the left. Just keep your face hid."

Joe pulled off the road.

Vol took a long look at Joe pretending to scratch his eye, cough, one thing or another to hide his mug, and left him in the car to perform these acts while he ran into the Shop 'n Save. Into his basket went several items, including a loaf of bread and a couple of steaks, some charcoal, and three cans of lighter fluid. Vol was racing, but all around him people were moving slowly, like stunned animals in the heat and the air-conditioning, not adjusted to either. It made him crazy when people were slow, made him want to blow them away. While he was checking out, he had a brief, fearful fantasy of Joe driving off without him, and then what—him, Vol, just walking along the highway carrying charcoal and steaks and unable to report the disappearance of his vehicle. He saw this as if seeing a movie and practically couldn't wait for the cashier to make change.

But when he got out to the parking lot, Joe was sitting there with his sunglasses still on and a fishing hat fringing his face. The hat he must have unearthed from the small nylon suitcase he had in the backseat. Joe looked weird trying to be normal. Vol said, "Let's go to Keystone State Park before the supper hour is over. Grill ourselves a steak."

"At a state park?"

"They have charcoal pits. I got all the stuff."

"I'm tired of eating bread and meat," Joe said.

Sometimes he wondered where Joe came from. "You want me to go back in for a salad?" Vol meant this as a joke.

"Yeah, why don't you?"

"You're fucking nuts. Your face is all over the news, and you want to have a salad. Drive. Don't sit in any one place where people can see you and put two and two together."

"The picture doesn't look like me. Both of you said so."

"Get moving. Maybe somebody else has better eyes than I do. And get that hat off while you're driving in eighty degrees. It looks fishy."

"People probably think our air-conditioning works. People get it fixed when it doesn't work."

After a while, Vol asked, "How did you feel about hitting the girl?"

"It had to be done."

"How much of that you done before?"

"None of your business."

"You were smooth. I have to hand you that." When Joe didn't answer, he said, "I hated that bitch, didn't you?"

"I guess."

"What? You liked her?"

"I was thinking about something else."

"You want that salad. Don't want no bread and meat. Want salad."

"You think everything is funny."

"I'm starved. I need something solid."

Hunger tended to hit Vol every couple of hours and he fed it. He thought maybe if no one was around at the state park, he would toss the contents of Marina's purse into the charcoal pit and incinerate them before he ate anything. A lot of plastic, though, the more he thought about it, the cards and such, which would send up a smell. Then he thought maybe that wasn't such a good idea. The purse wouldn't burn easily, either, since it was leather. And it would smell, too. Maybe it would come to mostly burying the things Anton had given him. Anton was a nut anyway. He said to do certain things, like burn the purse, but he didn't know what it actually took to do them because he never actually *did* anything himself. Christ, do it Anton's way, he'd be working half the night. So, yes, he'd keep Joe with him for the first part. Then get on the road again even though Mundy's Corner was only another hour away. He couldn't go to the body shop in the middle of the night. Just drive around. Rat in a rural maze.

He thought what to do. There were some shaggy overgrown properties on the way to the garage he was headed for. Maybe, about midnight, say something to Joe about looking for a place to camp out for the night, do it, do the thing, then go the rest of the way to Mundy's Corner in the morning. Say to Joe, "Let's just sleep in the woods. It's safer." Joe shrugs okay. Walk into the wooded area. Joe gets in front of him. Then.

"I hope you weren't using my half of the money for steak and bread."

"You're going to fight me about twenty bucks?"

In Vol's wallet is the five thousand Anton gave him before they left. Joe believes they're going to split the five thousand and get more later, but of course Joe will be out of the picture, which means Vol will be set for a while.

That's why they're all with Emelia. She pays up front and she pays well.

The sky is gray and rains are threatening again. It's been the rainiest summer ever. Except for earlier today with the sun burning through all the humidity and haze.

Like a Florida day. The earth is wet. He'll have to dig in wet earth.

Plans and rules. Leave no prints. No shoeprints, finger-prints, nothing. Move on. Paint the car *green*. Find a room for three days or sleep in the woods. Car's done. Drive away. Pull over somewhere. Put on the third set of plates he's got stored under the trunk flap. On the road. Beer and a couple of whores. Live it up for a while. Pick a phone at some bar or whatever. Call Anton from a differ-ent phone. Go back to the first phone. Wait for Anton to call back.

Rule: Always have a story. Anton's rule.

Forty-five minutes later, Vol and Joe pulled into Keystone State Park, and Vol pointed the way to the pic-nic tables, which had stands nearby for charcoal. They saw a free table, near some bushes. Unfortunately there was a family at another table about fifty feet away, so they drove down the road, looking. But the clusters of tables were occupied with people doing the summer thing, plas-tic bags everywhere, radios playing, so in the end, they went back up the road to the first spot, where there was only that one family to avoid.

Vol sighed. "We'll be burning nothing but charcoal here. I wanted to get to work."

"We should just bury the stuff."

Vol felt sweat break out.

They got out of the car and Vol told Joe to keep his head down and keep pretending to do something with the groceries.

Joe sat on the end of a picnic bench with his head turned away from the people who were fifty, sixty feet from him, and turned away from the grill, too. He looked odd, facing away from everything. "How long can it take me to get the cellophane off the steaks?" he asked.

"I said, 'pretend.' "

Vol took two slices of Italian bread from the bag and ate them, plain. He'd also bought a square of cheese and a car-ton of eggs because he kept an iron skillet in his trunk,

along with some fishing gear and a sleeping bag. He was
prepared, if necessary, to go camping for a few days.
Probably have to camp out while the car was being painted.
Joe had apparently tired of taking off the cellophane from
the steaks; now he turned over the cheese and checked the
eggs in their carton. "Steak, cheese, eggs," he said bitterly,
shaking his head.

"What's the problem?" Vol asked.

"Nothing," Joe said. "Not a thing."

Vol put some coals on and started a fire. He just sat
quietly until the flames calmed down and then, while he
waited for the coals to get hot, he fiddled around in
the trunk to see what all he had. He gingerly put aside the
garbage bag he had brought from the apartment. That he
had to get rid of, and fast.

"Supplies, supplies," he muttered to himself. No rope,
in case he had to drag the body for any distance. Fishing
rod and skillet were there. Salt and pepper, always salt and
pepper. He plunked the salt and pepper on the table.

With great relief, Vol saw the family of picnickers start
to pack up their stuff.

Then, with a certain amount of alarm, he saw the overweight woman, presumably the mother of the family,
start to waddle toward him and Joe. Vol went forward to
keep her at a distance from the face in the news. "What
can I do for you?" he asked.

"We were going to throw out potato salad and bean
salad, but then, I hate to waste, so I thought I'd come over
and see if you wanted it." She held out two plastic containers of food.

"No, thanks," he said.

"You sure? I can just dump it on one of your plates
and take my Tupperware home. I'd want to keep my
Tupperware."

Vol scrambled to think. "Tell you what. I got a skillet
you can dump these things in. You go on and finish up.
I'll run it over to you."

He backed up toward the car. He felt Joe watching him.
"Christ," he said under his breath as he rooted around in

his trunk. "Bean salad." He wished he'd just told the woman no, but he had been afraid to be unfriendly. Now he just wanted to hurry. She was creeping closer, in little shuffling steps.

"Did you guys forget plates?" she asked when he cut her off before she got over to their table.

"Uh, yeah. It's okay. We're just camping. Rough." He brandished the iron skillet.

"Wait a minute, then, let me rescue our plates. You just need to wipe them off. They're perfectly good. Plastic ones." Vol began to follow the woman back to her table. "We shouldn't have thrown them away. I always want to keep them, they do real good in the dishwasher, but my husband tosses them. So, go ahead. With a little water . . . We're not germy."

"It's real thoughtful of you."

The children and their father watched. Two young boys in shorts, preschool age, and a man in shorts, forty or older, overweight. The children were overweight, too, but all four people seemed comfortable with their size, proud of it, in fact. Satisfied. Right with the world and wanting to show who they were. Vol took the plates, looking at the smears of mayonnaise on them. The woman paused and took the plates back from him, holding up a hand to indicate he should wait.

"Whereabouts you been camping?" the husband wanted to know.

"Oh, just everywhere. Off the beaten track," Vol said.

"You staying here tonight? At the park?"

"No, I don't think we will. Think our wives are pretty restless by now. We'll head back to Erie, visit my sister tonight, go on home to the wives tomorrow." He watched the woman douse the plates with water, shake them, and dump food onto them.

"Where's home?" the man asked.

"Wisconsin." Vol thought about the license plates on the Chevy and wondered if the family had seen them. He thought not.

"Well, good luck."

"You, too."

Man, he hated friendly people, hated them. For twenty years he'd lived in the dark, one way or another, and people who went stupidly forward in the light drove him mad.

He ate a long supper with Joe, who was grateful for the two salads. They talked about the garage in Mundy's Corner and paint colors. Joe said he didn't think green was a good choice. Wasn't natural, he said. Green wasn't a common enough color and would stick out on the road.

Around nine-thirty, Vol was getting ready to burn the things inside Marina's purse—credit cards and slips of paper. He stared at her license. "Bitch probably never had a day of trouble in her life," he said. "What kind of a nut was she, do you think?" Vol handled everything with a tissue in his hand.

"What are you going to do with the lipstick and mirror?" Joe asked. "They won't burn."

"I know. Bury them somewhere."

They heard a new car behind them and looked around to see a marked car, a park ranger's vehicle, make a slow circle of the parking area behind them, a place big enough for four or five cars. The ranger's car stopped and the ranger got out, nodded, looked around, then went back to his car.

"Shit," Vol said. "I can't make a new blaze now. He can see we've already eaten."

"He's probably not paying attention."

"Good thing you're not running things."

Vol packed up Marina's things again in her purse and put the purse in the bag with the baby clothes. "Just keep your hat on and your head down," he said. Vol packed up the car, rinsed out the skillet, kept an eye out for strangers. Joe hardly moved. Which was what Vol had ordered. But Vol thought distractedly, Joe should move *some*; he looked strange going still like that.

Finally the two men got in the car and started out, not north to Erie, but toward the garage Vol had heard about in Mundy's Corner, and hopefully before that to a place in the woods where two guys could wander in for a piss and talk about the virtues of just camping out for the night, and talking, talking, talking, get deep enough in to where one of them could be buried.

■   ■

ANTON KNOCKED ON THE DOOR OF A SUBURBAN TRACT HOUSE outside of Detroit on Saturday, long before they were attempting to draw a picture of him in the hospital in Pittsburgh. The woman who answered the door had a little girl holding on to her leg. When the woman saw Anton, her muscles tensed. She held on to the wooden door; there was still a screen door between them.

"You shouldn't open the door without looking first," he said.

"You ought to know."

"Let me in." He rattled the handle of the screen door. "Come on, Elise."

She unlatched the handle and he let himself in.

"Where are your car keys?" he asked.

"Shit. Why do you want my car? Now what?"

"I have to put my car in the garage." He pointed out to the street to the white Buick.

"Stolen?"

"It's not stolen. It's the same car I had before. What's the matter with you?" He took her arm and pulled her toward the door. "Look. Look at it. Same car. It's just that some guys are after me, after this." He opened his jacket and let her feel the wad of money in the inside pocket. "If they can't see the car, the money is safe. I earned it, but people don't always play fair."

Elise took her car key out of a drawer in the wall unit that held the television and stereo. She held on to it. "What did you do? Are you carrying?"

"No."

"Because I don't want to go through any of that ever again with anyone else."

"That's not my bag." He took the key and in moments

had her car out of the integral garage. He parked it on the street. Looking around him, seeing nothing, he drove his own car into the garage. A great relief overtook him as soon as he pushed the garage door opener and the door rattled down.

He went up through the garage and said, "I have to use your car for a while, okay?"

She shrugged.

He said, "Here's what we're going to do. I'll give you money. You go buy a car. Something used, but not too bad. Put it in your name."

"Where am I going to park it?"

"Out front, out front. As soon as I can unload mine you can have the garage." He hated the way the little girl held on to her mother's leg and kept looking at him. She was four. Why was she such a cowardly kid? He hated the look of her, her fat face, an angry face for a kid her age. "Come here, honey," he said. "Come here, Ashley." What kind of name was that for an ugly, half-spic kid? "You want ice cream? You want Anton to buy you a lot of ice cream?"

"No."

Anton had to laugh. "Friendly place I've landed in. I'm going to go lie down. By the way, I brought a TV for the bedroom, but I'm too tired to carry it in now."

He got into the bedroom and lay on the bed, knowing he wouldn't sleep. From experience, he understood he would lie awake for a week, planning, fixing, until he got comfortable enough to go to dreamland. Things to solve kept him awake. He had to stop using his cell phone for a while. He had to avoid her phone, too, just in case anyone was onto it.

Anton would sit Elise down later tonight and instruct her about buying a car and getting a cell phone in her name. The car—anything would do so long as it had enough power to do speed. The Buick, if he kept it, would have to sleep quiet for a year until nobody was looking for it anymore. Two babies due in a month and a half or two. Would things be quiet enough by then? If not, he'd have to do something for money. This last job for Manny wasn't going to net enough.

■   ■

THERE IS A GARAGE ON THE WAY TO MUNDY'S CORNER THAT IS fairly small, built of brick, painted white. The paint is old and chipped. The man who owns the garage makes less than he would on welfare, but he'd rather work. His name is Buddy Kinder.

Buddy Kinder lives alone, having buried his very ill sister, and more recently his old mother, both of whom he'd supported. The father was never in the picture. Buddy has been described, by Vol, by others, as having a slightly moonish face. He will appear not to hear or understand for some minutes, but if you wait patiently you will find out Buddy is just processing things at his pace. "His mind goes slow," Vol said, "but his hands go fast enough and he keeps a reasonable number of paint colors around, last I heard." Vol talked a lot about Mundy's Corner and Buddy Kinder the night before last, as he and Joe drove and dug and buried and walked in the woods.

Now it's early on Sunday morning and because the car radio is broken along with the air-conditioning, Joe has heard nothing. And because he has stayed in the car for a day and the better part of two nights, eaten nothing but bread and cheese, he knows nothing much except that here he is finally at the place in Mundy's Corner and that he has, alone, himself, figured out this next step.

Joe drives past the garage the first time, sees that even though it's a Sunday, Buddy is in there, doing something or other. Joe turns around in a side street, and goes back, this time driving right in. This is what Joe is good at, doing things as if he has a right to them. From the time he was four, he took *things* and put himself in places with the air of the utterly natural.

He is once again wearing the gray wool pants, and the hard shoes, but this time with a blue polo shirt. "I came to get painted," he said. "This is the Chevy. My pal called, I think. About going from black to something in the blue range." He could not bring himself to say *green*. "I know it's Sunday, but I just happened to be a . . . day early, passing through, and . . ."

Joe waited while Buddy moved paint cans from the floor to the shelves. Buddy read the label of one can for a long time. "Did I know about this?"

"I thought my buddy Vol called. I got a niece just finished her junior year in high school. I promised her this can on wheels for her senior year. And I promised to spiff it up for her." These were the lines Vol had rehearsed. Joe thought they sounded too jolly, but he didn't know what else to say.

"Nobody called."

"Oh."

"No. I don't keep too much inventory without money up front."

"Well, I have the money." Joe looked at the seven or eight cans on the shelf, seven more and a spray gun on the floor.

"What color? Most of these aren't full."

"My niece wanted like that blue-green color. You have anything like that?"

After what seemed like a year, Buddy said, "It's a popular color. I don't have it, though."

"I guess she's with it."

After another year, Buddy said, "I'd have to order the paint. Might take a day or two."

Joe thought about this. He said, slowly, "I was on my way to Florida to give this to her. I hate to get stalled for too long. What color could you do, if you started as soon as possible?" He looked around the shop. There were no other cars or doors or fenders to be seen. Buddy kept moving cans from one spot to another.

"I have a lot of red. Apple Red, it's called. Some woman canceled out on me."

"My niece will get used to it. Sounds good for a young girl." He put the keys on the counter.

For a moment it seemed Buddy was going to refuse the job. Joe waited, trying to read the signs, as Buddy began to assemble scrapers, sander, solutions, lining them up. Joe wandered over to the steps leading out of the garage at the back, presumably to the house behind the shop. He sat on the steps. He tried to figure what to do next. He felt wired. Words were coming out of him in a scary way, as if he were somebody who chatted with people all the time.

Buddy reminded him in some way of Vol. They didn't *look* alike. Buddy was shorter, stouter, and he had a shock of red hair turning white. His skin was very pale. Maybe it was the pallor? Maybe it was the small nose and the thick shoulder muscles that caused the ripple of familiarity. Funny. Vol was almost all temper, while Buddy seemed somehow like a religious figure. Yet there was something.

Buddy asked Joe to clean out the trunk. He handed him a cardboard box and Joe put the few small things he had kept into the box. A jumper cable, a first-aid kit. Skillet. There was a carton of eggs and some bacon in a plastic store bag. He took the blue bag out, wondering if Buddy was paying any attention. There was some white bread left over from the picnic. Even though Joe was hungry, and the bread was something he could eat right away, he didn't much want it.

The sleeping bag and his small suitcase were too large for the cardboard box. Joe took them out and put them aside.

He wondered all the while if he could pull off the idea he had of staying here, right here, instead of camping out as Vol would have done, while the painting was in progress. Don't rush, he told himself. If it is to happen, it must be as if by accident. He sat on the steps for another ten minutes before saying anything.

"I'll leave you be in a little while," he told Buddy. "Anyplace much to walk around here?" He got up and sauntered over to the door. There was nothing but left-over steel mill sites and a strip of old houses with shingles falling off. The country was supposed to be in great

shape, but everywhere Joe went, he found derelict housing. It reminded him of where he'd grown up, some eighty
miles from Mundy's Corner.

He edged out the front door onto the street and
squinted into the sunlight. A dirty window two blocks up
the hill seemed to belong to a bar. There'd be something
to eat in there, if only beef jerky and potato chips. It
wasn't what he wanted, but he needed to get something.
"What time does the bar open?"

"Noon."

"They serve food?"

"Nope."

Joe sighed and came back indoors, where he got a piece
of white bread out of the bag in the cardboard box. "I
should have eaten on the road," he said. He was glad to
see two of his tires were already off.

"You like McDonald's at all?" Buddy asked.

"It's okay. Why?"

"There's one down in the town—maybe . . . four miles. . . ."

Joe said, "Sounds like a long walk."

"You can take my truck. It's around the side."

He couldn't tell whether to trust Buddy or not. On the
other hand, he couldn't sit in the garage and watch him
forever. "You want me to wait till you're ready to come
along?"

Buddy shook his head. "Go ahead."

Joe didn't see a phone in the garage. He backed out of
the shop and made his way to the side of the building
where he found a black Ford pickup with the keys inside.
He climbed in, thinking what a relief it would be to just
take off in the truck. Drive out of the state. Buy new
clothes, get some decent food.

Minutes later he bounced over the railroad tracks and
felt as if he lived here. Just another guy going in for his
morning coffee and his Sunday newspaper.

Most McDonald's had drive-thrus. He counted on not
having to show his face much. After a couple of turns
around the couple of blocks downtown, he saw the big

yellow M. He was glad to see a steady line of cars stopping before the order microphone. When it was his turn, he talked to a machine and the machine talked back—"That's two Egg McMuffins with sausage and cheese and one with bacon and cheese. Two large coffees. Two large o-j's. Is that it?"

He thought he sounded frightened when he said yes.

"That'll be $10.33 plus tax. $11.05. Have a nice day," he was told.

He reached into his pocket for cash, peeled off two tens from the wad of bills, and slid the rest back. He put on his cap and his dark glasses and drove to the pay window. Neither the teenager who took his money nor the one who handed over the bags looked at him at all. If he'd been wearing face paint, they wouldn't have noticed. He felt relieved and let down all at once.

He did not go directly back to the body shop, but drove around the block looking for a newspaper box. He saw one for the daily local paper, the *Tribune-Democrat,* but it was empty. He parked the truck at a metered spot and went into the Thrift Drug Store. He was in luck. There was still a pile of thick Sunday *Pittsburgh Post-Gazettes.* He could see, even before he paid for his copy, that he was on the front page—a different sketch, not like the one on the television, a better one, and next to him was Vol and next to him Anton. He felt the bottom drop out of him and didn't know how he could go on pretending anything anymore. He forgot to take his change and the boy had to call him back.

Shaking, he tried to saunter out the door to the truck as if he were not in a hurry. He opened the door and tossed the paper casually toward the passenger seat as people did who only intended to check it later for the lottery results or the obits. He started up the truck; he opened up one of the coffees and took a sip, letting the motor idle, just sitting. He'd seen enough rednecks over the years who sat in cars, tired, hungover, didn't want to go to work or to church or back home. He figured he knew how to pass for one. He could always perform better when he was alone. Vol would have made him self-conscious and apologetic. He checked the lid on the coffee, put the whole cup back in the bag, and started out.

When he got past the city streets and could move more freely, he pulled the paper onto his lap and tried to scan it while driving. This he was unable to do. The lines of print blurred. The headline, *Men, Pirate Baby Disappear*, was all he could read. He reached around to the emergency blinkers and pulled over to the side of the road. He was not a fast reader, so he decided to take the article with him. He tore out the two pages that covered the kidnapping—the second page had Marina's picture—and almost by accident turned to the sports page. Yes, an article was there, too. He knew enough from the paragraph he'd read and the caption under Marina's picture to figure she'd lived long enough to tell them everything she knew. So, he'd screwed up worse than he could have guessed. There was no way to read fast enough. He turned in his seat to see if anybody was coming down the road. While he watched, he made rips to remove the sections that had articles about him. Still, no one came by. There was a small ravine to his right. He ducked out of the car and threw the rest of the paper down the hillside. The paper threatened to open up, but in the end it folded in on itself and slid under a bush.

He pressed the pages he had torn out into a small thick square and tucked the square into his pants pocket. The unfamiliar motor made a roaring sound when he gunned it. He thought he saw newspapers flying up in the ravine, like large birds, but when he looked harder there was nothing moving. Another four-wheel-drive vehicle passed him, tooting the horn, maybe thinking he was Buddy. He raised a hand and kept going and in minutes was back at the shop.

If an army of police had come out of Buddy's shop to greet him, he wouldn't have been surprised. All his life he'd been expecting it.

His car was wheelless, down from the hoist and being sprayed off.

"I'd say that was a quick trip," Buddy said.

Joe told Buddy to take whichever two of the three sandwiches he wanted. He wasn't sure he'd be able to make a show of eating the third, but he would try. What he really wanted was something soft, like a bowl of oatmeal.

So, in moments, Joe sat on the steps, swallowing with difficulty, planning. He would have to burn the clippings once he'd read them. Feeling in his pocket, he found he had matches. Good.

He asked for a bathroom and was gratified when Buddy motioned him up to the house. He turned around and climbed through the wooden hatchlike door at the back, across a broken sidewalk of about ten feet, and into a small, shingled cottage. He entered the kitchen. Looking back to the garage, he could see Buddy moving around. He opened cabinets. There was food. Spaghetti, sauce, some meats in the freezer. Cereal. Cans of soup.

The house was remarkably clean. Old Buddy was a bit of a housekeeper. Either that or he had a girlfriend. "Hello," Joe called out. "Anybody home?"

The house answered him with silence.

He was happy to see there were three small bedrooms and that only one showed signs of recent use.

He sat on the edge of the tub and read everything twice.

The woman had lived, that was for sure. Marina, her name was. She'd provided the sketches.

He burned the bits of newspaper over the toilet and flushed away the ashes. It took several flushes because the ashes kept floating back to the surface. After washing his hands, he returned to the garage.

Buddy was removing the bits of metal and plastic that were not supposed to end up Apple Red.

"I feel awful my buddy Vol didn't call you," Joe began. "He can be so irresponsible."

"I got the time, so it don't matter."

"I like it that you're such a good worker. You got a nice house, too. Kept real nice. I swear I just wanted to lie down on one of those beds. Hey, I wouldn't be able to rent a bed for a couple of hours, would I? The motels don't even take a person till way after twelve, and I hate to call a cab and then get there and can't even check in."

"Go on, lie down," Buddy said. "Take the middle room. The first one's mine."

"I'll be happy to pay."

Buddy shook his head.

"I won't mess anything up. I don't know what it is, I'm just tired this morning. Got up too early, I guess."

Joe did not intend to sleep. He was living ridiculously, dangerously. But he didn't want to go to a motel. Motel people were supposed to look at their guests, and he didn't want to be looked at.

And he didn't want to move any more than he had to. He almost didn't care if they caught him.

Could he buy Buddy another meal, then maybe come around again to the question of renting a room there? This was a scheme he proposed to Vol the other night when they drove around on back roads. Vol kept talking about how he was trying to stay out of motels, that he'd maybe camp out while the car was being painted. Vol said "I" instead of "we" at one point. Then Vol asked Joe to walk into the woods so he could take a piss. Joe said he'd wait in the car. Vol said, no, they needed to scope out the location for camping, sleeping the night. He insisted Joe come with him.

Joe hadn't exactly liked Vol. No, Vol was hard to work with because he had a terrible temper and he *thought* he was smart. And yet, Joe was sometimes aware of a feeling of *needing*, if not liking, Vol. The feeling was a child's wish to let go and let the other, larger, person take over.

One day Vol had rubbed the top of Joe's head as if Joe were a little kid, and along with irritation, Joe felt almost gratitude. He did not like to think about what he'd had to do last night. Yet he understood Vol's thinking and Anton's, too. He'd known the moment his picture appeared on television what he was in for. He

knew when Vol called him into the woods that if he fell
in step in front of Vol, he was a goner. So he made
sure he never got in front. He stayed beside Vol and got
Vol to talk. And talk. And talk. Then he'd pulled his
own gun.

He'd had to bury the jeans and shirt and shoes he wore,
because they were full of blood and muddy from the digging and then the branches he'd pulled over Vol's body.
He'd had to wash his bare body in a stream. He put on the
more formal clothes again. Different shirt, his only other
shirt. He'd had to work very hard and that's what kept
him from collapsing. He walked a mile in one direction to
bury his clothes and he looked around and figured that
was about two miles, maybe three, from the direction he
and Vol had gone to bury the contents of the garbage
bags they'd brought from the apartment. Those they
hadn't burned finally, either, but just buried, afraid the
smoke would attract attention.

After he buried Vol, Joe sat in the car in the dark from
three in the morning until the light came up, thinking
out a plan. He'd taken everything from Vol's pockets. Vol
had been carrying two fresh sets of identification, one
scrap of paper that held the name and phone number of
the body shop, and another scrap with Anton's phone
number on it. There was the money, of course, too. In a
back pocket was the woman's jewelry. Joe took everything,
including Vol's wristwatch.

There were maps in the car. At dawn, he drove along
another mile or so, then let the car drift into a clump of
bushes, and sat there for a whole day, watching the sun
come up and go down and hearing the hours ticking off,
slowly as death. For a few brief minutes, he studied a map
and a couple of squiggles Vol had drawn. Finally, when
the sun came up again, he drove the couple of dozen
miles to Mundy's Corner.

He'd also kept the lipstick, the mirror, and a couple
of Marina's cards in case he needed them for something.
He'd slipped them into his pocket when Vol wasn't

looking. He'd told himself, emergency situations, you never knew what little things you could use.

He'd hated Vol. That was the truth. How could he not hate the big stupid brute? He began to cry in the bedroom where he hid out at Buddy's place. From the little doilies and the photographs, he figured the room had once belonged to Buddy's mother, the odd-looking woman who shaded her eyes against the camera and clamped her hand on top of a boy's head. Funny place to end up. His whole life was strange, mixed-up feelings for people, and then, after knowing them for a while, alone, always back to that. Soon, and suddenly, he fell asleep. When he woke up it was four-thirty in the afternoon and Buddy was looking at him from the doorway of the room. His moon face looked worried but not unsympathetic. "You're sure bushed, huh?" he said.

THAT AFTERNOON, WHILE JOE SLEPT, MARINA STAYED AWAKE in her hospital room for four full hours. She watched some television, using her remote control to breeze by many of the same movies and nature programs Anton scanned in Detroit. And she read the newspaper; several times over she read the same words Joe had devoured and burned earlier that day.

■ ■

CHRISTIE HAD AN ARMY OF INVESTIGATORS REPORTING TO him about credit cards, phone messages, road reports, motel check-ins. By Monday, he knew about missing children reports in Arkansas and California and a lot of other states. As he climbed the slippery mountain of facts, he hung on to the notion that Marina's overheard conversation was right and that the baby had been taken to Ohio. That wasn't Tahiti, anyway. The Feds were checking adoption lawyers and agencies, but the list was long and the people who tied up Marina and left her for dead were the types who would sooner do a handover in the street.

Dolan came in, wincing an apology, put a couple more sheets on the stack, and left.

"If this is on the Ted Bundy end of the scale," Horner said in the task force meeting, "we all look bad for about ten years until a pattern emerges. Shit."

Christie wondered, not for the first time, about his line of work. He often told people—he'd told Dolan—about the funny way he'd gotten into it, when he didn't know what to do with his life and his best friend at the time, a guy named Will, talked him into going to the Police Academy along with him. Christie had thought then he'd do police work for five years, six, then something else. Social work. The priesthood. These had crossed his mind. Funny story. It turned out Will was the one who quit after three years. Christie instead found himself promoted again and again. Pretty soon he realized he'd gotten fond of the people he worked with. Now this was who he was. Meanwhile, Will got married twice in five years and went off to live in Australia. Who could guess these things? Did any life go according to plan?

He ran home for less than an hour at suppertime so his kids would know he was alive. His daughter, Julia, pulled the top of his ear toward her to tell him a secret while he wolfed down some spaghetti. "Bend my ear," he'd told her once, forgetting how literal four-year-olds were. Catherine was in a bad mood and he didn't want to touch it, didn't have time to touch it.

For a couple of days everything went just about like that. He slept two, three hours a night. His team was efficient. The FBI handed over more printouts on missing cars, missing license plates, missing children. The amount of paper was staggering. He assigned three people just to write up summaries and get them onto Rapid-Start.

Nobody reported seeing any of the men. Christie assumed they were holed up somewhere and their cars had been ditched. Luck or cleverness was on the side of the kidnappers. Which?

The print media harangued Christie about having

nothing new to report, but then, they were in the business of selling papers. Karen Graves looked funny, dazed on sedatives. The Pirates played ball.

◼ ◼ ◼

AT THE SHERATON HOTEL, MARINA ORDERED COFFEE FROM room service, and sometimes food, even though she didn't have much of an appetite. Officers Anita Wood, Bill Beesie, Lorette Simmons brightened when she mentioned putting in an order, so she got things for them. French toast from room service. Chinese delivered from a local place Simmons knew. The television droned on, more for the police than for her. Wood liked her soaps, Simmons liked the talk shows. Marina switched to news channels as often as she could to check on the state of the case.

On her second day at the Sheraton, she put on the sports news midafternoon and strained forward when they began to cover the Pirates. Bill Beesie was the officer on duty that day and he stood up when Gene Lamont announced Ryan Graves would continue to take his turn in the bull pen. Beesie let out a large *shhhhhheeeee* of exclamation. "Man, I didn't expect him to be *pitching* again. That's gross."

Most interviewees on the street agreed with Beesie; they were offended. Newscasters, taking their cue from their interviewees, shook their heads and quietly questioned Graves' ability to perform in the midst of this horror, adding in low voices that nothing at all had surfaced in the case of the missing Graves child. At the Pirates' clubhouse, reporters asked Graves why he had agreed to pitch.

"It's what I do," he said. "If I'm needed in the seventh or the eighth or the ninth, I'll do what I can."

He was young. Boyish. The openness of his face broke her heart. She understood that he needed to hold on to something familiar. What did people want from him? Couldn't they see he was almost out of his mind? Shattered?

The window of Marina's room at the Sheraton looked

out over the river and toward the baseball stadium. She often thought of Ryan and his wife trying to keep from going crazy, and she wondered ten times an hour if there was something more she could have done.

It had taken her half the morning to bathe and dress, but this was good in a way, since problem-solving distracted her. She was not allowed to wash her hair, for instance, but had to use a dry shampoo, and even that had to be kept away from the wound. She was still allowed only a sponge bath. It hurt to get dressed. All this took time. Still, underneath, she thought about the baby she had not been able to save.

Courageous? It didn't seem so to her.

She phoned her mother and sister, playing everything down as much as she could. She told them she was fine and they didn't need to bother driving up from Virginia.

Otherwise the only person she called was her friend Lizzie, who also checked on her several times a day.

Nearly a week had gone by since the event.

When Lizzie called on Wednesday, Marina said, "I couldn't find it on the news today. Less and less."

"I know," Lizzie said. "I know. You feeling any better?"

"About the same."

"I wanted to call earlier, but I had to take the kids to register for camp."

"You sound like you're crying."

"Jason stuck his finger in my eye to wake me up this morning. You know how they do that peeling the eyelid back to see if mother is alive?"

The things children did, small events, were interesting in and of themselves. Humorous, tragic. Little one-acts of experience. Marina thought so, anyway, honoring childhood as she did, with no daily reality to take the romance out of her ideas—as various well-meaning people had pointed out when she didn't conceive.

"He's been into that lately. Anyway, I have an abrasion. I keep washing it out, but it's like I've been crying all day long." Lizzie sighed. "I wish I could get over there. I'm sorry. Doug's away till tomorrow night. Business."

"It's okay."

"Is Michael being okay?"

"He's trying. Mostly he doesn't want to talk about . . . where we are." She saw Officer Beesie trying to look as if he weren't listening to her.

"But he's being decent?"

"He's at work most of the time. He calls a lot."

"Policeman there?"

"Yeah. It's so, you know—"

"You can't talk?"

"Ummm. How's Annie?"

"Sensitive. As usual. She keeps asking me why I'm crying. I tell her it's because she made me read *The Little Engine That Could* twenty times yesterday. I wish I could come over and just sit around and watch TV with you."

"Don't worry about it." Marina looked at her watch. News and then order some lunch. It seemed impossible, even wrong, that her life had already assumed an established routine in this new setting.

"I'm sure you're getting bored."

If boredom could be defined as the need to do something, fix something, yes. She had agreed not to go out. She had let them talk her into being protected. "What am I going to do?" she wondered aloud. "I've always worked."

"Could you maybe do telemarketing or something?"

Could she maybe do telemarketing? Give up the protection program, go back to school, and study occupational therapy? Maybe just get a job at Saks? Surely the thugs who wanted her, if indeed they did, did not shop at Saks' perfume counters. Marina thought herself into various jobs, like an actress imagining, but imagining everything but acting.

"The news is on again," she said.

"Call again later," Lizzie said. "Or I will."

But there was nothing about the Graves case on the news.

With Beesie watching her, and the television still on, Marina closed her eyes and tried to think what she should do. About a job, about Michael. She was desperately lonely and yet she did not look forward to his return each day from work. He tried to do things for her; it made her uncomfortable; he couldn't meet her eyes. She sensed she could just let things go on like that for a long time and there would be a kind of patching up that happened over time, imperfect healing, the way wounds and marriages both were mended a hundred years ago. The doctors had said it was important she have someone to care for her, but she didn't see why that was true. There was enough falseness in the world; why must she have it with her husband, on top of everything else?

SO, ON HER THIRD EVENING AT THE SHERATON, A THURSDAY night, when Michael put his briefcase down and was looking at the room service menu, Marina asked Officer Lorette Simmons to go into the hall for a while to give them some privacy.

Michael turned toward her, surprised.

Simmons said, "Sure. You just open the door as soon as you want anything."

Marina asked Michael to take one of the chairs on either side of the round table in front of the window. "It's time to face all this," she said quietly.

"What? All what?" He looked at her, but he continued to stand beside the bed, his hand on the phone. His face was haggard.

"How bad it is between us. Sit. Please sit. I have things I need to say."

He put down the room service menu, crossed around the bed, and sat reluctantly.

As gently as she could, she said, "I've thought a lot about the night everything happened to me."

"I wish I could go back. I wish I could erase it."

She waited a moment. "I've been trying to put myself in your place—what you must have been thinking. You thought I'd already left, didn't you?" She thought she saw a small attempt at protest. "I know you did. I know you weren't at home in the middle of the night. I know about all that."

Michael shoved a paper cup that sat on the table. It flew at the bureau. Water splattered the front of the bureau and the floor. He shifted in his chair, looking away from her. "This isn't the time to talk about it. We're neither of us in the right shape."

Eventually she would explain to her mother and sister. The history. How for *years* he'd insisted their childlessness was her fault. Said she was too thin. Said she put out an enzyme that discouraged conception. But then they showed him pictures. They made drawings. Still, the denials. And the anger, blaming her, as he had been doing for years, for everything—things at school, his job.

He never did let himself believe the doctors. He gradually stopped sleeping with her. Even though he was physically there, in the same house, she was so lonely she couldn't bear it.

She'd tried everything she knew to try, talked to him about adoption, but he said no, he had no parents left, he was the last of the line. She suggested they go away for a while. He said he couldn't get the time away from work. She'd made the appointments with Dr. Caldwell, and after a long resistance, he'd gone along with her, but what she learned from counseling was that his violence was real, not something she was imagining, and that already too much was ruined to repair.

She looked at the water dripping off the bureau.

"I want to make sure I say this the right way." She paused to see that she had his true attention. "I still need to live alone for a while. Do you have someplace you could go?"

"I'm here with you. Or wherever, with you. We'll find a house or an apartment. We'll figure it out."

"Look, are we going to tell the truth here?"

Michael got up abruptly and pressed himself between the table and chair to stand at the window. His hands clenched. If Officer Simmons weren't outside, Marina thought, Michael probably would have grabbed and thrown something else. She told him, "I'm going to ask the police to find me a place to stay. For me alone."

"You don't know how these things work. These people aren't going to pay for you to be on your own. They want me with you." His face tightened with the distance he put between them when he talked to her this way. Rage. She now knew it was rage.

Michael, Michael, she thought, how can I help you, how can I say the right thing? Again, she had the feeling of wanting to reach out and solve it for him, to end the violence by capitulating, letting him blame her dim understanding, but she managed to stick to what she was trying to say. "I'll figure out how to make some money. What they don't handle, I will."

"Why do you keep cutting me down?"

"That's not what this is about."

"You're making me out to be scum. This isn't my fault."

"I never said it was."

Outside their window, a large ferryboat was taking passengers to the ball game at Three Rivers Stadium. She reached over to try to touch her husband's arm, but he pulled away. She said, "If you get angry, I'm sorry, but we need to make plans. You probably don't want to stay here at the hotel when they aren't paying the bill and you can't go back home. You've got to find someplace to go, too."

"So this is, what? . . . You're trying to punish me?"

"Oh, Michael." She put an arm around him, but he shoved it away.

"What's the matter with you? They practically kill you and you won't let anyone take care of you. That's your problem in a nutshell. You hear? What kind of a nut are you?"

"I know you don't want to tell me what's going on with whoever you're seeing . . . you think I can't take it. But I'm glad. I'm actually relieved."

"It hasn't been that bad between us."

She sat down on the bed. "It's been very bad. The last thing we said in Dr. Caldwell's office was—"

"You were going to leave me."

Finally, she asked again, "Do you have someplace to

go? Is there someone you could stay with?" When he didn't answer, she asked, "Are you in love with someone else?"

What were the stages, anyway—confused, innocently smitten, infatuated, in love, married, disappointed? Did it have to be that way?

"I'll stay here at the hotel," he said angrily. "I'll pay my own way. So nobody bumps me off," he muttered. He went to the phone and took up the room service menu again. While he waited for them to answer, he shouted, "I'll just stay here. Live on room service. Fine. Just so you know, I don't want this. This is all you."

Talking to him was hopeless.

Marina felt on the verge of terrible tears that wouldn't come and also on the verge of laughter that she couldn't explain. In a dream, stuck between two rooms, unable to move. She wanted to move.

THE NEXT DAY—THE THIRD OF JULY, A FRIDAY—SHE CALLED Christie to tell him she definitely wanted an apartment and pretty much wanted it immediately. She asked if she could have the on-duty officer drive her to look at possible places to rent.

He told her he would drive her himself.

He came to her room at the Sheraton to pick her up. As she opened the door, he was taking a call on his pager.

"It's okay if you have to work," she began. "I can wait. Someone else can take me."

"It's okay," he said. He clipped the pager back on his belt.

Marina handed him a piece of paper. "I called the university—my friend Lizzie suggested it," she explained to him, "because graduate students rent their places out in summer and the places are still furnished. Here are two addresses the University Housing Office had. They're both sublets. What do you think?"

He looked at the paper, saying he didn't like the Dawson Street address. "Too rough. Besides, it's a studio. About four feet square probably." He looked at the paper a second time. "I think I know these buildings. They're these ugly mustard-colored—"

"I could handle a studio. It's just for me."

He looked at her. "Just for you? Are you sure?"

"I know it complicates things. I want Michael to be safe, too."

"Come on. We'll look. I have an idea. Couple of ideas."

As he put her into his car, an unmarked Ford with a ton of papers on the seat and flashing-light contraptions on the floor, he said, "I've got something else I want you to do first, if you're willing."

"What?"

He motioned for her to wait a second and walked around to the driver side of the car. When he got in, he said, "Karen Graves came to see you in the hospital one day. You were asleep and she was crying pretty hard, so she left."

"Oh."

"She wants to meet you. She wants to thank you for what you tried to do. I have to go over there now for a few minutes. I check with them, one way or another, every hour or so. It helps. Do you think you can handle it?"

"Oh, yes." She felt anxious, nonetheless. "There's no news for them?" No gift of news to take.

He shook his head.

"How do they—?"

He shook his head again. "Faith is part of it. The rest is sheer grit."

They drove over Smithfield and down Sixth and over Penn to Gateway Towers. People who were dressed for work seemed to be walking in a hurry. The poor, out-of-work people shambled along or stood at bus stops. In normal circumstances, Marina would have chosen to walk it—a shorter route by foot. The pager beeped three times. The cracked, mumbled voice of the police radio made a more regular contribution to the sound in the car. Garth Brooks sang on the other radio about having friends in low places. Every once in a while Christie hummed tonelessly.

"Do you," she asked, "have really scummy friends?" He didn't know what she meant at first. "Friends in low places? Do you?"

"Well. I *know* all kinds of people. Unfortunately, I sometimes like the scummy ones as much as I like anybody. To be truthful."

She'd meant her question as a kind of joke, a distraction, and was sorry it had fallen flat. She studied the way he moved his mouth, as if he were going to speak and then changed his mind. She thought he seemed humorless and literal.

"Ryan Graves is probably going to pitch tonight or tomorrow," she said. "A lot of people think that's wrong."

"I know. I told him to go ahead."

"He consulted you? How did you come into it?"

"Well, there was the question of visibility. Was it a bad thing? A good thing? We talked it over. The bottom line is, he needs to do it. Between you and me, I'm not expecting any ransom note. If I ever was. It sure doesn't seem likely. I'm buying your interpretation, just between us."

"If you could find something I could do to help . . ."

"You already risked your life."

"Stupidly."

"I'm not sure anyone could have done better."

"I guess I'm still hoping I'll remember a word or an object that would justify—"

"You don't need to justify. If there's something to remember, it will come better if you don't force it."

As they pulled into the driveway at Gateway Towers, she thought of something she wanted to ask him.

"Two," he answered. "Four and six. Girl and boy."

Four and six. Two children. Four and six.

She felt eighteen, on a date, but somehow the script was wrong. Or she was in one of those theatre dreams, lost, unable to figure out the role, the play, but being pushed out onstage anyway. Two children, four and six. "Do they like baseball? Do you take them to ball games?"

They pulled into the garage at Gateway Towers. He

took the parking ticket the machine sentry spit out. He shook his head. "I'm a terrible father."

"Somehow I don't believe that."

"It's the old story. I'm not around enough." He pursed up his mouth. "Funny you should ask. Ryan Graves got me tickets for tonight, so if nothing new comes up by late afternoon . . . I can't sleep. I'm supposed to take off a couple of hours a day . . . maybe I'll manage to take them to the game tonight. It's not that I never take them—"

"Not as often as you'd like."

"Not nearly often enough. It's the job, yeah, I could blame that, but it's also the kind of cop I am. I have to go on vacation in a month and I won't want to leave. They'll have to send a crane to haul me out. It's not a virtue." They pulled into a parking spot and he shut off the engine. "How are you doing? This in and out of the car can't feel good."

Marina unbuckled the seat belt, waving off his concern. She felt awkward, moving stiffly. And she still had a bandage on her head, now more or less covered up with a mass of hair, but not invisible.

Workaholic, two children, four and six, girl and boy. And a wife. But he doesn't mention the wife. And why not? Is he the usual sort of creep, then? What does it mean? If this is a dream, she is floating around at a big social gathering, his wife is in the corner, but the crowd keeps mixing and the situation keeps progressing and the wife hovers, sips her wine, and does not come up to be introduced.

Christie hurried around to open the passenger door. He supported her by the upper arms to help her out of the car, then let go as soon as she was on her feet. "You'll like Ryan and Karen," he was saying. For a moment she thought he meant his children. "They're both trying very hard to be strong. They're religious, as I said. They're holding on tight."

By now Marina knew that Graves had come to Pittsburgh only two weeks ago. Next to their marriage and the birth of their son, the greatest day of their lives, they said, was when Ryan got called up to the major leagues. Team members told about the wide-eyed kid who came into the clubhouse and practically cried when he saw his shirt already made up for him, the kid who was amazed to see an old guy fixing up a locker for him, people bringing things—shoe polish, bats for him to try. This was his lifetime dream come true. He'd asked for a phone and called his wife right away. Now the Graveses' lives were completely wrecked.

"Karen Graves told me that when she saw you that morning in the Clark Building, she thought you were beautiful. She was really thrown when you were officially under suspicion at first. Then you turned out to be a heroine." He helped her up over two steps in the parking garage and back to the sidewalk outdoors.

The sun hit her hard in the eyes. She worried that underneath the gratitude, and way underneath the transcendent strength, Karen might wonder, as she herself did, if she could have done better. After all, Justin was lost, and how could a mother measure anything but that? "Right now I just want to run away," she said.

He grimaced, from the sun or irritation, she couldn't tell. "They asked for you. It's going to bring it all back for them. It's going to be emotional." But he seemed eager, expectant.

Through the glass doors, a thin woman with a clipboard rushed past a well-dressed man with a clipboard. Building personnel, probably, doing their 110 percent. The Gateway Towers was for people with money. "How about finding me an apartment in here?" she joked.

"They can't afford it, either," he said, as they walked in. "They were loaned the use of this condo—well, they *rented* at a very reduced rate—while they were looking for a place to stay, and it already had its own furniture, which was convenient since their stuff wasn't even packed yet to come up from Georgia. Now they have to stay here because of what happened—the phones being tapped, and all that—and the condo association had to meet about them.

Because you can't rent here for less than a year and the owner is supposed to be charging them $1000 a month at the very least. All kinds of rules at a place like this. Well, you don't need to know all that, but it's a mess. In every way. I feel so bad for them."

Now Marina sighed. She saw the woman with the clipboard looking hard at her, perhaps because of the newspaper photo. Maybe because of the bandage. Christie steered her around a corner and out of the woman's sight.

He said, "They're neither here nor there. The other day, wouldn't you guess, their stuff arrived and they had to put some of it in storage, take some of it off the truck. You can imagine—they don't feel like unpacking. You're going to see quite a few boxes."

"I'm just nervous about meeting them."

"Her parents are here, too, and his father, by the way. Her two brothers just left. It's a full house."

Christie punched the elevator button and stood back. The elevator, a mirrored thing, silent as death, slid into place and the doors opened soundlessly. Marina got on first and turned to see Christie look around, get on, punch the buttons. There were times, she noticed, that he had a kind of syncopated, jerky movement. It seemed like an apology for something. A group of boisterous people got onto the elevator on the second floor, pressing her against him. He flinched, then relaxed. Nerves, she thought. He'd be nervous all the time in his line of work.

■   ■

VALERIE EMMONS PRESSES JOSHUA AGAINST HER. HE SMELLS sweet from his bath. She pushes aside the book her husband has been reading about how and when to begin solid foods and she sits on the couch, lowering the baby to her lap. She told Stephen maybe the baby is only three months old and Stephen said the girl lied once so why not assume she lied more than once. He thinks it might be time for solid foods. He is in favor of experimenting with a minispoonful, one-one hundredth of an ounce. She wants to take no chances. The other child, he tells her, was not healthy to begin with. This one is different.

She knows this is true.

Joshua is not her first adoption. The other one, ancient history, back when they were still young, happened in Lexington, Kentucky. Bad luck all around. They hardly got used to having the child around, two weeks, not even time to get comfortable with him. He died in his sleep. Even the agency wrote it was not her fault. The child was sickly, they said. SIDS. It even happened to healthy babies sometimes. She swore never again. Not her fault, but there was something lacking in her, nevertheless. Love. Peace. She's been through a lot in the last years. So, is she calm enough now to send out the right messages?

The book is halfway under her on the couch, poking into her butt, which irritates her more than she can explain.

She scowls, and Joshua immediately begins to cry. He catches her every expression. How can she control everything about herself? She lifts up, gets the book out from under her, saying, "Shhh. Shhh," to no avail, and reaches over for the phone book she's put on the table beside the couch. The phone book looks terrible there because there's nothing else like it around. In a decorated house, each item is chosen for size and shape and texture.

The cleaning woman, Mrs. Moziak, knows how Valerie feels about clutter, and when she gets here, she will put the phone book and Joshua's bath things away.

Joshua screams.

In spite of the things she tells herself, Valerie begins to lose her confidence. He will feel it. She must find the right touch, not too harsh, not too soft. She manages to get the phone book open to the page she wants, then she scootches over to grab the portable phone she's put on the table behind the sofa, almost out of reach. "Not a good time to scream," she whispers, in what she hopes is a playful manner, "or you'll blow it." But Joshua does not take criticism well. He tunes in to criticism no matter how she jovializes the tone.

"Okay then, okay then." She gets up and hurries him into the room that is now his. She puts him into his crib, a beautiful white thing, which she calls *jail*.

She stands looking at him, worrying. It took her half the morning to get him cleaned up and dressed because she is still not fast at these things. Having help will relax her.

At first, she considered asking Mrs. Moziak, who comes twice a week, to come daily, to become more nanny than cleaning woman. But Mrs. Moziak did not seem particularly interested in the baby, even when Valerie asked her to say a few words to him in Russian. Anyway, Moziak is a sourpuss. She doesn't even say hello when she comes into the house, just cleans and polishes like a demon, grunts a reply to whatever Valerie asks her, and trudges out.

Valerie and Steve have often talked about replacing Mrs. Moziak with someone more personable. But who else could they find so thorough and passionate about cleaning house? It's an old-world virtue, very seductive.

Joshua, crying a little less vehemently, gives her that punishing look of his. When she tries to imagine the mother who has given him up, she gets a very specific image of a girl, plump and just slightly slutty. Maybe even sour like Mrs. Moziak. She no longer believes what the lawyer said about the *beautiful* child-mother. Her husband does, but for her, that part of the story has slipped.

Now Valerie reaches up to spin the mobile—abstract shapes in bright colors—and Joshua cries out as if these shapes threaten him. She can't do anything right, no matter how much she wants to please him. What if he simply doesn't like her? Stopping the mobile, she tries to imagine herself from his point of view—a new face, a new voice. He would try to substitute her eyes, nose, crow's-feet into the picture of his real mother he was carrying around. Just as *she* was always redrawing images of the child-woman who was his mother, trying to come to some balance between her worst fears and what the lawyer had said.

He is crying because he doesn't understand his dream.

Hopefully soon he will figure out how to erase the old face and accept the new.

Well, Steve had wanted *fast and private,* and they had gotten *fast and private.*

"Please stop crying," she pleads. She backs out of the bedroom door and passing the bathroom sees the towels, the plastic tub, and toys she's just used. The mess bothers her, and she hates herself for that lack of flexibility. She pulls the bathroom door closed. People learn, people adjust. She will get better at this mothering business, Steve tells her, and meanwhile he is so happy.

Her friend Debra thinks she's nuts to be doing this to herself at her age. *Their* ages, mid-forties, for Debra's two kids are grown and out of the house. *They* don't much like *her,* either. "So you had the need," Debra said, "he had the need, but did you have to fill it? You should have just told him no. Men shouldn't get their way about babies. Women should get their way."

But Debra doesn't know about the little boy fifteen years ago or about the years of hashing out whether to adopt again. In the twelve years she's known Debra, she's thought to tell her about the child who died, but Debra represents something else. Getting on with it, good times, cynicism. Mostly good times.

Bottles in the kitchen. Valerie stands there, almost paralyzed. Yes, things have changed. Down the hall, Joshua is still crying.

She goes into the living room and consults the phone book. The other one didn't cry. Never. Never cried. Finally she punches in the number of the local weekly where she one day two years ago saw the number of the agency in New York for which LaPaglia was a local representative. *In Pittsburgh* answers with voice mail. Wearily, Valerie punches one, then two, then one again. Finally a person says, "Classified."

"How do I advertise for a nanny?"

"Help Wanted. We can run fifteen words for sixteen dollars for one week. Additional words are sixty cents apiece. It's a special."

"I don't care about the money."

"Oh. Okay. What do you want the ad to say?"

Valerie says, "Help me. Isn't that what you guys do?"

She hears a little snort at the other end. " 'Nanny Needed. Good home. Reasonable hours. Pleasant children.' What else?"

Valerie has to laugh. Because there's old Joshua screaming in the background. " 'Pleasant *infant.*' I don't *know.* What else do people want to know?"

"Well, you'll want to be careful. You should probably say, 'Mature individual with experience. References required. Long-term employment position. Pay commensurate with experience.' Scare off the loonies."

"That sounds fine with me. How much do you think I should offer?"

"I wouldn't put anything into the ad."

"I know. But how much?"

"I couldn't say."

"Sure you could. What do others offer?"

"We don't get many ads for nannies. This is not a nanny kind of a newspaper. Not even a nanny kind of a city."

True. Not too many people in Pittsburgh can afford a house like hers or a twice-weekly cleaning woman.

"I really could use some advice. So you think it would be about the same as I pay my cleaning woman?"

"How much is that?" Curiosity leaks through the young woman's voice.

"She stays all day. It's a hundred a day. We wanted her to come every day and we were ready to offer six hundred a week. So I guess that's what I'd offer a nanny."

"Plus benefits?"

"My husband could answer better than I could about that. I think so."

"Cripes, what am I doing here? I could take care of a baby. It would be more fun."

"Oh!"

"I'm just kidding."

"Really, because if you're not—"

"I couldn't just leave these people in the lurch. I was just kidding. I'll get this in Monday for Wednesday's paper. Okay?"

"I'll leave it to you. The phrasing. All that. I need to get somebody good."

"Nothing against the rag I work for, but you might want to put your ad in the *Post-Gazette*, too."

Valerie puts the phone book away herself and takes the phone back to its stand, off in the corner. The crying has stopped, but little complaining sounds remind her Joshua does not like being in jail. She will have to spring him. In a week, things will be different. If she can just go out to lunch with Debra every once in a while, she will get better at this new job of hers.

She looks at herself in the hallway mirror. Does she look different now that she is a mother? Older. It has made her older rather than younger, this having a child.

She walks to the kitchen, opens the enormous Tupperware tub that contains a smaller Tupperware tub that contains a smaller one that contains a small bottle of vodka. No, she doesn't need it yet. But it's there.

Debra always drinks daiquiris and margaritas when they go to lunch. Right in front of her. Debra wears the wrinkles around her eyes with a kind of pride. The last time, Debra looked at the drink glass in front of her, ate the fruit out of it, closed her eyes, and said, "I got my wrinkles, and my thinness, and my kids hating me from this. It's very me. It's as much a part of me as my blood is."

Yes, Debra looks at her as if she is somehow less than she used to be. She knows she is supposed to cut off her relationship with Debra to make the recovering go more smoothly. But she doesn't want to give Debra up.

Joshua screams again.

"Cripes, I'm coming," she says. She shoves the Tupperware back, thinking that maybe when Steve goes to Denver . . . maybe then, just for one evening. She dreams about having a drink. Some nights, she literally dreams about it. For a long moment, she thinks to hide the bottle of vodka in a new place. But it's so near at hand, and likely not to be discovered. Even Mrs. Moziak isn't going to look through layers of Tupperware unless they throw a huge party and she has to store a colossal number of biscotti or something.

■   ■

RICHARD CHRISTIE HAD ORCHESTRATED MEETINGS LIKE THIS before, where emotions were running high from the start. He liked making them happen. They stirred him. He liked staying apart, as if he were in the audience at a play.

He opened the door and introduced Marina to the Graveses.

Karen, pale and thin, reached for Marina's hand to lead her into the room. When Marina followed, softly, willingly, Karen studied her face. Then she put her arms around Marina and hugged her hard, sobbing, "You're the last person I know who held him, who took care of him." Christie saw Marina fall apart when Karen said that. Eyes closed and then tears washing over her face. Women! The way they could just stand there and do that!

He stood in the open doorway and watched them. Finally he closed the door.

Karen asked him to come in and sit down. When she got him and Marina seated, she said, "I made coffee. Let me get you a cup." He already felt wired up, but he nodded. She left the room and the men began to speak.

The men in the room—Ryan Graves, his father, his father-in-law—congregated around Christie and counted out brightly colored tickets. He took them, kept them fanned out in his hand.

"Good seats," the father-in-law said. "These are the best."

"For your family, and if you ever break away . . ." Ryan's father, a trim, mustached man, nodded toward Christie's radio, pager, cell phone. Christie was touched that they could understand even a minute away from the office, even though he'd already explained to them he was never away from the case and there were hundreds backing him up. But how decent they were.

"My kids are used to the peanut gallery. This is such a treat for them."

"When they get the new stadium built, all the seats will be good. Not like it is now," Ryan's father added.

Ryan shrugged.

"Money. If they get the money," his father said knowledgeably.

Maybe because Marina was there, and emotions were running high, the men seemed to grab at anything to keep the talk flowing. Karen's mother came forward from the kitchen, in front of Karen and carrying a tray with coffee. She introduced herself quietly, then sat across from Marina. "Thank you for trying," she said. "You are a remarkable person." Karen, looking dreamy and uncertain, took the seat next to Marina, while her mother handed around cups of coffee. Christie found himself saying something dumb about the fancy colorful tickets and how plain the tickets had been when he was a kid. This was one of his commonest jobs as a policeman. To sit. And talk about one thing and watch something else.

He studied Marina's beauty, which had emerged again as her injuries began to fade. But it wasn't only her beauty stirring him, it was really the whole scene, the accident of it: the women sitting on the sofa, the light behind them, their combined beauty, two different kinds, the one young and athletic and blond and simple, the other complicated, darker, and stranger; his choice, the dark one.

He sat with the game tickets fanned out in his grasp. He told Ryan and his father-in-law that his wife hated baseball, and he saw Marina's quick attention to that statement. His heart went crazy. For a second, he almost offered her the other ticket even though right now she was not supposed to go out in public at all. Ryan Graves must have seen him look up at Marina, for he quickly suggested he also get tickets for Marina and her husband—that is, he said, if Marina was up to going out. Marina thanked him and said simply that she did not feel ready for any of that.

When they left the Graveses' apartment, Christie told her if she ever wanted to go to a game, he'd figure something out, some way of protection. Any excursion had to be something special, an exception, but with planning, it could be done. She shook her head. He didn't know what it meant. They got into his car, in the cool dark of the parking garage. When they drove up into the light, they both shielded their eyes.

He had to stop at the office before he could take her around to apartments. One of his detectives wanted him to look at two photographs of a crime scene from an old case. An old case with some new ideas in it. "Do you mind stopping off where I work?" he asked Marina. "It will only take a minute."

The Investigative Branch was a shabby place. He hoped she didn't mind it.

He had to leave Marina out in the Homicide Department while he consulted with one of his men in his glass-walled office. She could have chosen to sit while she waited, but she walked around and looked at things. He liked that. When he shuffled a photo to the back of a stack and looked up through the ribbed glass, he could see she was like an exotic bird trapped in an old schoolroom, with its ancient metal and wood and green institutional walls. All the while he studied the two particular photographs side by side, holding them up at eye level, he was aware of where she went, the bulletin boards she looked at. She stood for a long time in front of the one they called "the philosophy board." "The prayer board," one detective called it. When she turned around, he knew she understood the idealistic part of his job, the part with sentiment. He was glad she'd seen it. Because the rest of it, his life, was dizzy stories and dead-end types, desperation, lies. He liked that, too, in a way, hitting rock bottom almost every day, knowing the worst about human nature.

"I'm almost ready to sign on," Marina said when he came out to fetch her into his office.

"Why is that?"

"I don't know. I liked the people out there. I was surprised by the—"

"Brains?" He could see she couldn't come up with a noninsult fast enough.

"The phrasing of some of those quotes was beautiful."

"We're not all idiots."

He told her his speech about how *some* of the time officers deserved the bad rap they got, but not every single time. They came in the same packages as the rest of society, no better than the average. There were good policemen and bad ones and mixed-up ones. There was graft and bribery and prostitution, the whole roster. Dreams of license and a struggle up out of it toward their better selves.

"Would it be possible—could I just come here and work on the Graves case? There must be some routine jobs. Boring things nobody wants to do. I'm good on the computer."

Talk about a distraction. It would take a good month to get everybody used to having her around and just letting her work at whatever. People'd be bringing her coffee and asking her this and that. Staring at her over their file folders. It would be very unprofessional. "Can't. I can't allow it," he said gently. "We'll have to think of some activities for you."

He could see she was miffed. For a while she didn't say anything. And he sympathized—she'd said it was like she was in prison and the criminals were all free. That was true enough. Eventually she softened, and asked about lists of adoption lawyers and what kinds of computer programs were available for checking baby stores, adoption agencies, lawyers, charges against lawyers. And she wanted to know, had they found the owner of the Manchester house yet, where she had been shot? He told her the names—Anne Pinkus, the owner, and Emily Roderick, the tenant. Could they forge a connection, she wanted to know, between the names he'd revealed to her and *anything else* about the case?

"Not yet."

He thought, If she were a spy, I'd be a goner.

By the time they left the building, it was already one o'clock. She looked tired. He was hungry. And he couldn't take the whole day off, squiring her around.

He was judging his men by his own behavior. Maybe if she came to the office, she'd be a distraction only to him.

He looked over at her. No, she'd be a distraction in general.

"Sorry about this," he said, pulling into the McDonald's next door. "We can do better than this usually, but I kind of have to eat on the way."

He was grateful that, without hesitation, she ordered a large milk shake and a double cheeseburger, explaining she had orders to put on weight.

He paid for her lunch even though she tried to give him money. "This is work," he said, feeling like a jerk. He imagined the case being solved finally with a happy ending and him taking her to a nice celebratory lunch. Then he stopped himself and tried to erase the last hour. What am I doing? he thought.

They were still eating in the car when he drove past the six-unit apartment building in lower Oakland that he knew in advance he wouldn't approve of. It was exactly the one he'd thought—a yellow-brick, ugly thing, just a big dirty square with eight apartments in it. It flirted with poverty, trouble. "Forget this," he said, and drove off.

The other possibility was in upper Oakland, a sublet, which a downstairs neighbor could let them into. Christie didn't want Marina seen by anyone if he could help it. At first he intended to fetch the key from the downstairs neighbor, go out to the car, and get Marina, but he thought better of it. There was no guarantee he could keep the downstairs neighbor from following him around.

"I'll stay in the car," she said. "Go on. Look at it. I'll be okay."

He didn't like that much, but he agreed, saying, "I'll be quick. Sit tight."

The apartment was so full of the life of the regular

tenant, he wondered where there was to be room for the subletter. Toothbrushes, perfumes, stray shoes. And it wasn't very clean.

He turned back the key and hurried to the car. He had an idea. He'd been looking at a sign every day for how long now? He wasn't sure. It was one of those things you see and see until you stop noticing it. He passed it every day on the way to work—a handsome handmade sign that said FURNISHED SUBLET, and in much smaller script, a phone number. The apartment was on Emerson, in a large house that had been converted to rental units, probably two on each floor. He pulled up in front of it. "I have no idea what size this is," he explained, "but if it's reasonable inside, what do you think?"

Marina nodded. It was clear she didn't care where she lived. He worried about that. Not a good sign. He wondered if she was going to be able to discipline herself to stay hidden. Almost nobody lasted, but he didn't want her to know that.

He told her he'd feel good about the place on Emerson since it was on his way to and from work.

He squinted to read the number and dialed it from his cell phone. He got an answering machine that gave him another number and an explanation. Good news.

"Friend of the tenant," he explained, "is the person we have to see, because the tenant's already gone. This is good. This is luck talking to us. Tenant is a professor. She had to go to Africa to do research." He dialed the other number and arranged to look at the place later in the afternoon.

He drove her back to the Sheraton, watching her with side glances while he drove. She was restless, he could see that. He made her promise that, no matter what, she would never try to go to her own house. Not to look at it, not to do the garden, not for anything. After a pause, she nodded.

THE APARTMENT SEEMED PERFECT TO HIM. HE COULD SEE Marina there. It was a feminine place, attended to. The tenant had left the furniture—a floral-print couch, Ikea

tables, a decent bed, and a television and a microwave—
but had taken everything out of the drawers and closets.
Phone was operable. A big plus, since using someone
else's number had a safety factor built right in.

Christie shifted the coffeepot on the coffeemaker to
see that it wasn't sticking to the burner. He opened the
cupboards and found sets of dishes. A very acceptable
place!

He called the office and asked for Janet Littlefield to
come and sign the rent papers and make out a check in
her name, for which she would immediately be reim-
bursed. Then he called Marina to tell her to pack her bags.
He'd get someone to drive her over later that day, around
suppertime if she really wanted to move that fast.

She did. She sounded joyful.

■ ■

RYAN GRAVES HEADED FOR THE CLUBHOUSE AT THREE IN THE
afternoon, to practice, warm up. Get away from the mess
at home. He walked past the photos of Bob Prince and
Roberto Clemente and the folded shirts and the baseball
cards in the lobby at Gate D, and once more thought
about his bargain. A place on a major league team had
been his dream of many years, the only thing he had
wanted for most of his life, and now, in the lobby with the
memorabilia, he vowed he would give it all up if his baby
could be found alive. He would sell windows. He would
never seek this particular kind of joy again.

Last night he had almost given up. He had gotten a vision of his baby in a ditch, dead, and he couldn't shake it.
He's not sure how he made it through that visit this afternoon with the policeman and the woman who tried to
save Justin. Could they see the nightmares going on behind his eyes? Karen, well, she just sat and cried whenever
she wanted to. She'd gone crazy, that was the simple way
to put it. Her eyes were glassy, like something out of a
horror film, when he tried to talk to her. It was guilt in
her eyes, he knew that, because she'd been careless and

nothing she could say would erase that. Not that she would admit to the carelessness, not that she said anything at all significant when she talked to him. How could he stay with her knowing in his heart she had deliberately walked away from their baby? But he couldn't say the things he needed to say with her parents and his father hanging around and FBI and journalists everywhere. Even at breakfast they were there. When he looked up over the plate of bagels this morning, Ryan saw that none of them really believed anymore that Justin would be found. Deep down. Deep down they thought his wife had made a costly error a week ago and there was no way to recover from it. They would all put in their time, and would say all the right things, and days would stretch into weeks and months until they got used to the idea of a child gone. People told him it was one of the things parents never got used to, but he didn't believe they were right. He thought how much his thinking had already begun to accommodate the idea in one week.

He and Karen had hardly found a moment to say anything to each other privately. And yet they understood each other. She could read the message on his face: A stranger fought harder than she did to make Justin safe. She would look at him and then look aside, message received.

Better to be here, in the big circular hallway, passing Cam Bonifay's office with its big leather chairs, passing the places where work continued as if life would go on.

McClatchy was at his desk, on the phone, just standing, his hale posture caught and deflated as Ryan went by. The people in PR said hello as he passed, small gentle smiles on their faces. People were afraid to be happy around him. He'd overheard a conversation in the locker room two nights ago, about how babies were almost never found, how bad the odds were against him, and then he'd had to go down the hall and pretend to have some other business before coming into the locker room with a shout so they would stop talking.

They were just guys, ordinary and hardworking, like

the commercials said. Better than most, he told a sportswriter who interviewed him. The writer looked skeptical
and suggested, "Maybe just young enough and poor
enough to be still innocent."

Cam Bonifay, quoted in the article that eventually
came out of that interview, said if they'd wanted a poster
boy for the Pittsburgh Pirates, Ryan Graves would have
been it. The sportswriter said Ryan had a face of incredi-
ble innocence, an "I'll try my best" expression.

He'd never asked for his face. Every grandfather and
great-grandfather in his family had looked the same.
Stupid. Country boys. They didn't know the kind of violent thoughts he had. Scary thoughts. The way he wanted
to shake his wife until he could bring her awake. All they
saw was country boy.

He passed the visitors' locker room and then came to
the clubhouse.

He looked at his mail, which had already been opened
by a Fed, a young one, something like him, just in case
there was a ransom request or a bomb threat. But he knew
all of it would amount to more sympathy mail, and he
couldn't face it. He put the envelopes back in the slot,
aware of the huge stacks of unopened mail in the other
players' mailboxes. He'd heard the story of how it took
Lieber and his wife all winter to answer the fan mail
he got.

Ryan thought he would cry when the old guy who
cleaned the lockers in the club room clapped a hand on
his shoulder and said, "You show 'em tonight, kid."

He again thought he would cry when he practiced in
the batting cage and any child of fourteen could see he
was way off, swinging too high, and in one case, just losing grip of the bat. And two other Pirates saw him swinging that way, like an amateur. He wanted to hide, but he
kept making his rounds. In the exercise room, he chose a
bicycle and began pedaling. He could see other players
through the half-open door, beginning to trickle in.

The baby was not found, not found, everybody was
thinking, and time was going by.

If only he could reverse things. If he could turn back the world, like Superman did, and make what had happened not happen. If only that policeman, who seemed like he could see right through everyone, would see through to who'd done it and find his child.

Two days ago, he'd yelled on the phone to Christie that the police had to find and question the woman who owned the old house where his son was last seen. Stupidly, stupidly, as if they hadn't thought of that.

"Found her yesterday in Florida," he was told. "FBI ran her over the coals. She's an alkie, doesn't know her right hand from her car."

In a ditch somewhere, no life left.

He must not think it. If he thinks it, it will be true.

Does he pray? the team counselor asked him, something in the smudges under his eyes seeming priestlike. Yes, always, always, he answered. So did most of the others. They prayed for good games, for him, for good weather. They were a praying lot.

And they were superstitious, too. Prayers and hocus-pocus. One guy kept six cents, nickel and penny, on the floor of his locker. Players would leap on facts like "The Dodgers have never won a game in Chicago when a left-handed pitcher from the Cubs got the better of them by the fourth inning." And what could you do but roll your socks the whole way down as you had the last time you got a blast of wonderful luck? Who was to say this was illogical? Maybe it was the only logic there was. Feelings, routines maybe amounted to magic, maybe everything counted in some mysterious way. Maybe there was a big machine, with its own rules, and the way you rolled your socks and said your prayers and ate your breakfast *counted* and the machine was parceling out your rewards and punishments.

Just like how he felt inside, that if the Pirates could get on a winning streak and then could *stay* on a winning streak, something good would happen about Justin. Just as he had believed several months ago that if he nurtured and kept a certain feeling inside him, the Pirates would

root him up from the minors and plant him permanently
with them.

And that willed confidence, that purity of wishing, had
borne fruit. They had flown him up on a moment's notice, handed him a shirt already made up for him. (Shirts
of all the hopefuls hung from the ceiling in the clubhouse, a shirt with a number for every minor league
player who *might* get called up.) Most of the shirts stayed
up there untouched, most of the players stayed in the minors and eventually went off to do some other job, but
his, his was pulled down. The old guy who did the laundry, Vince, handed him a couple of towels, a pair of pants,
and then took a black marker to blot out the red on his
running shoes. Two more guys came by with bats for him
to try out and said he could borrow one from Adrian
Brown that seemed about right for him. If that could be
real, couldn't he get his son back?

Old Vince took him aside a couple of days ago and
said, "It's all in how you concentrate. Keep picturing his
face. Keep thinking about him." So he did this, squeezing
his eyes shut and calling up the fuzzy wisps of hair, the
round cheeks, the gurgling sounds; panicking when the
picture faded. He believed in magic, any kind, any relationship of thought to the outside world.

If the Pirates played well, he would get his son back.

After he worked out on the machines, he went to the
cage and pitched for twenty minutes. Several of the
Rockies were in there, as well as two of his own teammates. They stopped joking when he entered and the silence that came over the little cage was terrible. Finally a
couple of them asked him about the investigation, and
that helped.

By the time he got back to the locker room, the radio
was on and the slamming sounds and joking voices had
set up a big din.

"How you doing, kid?" a couple guys asked him.

He answered, "Hanging in."

"Want to watch the news?"

"I don't care."

For an ordinary rookie, well, it would have been a whole season before he heard too much from the more established players, the Youngs, Kendalls, Martins. But because of his special circumstances, every day the players asked him, "What are you hearing?" "Anything yet?" "Anything I can do?" They told him, "Hang in there." "Keep the faith." They asked him about his background, they talked fast food with him, they kept up the chat. They tossed him packs of bubble gum, hustled him along to the clubhouse kitchen, where they took potato chips, licorice, Mounds bars, chocolate chip cookies from the big jars or hanging racks and poured Slushies from the machine.

Pretty soon it was time to go out there and play.

For a long time he watched.

A ball would fly out, far, seem to be fair until the last moment, when it would go foul. He would *not think about* so much as digest the idea of it—surprise, wind, accident—what was almost inevitably safe and good turning off course. And the way a ball would sometimes get an odd spin so that what seemed like a simple grounder, an easy out at first, would roll, tip off a glove, roll again, until it rolled right to the back wall and back to the field, behaving more like a billiard ball than a baseball—that was something to do with time being elongated, with the inadvertent collusion of the opposing team, reminding him the world was full of strangeness, strange things he didn't know how to measure. Help would come from somewhere, the unlikeliest sources, maybe.

At one point Jason Kendall, muddy and intense, asked, "Everything okay?"

"Just waiting to play," he said.

Balls, in the air, in the dirt, *squirming* balls, caught once, thrown, caught again. Safe. All had their meanings.

Miracles. Baseballs that looked impossible to catch—caught spectacularly. Something in the muscles and mind knew how to do the impossible. An inner rhythm that defied the odds.

He got a part of the eighth inning when the team was

losing 8–2. He walked two guys, one flew out, and one hit a double. They eased him out. He didn't get to bat himself. The score stood through the ninth inning. He didn't think so much as feel, somewhere deep in him, that the evening's ball score was a sign of the odds against him, 4–1 odds.

■   ■

JOE PROWSER HAD HATED TO LEAVE THE MOONFACED ME-chanic's house in Mundy's Corner. Somehow he'd stretched his stay out with comments about how his niece could wait a little longer, letting the work on the car bump along at a slow, methodical rate. Buddy Kinder never bought a newspaper, never put on the old black-and-white television in the living room. He didn't look for conversation. He appeared to like the blasting noises of work, and silence, two sides of the same coin.

Not that they hadn't talked. Joe had flattered Buddy with questions about the business, how he'd learned it, how he kept it going on his own. Joe had also made up a life, in case anyone ever asked Buddy about him. He said he'd been born in Oklahoma and worked on a farm through his youth, then sold farm supplies, then went to a company that sold potting soil to places like Kmart. He made up another name for himself completely, one he'd never used before and had no cards for. He called himself Henry Quayle.

He slept at Buddy Kinder's house, gathering energy, and paid twenty dollars a night for three nights. He told Buddy it was better than any hotel he'd ever stayed at and he stayed at a lot of them as a salesman.

He slipped into the living room and turned on the old television when Buddy was working. And he took the truck for takeout each day, always checking a newspaper. So he now knew odd details about the woman named Marina Benedict, which awards she'd won, where she had taught acting classes. He'd buried most of her cards, but kept a few odd things, like AAA Road Service. Her address and social security number he had penciled in lightly on a restaurant card he found in Vol's pocket. He knew she had talked, been lucid.

It meant he must never come near Anton again. It meant he must disappear, him and his now red car with its ancient stolen plates. He must not speed. He did not feel the red car was particularly safe. He had no owner's card and it was going to be clear it was a new paint job.

When he got on the road, early on the first of July, he drove south to West Virginia, into the mountains, stopping at small-town fast-food chains for his meals and pulling the red car off into woods or bushes to sleep. He was planning to go higher up into the mountains, where he figured he could get really lost for a while. But by the time he'd got the new paint job nice and dusty, he changed his mind, and drove north again. He drove up to Erie, where he managed to beat the worst of the knot of drivers going to the lake for the holiday. After stopping at a Kmart, where he bought a pink-and-purple surfboard, green plastic sunglasses, a pair of swimming shorts, two pairs of casual pants, a couple of white polo-style shirts, three pairs of white socks, and a pair of cheap athletic shoes, he found a motel called the Moon-Lite and checked in as Henry Quayle. He noted on the check-in card that he had a red car two years newer than it actually was and he just happened to miswrite his license number, close, but not exact to the stolen plates he'd put on. He parked near the room, in the corner spot with the tail end of his car facing toward the woods. He left the glasses and the surfboard in the car.

From the motel room, he watched people come and go. Nobody gave his car a second look. He changed to his new green pants, white shirt, white socks, and shoes. In the mirror he saw that his hair was not very changeable, nor was the face that had made the newspapers. Glumly he ordered pizza and kept the drapes closed and his hat on when he paid the delivery boy. He sat at the window eating it while the air conditioner whirred loudly. He thought and thought.

How had he managed not to kill Marina? A shot to the heart, a shot to the head. It was the way she squirmed, he told himself, and how thin she was, so that under the sheets, even though he aimed well . . .

In spite of himself, he'd thought she was pretty. Well, beautiful. She threw him off balance, the way she acted as if she had something to say about the baby. The newspapers had said she never even knew the kid, just felt something was wrong. He wondered how people got that way, so sure of themselves. He decided it probably had something to do with being an actress. And being lucky and being loved all your life. Feelings he couldn't know about.

When it was dark, he counted his money again, put most of it in a spare pair of socks, and went out for a walk. He felt good—that is, invisible—being out in a crowd at night, so he stood in line for an ice-cream cone. Vanilla. The night was muggy, but delicious, too, in some way. Or maybe it was just that he was outdoors, finally, like a free man. The stars were vague and muddy in the haze and the lights, but he didn't mind; he looked up at them anyway.

■　■

RICHARD CHRISTIE PROPPED HIS HEAD HIGHER WITH TWO PIL-lows and watched Catherine struggle into a pair of shorts that were a size too small for her. He told his wife, "I want to do something with the kids today. Something special." Chief's orders, let Horner take over for six hours or so, keep the Feds happy, clean out his mind.

"I thought you'd go in. What do you mean, special? Oh, shit. I did gain weight. I look horrible."

She did not look horrible. She did not look wonderful, but only because she was so angry all the time. And also it wouldn't have hurt her to buy a new pair of shorts. Sometimes it seemed she wore tight or outmoded things on purpose, as a sign or a signal of something. Depression. Her present self not fitting her old self.

She did not seem particularly happy about his announcement. "This doesn't give us a lot of notice. We were going to hitch a ride with the Hendersons and go to Kennywood. With the mobs. But at least that would shut the kids up for the day. They'd feel they were out somewhere; they wouldn't be whining for something all the time."

"Come here."

Catherine obliged. "What?" she said, sitting on the edge of the bed.

"I'm trying to remember how it was when you said you didn't mind being married to a policeman. Remember? How you said you could make all the sacrifices that were needed? Remember? You said you were sure?"

"What is this?"

"Nothing. I want you to remember the feeling."

"Why?"

"I'm still a cop." He took her hand and placed it on his heart.

Absently Catherine began tracing his chest. Her touch felt good to him, softer than usual. Lately, they tended to grab at each other and hurry each other to climaxes before one of them was needed somewhere else. At first he'd found it exciting, the rough, quick, functional sex, but he soon tired of it.

"That was before we had kids," she said.

They'd had this conversation only a hundred times, maybe more, since life had dealt them children, and children had dealt the marriage a blow. Catherine did a lot better as a young, outgoing woman with time on her hands and a husband in a dangerous job than she did as a mother with a house-and-kids routine she couldn't see a way out of.

"I like how you're touching me."

"I'll bet."

"What are they doing?"

"I don't know. I don't think I heard them *up*. If they are, they're pouring cereal all over the place. Or sticking firecrackers up each other's asses."

He kept trying to ignite. "Lie down for a minute, okay?"

"Now?"

"Yeah, now." She lay there stiff and suspicious, in corpse position, hands on her belly.

Richard got up on his knees in bed and leaned over her to slip her sandals off. He had nothing on. His cock was partly hard. He wished she'd touch him or reach up and take him in her mouth. But she kept looking at him curiously. He tried to remember when she had cut her hair in this way. It didn't quite suit her, a short boyish cut with a shock of blonde that swung way out to the side. When he'd met her she was a petite, longhaired dynamo with no ambitions but to be with him as often as possible and to make enough money working at Pitt as a temp to buy herself clothes and take a trip every once in a while. He was glad when she got ambitions about school; that was good, too, and it carried her for a couple of years. Then suddenly, she stopped, gave up. Now she sometimes looked like a slightly pudgy adolescent English schoolboy, disgruntled about everything. Had he done it to her? He knew he had.

He unzipped her shorts. "Let's go shopping. I'll buy you a new pair."

"These look awful. I know."

"No, no, I didn't mean that. Come on, honey." He touched her breasts and her eyes hooded over. While he was slipping her shorts off, she said, "Lock the door if we're going to do this," but her voice was soft.

He came back to the bed. She began touching him again in the way he'd said he liked. "Your scars," she said, tracing two lines across his left shoulder. "They got to me."

He saw her trying to remember, but as she touched the lines—a knife had made them when he was young, a freshman on the squad—he thought of Marina, with her new scars. He fought to get her out of his mind, but she kept sneaking back. A moment's guilt softened him, as Catherine lay against him. He pressed forward, willing himself to love the woman with the chopped-off hair, the caged, angry eyes. He let himself think of a trio of buxom women blowing him, an image that had released him since he was a boy. In the end it was a good, energetic, not very happy fuck.

"We'll go to North Park," he told his wife. "Battle the crowds. Swim, hot dogs, the works. Don't try to pack anything. We'll just buy what we need."

"I have charcoal, hot dogs, and Kool-Aid. Some Coke. I just need to get buns. Chips, I have chips. Should I make potato salad?"

"I want to buy things. No effort, no trouble."

■ ■

THE NEW APARTMENT WAS SMALL—PRACTICALLY AN EFFI-ciency—but full of light, so that it seemed more spacious than it really was. There was just a nook big enough to hold a dresser and a bed and a chair, a living room with a dining area, and a Pullman kitchen. But everything was new and bright. It was her first day there, and it felt right.

She had brewed a pot of coffee. On a plate she had a pecan roll and a croissant that Commander Christie had brought by from the bakery last night after he moved her in. Soft baked-goods tended to go down better than heavy or raw things, she'd told him, and he'd come by with this. She'd seen a lot of rice and milk shakes, soups and cereals so far in the last week.

"Anything new?" she'd asked.

"Nothing yet."

"I can't stop thinking about it."

"I understand."

She tried to read, but her mind kept blazing. A sentence presented itself to her three times, four, and made no sense. She looked up, and all around her everything was unfamiliar. She read the sentence again, black ink symbols marching past her. Flashes of the day she tried to rescue Justin Graves edged out the sentence. The feel of the baby in her arms, the sweet-sour smell of him, his hic-coughy cry, the way she'd caught his eye from the begin-ning, or he hers. The longing to take care of him, even now. And she remembered, too, the brutal way she was thrown around the room by Vol, then tied in the chair. The layout of the room. These things kept coming to her. She would slow her breathing and concentrate, in the hopes of remembering something new.

And just as she would look up and take in her unfamiliar surroundings, take in the astounding fact that, after all, she and Michael were living apart, separating, finally, she would try again to remember something that would help the Graveses, and she would come inevitably to Detective Christie.

"You have to take care of yourself now," he'd said. "I'll tell you as soon as I know something."

" 'Commander' or 'Detective,' " she asked, "what should I call you?"

"Richard," he said.

She conjured his face, imagined his knock on the door, his whole person, coming into her place, sitting down, confiding in her about the case. In her fantasy, he said, I can't do this without you. You hold the key, you will figure it out. When she imagined she could help, she felt special, special.

It was a joke. She had never thought of a policeman as anything but dull: the defensive young traffic cop who had pulled her over for going too fast in a school zone, the burly embarrassed officer she'd summoned to the house when she was a child worried about her mother.

Attractive? No, not in any conventional sense. He caught her fancy in that tricky way extraordinary people had of taking you by surprise. His ordinariness was so blatant, the book of him so open, she felt cleansed in his presence, as if she'd gone to church. He had the same quality great actors had, of being utterly seeable, letting you in. Or seeming to.

On the third of July, she'd watched the evening ball game from her new place—only hours after Christie had found the apartment and moved her in there and gone to get her baked goods and then run off to take his kids to the ballpark. He told her to make out a supermarket list and he would send a policewoman to get the things. When the camera panned the stands, she tried to see him in the crowd.

The Pirates lost their game, 8–2. Ryan Graves looked like any other pitcher, intense, a small player in a big world, Orestes, all of them.

Now, on this morning of the Fourth of July, only a week after the kidnapping, there was nothing at all about the event on the news. There she was, wounds to prove it had happened, three men had split and gone off somewhere and they couldn't be found, a child's whereabouts were unknown. She put down her book and skimmed the channels, searching, searching, and seeing nothing.

■   ■

THE SUN SHONE BRIGHTLY OUTSIDE HIS WINDOW AND HE DEcided to go out in it after all. He slipped on the swimming trunks and decided not to bother with pants or shirt. Nobody else did.

He was upset, had awakened upset, early in the morning, and been afraid to go five doors down to the little office lobby for free coffee or to go to a restaurant for breakfast. He knew he'd have to do these things sometime, but he was afraid. He'd had bad dreams and realized now that it was not only Anton he had to stay away from but Emelia, too.

Emelia would be angry with him. He could never call her again, never do jobs for her. He had done something stupid, he saw that now, now that he had time and was calmer. She had frightened him that day in the car, made him feel he had to do something quickly or all of them, wherever they were, would be caught, killed. Now he didn't remember what she said that so frightened him. He supposed he loved her in a way, maybe because she always touched him when she spoke to him, and now he was sorry he'd never be able to talk to her again. Now he had nobody at all.

He could never go back to the place in Pittsburgh that

she had let him live in. He had fixed it up, made it almost presentable, and now . . .

It was the Fourth of July, and "that means everybody goes outdoors," said the woman on TV. He would go swimming in his new swimming trunks. He took a key and some money and put them in a paper bag. He grabbed a towel from the motel bathroom. He rolled up the tiny threadbare white thing, partly damp still, and carried it under his arm. He closed the door to his room quietly behind him and trotted off toward the beach.

His eye automatically went to people's back pockets, women's purses put down on counters or benches, strollers with babies in them. Most parents held on tight to strollers, he noticed. How easy it had been, how easy. Because Emelia told him to . . .

He estimated he could live for a couple of months on the five thousand, because he spent next to nothing, but then after that, he'd need to find another source of income. No Anton. No Emelia.

Purses, he decided. Purses and wallets. That was it from now on. Like the old days.

He turned a corner, away from small shops and toward the water. He expected to see the army of policemen come to take him, but there were only people in shorts walking in the same direction he was walking.

At the beach, he chose a place about twelve yards from the water. He put down his towel and his paper bag and he sat. There were babies and small children all around him. Some reached up to take their parents' hands, some did not. Some didn't look like their parents at all. Which were adopted? He couldn't tell. The parents came in all shapes and sizes and moods. Fathers looked away from their kids more often than mothers did. He liked to observe things like this.

Did it really matter where a small baby ended up? Emelia had asked him. Babies don't know. Give them a good life and they're happy human beings.

Joe had not known either father or mother, all his life. They had handed him over to his mother's half-sister, a single, slightly retarded woman who never complained about anyone or anything. Joe understood things nobody thought he did. He knew his comfort at Buddy Kinder's garage came from something in Buddy that reminded him not only of Vol but also of his aunt, who had told him bluntly, from the earliest age, how things stood: His parents didn't want *him* and nobody had ever wanted *her*. Neither one of them was too pretty to look at and that didn't make it any easier to get along in the world. She'd try to put food in his mouth and maybe he'd one day do the same for her.

They lived on welfare some of the time. When that ran out, she took in washing and ironing. By the time he was six, Joe was making the decisions for both of them. By the time he was eight, he was taking what they needed from markets, school supply closets, neighbors. He was a provider, a miniature quartermaster, and good at it.

When he was fourteen, she lay down one day and didn't get up again. A heart attack, he was told. They put him in a foster home, but he ran away and eventually, after they'd stopped looking, made his way back to his aunt's house, where he managed to live, by theft mainly, for two more years. Then he worked for twelve years as the janitor in a machine shop. He took what he could from supply closets. He didn't do much to keep up the house. It was a tiny thing, only three rooms, and dreary ones at that. One day he sold the place for three thousand dollars and went away.

Joe sat on the tiny towel that had come with the room at the Moon-Lite. He looked at the lake. He had always found a way to survive, he told himself. He would need to be strong again.

■   ■

MARINA DISCOVERED THAT THE PHONE IN THE KITCHEN reached to one of the dining chairs. Lizzie was saying, "He wants to see you. He wants your address, your new phone number."

"He shouldn't have bothered you."

"Of course, I won't give it unless you *say* I can."

"Don't. Not yet, anyway."

"You aren't just being stubborn?"

"No. I'm following my gut."

"Okay, whatever he did that night, whoever she is—"

A loud burst of noise told Marina that Liz's children had come into the kitchen. "I'm sorry," Liz said. For what seemed like a long time, she was caught up in giving them rules for the day. Play only in the yard. No television until she showed a movie later. A normal life, so normal it seemed unreal. She pictured Liz, the new haircut, a long pixieish style that she looked fantastic in—but it didn't matter what Liz did, she had timeless, classic good looks. A perfect mathematics of symmetry going on in her face.

When Liz got back to the phone, she said, "It was shitty of him, I could kill him for it."

"It's Kendall, I'm sure it's Kendall—from his office. She always liked him."

"Well, I could brain the both of them."

She couldn't explain to Liz the affair with Kendall was nothing, nothing. Sweet, kind Liz. Her life had been blessed. Everything in it, so far, was fixable.

Then Marina could hear Liz talking to her husband, Doug, although she couldn't hear what they said. Liz got back on the phone and announced, "When he takes the kids to see fireworks, I'm coming over. I'll bring food."

"I have food. Detective Christie had me make out a list and then he sent a policewoman last night to the supermarket. She was on duty until eleven. Some service, huh?"

"Yeah!"

"Anyway, I have ice cream, milk, lots of bread. Everything. I have cereal, rice, vegetables. They showed me how to order things in. They gave me a phone number."

"Well, I'm coming over with beer and hot dogs and some other things tonight. I'll have everything cooked. We can heat it up in the microwave. We'll have our own little party."

Doug got on the phone. "Hey, tiger. How are you?"

"I'm okay." Marina sat down at the dining table again and pictured Doug—blond, innocent-looking, standing in his kitchen, trying to figure out how to cheer her up.

When Liz got back on, she said, "In our house, you're known as Sigourney. And Superwoman."

ON THE TELEVISION, A MAN LINED UP HOT DOGS AND HAM-burgers on a grill, in an artistic arrangement, a dots-and-dashes flag of a design. Marina paced back and forth, wondering how she would fill all the time in her life now. She almost missed having the police around. She almost decided to let Michael come visit.

She leaned out the front window, thinking, Does this count? Am I breaking a rule? The street was quiet. Every-body had *gone* somewhere. Pull it together, she told her-self. She thought how that phrase made literal sense. *Pull it together*. Active. Things *come together*. Passive.

In the early afternoon, it drizzled. Later, it rained hard, and around suppertime, it stopped.

Liz arrived with her care package—food, red plastic plates, napkins that looked like a flag. "Wow," she said. "I like this place. I could stand this for a while."

"Tell me your whole day."

"You're kidding."

Marina shook her head.

Liz winced and told about Hula Hoops, crayons, flags, chases in the wet grass, slipping and sliding. "It couldn't be more ordinary."

"It sounds nice."

"You're the interesting one. Doug is gaga over you. Says those guys tried to kill you and you're still gor-geous."

"I have a bald spot."

"Eh. What's a bald spot?"

Liz heated up the food and finally presented Marina with potato salad, hot dogs, and baked beans. "It's all go-ing to be okay. One thing I know is, Michael still loves you."

Marina looked across the table at beautiful, sane Liz,

who had never done anything stranger, to Marina's knowledge, than get in the car and drive around for an hour late at night when she and Doug had had an argument. That's when she told Liz she found herself thinking a lot about the detective, Richard Christie. She'd wanted to say it aloud so she could break the spell of the secret. In her experience, it worked, for all kinds of things. How many times she'd had to say, "I know I'm not pregnant, but I keep thinking I am," so she would not think it anymore, torturing herself.

Lizzie looked very worried. "He's been making moves on you?"

"No, not at all."

"Oh, sweetie. He's just been nice to you, that's what it is."

She'd had to say it, embarrass herself, to make it evaporate.

■   ■

IT WAS TUESDAY MORNING, JUST AFTER THE FOURTH OF JULY weekend. Michael closed the door to his cubicle of an office. He knew the thump of the door could be heard over the phone line. He picked up the receiver.

"A couple of things," Christie said. "If I can get her to agree to accept phone contact—?"

"Look, I'm not some criminal. I'm her husband. I don't even have an address. At least if I could hear her voice every day . . ."

"I want you to be careful where you call from. If she ever agrees to let you visit her, and if you go to visit her straight from work, do a long, hard check in your rearview mirror."

"Right, right. I *do* anyway."

"Fine. But the other thing I wanted to talk to you about—apparently you checked out of the Sheraton last night. You're not back at the house, are you?"

"No. No, I'm not."

"Where you go is not my business. Having a contact

phone number for you is. You want to give that to me?"
Michael gave him Kendall's number, saying only that he
was staying with a friend from work. He hated having to
report to the detective, as if the guy were his boss, his father, a priest. And some things were almost impossible to
explain. The way he and Marina were working things out
even over the distance and silence. How could he explain
that?

When Michael put the phone down, he was sweating. It
had been much harder than he'd guessed to stay at the
Sheraton alone, and easier than he'd guessed to stay with
Kendall. Alone, he had felt anxiety so great, he had trouble driving, sleeping, eating. He thought to see a doctor,
get something to calm him, but sitting in the hotel room
with Marina gone was part of the problem.

Kendall was practical. And fast! The way she could
make decisions! On the Fourth of July, she had called him
and said, "What was the matter with you yesterday? You
okay?" "We've split. She's not here," he admitted. Kendall
said, "I'm coming over to visit." She took a look at him
sitting in the hotel room. "This is not healthy. Let's get
out of here." She drove him to her place, made up a bed
on the couch, tugging and slapping the sheets. Rented
Airplane. Man, to think they laughed the way they did!
They drank margaritas, which she'd made late into the
night on Saturday until all the fireworks sounds were
gone, and the buzz, the salt, the sour was all sensation,
and falling into her bed, the real bed, was just one more
sensation. They'd had a more modest amount of beer on
Sunday night, but they'd ended up in bed again, keeping
up some kind of contract. He wondered if he was being
bought or sold or blackmailed into leaving Marina for
good.

When she went off to make dinner last night, Kendall
handed him a photo album with pictures of herself as a
child and as a high schooler, and other photos of the
house she grew up in and vacations she'd taken with
friends. He wasn't sure why he was supposed to look at
these, but after he had, he was jolted by how well he felt he

knew her. "This is happening too fast between us," he said. "I can't catch my breath."

"What, then? Back to the hotel?"

"No. Just thinking time. Don't you think we need it?"

"The *last* thing we need. We need to have some fun. Find out if it's fun together. If you tell me you're still in love with her or that you're sure you're going back to her, I'll cry, but I won't butt in. You can sleep on the couch after all. I'll go out with friends. What are you trying to tell me?"

"I'm not sure."

"Well, hey, we might as well have a pitcher of margaritas and watch these three dumb movies I rented. We'll be in hiding together and we'll make it fun."

After supper, she drove him to the Sheraton, where he checked out and packed up his things.

"How did you get so sure of yourself?" he asked her.

"I don't believe in suffering. I can't stand suffering, so I don't suffer."

That's what she'd said last night. He knew it wasn't true.

The call from Christie did not come until the next morning, Wednesday. "Use the old number. It'll forward after two rings. So you don't need the new one." For several minutes, Michael stared at the piece of paper he'd had ready for the number. Then he put it aside and tried to prepare the brief in front of him, but he wasn't thinking. He couldn't think.

He took a deep breath and dialed her.

Her voice. Her voice went right through him. Butterflies filled him just hearing it.

"Are you okay?" she asked him.

"Me? Yeah. You, that's the question."

"It's hard to be locked up."

"I'll bring you dinner and a movie."

"No. No. That's not what I meant. No, don't." Before he could argue with her, she began to explain the voice mail and call forwarding systems that would channel their calls from the old phone. His calls could be retrieved by punching the number two, hers the number one, except she'd never have to use it because she was never out. "They seem to have thought of everything."

"Let me come by. Tell me where you are." He felt like an eager lover in a play.

"I agreed to the phone calls because Christie said you were in a lot of distress, but that's it. No visits. Not yet."

When he hung up, he threw the pen he was holding across the room. It clattered against the wall and then fell to the rug. A small sound. Why was his throwing things so hard on Marina? It wasn't the worst thing he could do. And she wasn't *that* delicate. Princess ideas, she had. He dialed Kendall. She made murmuring sounds—humming, "Yes," and "I understand," in a way that was supposed to keep the other women in the front office from figuring out whom she was talking to. Michael was pretty sure the women would figure it out anyway. Had figured it out, no doubt. He actually laughed at the funny sounds Kendall was making. His life was completely out of control. And all because they'd joined the baby chase. The world was crazy and he wasn't sure why anybody would want to bring another person into it.

SO ANNE PINKUS HAD RENTED TO EMILY RODERICK FOR SHORT hauls a couple of times in three years. Roderick made the arrangements by phone and paid her rent with a money order.

Christie had asked Special Agents to search Pinkus' bank account to get a signature and a place of purchase for the money order. Even a vague address was a beginning. He could let the Feds circulate the sketches of the men around, and near the place of purchase. The FBI had that kind of reach and manpower; give them a neighborhood to focus on, some little village in Iowa or all of Los Angeles, they could cover it pretty well. Christie accepted the FBI like he accepted death and taxes. You might fantasize about circumventing both, but mostly it was easier to go with the flow. Of course, in a high-profile case like this, they'd look for their chances with the evidence before dumping it on him. Even though he considered Horner a friend. Even though he was in charge. Even though.

Yet, in his experience, when one thing broke, everything else followed.

On Wednesday, Horner came to Christie's office and lowered himself into a chair. He said, "The money order came from one of those check-cashing places in New York City. Talk about anonymous." They were scanning all FBI files for an Emily Roderick, he assured Christie.

The men in the North Side apartment had referred to someone, a "she." Was this Roderick? Christie looked out the window. Both men were putting all the pieces together, like chess players. Memorizing the board.

Horner said the surveillance camera in front of Marina's house was working fine and that the tapes had been checked regularly.

"Thanks. I can spare a man to watch the tape if you want."

"Not necessary," Horner said. "The truth is, I need to go have a long sleep. Know what I'm thinking about? A nice poker game when this is all over, if it ever is. Taking your Popsicle money."

Christie looked at the coffee stain on Horner's nice white shirt and picked up the sense of bravura in his matter-of-fact reporting, and found it hard not to like Horner in spite of their inevitable competition with each other.

■   ■

AT TWO IN THE MORNING ON THE TUESDAY AFTER THE FOURTH of July, the newly painted, but dusty Apple Red Chevy made its way down Pine Street and briefly slowed down in front of 211, as its driver pretended to be reaching over to the glove compartment for a map. Nobody was out on the street at the moment, this being an advantage of the humidity and the lateness of the hour. Joe sweated even though he usually didn't sweat easily. From what he could see, the house might be inhabited, although he doubted it. Lights were on on the first and second floors, but they were not very bright bulbs.

He wanted to drive by a second time, but something told him not to. He drove down the next street, the one parallel to Pine, a couple of times and slowed to look through the side yards toward the house at 211. The first-floor light was still on. No, he did not find the pattern of lights believable.

Next he went back a block and a half to the alley he'd spied on the way to Pine Street and he drove down it, counting houses. There was a detached garage behind 211. Good news. A garage with a wooden door was a good thing for a man with his skills. A wooden door and a padlock, very good. The house at 211 Pine Street had his name on it.

He kept driving, out of the alley, up a street, down a street, until he saw a service station that did car repairs. Several cars sat in the small lot to the side of the garage. He drove in and parked there next to a dusty Tercel.

The night was absolutely quiet. It was amazing that people lived in sections like this that were so quiet. Joe walked back down the hill, hands hanging at his sides. Emelia had taught him to always have a story. She had taught all of them this lesson. He practiced phrases: *grew up here as a kid, thinking of retiring back in the old neighborhood, just passing through. Like night driving, nobody else on the road except a few good old truckers.* Working not to be stealthy, he sauntered up the alley behind Pine and located the garage. There was no way to hide what he did next. He slipped a thin flashlight from his pocket and directed it through the crack between the door and the wall of the garage. Unsatisfied, he looked around him, squeezed between the bushes and the side of the garage, focusing the light at the only window. Good. Better than good. The garage was empty. His heart pounded.

Taking a chance, he felt around along the rocks and bricks and above the molding of the door for a key. He did not find one. He let out a curse. People like Marina

Benedict always hid keys. He stopped and looked around, worried that light would be coming into the sky soon. Heaving a sigh, he looked under the decorative rocks around the neighbor's garage. Nothing. He thought about what to do next. A broken window was not an option in a neighborhood like this. At times in the past, he'd carried a ring of skeleton keys, but he had nothing now.

He stopped and breathed, trying to find his magic—the innocent manner he used to jockey his way in and around situations nobody else would touch. Breathing in the night air, he noticed things. The garden had been recently well tended, but now the flowers were beginning to fight the weeds. Something smelled wonderful, though, like perfume. The ground was wet, but he figured that was from rain. Marina Benedict was the kind of person who would take care of her flowers or make her husband take care of them. No. Nobody was home. Why not look for a garage key inside the house? Or at least something to pick the lock with?

In moments he was in the yard. He found a basement window very easy to jimmy. The first cool breeze of the night lifted the leaves of the tree as he slipped in. He hated to close the window behind him, but he did. He would have to work fast. It was nearly four in the morning.

Still using his flashlight, he searched the basement. He gathered bits of wire, thin nails, in case he needed to jimmy the lock. On the way upstairs, he found a Peg-Board with keys, but none of them looked right for the garage lock. Still, he memorized which went where and took the smallest ones. The door to the basement was locked from the upstairs side. He listened for as long as he could stand to wait. Every once in a while he thought he heard shuffling, but he decided each time it was his imagination. He threw himself against the door several times before it gave, and when it did, finally, he fell against the kitchen cabinet so hard that he bruised his arm badly. Panting, he listened again. Ha! There was nobody there to greet him. He examined the basement door, but there was no sign of his violence with it. He opened the freezer. Empty, almost. He grabbed at a blue freezer block and clapped it on his arm. Then, very quickly, he went to the top floor and searched the whole way down. His right hand held Vol's nine-millimeter gun.

He checked bowls, drawers, looking for keys or sharp implements. Finally, in the dining room, he found a complete set of house keys, and it looked as if a garage key was included, too. He opened a few cabinets, opened the refrigerator, assessing.

Moments later, he let himself out the back door and tiptoed through the yard again. Fumbling, he tried the small key on the garage door, but before he could fit the key in, the lock opened in his hands. The thing had not been locked to begin with. Breathing raggedly, he warned himself he was losing his touch. How had he not seen the open lock?

He moved quickly. Out to the alley, down the alley, up the street, up the hill to his car. Four-twenty. Some people's jobs made them get up at this time. Careful, careful. But he had to be fast.

He drove to a nearby supermarket, knowing he would be all the more visible for the hour of the night. Surveillance cameras on. Clapping on his funny fishing hat, he pulled it low. Into his basket went fruits and vegetables, milk, cereal, bread, eggs, pasta, sauces, a couple of packages of soups. Take the perishables in first, he told himself, leave the other things in the car if necessary. He practiced phrases: *her uncle; bringing her a car; all she's been through, wanted to help her stock up; oh, yes, she'll be staying here again in a day or two. Oh, she's fine, she's strong.*

And if he dangled the keys as he talked . . . Very natural.

Then he'd dump the food and get out. Leave the car or take the car, depending on who questioned him.

He packed everything onto the passenger seat, hurrying, hurrying, worried about light coming into the sky before he could get inside. He doused the lights and started into the alley.

He could not believe his eyes. The man across the alley from Marina's house, some fifty yards away, was washing his car. Washing his car at five in the morning. What kind of a nut was he? Joe backed up and drove off, cursing that his perishables would perish before he could eat them.

■   ■

IN THE DOWNSTAIRS CONFERENCE ROOM, CHRISTIE NODDED to each person there, and they summed up: investigation of adoption lawyers ongoing; APB on the cars that by then may very well have been ditched, particular attention to Ohio adoption practices, best lead so far is the name Emily Roderick. New focus on Pennsylvania, Maryland, Virginia, West Virginia.

Four o'clock. Even though things were nearly stagnant in the Baby Graves case, there were no new murders in the city, so the efforts of the police could still be as intense as those of the FBI.

I'll never bury this case, Christie thought. This one's going to be with me forever. Solved or not. He often thought about how he got to Ralph's Discount City twelve minutes after the baby disappeared and that had not been enough to help the woman who had lost her baby.

"Pray for some luck," he said to the task force.

He saw one of the FBI men raise his eyebrows. He thought it meant, We use our wits. We don't pray for luck. We understand the size and frequency of failure, having learned about percentages in our advanced math classes. We have QPAs to back us up and don't need to fuel on emotion. We move on.

"Thank you, gentlemen," he said, standing. "Tomorrow."

He went back to his office, greeting people along the way. "Hello, Commander," each one said. The ones from other divisions asked, "How's it going?"

"Bits," he said. "Still bits. Not a lot." Their faces showed they wanted to talk, but he was talked out.

"How did you choose to do this?" Marina had asked a

week ago, when he'd showed her the office on the way to apartment hunting.

"One thing followed another," he said. He remembered that moment now as he stood among the desks where she'd asked him that question. He hadn't had time to explain about his friend Will, nor about how, on a case years later, a priest had told him the story of St. Basil, who was tricked by his best friend into becoming a saint. According to the priest, the friend copped out at the last minute and left Basil to go it alone for sainthood. Christie was amused by this story.

Marina had not looked satisfied with his one-line explanation. But there were certain intricacies in answering "How did you choose to do this?"

He stood now in front of Coleson's desk, halted by McGranahan, who wanted to show him a new "wanted" photo. "I don't think there's any likeness," McGranahan said. "Do you?" Christie shook his head, went into his own office, and closed the door.

He was flattered by her. That was part of it. Cripes, everybody needed to be flattered, he knew that. She'd honed in on the part of the bulletin board that was *his* section without knowing it was his. Or she knew instinctively. A child's drawing with a picture of a house in the background and a family holding hands in the foreground—an "all is well" crayon drawing. His son, Eric, had done it.

He leafed through pieces of paper on his desk until he found the one he wanted. He saw through the window of his office the bulletin board she'd pored over. *No greater honor will ever be bestowed on an officer or a more profound duty imposed on him than when he is entrusted with the investigation of the death of a human being.*

"I memorized that once," he told her. "Like a good schoolboy."

. . . *regardless of color or creed, without prejudice, and to let no power on earth deter* . . . What a goofball he was. He still knew it.

She'd smiled.

"By Anonymous," he'd said, to cover his embarrassment.

She told him she liked the Ramsey Clark quote best, especially the part that went "We cannot let the 'corpus delecti' diminish our capacity for joy. We should not faint at death. Death is truth and while all truth may not seem beauty..." Ramsey Clark, she said, got downright Shakespearean. Christie had taken the thing off the wall, Xeroxed it, and put a copy on his desk. This one he didn't know as well.

He lifted the phone and dialed.

Words danced in front of him. *A warm humanism...
cannot face death cannot revere life...*

He asked how she was holding up.

"...about out of my mind."

"It must be awful."

"It's inhuman."

"Maybe you were... hasty," he said. "Maybe you should try to work things out with your husband."

What he said hung in the air for a minute.

"You don't understand," she said angrily. "This isn't some vengeance thing. We were *planning* to separate. And why would I want him to come around out of pity for me?"

Her anger caught his breath.

She said, "Pity and boredom. That would really do the trick."

What's the trick, he wondered, what's the trick? He said, "I'd come by if I could, but we have a guy from the prison says he wants to give us a name, tell us something about a kidnapping, he says, from ten years ago. I think it's going to turn out to be a lot of bull, but I've got to be here. I'll try maybe tomorrow to look in on you. Okay by you?"

"Sure. I mean, it's very nice of you. I don't want to be a burden."

"You're not a burden."

He would have to think of ways she could get out of the apartment from time to time. Tomorrow afternoon, he would just talk to her for a while. Take her her mail. Maybe some little candies. Tell her some funny stories. St. Basil, or whatever amused her.

3

HE LIES IN BED, AN UNFAMILIAR HARD MATTRESS BENEATH HIM, some sort of foam pillows that hurt his neck, and he listens to Kendall breathing. No, he does not love her. He could never love her. The bottom dropped out of the earth when he met Marina eight years ago, and this, no, this is nothing like it. He tries to lie still, but he keeps thinking, If I could just roll onto my left side, just get this cover off me, just . . . When he does roll onto his left side, Kendall stirs and puts one arm and one leg around the hillside of him and keeps moving closer, closer, seeking some connection in her sleep.

Kendall's apartment is not very large. Michael usually retires to the bedroom when he calls Marina in the evenings before supper. Or he calls from work. Not that he hides the fact of the calls from Kendall, only that he wants privacy. Now, in the middle of the night, he wishes he could call, but it makes no sense to wake Marina to find out how she is. . . .

He's been thinking. He must tell her slowly, over time, over the phone, and then in person, how he is changing. That Saturday morning, months ago, when he threw things toward her, not *at* her—just audio- and videotapes, but a few of them ruined, and Marina seeing all over again her father, her father's temper—that was bad. How clearly he sees himself now, from outside, from her point of view, as if he stepped over to stand beside her and look dispassionately. His inability to apologize, the way he's been stuck in *resistance,* and then his indirect way of solving things—that first loopy drunken evening with Kendall that led to everything else. Marina always hated indirection. He wants to admit to this terrible anger of his. He wants to be rid of it once and for all.

He carefully slips out of bed and makes his way to Kendall's living room with its surprisingly expensive furniture. She has trendy good taste, but how does she afford these things? Thick wide wale corduroy for the couch upholstery. Large chenille-covered reading chair. Everything in muted sage greens and brick colors. "I like a place a man can be comfortable in," Kendall said in that cigar-smoking voice she has, a comically sexy voice. "Even I get freaked out with little doo-da-*das* around and delicate furniture that looks like it's going to break if a guy sits on it."

"You've been dating football players." He laughed. He thought it was a joke.

But she said, "Well, yes, some." It turned out she had for a while been seeing one of the Steeler linebackers, who got traded to New England. "A sweet guy," she said wistfully. "Awfully upbeat, though."

If he leaves here, he can live at home. . . . What can the police do?

No, not even in the old days was he any good at breakups. Tonight Kendall was trying to be brave, coming up with funny little phrases. He will still have to see her at work—it's going to be messy, messy. And yet it must be done, before she gets any more attached, even if he has to go to another law firm.

When he slides the bedroom door shut, it makes a noise scraping over the thick carpeting. He slows it down and stops just before the click of the lock. He puts the television on so low, he has to lip-read, but it's sort of fun, keeps him concentrating. He flips around from one channel to another and then settles on *Spellbound.* Marina always liked Ingrid Bergman. And no wonder. She, too, looks like she holds a boatload of sorrows, a romantic—the most dangerous kind of woman there is, his father said once. Yep, shake you to the core. Make you question your very existence. Shame you and blame you. Must be a song like that, and if there isn't, there should be. Yes, why was it men fell for that aloof sense of *right* in some women, beautiful women especially? Was that the way the world kept going? God planted dread goodness in a few people to whom he also gave physical beauty and that took care of some of the policing of inner lives. Externalized conscience.

He hears a step and then the sound of the door scraping over the rug.

"Bad night?"

"I'm wide awake."

"You can't call her tonight. Call her tomorrow morning."

"You shouldn't have to put up with me," he says. He looks away from her, thinking how disappointed she would be to know his longings, his thoughts. Not even just for Marina, but sometimes for his street, lawn, home, living room, images that sometimes come to him faster than a camera could make the journey, faster almost than thought. A longing to turn things back, for the past. "I need to go home."

"I know. Here, have a bourbon or a brandy." She is already at the cabinet, already pulling out bottles. "Give it three days or so. If you still feel that way—"

"I don't want anything."

"Sure?"

He says, "You hit that stuff too hard. You probably should try to quit it." He watches her put the bottles back, a wary look on her face.

"What?" she asks finally.

"AA. Have you ever gone?"

"Once."

He feels a great relief that she has admitted it.

"I can't stand the wimpy types who go to those things. You never heard so much whining in one night. I think they're victims, people who are afraid to live!"

"Give me a break. There has to be more than one type."

"I don't think so."

She goes to the kitchen and he hears the water run for a long time. When she comes back into the room, she is finishing a glass of water. "Maybe you need your own apartment. So you don't feel trapped. This has been too much of a jolt."

He nods gently. "But what I really need is familiar *things* around me. I'm no good at work the last couple of weeks. I'm all out of whack."

Kendall struggles for a reply. She goes to the cabinet and pours a splash of whiskey into the large tumbler, more thoughtfully than defiantly. She sighs, takes a drink, then says, "Call her as soon as the light comes up. Make sure she's all right. When you get the willies, you have to act on it. And move back home if you want to. I'll support you no matter what you decide. What the police tell you about 'you can't go back' is half to protect them. So they're not responsible. Whatever. I'm . . . sorry this isn't working. How could it? You were angry. You only came on to me because you were angry. What did I expect?"

His eyes follow the tufty rug to her toes. Her toes lift with tension. He isn't sure what to say.

■   ■

WHEN KAREN ARRIVED THE FIRST TIME AT THE EMERSON STREET apartment, she stood rooted to the spot just inside the door. The shirt and pants she wore looked too big for her. She'd lost five or eight pounds already. Her skin had lost its healthy flush. Fumbling with her purse, she thanked Marina for inviting her over. Marina led her to the sofa, sat her down, and took the space right next to her so that she could catch her when she crumpled.

"When you saw him," Karen asked, "tell me again. He was still all right?"

Like a litany, the few facts rose up again and again between them, comforting in their repetition, measures of how many minutes had gone by in which Justin did not cry, descriptions of his hungry cry, the strange fact of his being able to sleep, the way he looked around.

"He was used to me, my voice—"

"Of course he was."

"He didn't cry in the store when . . . I don't understand. He must have been terrified."

Something about Joe. On his own, with the baby, he had been very matter-of-fact, almost gentle. Marina kept this observation to herself.

"But he was all right when they left with him?"

"Yes." Alive.

Karen breathed in the possibility of hope.

"We're going to have something to eat while we talk. I made us some lunch." Marina went to the kitchen to cut the bread. It felt good to be doing something. Just a pasta salad with sun-dried tomatoes, but a feat of spirit to make it, for it was all too easy to eat poorly. She put large chunks of bread into a basket. She could remember times in her youth, in love with one wrong person or another, when she had forgotten to eat, forgotten how to take care of herself.

"This is good of you to . . . all this." Karen's voice rose up from the next room.

"It's nothing." The truth was, she had needed the company, the activity. Her life now was a matter of waiting for visits. Lizzie came by every four days or so, bringing treats. She was evidently attracted to red—scarlet dahlias, bing cherries, strawberries. When she brought raspberries yesterday, she asked about Richard Christie. Marina said, "It's okay. He's just very nice. Thoughtful. One of the kindest people I've ever met. It went to my head." Lizzie seemed relieved.

In preparation for today's visit, Marina had put out place mats, not hers, of course, but those owned by the anthropologist leaseholder—flowered things, cheerful elongated octagons of double-sewn cloth—and luncheon plates with a border of fruits and vines.

She thought it was important to keep Karen talking. She made her review what they both already knew: FBI files, computers . . . airport checks. "How can I . . . make *sure* they don't slow down?" Karen whispered. "He could be anywhere, in any town or city. . . ."

Marina emerged from the dining nook for a second so Karen could see she was listening.

"I mean . . . how can they possibly *look* for him?"

"They must have things we don't even think of," Marina said weakly. Inside, she thought sorrowfully, one baby among millions, hidden away. How many years had she noticed and not noticed the milk cartons, the ubiquitous mailings. . . . She slipped back to the kitchen to fetch the bread and the bowl of pasta. She had been wrong to think she could comfort this woman. When she thought about the usual busyness of life—the crowd at a ball game, the number of people in university classrooms, the number of cars going down the street where her apartment was—she, too, lost heart. Why, she had known people well and not run into them for ten years although both lived in the same neighborhood and liked the same activities. How could one small baby be identified, found?

She came back into the room and placed the serving bowl and the bread basket on the table. "I'm just going to pour us some water and then we're ready."

Karen nodded absently. Food, water, it meant nothing to her.

Marina stood as close to the doorway of the kitchen as possible so that Karen could see her while she poured the tall glasses of water. She forced herself to imagine armies of people combing the supermarkets, the day-care centers, the baby departments in stores *everywhere*, searching.

Another image overtook it: Joe, Vol, and the other one swimming through crowds, overturning mathematical probabilities, to find her.

Disappearing *was* possible. Being hunted, found, possible, too. So they said.

"They keep sending me the trauma counselor," Karen confided, as Marina carried the glasses of water to the table. "I know they want me to prepare for the worst. I'll never be able to believe it."

Marina thought of Cherry Mahan's mother on the news every year saying she was still waiting. Her child gone for ten years, fifteen, but hope not totally gone. How could a mother kill hope?

"Come to the table. Try to eat something," Marina said, feeling stupid. Wasn't there something better to say?

Karen followed her and sat down.

"Are you having trouble eating?"

"It's like there's a spot right here"—Karen pointed to her breastbone—"that closes off and won't let the food down."

"Take a deep breath," Marina said. "Try to think of clearing that spot. Yes, right there. Just like that." Gratified, she watched Karen try to breathe. "You have to keep up your strength. You have to."

Karen ate slowly.

"There you go."

They ate for a while in silence.

Karen said, "They brought back his stroller. It had fingerprint powder all over it. Why would they bring it back that way?"

Marina's heart swelled. "They don't consider things like that."

"Can you think of anything we can do?"

"I think and think all the time. I'd do something if I could, I promise you."

"I'm sorry. I didn't mean— It's not your problem anymore."

"That's not how it works. I'm involved." Marina added another spoonful to Karen's plate and her own. *Eat. Live.*

"You're such a strong person," Karen said.

"It's not that. I'm just unused to sitting tight." And well, yes, she had an ego of a certain size and difficulty and thought she could *solve* things, make them better. It came with the baggage—that narcissistic stain or blot or whatever they called it.

Marina felt Karen looking at her.

"Are you, do you think you're healing all right?" Karen asked. "You don't get faint or anything from the—" She pointed to her own head and it was a perfect comic gesture, a gesture an ingenue would do in a play with froth.

Marina laughed and suddenly felt a disorientation she couldn't even begin to describe. "The way you pointed," she tried to explain. She had a hole in her head. Not a big one, not even a serious one anymore, but she was losing her mind all the same and she knew this. The craziness was music swelling underneath a film and about to take it over. "Bandages off tomorrow."

■   ■

A WATCHER. HE HAD BEEN AS A BOY, WITH HIS FATHER GONE, his mother a busy woman without time for feelings, and him, a worried child. It comforted him even back then to know what people did, to watch their routines. One friend pulled up his socks when he took an exam. Another ate his pencil. One of his mother's neighbors took the garbage out every night and stood in the alley for a few moments, sighing. Another shook her kitchen rug out each evening. These things became part of his clock.

He knew Marina checked the newspaper every morning, looking for the small mention; she watched ball games on television at night, listening for the helpless frustration in the voices of Lanny Frattare and Bob Walk.

He knew Marina's husband wanted to move back to the house because he needed to put *something* back to the way it used to be—even if all it meant was the customary drive after work, the feel of the familiar couch, the sound of the living room clock ticking, little things. "You have to hang on," Christie told him. "Maybe something will break soon."

Coleson was overeating lately. McGranahan was fighting with his wife. The young hotshots from the FBI were getting that alienated look in the eye.

Karen. He called her every day before lunch even though he didn't want to tell her there was no news. She sounded a little better after she'd visited Marina, so he encouraged another visit.

He felt a failure. He had had a childhood, imperfect as it was, and he'd been allowed to grow to adulthood.

He thought of his aunt, his mother's sister, a nice woman, who always had a bowl of assorted candy on her coffee table. He met with his task force, at once seeing what was before him and remembering his aunt leaning forward to offer, his mother choosing, him waiting his turn, the paper crackling.

■   ■

ON TUESDAY, KAREN CAME AGAIN TO VISIT. IT WAS CLEAR SHE had been crying. She moved around, looking at the apartment as if for the first time, touching things.

Marina didn't know what to say, so she let her go. She put down the plates that held the tuna salad sandwiches so carelessly, they made a clunking noise.

"Ryan believes . . . I don't know, he keeps asking me how could I walk away from the stroller." Karen took a napkin from the table and wiped her eyes with it. "He says maybe I wanted to lose Justin. How can he say that to me?" Karen looked twenty years older, someone who'd had no luck or love—tight, embittered.

"He doesn't mean it. He's stuck."

"I'm sorry. I don't want to cry."

"I think you should. I believe in it."

Karen cried, awkwardly at first, saying, "I could live with a divorce if I have to. I could live with anything if I could get my baby back."

Divorce, so quickly.

"I could stand anything if . . ."

"I know."

"I miss him so much."

"I know."

"You invited me for lunch. I'm sorry."

"Don't worry about me."

Karen wandered the room again. When she came to the photographs of Marina, she looked puzzled, and then moved on, straightening a pillow, touching the fabric of the sofa.

"I'm supposed to talk about my family. Show you pictures."

"Says who?"

"Commander Christie."

A few moments later, after they were settled at the table, Karen took a brown envelope from her purse and handed it over.

"If you trust me to look at them while I'm eating."

"They're just ordinary prints."

There were about twenty photos in all. Marina studied them: the parents, the father-in-law she'd met over at Karen's apartment, the brothers whom she hadn't met, the brothers' families. How they had all come to Karen, flown in immediately, stayed, first at the team's expense, but then at their own, in a suite at the Hilton. Marina felt pangs of jealousy. Brothers, too, doting brothers. Family love. People who made flights, connections. People who came to embrace you. She'd never had that.

How could she feel jealous of this woman who was suffering the worst loss of all?

She turned over more pictures.

Church elder. Salesman. Heating engineer. She wished she belonged to them. Smiling people who didn't seem to be wrestling with some monster of ambition.

Family reunion, wedding, reunion, family vacation.

Karen's voice calmed down, her face softened. She began to ask questions.

Marina's answers to Karen's questions fell like coins, petty losses. No, she did not want to reconcile with Michael just now, if ever. No, her father was dead, and there were times she felt it *was* her fault, the things she'd said to him; no, her mother hadn't come to see her in the hospital or since, nor had her sister, who lived in Virginia near her mother. But it was better that way, both were too easily upset.

Karen looked at her with concern. "But, just to be with you," she said.

How could she explain to Karen Graves that neither mother nor sister could get on buses or trains or in cars and go from one place to another? That her mother and sister could not move forward to show love, interest, anger. They'd taken abuse and not fought back. They were stuck. They were stuck.

Karen rose and studied the theatre photos of Marina again. "Don't take this wrong, but you don't seem like an actress."

Other people had said so, too. Perhaps it meant she wasn't one, in the large sense, after all.

"What's this from?"

"*Phaedra*. And the other is Portia, in *Julius Caesar*."

"Hard parts, I bet."

"The old, big, angry plays, the terrible people, that's what I do best. I look like comedy, but I'm better at tragedy. I don't know why. I have a huge voice in me for one thing. Clytemnestra, Medea, I can play the hell out of them, you know, raging at the heavens. Only there aren't that many productions of those plays around. At least not in professional circles."

"People like to be happy," Karen said. It made Marina smile. "You'd be good as, like, the Julia Roberts character in love."

"You like romantic comedies?"

"They're my favorite thing. In the movies. Are there plays like that?"

"Some."

"Don't you ever do things like that?"

"Here and there. Well, actually not for a number of years. Once I slid by as a happy shopper in a Shop 'n Save commercial. Once I was a witch who loved nacho chips. Not the same thing as a romantic lead."

"Couldn't you try, though?"

"I'm not good at those roles."

"Maybe with a little practice."

"Maybe." If she'd known how to access the life of an

ingenue, she might have done it a long time ago, then moved on to leading ladies in comedy. When she was seventeen—she remembers this so clearly—she was eating an ice cream cone in the theatre lobby one minute waiting to be called in for an audition, and moments later, on the stage, violent, huge, emotions came rolling out of her. "You have a gift," they told her.

If she had a gift, what good was it? Wouldn't some "act" have been better with Joe and Vol and the other one? A role. A crazy woman, a relative, a journalist, a nurse? Something to throw them off?

"I guess I haven't been to plays. Not since I was a little kid. I should go sometime," Karen was saying.

Pretty soon nobody would go to the theatre anymore and it wouldn't matter. Pretty soon it would all be film and TV, adventures and sitcoms.

Marina lifted a bowl of hard candies from her coffee table and handed it toward her guest. Karen chose one solemnly. "Commander Christie brought them to me last week," she said.

■ ■

THE NEXT DAY CHRISTIE CALLED TO SAY HE WAS BRINGING over a couple of pieces of mail himself.

When he walked in, he asked how she was killing her days and she said something foolish about how often she cleaned.

Like Karen Graves, he stood for some moments awkwardly. He looked stuck. He said, "Maybe I should have found you someplace else. Out of town or something. I was in such a hurry to solve everything. I didn't help, did I?"

"I think I would find this place perfect—for right now—if I could come and go."

He touched a small table with his fingertip. Shy, awkward. He had a funny movement, something like hitching his hip before he moved. Maybe an old injury, she thought, maybe a back problem. Some people carry a trace of an

endured physical pain in the face; he had that. He moved
with an odd rhythm, almost jerky. He handed her the mail
and waited while she shuffled the envelopes. "Anything
good?" he asked.

"Maybe. Looks like get-well cards, bills, a couple of letters."

"Check the letters and cards while I'm here."

"Oh?"

"Probably nothing, but look them over. A couple of
crazies write to everybody. Anybody asks to meet you in
person, of course, you alert us."

"That'd be wild," she said, hardly able to think what
she was saying because he watched her so closely.

"Some little old lady who just wants to talk to you
could be one of your guys."

"I see. You're right." She read through them quickly
and tossed the envelopes onto an end table. Was there to
be anything she didn't have to suspect? Was there to be
any part of her left private? She started toward the
kitchen, looking back at him. "I'm going to get you a
Coke or a beer or something. What do you—?"

"Just water."

She thought he visibly relaxed when she offered him a
drink. She tried to get her voice comfortable and sure. "I
need to ask you a favor," she called from the kitchen. She
had been thinking hard and knew what she had to do to
keep sane. Like Chekhov's women, she had to work. Like
Olya Prozorov and Sonya Alexandrovna, she had to work,
work, work. She stopped moving to listen for his answer.

"Anything."

"Could you get someone to take me to my house for an
hour or so? I want to pick up a couple of things, but
mainly the computer. It's a little heavy. I probably
shouldn't lift it." She wondered if maybe she should try to
get hold of a new laptop. But she was used to her larger
machine.

"How about tomorrow. In fact, if I can do it, I'll take
you over myself."

Tomorrow was better than she had hoped for. "I

appreciate it," she called out. She took a couple of ice cubes from the freezer and plopped them in his glass. Halfway out of the kitchen she got an inspiration, and reached into the refrigerator for a lemon half. She sliced a thin crescent from the lemon, dropped it into the drink, and watched it float downward until it caught like a parachute on the rocks.

Richard was pacing when she returned to the living room. He turned to her expectantly.

"Pretty," he said when she handed him the glass. His eyes clouded. He turned to search the room.

She sat.

He asked, still standing, "Could I bring you some books, maybe?"

"That's a nice offer. If we have enough time, tomorrow, I could get some — I have a lot of books at home I never got to. Like everybody else. They'll hold me for a while."

He nodded and came to sit beside her on the sofa.

Every time she talked to him on the phone, she asked him, "Is anything happening?" And every time, he said, "It's slow. Very slow. But we're moving." And every day, the things his voice did to her, when she was trying to get back to the hard facts of what they discussed—the lack of clues about Justin.

"How could those men completely disappear?" she asked now.

He winced and laughed. "You must think we're a bunch of incompetents. We're puzzled. We're puzzled."

"Karen is out of her mind."

"Of course." He grimaced—"made mows at the moon" was the phrase that came to her. From some play or other. Faces at the moon, as if alone. He would probably hate classical plays, but he acted them, a bit.

A sudden wave of loud music came to them from outside, somebody's car. It receded. "Arrest that man," she said.

He smiled. "You like living in a city?"

"Yeah."

He moved his tie back to center, a nice tie, she thought, navy with small cream-colored diamonds. How did he feel about dressing so formally every day in hot and cold weather?

"What else?"

"Emily Roderick. Is she a real person?"

"Maybe. Slips through a lot of cracks."

"I think about that place. Nothing personal in it, and yet it was more or less clean. Who would use it that way? It was almost *presentable.*"

He shrugged. "A sublet, maybe. Like this. But low end of the scale."

"But somebody neat. Maybe the guy, Joe."

"Possibly."

"How did the owner get paid?"

"Money order drawn in New York. Turns out after all our effort it wasn't in the name of Emily Roderick, the tenant, but somebody name of Tony Anderson paying for her. So far we're coming up empty on the Mr. Andersons we've questioned. Also on the Emily Rodericks. New York, you get at least twenty of everybody, no matter how weird the name."

Marina studied the gray coming into his hair, evenly threaded. Pale eyelashes. A worrier's face. She thought, A delicate boy, probably, in the early years. Dreamy and worried about school. She pressed, "I asked the FBI how the traces were run. They wouldn't answer me."

"They don't." He shrugged. "I didn't take the silence vow. We have computer programs for just about everything. Real estate ownership. Maps. Addresses. Zip codes. Not rental agreements, though." He chuckled. "Not informal sublets. That would be some large data bank." He put his glass down carefully on a magazine that was sitting on the coffee table. "You don't have any bourbon, do you?"

"No. Sorry. Maybe back at the house. I'll look tomorrow."

"You drink bourbon?"

"Not usually. My husband does sometimes. He might have taken it when he packed. I'm not much of a drinker."

There was a long pause. The phrase "my husband" hung in the air. Pluck it back, she thought. But there was no way to do that.

Christie began to say something, stopped himself, and then went ahead, blushing. "I talk with him every other day on something—what with the switch to voice mail and then the problem of your regular mail. . . . He's having a hard time."

"I know that."

Christie reached over and lifted the glass, but did not drink. "I won't pry."

She mumbled an apology about needing to separate just when she went into the relocation program.

"People separate all the time. Life proceeds." He took a good long drink. She watched the lemon bump against his upper lip and his momentary look of confusion at the change of texture. She reminded herself to look for the bourbon. "The fact is, it makes it easier. We don't have to worry about somebody following him from work to get to you."

"This other woman—Kendall, from his office—is she in any danger?"

He looked embarrassed. "We more or less ordered him to arrive and leave with her so it's clear it's *not* you." He shook his head. "Mighty nice of you to ask." There was a long silence. "What did you ask the Feds that they wouldn't answer?"

"How they were pursuing black-market adoption."

"And?"

"After they asked me why I wanted to know, which is a stupid question"—she felt her voice go up, childishly uncontrolled— "they just said something about the usual channels. Boy, are they buttoned up! I said, 'Do you have women pretending to be looking for a baby to see what surfaces?' and they said they couldn't talk about it."

Christie laughed. "Maybe you'll end up on the force after all. We could use a beautiful actress in homicide."

Marina stopped and stood back from the scene. She realized with relief that she would not be tempted by him after all. He was too different from her. He came from a conventional and sexist world. A bourbon drinker. Unused to lemon in his water.

"Former actress," she said.

"Maybe you'll surprise yourself. Land something big."

She tried to tell him in terms he would understand how it was. How good it felt to stop trying. "Timing, luck, the stars, whatever. When you decide to say *good-bye,* it's very, very freeing. I'm done with it. Really."

His eyes told her he thought the conversation was about something else—but it was too late to retrace her steps.

"What are you thinking?"

"Nothing," she lied. "Nothing much. Sometimes I go blank. . . ."

"Why don't I believe that?" His challenging look made her laugh. "It's so nice to see you laugh."

"I used to do it sometimes, believe it or not."

"When?"

"I don't remember. A long time ago."

He stood abruptly.

"It was nice of you to come by," she said.

"My pleasure."

My pleasure. Beautiful actress. And. He had a family.

He was a simple temptable man performing a kind gesture and she had not been cautious enough with him.

She followed him to the door. "Tomorrow, I want to go to the library, too," she warned him. "So send me someone with *a lot* of time. Someone whose time is not as precious as yours."

"We'll see."

"I have to make a life for myself in this prison!"

He laughed. "That sounded like an actress to me."

"It might be a line from something. After a while, you forget where you get these phrases."

He looked fascinated, happy. She thought of him,

amused like that, lightened by her, all night. She read the cards and letters from people she knew and people she didn't know. And all the time, he would pop up in her mind, laughing in that awkward, surprised way.

WHEN HE CALLED AT ELEVEN THE NEXT MORNING, HE TOLD her he could pick her up at one. He had about an hour, his lunch hour, a little more if she needed it. She should have something to eat before so they could spend all their available time getting the things she needed. The library, hadn't she said, too? What library did she need to go to?

Carnegie in Oakland, she told him. She was frustrated that she would have to rush. She'd have all of fifteen minutes to spend there.

Dark glasses and a hat, he'd said, wouldn't hurt, clichés though they were. Sometimes tried and true was the best way, he'd said.

"Blond wig, maybe," she joked.

Then he said seriously, "If you have one, that would be excellent."

"I have one at the house. It's a terrible wig. It cost about ten bucks and was meant to be seen from an auditorium, hundreds of feet away."

"Okay, but you might actually want it sometime. Get it today. I'll give you an opinion."

Since her hair was her most noticeable feature, she rolled it into a twist and hid it under a scarf. She didn't have a hat with her. Michael had packed her nightgowns, T-shirts, dresses, shorts, shoes. No hats. No wigs.

She was pale from sitting indoors. She put on a pair of calf-length pants and a light, loose cotton blouse because the side wound was still easily irritated. When she added sunglasses, she looked, even without the suntan, as if she were advertising tropical drinks on a Caribbean beach.

She felt her breathing shorten and a familiar flutter from her heart on down. Stage fright. The feeling of being utterly, completely spotlighted and seeable, even in disguise. Danger, she was in danger. From Joe or Vol or the third man combing the streets for her. From Richard looking at her, watching her every thought. She felt naked. From the bedroom closet she got the one large suitcase Michael had packed for her. She might as well take it and pack it once more. She chastised herself a million times for her nervousness. Still, she shook when the doorbell rang.

When she opened the door to Christie, he was taking a squawking radio from his belt. Moments later he was speaking into it. His sport coat opened and she saw that he wore a gun. This was work. *She* was work. He was on a job. Good. Her breathing slowed a little.

His eyes met hers and quickly looked away.

"You look different," he said when he'd finished the call.

"I was trying to hide my hair."

He nodded. "You're very hard to disguise in general. Hair can be cut, but eyes, bones. Let's go. If you're ready?" He lifted the suitcase and led the way outside.

Already the car felt familiar. This time the front seat was clear of debris, but she had to rest her left foot on two flashing-lights systems.

"This is going to be strange, seeing the house again and having to leave."

"Ohio River Boulevard?" he asked.

"Yeah. Don't go any faster than you have to. I'm in love with everything. Cracked sidewalks. Everything."

"Cracked people."

"Everything." Her eyes ate up everything on the road. Buildings, people, traffic lights, flowers in yards.

"You want me to go through downtown and drive the bus route? Where you got on and off?"

"Do you have time?"

He looked over at her and added, "We could even drive by the apartment. We like to debrief people when we can. We never had a chance to do that with you."

He took Bigelow Boulevard to downtown, moving expertly through the city lanes. The city had never looked more beautiful to her, the old architecture, gargoyles and cupolas, steady old square buildings poised against the rusty elegant U.S. Steel building, and the glass cathedral that housed Pittsburgh Plate Glass. The bridges everywhere she looked. Ramps and highways crisscrossing over each other.

She had never fully looked before. Now she took in everything. It was a breathtaking city, with height and contrast. Carved out by the rivers, three of them.

The 16A bus stop served several other lines. A long queue for one of the buses was forming. It looked much as it had on that day. She remembered how she hadn't wanted to take the bus, how distracted she was by the events of that morning—with Michael, with Dr. Caldwell.

"Okay?"

She gestured that she was.

"Better to talk," he said. "I can stand to hear it all over again."

"Well, let's see. I got on the bus and then I went through a bunch of changes."

"What changes?"

"Surprise, denial, withdrawal, deciding on an action, withdrawal, covert action. Something like that."

He was all business today. "You're very aware," he said. "You have all the words for things. You have to slow down and allow a few other things in."

"What?"

"Come on! You know what. The nightmare part of it. Where are your feelings?"

His words chastised her. There she was, hiding again. She tried to let in the feelings. What was I doing? she asked herself. *Saving the child.* And when she thought those words, tears came to her eyes. Because it was about her and what she didn't have, as well as anything else. What a mess she was. Eventually she pointed out the spot where she got off the bus and ran after the man. Joe. "Hard to believe I did that," she muttered.

Christie made his way around a couple of blocks and stopped the car in front of the house she'd run to. She saw how tattered the neighborhood was. The house was the nicest one on the row. The brown paint on the win-

dowsills was chipped but intact. There were several old
metal garbage cans at the side.

"I didn't see much of this before. I just ran in. Dumb,
foolish."

"You did well." He reached over and patted her left
hand. She wasn't sure if he meant in her recitation just
now (had she done it with more feeling?) or in her en-
deavor to figure out what was going on in that building
on the day she entered it.

"Ready?" he asked.

She said yes, and they started out again.

The bleak road gave way to a commercial strip with
Wendy's, Long John Silver's, KFC, everything fast in food.
Trucks and vans zoomed in and out of these places, making them slow down repeatedly. When she saw a big white
sign that said simply SUBS, she said, "They might have gotten takeout there. What they got didn't have any logo on
the bag or the wrapper. It didn't say 'Subway' or anything
like that."

"Hmmm. We've probably been there, but if we haven't,
I'll send someone with the sketches. Don't get your hopes
up. People sometimes recall what you want them to recall,
but they don't usually have anything new to add. The
woman in the Rite Aid, remember?"

"I want to find Justin."

"I know you do."

"Karen Graves came by a couple of times. She's going
to visit me again tomorrow."

"Good. Don't worry. We're making sure she's not followed."

Marina watched him drive. He checked the rearview
mirror constantly. He said, as if deciding to trust her,
"Just between us, the Feds put a camera on Pine Street."

"On the street?"

"On your house."

"Where's the camera?"

"Outside. Up a telephone pole. It looks like telephone
equipment."

"I'm trying to imagine what they expect to see."

"Someone pretending to read gas meters, someone pretending to clip lawns." She watched him hesitate. "Someone just driving by. Looking suspicious. You never know what might turn up. Keep up your hopes."

A camera on her house. All of this still seemed like someone else's life.

"This is how it usually breaks when it breaks. License plates, driving infractions, motel registrations. Something."

"I wouldn't be a very patient investigator."

"You'd have to be. You'd learn to be."

"What if you find the men and they turn out not to know what happened to the baby?"

He let out a breath. "That could happen."

After a while, she untied the scarf and unpinned her hair.

"There, you look like yourself."

"The pins were tight. Starting to hurt."

He looked over at her. "The scarf made you look so thin. Do you have any hats?" he asked. "You'd probably look good in hats."

She felt the tiniest wire of anger that he dared to play costumer with her. The anger made her feel safe. His luggish cop was no more appealing to her than her Caribbean princess in a tight head scarf was to him.

"I probably should cut my hair off," she said. "That's simplest."

"I'm not sure you need to be so drastic. Turn here?" he asked. She nodded. "This is going to be a little bit strange, going into your house but not being allowed to stay. Take a deep breath."

She believed in deep breaths. She tried to ready herself.

"If any neighbors come running, you don't tell them anything, not even the section of town where you're staying."

"Okay, where's the camera?"

"What's that movie?"

"Right." The movie, the musical, the whole tired joke.

When they got out of the car and walked to the front door of her house, she played to the camera—for his sake or her private joke (actress, scarf on her head, out of work), it wasn't clear. She faced the telephone poles and tilted her head upward. Christie chuckled. But mostly she felt shaky and wanted to hurry through whatever she had to do. Neighbors did not come running. In fact, nobody seemed to be around. It was the middle of a workday after all. She unlocked the front door. Her chest felt heavy.

Dust motes swam in the hazy light. The phone, the sofa, everything seemed just slightly off. The place looked like home, and yet not. Michael must have knocked a few things around on his last night here.

"Nice house. I like the way you've done it."

She thanked him.

He went to a library table and lifted a photo in a frame. "My God, is this you?"

"I'm afraid so."

He picked up another. "And this?"

"Afraid so." She felt embarrassed that Michael had put so many pictures of her around the house.

Christie studied photos of her as a child, as the Duchess in *The White Devil*, as a teenager on a sailboat. He might have been on a case.

Marina watched him impatiently. She was in more of a hurry to get in and out than he was, because if she stayed for five minutes, she would want to stay for an hour. She would begin watering the fig tree, dusting cobwebs. The fig didn't look as bad as she thought it was going to. She touched the soil. Dry but with a hint of moisture a quarter of an inch down. "I'll just water this. Two seconds." At the same time, she wasn't sure what to do with it next. Could Michael take it and care for it? It was too large for the anthropologist's apartment. She hurried into the kitchen and took a jug off the shelf, and began filling it with water. "Computer is upstairs in the spare bedroom," she called. "I want the modem, too."

"I'll do all that. Clothes, hats, books, I'll leave to you. You pack the suitcase, I'll carry. You have other suitcases somewhere?"

"Oh, I think Michael probably used them all—Never mind."

He was already on his way upstairs. She poured the jugful of water onto the soil and went back into the kitchen, where she found a box of large trash bags in the cabinet. Easier to put her books in them. And clothes, too, for that matter. The main things were the computer and modem.

She selected books from the shelves, dropping them hurriedly into one of the bags. Richard came downstairs with the modem balanced on top of the monitor. "I want to talk about this," he said, tilting his chin toward the modem. "Later. In the car. Computer is unplugged." He started upstairs again, nodding toward a wall where other photographs were hung.

"I think you should take some of those pictures with you," he said.

"I don't have much room, and besides, it is temporary—"

"Make the apartment feel more like home." He was halfway up the steps again, around the corner, when she heard that he got a summons on the police radio. She could hear the static and then the metallic sound of a voice say, "Commander Christie," a couple of times. She waited to find out what was happening.

As the call continued, he came downstairs into view. "Right," he was saying. "Paramedics are there?"

"They're here, but the kid is gone," the voice on the box said.

"Secure the scene. Who do you have?"

"Littlefield, Nellins, Hrznak," came across the crackly radio.

"Excellent. Littlefield is in charge. She should be able to get there in five minutes. I'll be there in"—he looked at his watch—"twenty minutes. At the outside."

Christie turned back to Marina. "You grab the clothes, hats, I'll get the computer to the car. You finished with the books? Can we do this in five minutes? Three?"

"We can try."

"Let's move fast, then."

They rushed upstairs, bumping into each other. "What is it?"

"Homicide. Kid got shot in Homewood. I need to get over there."

He headed for one room, where he lifted the computer box and cables, and then hurried downstairs to take these things to the trunk of his car. She saw him doing all this through the bedroom door and then the window. She hardly looked at what she was grabbing. She just grabbed. By the time he got back, she was dropping the last couple of things into a garbage bag. Jewelry, scarves, the blond wig—a strawlike thing.

"The books are in the bag downstairs," she reminded him. "They're heavy."

He took a bag of clothes and a suitcase from her. She ran back for a purse and into the study for a box of floppy disks.

On the way out of the house, Christie took the photos from the shelving unit in the living room and the others from the mantel, grabbed a throw from the sofa, and wrapped them into a secure package even as he moved out the door. "We can come back if we have to," he was saying. While Marina locked up, he placed the photos on top of the jumble of things in the garbage bag. She saw that even from the porch, he was watching the street, scanning the neighborhood.

"You have to come with me to Homewood," he said. "I'll get you a ride from there. Ten-year-old kid. Got shot walking his little sister."

IF THE CALL HADN'T COME, IF THEY'D SAT OR WANDERED around at leisure, if they'd had time to dawdle or for some reason opened the refrigerator, they'd have seen the evidence of a person living in the house. If they'd had to go to the basement for a suitcase, they might have seen Joe himself, in the flesh. But then, maybe not. During most of their visit he was wedged in a cubbyhole, hardly breathing and, having pulled a pile of tarps over him, very good at being invisible, as he had always been, all his life. As it was, they left, the detective and the past tender of the house, with vague impressions of dampness in the bathroom, less dust than they expected, and they both concluded separately that Michael had been sneaking back.

FROM THE CAR, MARINA WATCHED THE POLICE WORK. A CROWD gathered and tried to get close, but the officers kept pushing them back. Up on a small front lawn, an old woman cried. Another woman, possibly a neighbor, comforted her. Two other people, a uniformed policeman and a younger woman, stooped and talked to a little girl who seemed more puzzled than anything. There was a chalk mark on the sidewalk, photographers moving about. A classic, horrible scene. Television cameras arriving and setting up. All within half an hour.

Christie came over to the car. "I'm sorry you have to wait. I'm getting a ride for you."

"I can wait. As long as you want. It's okay." He didn't understand that being out in the world, even at something so terrible, was better than going back to the apartment. Protection? She was ready to give it all up.

"Now, you can't just go on the Net," he'd warned her in the car, "without talking to me first. We have to make sure you do it safely."

Even that.

And she'd thought, This is too hard. Let Michael go back to the house. Let me take a job somewhere, see people, talk. Let both of us take our chances.

A little later she saw Richard gesture to a uniformed officer, pointing her out in the car, and making gestures that looked like the counting off of orders.

The man came over to her. "I'm Palmer. I'm supposed to put your things in my car, take you to the library, then home. And if you need groceries, you should write out—"

"I know I'm not supposed to get that much service."

"That's what the boss said. I do what he says."

She thanked him. He lifted the surprisingly light suit-

case and carried it to a police patrol car. Then he came
back for the heavier bags of things, and finally the computer and its accessories. She thought she could hear him
swearing under his breath. Still, he shielded her from people and cameras as he moved her the ten feet from
Christie's car to the one that would take her on her errands.

■   ■

ON THE SAME DAY THAT THE TEN-YEAR-OLD BOY WAS SHOT IN
Homewood, Anton sat at a coffee shop in a little town in
northern Ohio. He jotted a postcard to Manny, using
Manny's home address. On it he wrote Elise's new cell-
phone number. The postcard went into a stamped envelope, which he sealed. He pushed aside his cherry Danish,
took a last drink of coffee, and went outside. On the street
corner was a mailbox. He dropped the envelope in, and
looked around. The good thing about small towns was
there was always a place to park. It was good to come to a
town like this every once in a while.

Bad to stay, though. People remembered you. He got
into Elise's Escort with its Michigan plates. Her car felt
good, safe.

He waited now only to hear from Vol. Contact which
ought to be coming soon. He hoped Vol was playing it
very, very safe. On the other hand, what if Vol had rewrit-
ten his orders? What if he'd seen all their pictures on the
news and thought, What the hell, let the jerk live? What
if he and Joe had gone off in two different directions?
That had been a problem in the past, Vol trying to think
for himself. Even with the girl alive, there were ways to
pin the whole thing on Joe, should it come to that: Joe did
this dumb thing, they were trying to protect him, Joe
had this contact somewhere, Joe took the baby with him.
They didn't understand what Joe had done, etc., etc.
Always a little odd. So long as he and Vol swore to it, and
nothing else was found, it would be okay.

Better, though, much much better with the girl gone, too, as he had ordered from the start. If he had to do it himself, so be it.

He started up the Escort, and before he was away from the narrow streets, caught himself creeping up to sixty miles an hour. He forced himself to slow down. It was a thrill for him, going fast on a small-town street. It would give him great pleasure, as a matter of fact, to drive seventy miles an hour right at Marina. Ha! Shame she didn't live here. Wide-eyed surprise, all right! He laughed. Those big eyes of hers. He hated her, everything about her, the way she dressed, the way she talked. Spoiled brat, he thought, really la-di-da, privileged all her life, loving parents, plenty of money. An easy life. An actress, for God's sake, and what good was that in the world, but it made her feel her shit didn't stink. When he thought about her having *no fear* of telling him what he ought to do, it made him crazy.

He let out choked sounds as he drove along. "Hate her," he said. "Hate the fucking bitch." He wished he had it to do all over again. He'd have the others tie her up by her la-di-da hair, then he'd rape her. Or maybe cut her up some, then rape her and let the others have her after. He didn't know why Vol and Joe were so easy on her. Even now, thinking about it, he couldn't figure why they all hadn't slapped her around more and had her a couple of times each. Well, not Joe. They'd probably have had to lift Joe up and put him on her. Joe was damaged goods. But not Vol. Vol was dumb, but otherwise . . .

Next time, next time. She made him sick. Little flowered dress, and her saying, *"Let me help you put this right."*

Suddenly he saw a cruiser in his rearview mirror. He was going seventy-five, maybe more. He slowed down immediately to sixty and prayed. Sweat broke out all over him. He couldn't breathe. Switching on the radio, he thought, *On my way to visit my cousin. My wife's car.* Always have a story. A chorus of women on the radio sang screechingly about a health plan. He switched off the radio. *Only doing sixty. So sorry. Had too much coffee and wanted to get somewhere to take a leak. Not thinking.*

The police car passed him. He didn't breathe for a whole minute. Then he let out a jagged breath.

So the card would go to Manny and he had to trust Manny was in it as far up the ass as he was. He had to believe Manny wouldn't willingly give up a lucrative trade. That they'd keep on working together. Emelia had three women in New York ready to give birth, so Manny would have to get in touch with him. They had kids to sell, and they could all live pretty nicely for about a year on three more sales. People wanted kids. Pah. He didn't get it, not for the life of him. Elise's kid was enough to make him want to ditch her, but Elise kept being so useful. She had a car, a job, a decent credit rating, and no arrests. And she didn't ask too many questions. He could sit in her game room and watch TV for twenty-four hours straight and she would just go about her business so long as he gave her a little money and a little affection.

He thought sometimes of the way Marina rocked that kid that wasn't hers, whispered to it, closed her eyes. He dreamed about her once, shaking her head at him. The way she sat there. They were three men with guns and she rocked this kid and told them where to get off. Until they slapped her around and she finally started kicking and biting. That was more like it.

He pulled over at a Wendy's and studied the map of Pittsburgh once more. He could remember her street, but not the house number. He found the street, not too long a thing, just a street. Pine. Start somewhere. Make friends with a neighbor. Find out where she is. Get in and get her. If she's not there, well, find the husband. Follow him home from work. Get a house, an address. Find Vol and get him to earn his fucking money and blow her out of the water. If Vol can't be found, do it himself. Gun, car, whatever the situation required.

This is what he loved about the courts. The whole thing could be obvious to any child—a witness, a corpse, and a pile of logic—but leave no fingerprints, and they can't get you, no matter what. Dress nicely, wear your moxie on your sleeve, deny everything.

He folded up the map and started out again. He thought about Vol objectively. Vol was a sloppy sort of a guy, maybe more trouble than he was worth. Maybe he shouldn't give Vol the job, after all, but should just plan on doing it himself. Maybe it was time to cut Vol out. More and more this seemed the wise thing to do. A downsizing. Just him and Emelia and Manny, who walked the walk and talked the talk of *clean*. Do things themselves, cut out the labor force. After all, Joe had fucked up big, twice on this last one. Leave no traces and there was nothing they could do to him.

As he drove, careful to keep to sixty-five miles an hour, Anton's thoughts slowed, too. He came up with the idea of relocating, to Montana or someplace really different, where he knew nobody and he could set up for himself. Bypass Manny, who wanted out anyway. Emelia might agree to that. Place the ads and do the transfers himself. It couldn't be that hard. Never meet the parents in the same place twice. Skip the paperwork.

Such a lot of fuss over ugly, crying brats. He firmly believed it was Hollywood inspired, all this baby lust, like the weird-named cars people just had to have, which then made them feel like they *were* somebody. They weren't. Every time he handled one of those ugly babies, he dropped a prayer on them that they would cry all night, drive their parents nuts, and then grow up to be delinquents.

Pittsburgh in a couple of hours. He had a spare identity card he could use for the hotel. One of Manny's little treats. For tonight he'd be Duncan Fox of Macon, Georgia. A man with no arrests, and no fingerprints on file anywhere.

Manny was awfully good with the paperwork end of it. If he ever split with Manny, he'd want to leave with a couple of passports and driver's licenses in his back pocket, and not just a couple, but enough for a lifetime.

So, Pittsburgh in a couple of hours. Then the search for Marina.

■   ■

SHE HAD THE NEWSPAPER WITH THE PICTURE OF THE BOY IN front of her. It was Saturday afternoon—his checking-in phone call, he called it—and he told her this one was fast. They had a suspect, another kid, obviously hiding out somewhere. When she asked if the FBI was helping with this one, he said levelly, "They would if I asked. They tend to stick with high-profile cases, though. They don't do too much about some poor kid in Homewood."

"You don't get angry at the Feds?"

"They're good at what they do. And besides, half of them are my friends."

"What are they up to now?"

"Interviews, lots of them," he told her. "New adoptive parents, agencies, looking for a disgruntled couple that might stick out."

She liked that, wished she could do it herself, reading silences and sounds, figuring personalities.

"I could probably swing by around five if you need anything."

"With my mail?"

"Nothing for you today. Sorry."

No newsletters from her casting agent, no pleas for money from the Eastern Paralyzed Veterans, nothing.

"I don't need anything," she said. "I'll have Karen Graves over for dinner tonight. The team is out of town."

"Good. How's the computer?"

"My friends Liz and Doug came over last night. I'm set up."

The solution to hiding Marina, even on the Internet, was an AOL CD in Liz's name for five hundred free hours. Liz was only too happy to be able to provide something: "Study, shop, surf, read weather reports," Liz had said excitedly. "Couple of hours a day. It should help."

"So long as you don't block call waiting, then, you can go ahead."

She promised.

He rang off thanking her for allowing him to check on her.

The computer, its screen quiet and dark, sat on a small table in the corner of the dining area, inviting her. She looked at it warily. "Spinning my wheels," she said to herself. "Killing time."

The novels she'd brought to read were lined up neatly on a shelf in the living room, next to the television, where they might wage a clear and open competition for her time. It felt wonderful to have them there, her things. The photos were out, too.

The library books, however, she had stacked in small piles under the bed. She'd hidden them purposely, feeling furtive, not wanting to explain to anyone, not Richard or Doug or Lizzie, what she was doing. Well, it was silly, laughable, to think she could find anything, do anything the detectives could not. But she couldn't stay away from it.

The books under the bed were all about adoption—how it was done, what paperwork was needed in each state. If she were to die and the books were discovered, people would assume she was trying to adopt. No one would be able to interpret accurately the meaning of the stage props. Who finds the vial that Juliet drinks from and what do they make of it? There are some things people can never know. Unless the person can explain . . . "Spinning my wheels," she chided herself again. "Trying to make myself feel useful."

Sitting on the bed, and then lying back, she read for hours. She did not identify with the voices in the first book; she did not feel the desperation they described. And yet she *had* felt such a desperation three years ago, and two years ago, and a year ago. Had those feelings changed, too?

What she was reading almost everybody already knew: There were many people who would do about anything to get a baby. Many of them were white people who wanted babies who looked like them. Healthy white infants were hard to find.

There were a lot of people in the world who still thought blond hair and blue eyes was the ultimate beauty. Marina's next-door neighbor back at the Pine Street house had declared, "God blessed me with my little girl, a perfect child—blond hair, blue eyes, just *perfect*," as if the coloring conveyed goodness, perfection. It was funny. Did the neighbor expect dark-haired people like Marina to agree they were inferior? Why was blondness so important to the woman?

Marina lay there letting her mind drift and tried to imagine the person or people who would take Justin from the three men she'd seen. More likely from the third man, since he was more presentable than the others, although his neat, almost dandyish clothing covered a compact time bomb. She hoped Justin was far away from this man. The thought of him made her shiver. He was much more mysterious than the other two—"the thugs," Christie called them— more frightening.

International Adoptions, Getting to Know Your Child, Adoption Procedure, The Hows of Adoption. She read as if she were studying for a bar exam. The people she'd run into would not have the patience for procedure, legality; no, not even the cocky, well-dressed man—the boss who had ordered the others around. No, with him it would be a back alley somewhere, an exchange of cash, and that was that. If she closed her eyes and *acted* the role of that man, could she imagine decisions he might make, actions he might take?

Two of her library books yielded the names of adoption lawyers from each state. She could call them and ask about how the whole thing was done. Tomorrow. Tomorrow she would call. Finally she got up and approached the computer. It made a singing noise when she turned it on, a positive greeting. "Hello," she answered. "Can you help me?"

Soon she was on the Internet.

■   ■

ANTON FOUND HER IN THE PITTSBURGH PHONE BOOK, EASY AS anything. He found the husband under attorneys in the yellow pages. Fine. Take his time, figure out the patterns. Get her alone and this time . . . He drove to a newsstand in Squirrel Hill and bought a more detailed city map and a lottery ticket. Since he was lucky enough to get a meter and some time on the meter, he went next door to the Squirrel Hill Cafe, known as "The Cage," and ordered a meat loaf sandwich and a beer. He'd grown a mustache. He wore a pair of glasses, slightly tinted. The Cage was dark, as usual, a complete shock to a person coming from outside, and nearly empty, save for two customers—an angry working-class drunk standing at the bar and a lonely, gregarious bohemian drunk sloped over it and trying to engage the barmaid in conversation about the proposed stadiums.

Anton felt invisible. Safe. He chose the bohemian. "Hey, what's happening in this town? Anybody got a newspaper?"

The barmaid, a hefty young woman with stiff, short blond hair, reminded him of some male rock star, but he couldn't think which one. She reached to a shelf behind her and placed a paper on the bar without a word.

"Little kid killed," Anton murmured.

"Yeah."

"City gangs. Terrible."

"Where you from, then?" the scraggly drunk asked.

"Illinois," Anton answered.

"So what's happening there?"

"Nothing much, believe me. It's so boring people buy tickets to look at Abraham Lincoln's grave."

"This is a good town."

"Yeah? Buy you a beer?"

"Sure."

"What's with the stadiums?"

"Some people don't want them—the idea is two new ones to replace Three Rivers. The mayor says it's good business. Lots of 'this and that' kind of fighting. What I don't like is, they want to make the baseball stadium fancy, with fancy stores. Should a stadium have fancy stores? I don't think so. So, what do you do in Illinois?"

"Salesman. All over."

"Sell what?"

"Baby supplies. Cribs, strollers, hanging seats."

"Is that a good line of work?"

"Good enough. Now, wait a minute, you guys had this horrible case with the kid of one of the ballplayers, right?"

Anton felt a kind of elation when they talked right to him, shrugged, and said, hell, the police didn't have a thing and the case was probably never going to be solved. "You can tell," the loose drunk said, "they ain't got diddly-squat, or there'd be something in the papers."

The waitress said, "Police in this town can't find their dicks with a map and a zipper down."

The friendly drunk said, "This is true."

The tight one nodded his head.

Anton shrugged and pretended to read the classifieds. "Guy's got a guitar for sale."

■   ■

AT THE BUILDING WHERE RICHARD CHRISTIE WORKED, THE staff moved sluggishly, with the weight of summer on them. They were either coming back from vacations or going on vacations or had one foot in lala land, taking vacations in their minds, or having weekend hangovers. It was hot and humid. The fans whirred at them. As Christie had told all the newshounds, they had a good lead in the case of the shooting of the child in Homewood, but they didn't have the suspect in custody yet, even though it was only a matter of time. How long could a restless seventeen-year-old hide out? Motive:

Revenge for something an older half-brother had said. Insults cut deep.

The Bureau had finally shared with him a list of people suspected of illegal or at least messy adoption practices. Doctors, nurses, bureaus, agencies, with one complaint or another against them—made too much money, showed prejudice, misrepresented something. The list was longer than he'd have guessed for a five-hundred-mile radius. No longer was the Ohio connection the main thing, they all wrote on their Rapid-Start reports. Ohio might have been, if it figured at all, only the first leg of some elaborate journey the baby was making. They were checking everywhere. Texas, Arizona. The shortlist the FBI had come up with for interviews included five particular places in Ohio that looked promising—three agencies, two lawyers. Seven in Pennsylvania. Three in Pittsburgh. Well, it was a long shot that any lawyers or agencies came into it at all, but he would check the Pittsburghers out himself, via Artie Dolan. Top of the list was James Rawson, very wealthy, once had a malpractice suit. Had done adoptions back in '88, but not since then. Sol Holzman, who had a lot of druggie clients and was suspected of passing the stuff himself. And a guy named Paul Furlo, who ran adoption ads regularly. There were others, plenty of others, down to a couple of attorneys who didn't seem to specialize in anything, but had done an adoption or two. He gave the list to his best investigator, Artie Dolan, asking him to work with Special Agent Terrence. Artie was the greatest, could get a confession out of a toenail. "Artie," he said, "work the shortlist this week. After that we'll see where we are."

It wasn't quite eleven in the morning. He was about to call Marina to check in when he looked at today's mail for her—with its little forwarding stickers addressed to him. Again, almost nothing. There was only a AAA renewal and a request for funds from the Fraternal Order of Police. He felt miserable. How naked he would feel, handing over the AAA renewal. And the other piece, funny anyway. Maybe she would laugh. Blush. In the little play that unfolded in his mind, Marina was saying what small amounts she'd sent to the police in the past, and she was wondering aloud whether the money ever went to anything worthwhile. He was returning phone calls and in his mind she was saying something, one of those funny little phrases of hers, somewhere between smart and angry, maybe something like she had to treat the police better in future. He shook himself. She was a beauty. Young and talented. Why would she look twice at him?

A current of life went through the place a little bit before noon. A person with any sensitivity would have known something was happening, even before any specific word came down. Voices lifted out of their lethargy. "Hey. Right." "Right away." "Got it." Phones rang at a different pace.

"For you," McGranahan said. "News, important."

The guys downstairs told him a print check had just come through on AFIS for a body that had just been found in Westmoreland County. Matched a guy who'd been arrested a couple of times in Wisconsin—car theft, illegal possession of a weapon, hit-and-run—and get the name, a guy named John Volbrecht. All that was left of this Volbrecht was some clothing, a tiny amount of blond hair, and enough skin to print him. Otherwise, bones, scattered here and there, with a bullet hole through the skull.

Moments later Christie was on the phone with the State Police, and moments after that with Marina. He asked her, "I don't know if you have a strong stomach.... You feel up to taking a look?"

"Pick me up," she said. "I can handle anything if it means getting out of this place. It's Vol?"

"You'll tell us, maybe. If it's at all possible. This isn't going to be pretty."

When he picked her up, she was wearing jeans and a long T-shirt and sandals. She had her hair pulled up in a ponytail and stuck through a Pirates baseball cap. Now he wouldn't have guessed that—the cap. He wanted to hug her—she looked great that way, so untroubled. Like a young mom cheering for her son at a game. A young person moving from one apartment to another, ordering pizza for the movers. He saw she wore sandals and said, "Lose the shoes, kid. Put on something solid."

She went to the bedroom to change her shoes, calling to him, "I'm trying to get into hats. Like you said."

"Your hat is *great*." It was one of the old ones, a black pillbox with three gold lines across the front.

While she changed her shoes, he looked around again, at her computer setup, the couple of pictures of her that he'd packed.

"You're on the Net?"

"Every once in a while."

The apartment looked more lived-in now. He liked that. It also smelled good, of food, garlic to be exact, and her perfume. She was alive. She was living. She was going to be okay.

"You're feeling better," he said. It was almost a question.

"I felt awful for a long time, seemed like it never would end, then I woke up one day and my energy was back. So sudden. Why is that?"

"I don't know."

"I don't either," she said.

Traffic was heavy on the Parkway East. Sweaty guys in orange jumpsuits kept waving drivers over to form a single lane. He considered using his flashers, but he decided the worst of it would be over within three minutes or so.

Marina shifted in the seat and asked, "They only found one body?"

"So far."

"And how bad is it?"

"It's very bad. It's summertime. There won't be anything recognizable in the usual sense."

He saw her hand go to her mouth automatically. Funny, the way people pressed back the nausea that way.

"You still want to do this?"

"I do. I want to."

Up ahead of him was a family clearly starting out on vacation. Three children peered out of the back of the van. There were surfboards on the top of the vehicle and bicycles on the back of it. And a look of anticipation on the faces of the children. "I'm not a good enough father," he said suddenly, and realized he was taking up the conversation he'd begun with her two weeks before.

He felt her hold her breath and then breathe again. "Why do you say that?"

"Those kids up there." He looked to the side and saw she was watching them, too. "I promise vacations, I don't go. I send my wife with the kids, and I catch up for two or three days. I should be playing in the surf with them, miniature golf, whatever, but I don't. I keep choosing work."

"I'm sure you're very good in other ways."

He was unreasonably happy to hear she thought so, to think she saw something good in him. "What ways?" he asked, too eager.

"A sense of reality. Truth. A wish for justice. A sense of steadiness. All those things you can't buy."

"You give me too much credit. I figure I should provide plain old fun, catch some baseballs, just be *around*."

"That counts for a lot, too," she said soberly.

The police radio saved him from reaching for something to say. He was shaking slightly, even to hear her talk about him. And yet he felt himself performing the role of "busy man"—not exactly the reality and truth she credited him with. "Excuse me." He took the question on the radio, confirming that he would be there in forty-five minutes at the very outside. He put on the flashers, checked the rearview mirror. "Cripes. I think we've got KDKA five cars behind us. I'm going to insist they keep you off the news. If this is your Vol guy, you see what I mean. The ducks are going down. Somebody wants rid of the actors in this thing."

He looked over and saw she was listening intently.

"Do they know when it happened?" she asked.

He told her what little he knew. "By the deterioration it looks like four weeks ago, but it hasn't even *been* four weeks altogether, so—Let's just say, if this is our man, probably right away."

"If it's Vol, then what happened to Joe? They were to-gether. But I think the third man had the baby, so"—her voice fell—"this could go nowhere, right?"

"It could go half an inch. You know about that tor-toise. He gets there eventually."

The children in the van began to wave at them. Traffic eased up. They passed the van, Marina waving back. "Cute kids," he said. "All excited."

Good. She thought he was good, and he was dragging her along partly because he wanted to be with her. They could have hauled the body to the morgue, and then brought her in for a look at it. He ended up saying, "There's some clothing, and they figure the deceased is a white male. That's about it. That, and there's not much hair. Maybe there will be some advantage to you seeing what's left of the body before they move it."

"Vol had baby-fine hair," she said.

"I remember."

He felt he was telling her too much, but he couldn't seem to stop himself. "They ruled out suicide because of the position of the bullet wound. It's in the skull, a precise hit, so not too likely an accident. Then the bullet hole is in the wrong direction for suicide. You interested in this?" She nodded emphatically. Her attention was flattering, not that he hadn't had that kind of flattery before, a mil-lion times. But he liked talking about what he did. "It's concave on the inside. The guy got shot in the back of the head."

He looked over at her. She had not blanched yet. He said, "What are you thinking?"

She said, "I'm thinking about the guy, Joe. On the bus, I would never have guessed he'd have a gun. Or try to kill anyone. It didn't seem like him."

"Unlikeliest people will pull a trigger. This guy was among the likelies."

"I suppose so. Maybe the other guy went with them af-ter all. Things were desperate."

"Whoever killed this guy pulled branches over him.

That brought water and rot. The flies would have been there in minutes."

"And?"

"You want to know?"

"Yes."

"The flies lay eggs. The maggots eat. They turn into flies. They lay more eggs. More maggots eat. They like the eyes, the nose, the mouth, the ears best. So, there goes the usual kind of identification. Animals come along and dismember the body. Very little left. What are you thinking?"

"Of things I've read. Of how undignified death is."

He drove for a while. He couldn't think of anything smart to say. He didn't know what she read. "It's summer. You wouldn't believe how much worse that makes things."

"How did they get fingerprints?"

"Ah. That's one of those lucky things. Fingers aren't that tasty." He heard her begin to laugh. Which most of the people on the force did, a lot of the time, in a situation like this. He was gratified by her reaction, and added, "Nothing left but his blue jeans and his fingerprints."

She laughed more freely, shaking her head.

This was good. She was tough. "Just be logical. Don't rush to any conclusions. Don't say anything you don't believe."

"I never do. That's the problem."

He tried to think how that was a problem. Had she said something to her husband that she couldn't take back? Could that be it? In his experience, you *could* take things back if you meant it.

They got onto Route 22 in Murraysville, one red sign after another. It was lunchtime and he was beginning to get hungry. He wondered if he should pick up something on the way or wait until the work was over. After, he decided, and explained, "People get very hungry at a murder investigation. You might think that's perverse—"

"It makes perfect sense."

"If you can wait, we'll grab something after."

She waved her hand, no problem, and they looked out at the day. He could see she took everything in. He was beginning to think she was like him in some ways. They both had absorbent personalities, took on other people's lives. He shut off the flashers and moved expertly through lanes of traffic.

"Do you like truth? I said you did. Do you?"

He was unprepared. He only half heard her. "I think so."

"Are you a little in love with me?" she asked.

He hadn't known how the truth would hit when it hit. He hadn't counted on her giving it a swat. "Yes."

"Well, that's a problem."

"I know it."

"I'm a lot in love with you."

He almost couldn't drive, the way his body seemed to hollow out. Was she watching the blood racing to his face? Did she know his voice was caught, trapped in his throat? Finally, he said, "I didn't think that was possible."

"And it may not be real. I'm saying that straight off. Nothing is normal right now. This summer's been lifted out of everything else."

So she was saying it wasn't real. Hardly a surprise.

"You've been so helpful to me. Maybe I don't know what I'm feeling—being alone most of the time, without contacts."

He'd thought of that.

"I'm aware I'm probably no good for you," she finished.

"I want to touch you so bad I can't stand it."

Saying it, he allowed the other truths in. He'd been afraid he would call out her name at night. He awoke thinking of her in the mornings. He felt endangered and reckless. He did not know, at all, what he was doing. He jammed on the turn signal and pulled off at a Pep Boys. The car sat panting in the parking lot. He could hardly look at her, the way her beauty astounded his senses, every time, every single time. She always seemed to be seeing his awkwardness, and yet he couldn't stay away from her.

He reached around and touched her hair. Leaned over and brushed her lips. His voice came out all raspy when he tried to joke, "Is this where I let you know things with my wife are not—?"

"Is it *true*?"

"Yes."

She was looking so hard at him. "Only say what's true." She seemed very sad suddenly.

He tried to look for the truth. "We don't get along very well. She's not happy. That's why. But we're not, however guys put it, 'virtually separated.'"

"Just unhappy. Normal."

He didn't understand her words. "Well, I hate normal, then."

"Are you romantic?"

He wasn't sure if that was a bad thing or a good thing. He wanted to be honest in this, if that was possible. "It's not her fault. It's mine, if anything."

"Is it? You've done something bad?"

He shook his head, feeling she could never love him, with his self-doubts and his vague sense of his own blame. "I . . . we've got to keep going," he said. He put the car in gear and tried to think if there was more to say. "It's just the way it turned out. She wants more. And I'm bored. I'm so bored I could . . ." His hands opened. Die, he'd almost said. "I resigned myself to it. . . ."

She was so beautiful. He couldn't help touching her. He reached over and touched her shoulder, her face, the place on her waist where she'd been hurt, and he didn't want to stop.

"My place this afternoon," she said. She almost sang it, but it had a sad note.

He looked up at her, unbelieving.

■   ■

JOE, OF COURSE, HAD NO IDEA WHEN VOL WOULD BE FOUND. He knew it would happen sometime. With luck, when all identification had faded. Without luck, sooner. He had started to believe he might have luck on his side in this. Other things were coming up lucky. The house he was living in, Marina's house, was everything he could wish for. And she'd been there and gone without finding him. That was luck in the works, and he felt the machinery was only getting smoother.

Joe had gone out at night twice since he moved in and set up house, slipping carefully through the yard, walking to the supermarket, carrying the food back. The bags of food were always heavy to carry, but it seemed a safer way than starting up the car in the middle of the night. He'd done one of his slippery miracles to get the car into the garage to begin with. Then he'd found electrical tape in the garage and newspaper and he'd quickly taped the paper over the windows so no kid goofing off in the alley would be able to see the unfamiliar car inside. There was always the chance somebody might call the police about the newspaper. This worried him.

Marina and Michael, he sometimes said to himself, trying to pretend he knew them, as if he *were* an old uncle come to bring her a car. He loved the large, wraparound porch that he would never be able to use. The antiquey picture frames and throws. The crisp, clean modern kitchen. Three couches altogether—and he'd tried all three, one in the spare bedroom, one in the home office, and one in the living room. He liked the living room couch best, a light-colored rough fabric, and seats he sunk into, although he didn't stay in the living room much. Sometimes he sat there in the dark, late at night, for a few minutes.

There were things in every drawer. Corks, pencils. Anything he wanted, he was able to find, eventually. This intrigued him.

He knew many particulars about Marina by now, all kinds of details. Who would have thought it? A woman he couldn't get rid of on the bus, and now he was in possession of the tiny facts of her existence. Ear infection. Angry letter to Kaufmann's about a drapery order that got lost.

He'd been through every piece of paper, every canceled check. He knew her doctors were located in Oakland, he knew how long she took to pay a bill (usually three weeks). He knew which items she checked in the *Cultural Arts* newsletter. Little red check marks. She was looking for work. Or had been.

Shot in the head. He'd meant to kill and had failed. That he knew. No television report, no news article he'd seen mentioned brain damage or physical damage. From his hiding place in the basement, wedged in a cubbyhole, it had sounded as if she moved and talked normally, but how could that be? Once in the heart and once in the brain. She had flinched, collapsed inward when he shot. That must have been how the thing went wrong. He wondered how long she would be allowed to live. Anton would not allow it. And if Anton found him again, the end of him, too. No doubt at all. He felt an odd commiseration with Marina, both of them hiding out somewhere, both marked.

He wondered what had become of the child he'd named Brian. Before Brian, everything clicked along as it was meant to. He or Vol drove to New York to pick up Emelia and a new baby. Then he and Vol rented whatever motel room Anton told them to take. Bill paid in advance. Fake ID given at check-in. Anton and Emelia drove up in another car and waited with the motor running. He and Vol cracked a window, drew their guns. Eventually a couple drove up. An exchange happened, at dawn, bundle for bundle, out in the middle of a parking lot, almost always eerie and quiet. He and Vol got an earful in the next sixty seconds, two minutes. Anton and Emelia pretended things, always talking very fast, talking over each other, confusing the couple. A fifteen-year-old Russian girl, they said, an airport, a plane to catch.

Anton and Emelia hurried the couple away. Then they got into their own car and drove away fast. Usually a branch or some scrap of paper hanging from the trunk, something almost innocent, covered their license plate.

He and Vol followed. Drove behind Anton and Emelia, making sure all was safe. Pulled off into someplace secluded and got their fee, cash.

It worked. It kept working. Joe got scared, every time, hoping he wouldn't be needed. Now he wondered, with Anton working this last case alone, had it looked suspicious? Had the baby been sold?

Or killed, the way they wanted to kill him for taking the baby. Easy to blame him, but hadn't Emelia told him to do it, or something like it? Or was he dreaming?

Joe did not want to go over and over what he'd done wrong. For the first time in his life, he was in a nice place, where the covers were soft and there were pretty little boxes, vases, artwork on the walls. There was one painting over the fireplace he kept thinking was a woman bowing down, but then he'd think, no, there is no head, just a dress, and then he'd think, no, not a woman at all, a great big flower petal. But then he would change his mind again.

He was living in Marina's house, moving about, sitting, looking at things. It thrilled him.

He discovered how much he liked baths.

He used only the plainest shampoos and soaps, and he'd already replenished some of them. He thought of these as the husband's things. There were others in fancy containers. Marina chose things that smelled delicious. He wanted to use them, but he didn't.

Even the laundry soap appealed to him. He'd done only one wash. Late at night. He used the dryer without a fabric softener so that he would pump no fresh soapy smell out into the neighborhood.

When the phone rang, on the Monday after the Friday Marina had been there, it rang only twice and then it stopped. The answering machine, which sat there in the kitchen with its single light on, did nothing. He stood over it, watching, listening. In the first days, he'd thought the volume was turned down, but no, that wasn't it. The police, he had to conclude, were intercepting all calls. He was sorry for this. It would help to be able to hear what calls came in. It would give him an idea how to move next.

He was sometimes tempted to make calls. He knew a phone number for Emelia, but she had said never to call, never. In all the time he knew Emelia, he could never imagine going against her. What if she wormed out of him where he was and sent Anton after him? He had emptied Vol's pockets and found a phone number for Anton in Michigan and one for Manny. He was irritated that Vol would be entrusted with these phone numbers when he wasn't. But he couldn't call Anton now. And Manny... no, he thought not.

He'd seen Manny once outside his office building. Huge guy. Huge and sad. He'd seen pictures of him in Emelia's place, way back when, way back when she lived in the apartment, before she started living in New York. And he'd first met Emelia, what? Fifteen years ago. Before the Mexican husband, before the guy after that, before Anton. She'd say, "Can you get me a TV?" And he'd get her a TV. That's how it started out.

It was lunchtime. Joe opened a foil pouch and poured the contents into a bowl. He added water, stirred, and put the bowl in the microwave. He had bought a lot of soup packets because they were light and easy to carry. Easier to dispose of than cans—since he had to sneak the garbage out when he went for groceries. He didn't know why, but even in summer he thought soup was the perfect lunch.

In the beginning he'd slept in the basement. Like a dog on a bed of blankets and rags. Then he crept upstairs while it was still light and lay on the bed with the two guns beside him. It was stuffy up there, but he couldn't open a window without alerting the neighbors. He saw a fan in the basement, but he was afraid to use it. At first he'd planned to sleep during the day and stay up at night, keeping watch. But after a while, a feeling of safety enfolded him and he began to make his way to the bedroom at night. He never got under the covers, though, even when he moved sleep time to eleven at night. Every morning, he woke up surprised at the tiny cameolike pattern on the bedcovering, the drapery swags at the windows. "Some hotel," he said to himself.

After a few days, he adopted the usual schedule, surprising himself. Breakfast, lunch, nap, dinner, television, sleep.

When he used the bathroom—usually the tub, but even the shower once or twice—he always dried it out afterward and put everything back so his presence would not be noticed if anyone came by. He had just used the shower the day Marina and her cop came in, but miraculously, they hadn't stayed long enough to notice any tiny changes—wet soap, the smell of shampoo, dampness hanging in the air—or to open the refrigerator.

Luck had been with him. There he was, in the basement, just hanging his towel. Suddenly he heard noises. Voices. He strained to listen. He thought with alarm about the steaminess in the bathroom; then he heard the police radio. He peeked out a side basement window and saw the antenna of the police car. He pulled his gun. Yet from the rhythm of the voices, the people above didn't seem to be searching. They sounded more casual. That's when he crawled into a two-by-four space in the laundry room and folded himself up. A policeman meant another gun, and skill, and experience. Better to be invisible. If she'd come unaccompanied, he would have had a chance to kill her, but then he would have had to leave, too. It was just lucky, the way it happened, them coming and going so fast. He wondered if she would come back alone sometime.

Hours after she and the policeman left, he went upstairs to see what it had all been about. Things were missing. The computer, more clothing. He knew about witness protection programs and victim protection programs from things Anton and Vol had said. So she'd be harder to find than a normal citizen. But according to Anton, anybody could be found if you wanted to find them. He had made a list of return addresses from her Christmas cards. He had the list folded tight in his pocket.

His eye kept expecting the missing photographs of Marina on the shelves and tables where he was used to them. His eye was constantly being disappointed.

He made some significant operations changes. Marina's visit had forced him to rethink his use of the refrigerator. He began freezing ice and ice blocks in the basement freezer chest. He began to put a couple of freezer blocks or a bag of ice with his milk and other perishables in the big red picnic cooler—which he then put right back on the shelf in the basement as if it were empty. If she came back and opened the refrigerator, if she went to the basement and opened the freezer, his invisibility would buy him time. A part of him knew this was an overly elaborate scheme, but that was also part of the pleasure of it. To be there and not seem to be there at all. Right in her house. His best magic trick to date. A way of living well while being hunted. Getting Marina to protect him without knowing she was doing it. Vol could never have come up with something this good. No. Not Anton either. He was not ready to do the work of pursuing the list. He would wait here.

Cereal and milk for breakfast, the one bowl washed out in the basement. At noon, either a packet of soup, like today, or he went to the basement freezer for a frozen lunch entrée. No cooking, no setting off kitchen alarms with smoke. He'd come to like the microwave, with its whirring noises and quick gratifications.

Later he would carry the fan up from the basement.

As long as the Benedicts did not shut off the electricity—which was unlikely since they had lamps on timers—he could live this other life. While he waited.

■　　■

ALL AROUND THE SCENE OF THE DEATH OF THE MAN FINGER-printed as Volbrecht, people worked. Men in rubber gloves took samples of dirt, maggots, hair fibers. What Marina saw was a few scattered puzzle pieces, but enough to convince her what puzzle they belonged to. The soaked, mildewed blue jeans were the first thing the detectives asked her to look at. "They're the right color blue," she said. "And they were cuffed at the bottom, just like that. I forgot, but now that I see it, I remember. It's odd since he was so tall. I'm sorry I didn't remember before."

"It wouldn't have mattered," Christie said. "If we'd put it on the description of him, he'd have uncuffed them."

"Do you recognize the belt?" The man who asked had on a State Police uniform. She understood he was supposed to be in charge, but it still seemed Christie was.

"It's pretty generic. I don't think I do."

"You want her to look at the rest?" the trooper asked Christie.

"I'd like her to look at the hair and the fingers." She felt his arm go around her shoulders to guide her in another direction. "Are you okay?"

She didn't know how to answer that. There was nothing good about Vol so far as she knew, and yet the end he'd come to saddened her. Or maybe it was the end everyone comes to that saddened her. Worms and dirt and grinning skulls. Good person or bad, what is the difference?

Except maybe if the ground itself is whispering the life story to anyone who passes by and a lesson can be learned.

Except if something good is handed on to someone young in such a way that it can never be lost or forgotten. Some people spoke of unbelievable amounts of love handed to them by their parents, of love that so filled them up they had plenty left over for the rest of the world. Those people had values. They recognized others as separate from them, deserving of respect. They were so filled up with a sense of self, they could look outward, at others, and see beyond themselves. They didn't cheat themselves either. Their lives were—

She stepped carefully over branches along the path she was told to take. She understood the investigators were fighting for footprints, packets of matches, fibers from shirts, hats, anything that might help.

"We'd like you to look at this hair."

Over to the side was something on a tray that seemed at first like a block of dirt, then like the head of John the Baptist. The hair they asked her to look at was not the hair on the skull, if any was left, but something that had come off the skull and was unlike hair. Corn silk, mud-caked. How could she know someone had not husked a dozen ears of corn and come up with this exhibit? "It's his hair," she said.

Somebody took her picture. She looked up. A guy with a Polaroid. "I'm killing this roll," he said. "That's all, doll. Don't worry. I had my orders about keeping you out of the news. Here's for your trouble." He handed her the developing print. She held it out toward the air, waiting.

The trooper called her over to another tray. Mushrooms, she thought, then roots, while the realization of what they really were tripped over the first thoughts, catching up. She shook her head. "They could be anyone's."

"Couple of digits," the guy said, laughing.

"I thought they were mushrooms."

"We *all* want lunch. That's how the mind works."

Christie took her by the arm. "You're doing great." The way he held her, she couldn't bring the developing photograph up to see it. When he let go of her, she looked. She could feel that he did, too. Had the photographer done it on purpose?

■　■

RYAN GRAVES AGAIN WALKED PAST THE PHOTOS OF BOB PRINCE and Roberto Clemente and past the folded shirts and baseball cards in the lobby at Gate D; the word was, the crowd was going to be large tonight.

His teammates were angry, the kind of angry that comes from losing. This year's advertising campaign—some of them liked it, some didn't—showed the players punching time cards, like ordinary laborers, like the people in the stands who had built the city. The voice-over said, "Let's go to work."

If only he could. One inning on the third of July. And one inning three times after that. And all the time they'd been moving inexorably to the basement, where they sat pretty squarely a week after the All-Star break, and except for a few hiccoughs, that's where they'd stayed.

They exercised, most of them, that is, and practiced for hours in the late afternoon, but the jokes were nasty. Loser's jokes.

Everybody was angry.

This time, around six o'clock, a couple of them went toward the kitchen, asking him if he wanted to come along, but he said, no, thanks. He'd had a big lunch. All by himself, too. He'd just gone out to a restaurant without much of an explanation, because Karen's parents had come back again a couple of days ago and left again this morning, and he was about ready to explode with all the hovering, the talk, the same things said over and over again. Cheese dog and fries. It felt good, eating alone.

He was checking off the items in his locker, several of the other players with lockers near him were jostling one another and talking rapidly in Spanish, nobody was really watching television when the little flash came on with its maybes. "The body found may be connected with the kidnapping of the Graves baby," the woman was saying. He heard just the end of it and started moving toward the television, but the newscasters had moved on to a story about city council.

Vince, holding about twenty-five of the night's two hundred and fifty clean towels, came into the room just at that point, not at all aware of the television, and said, "Hey, kid, telephone. You're supposed to take it in the office."

Ryan hurried past him, a few of the players looking up to notice his rush.

"Some news, a very small bit of a lead," Richard Christie's voice came over the phone. "I don't want to get your hopes up too much, but I just wanted you to know if you haven't already seen the TV—"

"I have."

"I tried to get to you before, but the newshounds were all over us. We're pretty sure one of the guys involved in taking Justin turned up dead."

"Oh, my God," Ryan said. "And Justin—? Is there anything?"

"We did a search of the grounds around him. We—we're doing a more thorough search. We think your son was nowhere near this guy at that point, so try to hold on to that. One thing usually leads to others."

Ryan swallowed hard. "I'll try."

"You doing okay?"

"Yeah."

"I mean, not just today. I mean, your wife, too. I just managed to call her and she didn't sound too good. Is there anything we can do for her?"

Ryan wanted to talk to Christie more than he wanted to talk to anyone. He didn't know why. It was just something about the detective that made him feel like a high-school kid telling something important to the one teacher he could confide in. So he said, "We're not doing too well, my wife and me. Her parents were back. I'm not sure it calmed her any. She still doesn't sleep much."

"Sleeping pills don't help?"

"I hate the things. But even when she tries them, she doesn't sleep right. She thinks she's going to hear something if she stays awake."

"When did the folks leave?"

"Close to noon today."

"She's probably better off with company, right?"

"I don't know."

"She's been visiting Marina Benedict," Christie said, pronouncing the name carefully. "I thought that might help."

"I think it's the only thing that's kept her from going off the deep end."

"I'll talk to her again. She wanted me to try to catch you before you had to go out on the field. We don't know anything except this guy was involved, and we're checking out his contacts. Marina . . . Marina made as positive an ID as she could under the circumstances."

"It means a lot, sir, that you called me yourself. I saw, we all heard, something on the news, but I couldn't catch it."

"I'm sorry all that got to you before I did."

Ryan hung up and went back to the locker room. He could sense the underlying tension there, although everybody pretended to be busy with shoes or towels or bubble gum.

Karen's father had accused him of not thinking much about his baby, but he did.

"It's . . . okay," he told the players. "They think they found one of the guys."

Ryan didn't get to play that night, although, as usual, he tried to communicate that he was ready to "go to work." He warmed up in the bull pen briefly, but he wasn't called. The team made a mess of almost everything and won.

■   ■

NINE O'CLOCK THAT NIGHT. THE LIGHT FELL FROM THE SKY. Children's cries rose up at the sound of the Good Humor bell and then their voices faded. The alarm clock ticked asthmatically, the sound of an old heart through a stethoscope. They lay in tangled flowered sheets that belonged to somebody named Amy Bissinger, who was almost a Ph.D. in anthropology and was now off in Africa doing research. One day Marina would live somewhere else. The wound at her side would fade and fade and become a white scar. Where she had her little bald spot, her hair would grow in again, and there would be just a scar underneath that would identify her skull as hers and nobody else's.

They lay together and held on. She had thought she wouldn't go through with it after all, after challenging him in the car. She'd only wanted to break the bubble of tension between them, acknowledge what was happening. Now it was too late. She'd seen the Polaroid, the way he looked at her, and it made her want to be good to herself. And to him.

He'd gone to the office until six, told her to eat supper, since food was being ordered at work for him. He'd had to meet with Horner and his men to talk about tracing out Volbrecht's life for further clues as to companions. Then there was a news conference. And Justin's parents to talk to, to catch them up on the development, Vol's body found. She hadn't eaten, though. She couldn't.

He held her tight. It was hot. Even with the crazy system—air-conditioning on full blast in the living room, fan pulling cold air into the bedroom—they sweated. But he didn't let go. She burrowed in, her face in the curve of his neck, her knee between his. The thought that he would leave her tonight seemed almost unbearable. But he would, of course, he had to, even though it didn't seem so from the way he held on. She wondered if the two of them would ever go on a picnic, dunk each other in the water, throw a Frisbee, have a hot argument and appear before each other hours later, laughing and apologetic. Would this thing that had begun so bizarrely become normal, or would it always be something else? She was hollowed out, with room for nothing but him to fill her up again.

The phone rang, then it stopped. Voice mail had intervened to keep the world out. Who? Lizzie. Maybe even Michael.

As if he read her thoughts, Richard asked her, "Will you tell him?"

"I suppose I will." She added wryly, "Loving the truth as I do. We don't talk every day anymore. We did, but I told him I didn't want him calling so often. I know he went back to the house. I could tell he'd been there when we went. But when I asked him about it, he denied it."

Christie nodded, unsurprised.

"He used to be honest. Anyway, we haven't talked about the actual divorce yet. Paperwork. And dividing our things."

"He's a lawyer," Christie said, almost teasing. "Gives him an unfair advantage."

She slid upward and reached for the lamp. "Should I put the light on?"

"Not yet. Come back. For a minute. I have to go soon. I should have gone already."

She slid back down.

"Do you still have . . . feelings for him?"

She was aware of not liking Richard's ready-made phrasing, but she put that aside to answer the question. "I don't know. I can't find them, the feelings, if I have them. I can't find them at all."

"And he has someone else?"

"He doesn't elaborate, but—Kendall always liked him. Women tend to like him."

"You aren't jealous?"

"If I am, I can't find that either." She turned over and lay flat, trying to sort out the truth of her feelings. "I think I'm grateful he's found someone. It was awful to see him falling apart. He wasn't . . . himself anymore. That's not quite true. . . . Anyway, he was falling apart, and I couldn't bring him back."

Richard got up on an elbow. "I have to go," he said. "I don't want to."

She looked the length of him, startled to see how vulnerable a policeman is, or can be—torso bent inward, protectively, penis lying curved along his leg. Muscles, scars, body hair—on him smooth, dark, long hair. This hair alone could identify him, she thought, for those who knew how to look.

Eventually she got up and made toast, buttered it, and brought it to bed. She knew he had to leave, but everything about time was upside down today. She hadn't eaten lunch, after all, hadn't eaten anything all day and needed something gentle to break the fast, toast, breakfast food.

He was mostly dressed when she got back. He shook his head to the toast.

Unbidden, she found herself saying, "My father was violent. He hurt the three of us, my mother, my sister, and me. He should have been arrested, but he wasn't. My mother and sister protected him. Even now they won't admit how bad it was. They'll say anything, anything— 'He was drinking that year,' or 'He loved us but didn't know how to show it,' or 'People from his background learned that behavior.' " She found herself shaking again, even to report it, this old thing. Richard looked at her, paying attention, which made her feel foolish. Wasn't domestic abuse the dull, daily rote of the police force?

"Go on," he said.

She shrugged.

"Your family? Your husband . . . ?"

"I don't know why I had to be the one to speak the truth. I was elected or something. That's why I can never get truly close to them. We always come back to *the subject*. Well, Michael understood that. He saw what I'd been through. I think I married him because I finally felt safe. He was the gentlest man until we started having trouble—one sort or another. Mostly, I . . . I don't want to talk against him."

"I didn't ask you to."

She got back into bed, pulled the sheet around her, and sat with her knees up. "What went wrong was we wanted a baby. Both of us. We wanted a family. It obsessed us. And we couldn't. And the relationship fell apart."

He came back and sat, touched her knee, said, "Promise me you'll tell me. . . . But I can't, not now. Promise me you'll understand. I'm supposed to be back at the office. Two hours ago. Home, four hours ago."

"I know."

"I'll be thinking about you all the time. I want to know everything about you. I'm leaving, but I'm not—"

"I understand."

She watched him put his coat on. She loved the muted colors of his clothes and the way it looked like his fingers cramped when he buttoned the top button of his shirt. He looked up at her from time to time as he pulled a tie on. Those quick glances of his made him seem as if he were embarrassed to be looked at.

"Thank you for starting to tell me something so important," he said.

"You sound so formal."

"I'm sorry. I don't talk very well. I don't talk the kind of lang—"

A panic came over her. She was losing him. "I know. It doesn't matter."

"It doesn't seem to. Not at the moment," he said with a quizzical raise of the eyebrows.

As she watched him strap on his gun, Marina thought how she wasn't afraid of him, nor did she feel any violence from him, but fear came back anyway. Fear, now, that someone else would be violent toward him, and she would lose him.

AFTER CHRISTIE LEFT HER APARTMENT, MARINA SAT FOR A long time trying to figure out what had happened to her. *Richard,* she said to herself. She was just learning to say his name. She was smart enough to know people did things— got involved—out of revenge, fear, to move on, to put a former relationship to rest. When she thought of Richard's face, she didn't want any of these motives to be what moved her. He could be hurt. She didn't want to hurt him.

When she saw it was eleven o'clock she put on the news, flashing back and forth from channel to channel. They all had it in some form or another, but all they were willing to say was that the deceased was a possible link to the kidnapping of Justin Graves and that police were continuing to comb the hillside for other evidence. She was on camera, on one channel, just a bit of her, a shoulder, her hair through the baseball cap. Richard had wanted to hide her. He would be angry about Channel 11 using that clip.

She sat up for hours, thinking about everything that had begun a mere three weeks ago. Her heart pounded and she longed for the next time she would see him again.

At two in the morning, when she realized she would not sleep, she went to the computer and turned it on. A moth flew in front of her, but every time she swiped at it, it got away. She let it tap against the lightbulb and the metal lampshade. Soon she was on the Internet, a middle-of-the-night excursion, the only kind she could take. She typed, "black market adoptions." The globe of the world whirled around for a few seconds and a box told her no entries were found. Hmmm. She typed in "black market" alone and got a thousand articles on gold, drugs, kidneys, just about everything but children. She typed in "adoption" and got six hundred thousand entries. Well, she thought, clicking off ten of them and beginning to read, this will certainly take up my time. Months perhaps. Minutes, hours, weeks, months.

Every state had laws about adoption. Most mandated waiting at least seventy-two hours after the birth before the birth mother could sign away her rights. And each state had laws on advertising. In Ohio, it was outlawed. In Pennsylvania, it was permitted. Yet people from Ohio adopted all the time. She thought about this, pretended she lived in Ohio and asked herself what she would do, how she would proceed, especially if she didn't luck out with the agencies. By the time she got to the sixtieth entry, it was clear that private adoptions went on everywhere. So. People who wanted to give up children and those who wanted to adopt had to get information from somewhere. Where did they start? They either went to agencies or they went to private adoption services or private attorneys or—? The phone numbers had to be listed somewhere.

When she looked at the clock, it was after three. She wished she could talk to someone, but there was no one she could call at this hour. Not Lizzie, who was usually good to talk to about most everything. Not Richard, who by now was probably at home.

She put a legal pad on her lap, clicked to start a fresh search, and typed in "adoptions, Ohio." This list was slightly more manageable. If a Web site gave her an 800 number, she wrote it on the pad. If the ad suggested a small or private operation, she wrote down the number. By morning, she had a couple of pages of phone numbers. She was also, finally, sleepy. She would do the same thing for Pennsylvania and West Virginia. She would start with the tristate area and move on from there if nothing panned out.

She went to bed, comforted that she had work to do. She put her notes in a drawer in the dining room. The African sculptures on the shelves, the mosaic jars, kept her secret. The pregnant woman in mahogany, the teak man with the long legs, stood there as before, without a whisper about Marina's middle-of-the-night work.

Her phone rang at seven in the morning. "I'm a block away," he said. "I'm practically there."

When she opened the door, he hurried in, got the door closed behind him, and held her in a crushing embrace. "We're losing our minds."

She smelled his soap, could feel his skin damp under his shirt.

"I didn't sleep."

"Neither did I."

He let her go and she felt herself floating, light-headed. "Give me a minute." She felt for the couch and sat down.

He stood across from her. She saw he was willing himself to let her go. She felt the possibility of a new contract between them. No touching. Fewer phone calls. A visit or two, then no more. Send some lackey with her mail. Get to important business. He was a man, a cop. He had to have thoughts like that.

"I need to get some coffee," he said awkwardly. "I left the house in a rush. I do need to get in early. It's just that you're right on the way. I had to stop."

She saw him again for the first time, hands in his pockets, awkward. Something made her want to challenge him. "You found this place for me. Remember?"

"I know I did. It's not lost on me, believe me."

"I'll make coffee. Don't go yet."

She stood, and everything changed. The new contract got thrown out. He held her again for a long time and then his hands were all over her. He moved her toward the bedroom, groaning, "I have no time."

"Then don't."

"Too late." He took time only to put the gun holster on

the bureau. Then his clothes were off, his carefully pressed clothes, thrown, landing somewhere between the chair and floor. He was hard, ready for her, touching her face, her breasts, trying to slow himself down.

"It's okay," she said. "I'm ready, too."

He seemed angry. He said, "I don't want it this way, fast."

"Yes, you do," she said. "No lies here." What was the use of lies?

They made love, but fast, so fast, you could feel the violence and impatience of it. In all her time with Michael, even in the early days, it had never been like this, desperate. Hard cock, gun, not lost on her. The way he came at her, separated her legs, touched her, entered her, rocked her so hard she almost couldn't breathe, it didn't escape her. The wanting to give up, the little death, she was very aware, only marveled that she had escaped it all her life.

They lay there exhausted. The clock ticked a breathless sound. The air had the hum of morning—cars, radios, a million coffeemakers starting up. His skin smelled strongly of sex. It mixed with the sharp smell of soap.

"You're not sorry?" he asked.

She shook her head. Sorry, no. Surprised at herself, yes, even shocked, unable to think what all this meant, yes.

He shook his head, laughing a little. "I'm not very interesting. I think you're making me up."

She didn't know what to say to that. Maybe it was true.

He got up and began looking for his clothes.

"I'll make coffee. Even if you can't stay."

"I'll be out there in a minute."

She heard him in the bathroom, peeing, and was touched by the simple fact of it. She tried not to think about his wife and family or about people getting hurt. She was someone else, not fucking saintly, not fucking saintly at all. She could hear him dressing. She saw him dragging his remaining clothes into the living room so he could see her while he buttoned his shirt.

He watched her while she measured and poured water in the machine for coffee. The way he looked at her did things to her. Ridiculous physical things. Stomach dropping, throat coated with phlegm, hands shaking, knees weak. Measurable, chemical, physical things. Would it all disappear like a dream? If she could get out into the world again and be her old self, would it all go away? If she got cast in something, got a role, would this fade? Just as easily as it had come on? Was it just lust? Or grief? The well-known reaction of the bereaved—banging death.

"We . . . think we might have something," Christie said suddenly.

"What?"

"It's crazy."

"What?"

"Well, one of the names that came up in connection with Volbrecht was Anton. There was an Anton Vradek, sometimes Vladic, sometimes, we think, Anthony Woods. Probably a couple of other names in there. And when they ran him, they discovered he's connected with a woman named Emily Rogers, and that's awfully close to—"

"The name of the woman who rented the apartment. And the guy who paid the rent. Tony Anderson." Something was happening.

"It gets better. Bigger and better. I can't tell you how, how hopeful I am, when things start to crack."

"You have that much?"

"I don't know. It's possible. The Bureau was running checks all night. One guy—he's pretty okay—I told him to call me if he saw anything at all. He called me at six this morning."

She wanted to know everything, but he was late already.

"There might be a group . . . a whole, what-do-you-call-it, ring, involved," he said, as if ordinary terms were escaping him.

She hurried to take the coffeepot off its burner and said, "Here. This has a pour and brew." She poured into one of the flowered mugs the anthropologist had left.

"Okay. So. What they have on Emily Rogers is a series of allegations, complaints, mostly, in an article by some guy from *The New York Times* about girls in Mexico who say she befriended them, got their babies, and then dumped some of the girls on the street in San Antonio. Others she left back in Mexico but didn't pay them. This was five years ago. The woman called herself Emelia Rodriguez, but one of the girls got suspicious and looked in her wallet and saw something with 'Emily Rogers' on it, and another person, months later, described the same woman. The FBI had a file on her from four years before: she was suspected of running a baby farm. Then she disappeared, and nothing else. Not for a long time. Oh, believe me, they called her up on this case, but they couldn't locate her. What they don't have is a clue about where she sold the babies or where she's gone."

"But if some guy in Ohio or somewhere," she said, "bought Justin—"

"What?"

"It means he's alive."

"Maybe."

"The alternative is something I can't get my mind around."

He nodded. "The names are linked. That's what we have. Volbrecht was arrested once on a possession of weapons charge and the guy who paid his bail was *Antoni*o Vradek. A woman named Selma Louise Jackson once served a little time for credit card fraud. Back a ways. The person who paid her bail was Anton Vladic. But get this. The photos of the Jackson woman match the description of this Emily-Emelia woman that *The New York Times* guy got from the Mexican girls. We only know that after the fact. This Emily then gets named in the black market baby trade. It's wild, like I said. FBI is stepping it up big to find her."

"Emelia Rodriguez," she said. "Anton Vladic."

"He has lots of names. They all do."

"I sort of had myself convinced Anton was half in my imagination."

Richard put his mug on the kitchen counter. "You can't think like that. The guy would like to see you dead.

You have to remember *he's very real*. And his honey Emelia can't be any sweetheart. And if they were working out of the North Side, they probably know the city."

Marina poured herself a cup of coffee, too. She still felt light-headed, jet-lagged, beside herself.

Richard drank his coffee very fast, too fast for how hot it was. "I've got to get in," he said. "I want to be with you differently, not like this."

She took his hand and walked him to the door. He looked over at her computer.

"Are you keeping yourself busy?"

"Kind of."

As she saw him out, touching the back of his head, then his shoulder, she wondered if he should be telling her anything of the investigation. She'd thought she wanted it, something to go on that she could do at the computer, something to help. But now she felt foolish and useless, a tiny unnecessary cog in a big operation.

She watched him walk down the stairs and out the front door. She could see him through the glass panels, and then he disappeared.

■   ■

"HE LOOKS GREAT IN IT, SEE," VALERIE SAID. AND THEN TO the baby Joshua, she murmured, "Don't I have great taste, huh? Don't I have the best taste? Oh, look at him. See how he laughs. He likes me."

Katie thought she was a little strange, this mother who seemed so surprised her child liked her. "Sure he does," Katie said evenly.

"Come on, let's go. You can carry him to the car if you like."

"It's my job," Katie said. One of her jobs. She had left *In Pittsburgh* to take the nanny job three days after Valerie called and before she ever typed up the ad, but when her boss protested, she gave him another week of her time, putting Valerie off. Then she got a brainstorm and told her boss she could do both jobs just fine if he bought her a cell phone. He agreed and she worked on the classified column in and around the baby care. She felt in her purse for her phone and then, finding it, lifted Joshua up and placed his head over her left shoulder. Classic position. He could see. He could feel her heartbeat.

Valerie wore a pantsuit of beautifully woven linen. Must have been mighty expensive. The woman liked to get decked out. Katie felt ridiculously awkward in her shorts and T-shirt, going off to lunch at one of the fancier places, but Valerie insisted they go. She said, "Face facts, the baby is happy if the mother is happy. My husband is always saying we shouldn't go out until we're more used to the baby and have our routines down, but then he doesn't stay home all day."

"Men!" Katie said on cue.

As they left, Katie felt Mrs. Moziak looking out the window, scowling, probably. Why did the woman frown so much? And why did Valerie Emmons keep her on if she was such a meanie? Surely there were other cleaning women.

Valerie said, "I'll hold Josh at the restaurant part of the time so you can eat."

"Well, it's up to you, but I'd like to do my job."

Together they strapped the baby into his car seat. He gurgled, making friendly babbling sounds. "I'm not very natural at using all this gear," Valerie said. And Katie could see that she wasn't, the way Valerie fumbled and finally let her take over. Still, the baby looked at his mother with—what other word was there for it?—love.

This was the third lunch out in a little over a week since Katie came on the job on July 13. It was already the second time for The Top Deck, the most upscale of the local restaurants. Well, money was obviously no problem.

The BMW hummed along. Katie said, "I promise I'll buy a few nice dresses with my second paycheck. The first I needed for some other things, but I'll get it together. I know I'm not properly dressed to go out."

"Oh, you're fine." Valerie waved a hand. "Tell you what,

I'll give you some things I'm not wearing. Or we could go shopping."

"Jeez. No, I wasn't trying to beg. I'm sorry I said anything. It's just that my crowd doesn't get dressed up much."

"I didn't think of it as begging," Valerie said. "Sometimes I don't know what to do with what I have."

Valerie had the kind of car seat that could be strapped to a chair. Katie carried it in with them. A hostess seated them on a back porch, where there was a complicated system of awnings in case of rain. A waitress came running to help Katie strap the seat to the chair next to hers. "Oh, your baby is so cute," the waitress said. "He looks like you."

Katie could feel a deep blush beginning. She said, hurriedly, "Oh, I'm just the nanny." And because she'd seen Valerie's face fall, she kept talking even after the waitress left. "You can be my little date," she said to Joshua. "My little guy."

Valerie said matter-of-factly to Katie, "He's a passport. Seems to be the way it works. Take a cute kid with you and you get the treatment." Then she ordered herself a martini and an appetizer of sausage and polenta. She kept staring at the menu long after she'd made this selection. "I'm planning on really enjoying myself this afternoon," she said.

Katie ordered iced tea and baby salmon crepes.

"Poor baby," Valerie said.

Katie didn't know what she meant. She would have sworn it had something to do with the iced tea.

"My martini is going to feel like too much of an indulgence. I think I'll cancel it."

"You want me to go catch her before they make it or put it on the bill?"

"Oh, don't bother."

Katie felt uncertain. She still could not get used to spending money needlessly. In the mirror on the far wall she saw herself and felt ashamed—she didn't know how to use makeup, she needed a haircut, she looked like a kid of eighteen, somebody who hadn't matured.

"If I end up drinking it, you can drive home," Valerie

said. "I have my rules. You wouldn't mind driving my car?"

"Heck, no!"

The baby laughed, as if approving.

"He thinks we're okay."

AT TWO-THIRTY, VALERIE WENT TO TAKE A NAP EVEN THOUGH she hadn't had the martini after all. Katie played with the baby out on the deck for almost an hour and as soon as Joshua went to sleep, she carried him into the nursery. Then she went back outside, passing Mrs. Moziak, who was still cleaning the kitchen but hadn't begun on the floor yet. The house was a museum of cleanliness. "I'll go back in through the other door," Katie assured her, continuing, "if he wakes up."

"Is no matter," Mrs. Moziak said. She gave the impression she was about to say something else, but then she didn't. Katie sat at the heavy wrought-iron table and began to retrieve phone calls that had come in for ads, and then she began making her return calls.

Mrs. Moziak came outside. She shook a few cloths over the balcony, taking a long time. Katie watched her, puzzled. Mrs. Moziak sighed.

"Everything all right?" Katie asked.

Suddenly, when Mrs. Moziak turned, the scowl was gone. She seemed not so much angry, but nervous.

"What is it?"

"Very glad you are work here," Mrs. Moziak said.

"Oh. Thank you."

"She isn't be good with the baby before you."

"Oh. Really? In what way?"

Mrs. Moziak shrugged. "Not . . ." She made a repeated jerky movement with her hands.

"Not quick," Katie filled in. "She said so herself. Seems to be kind of awkward. So much for 'natural,' huh? You wonder why."

"Because baby adopted."

"Oh. Oh. Now, that makes sense."

"Just got him. From Russia."

"Oh. Well, jeez. I'm getting the picture much better now. Wow."

■   ■

CHRISTIE TOOK THE CALL FROM THE STATE POLICE CAPTAIN, WHO had his troops combing the grounds where Volbrecht's body had been found.

"We got a baby," Captain Evans said. "Remains of a baby. And a whole bunch else. It don't look good."

Richard felt sick. Images of Ryan and Karen's faces flashed before him. "What else?"

"Blankets, purse, garbage. A woman's purse, which has some stuff with the name Benedict in it. That's the woman who tried to save the kid, right? And the big find is the outfit, the kid's overalls and the shirt with the sail-boats on it."

He hung up, called the Feds, gathered his men, and told them. He knew it would be on the news in a matter of hours, so he clenched his fists and called Karen Graves. He told her he was coming for a visit.

When he got there, he wanted more than anything to change the expression on her face. He couldn't think how. She would hear it on the news if not from him. A child's body had been found, he said, and that was all they knew at this point. He was going to have a look.

Karen asked if she could go with him.

"No," he said. "Not yet. I want to check this out. Could be unrelated." He didn't for a moment believe it. "Where's Ryan?"

"On the road."

"Your parents went home?"

"Yesterday."

He said, "I'm calling a car for you. I'll get one of the po-lice to stay with you. I don't want you to be alone."

"Could I call Marina?"

"Okay. Okay, but make sure she knows we don't know anything yet." It was clear the phone call woke Marina. Karen began to explain, but handed him the phone. He told Marina what was happening. He heard in the almost silence that she was crying. He asked her to be strong for Karen's sake. He looked up from the phone. Karen was straightening a plant on a table, plucking a dead leaf from it, and carrying that to the kitchen. He saw her go into the bedroom and come out with a sweater. He heard Marina say the police should bring Karen to her place, and he had to admit it was the best thing to do. He promised he would call her as soon as he knew something.

His stomach churned. After making his call, he left Karen and got into his car, which sat in the driveway of Gateway Towers with the lights flashing. Shutting the flashers off, he started out.

He wished it hadn't been the State Police. The body found out there. And so long after the fact. He didn't think the county coroner, who was not a doctor, but a mortician, could handle the case, and he hoped beyond hope that nothing of the evidence was destroyed before they got their men in. And that Evans and his mortician had put egos aside and called someone else in. He hoped it was Bruegger, the anthropology prof from the university that lots of the outlying areas pulled in on cases like this. Handsome fellow who handled the bones of the dead carefully, like artwork in his fine-boned hands. Bruegger hadn't been known to give a wrong answer yet, and everybody knew it.

He drove, thinking about Marina's purse, the garbage, blankets, a child's clothing, all being found together. Volbrecht and his accomplice must have buried everything to do with the apartment and the Graves child; they'd left the apartment "clean," in the sense of usable evidence. The prints and fibers the FBI had gathered there might be useful later, after the fact, as evidence once someone was found, but they hadn't been useful yet.

Joe and Vol—he and the other police spoke their names with split-second pauses before and after, as if they were naming cartoon characters—must have driven right away to Westmoreland County, found themselves some woods. Done a burial job that, given nature, didn't stay buried. And then the accomplice, Joe, killed Volbrecht.

Maybe the other way around. Maybe the two guys fought first. Joe killed Vol, then had to run off and bury the rest of the evidence himself. Big job and he was a slight sort of guy, according to Marina.

Or Marina was wrong, or had been purposely misled, as she worried the other day, and the third guy, Anton, went along with them. Anton and the baby. An argument. Maybe several arguments. The child more dangerous alive than dead ...

Maybe there'd be another body before the day was out. Anton, Joe, this Emelia Rodriguez the FBI was so interested in.

He passed the Pep Boys where he'd pulled off the road, where he'd first touched Marina in the car.

He didn't know what he was in the middle of. Lust, yes, definitely lust. He'd started this thing and he knew he couldn't go on with it. Other people did, but he couldn't. He really was losing his mind. He could hardly bear to go home. He did not want to face his wife, let her look into his eyes. The truth of what he was feeling must surely be naked on his face. And yet, to think of *not* seeing Marina. He couldn't imagine it.

He found his hands shaking. His greatest strength as a cop was that he could always figure people out—what they were doing, what they were trying to do. But here he was, in this thing, and he didn't understand himself. Was it just that she was so beautiful?

The day was steamy with drizzle. Even when the rain let up, there was a haze in the air. The ground at the side of the road looked spongy. Long before he saw the State Police raising arms in greeting, he saw them in his mind's eye, an army of sorts waiting for him. Sleepy, scared, well-meaning, flawed. Defined and focused only when there was something clear like this to get behind.

Bruegger was there. Thank God for that. He nodded and waved as Christie parked. His silvery hair and beard made him stand out from the cops.

"Human child, all right," Bruegger said when Christie approached him. "Boy. Boy child."

Christie felt revulsion rise in him.

Then Bruegger said, "Newborn. Not quite full term."

"What do you mean?"

"Not fully developed. Premature."

■   ■

THE THIRD WEEK OF JULY. MARINA WAS WORKING EIGHT HOURS, twelve hours a day—in the middle of the night, at noon. Just like the police. Just like the Feds.

The bones of a premature child had been buried with her purse and Justin's clothes and ordinary garbage. Time of death, roughly the same time as Volbrecht. Within days anyway. What did it mean? Justin was a substitute for a child who had died. She felt that. Saw it in the remembered image of Joe's face in the apartment.

The woman who answered her first phone call was bright and sympathetic. "You're looking to adopt?"

"I think so," Marina said. "It's a hard decision. I'm . . . I'm trying to gather information."

"Yes, I understand."

"I thought I should get started, anyway—since it takes so long."

"Yes. Our average is a little over a year, well, lately more like two years. We've had a large rise in clients."

"Why is that—the sudden increase?"

"Accessibility, I guess. We put in a Web page and we've been a lot busier. Is that how you found us?"

"Well, yes, but I also found your listing in a book." Marina looked toward the bed where she still had a stack of books underneath. On the legal pad before her was a page of Pennsylvania agencies listed in both sources. Underneath were pages for the other states. "The notation said you find infants."

"We do find infants, yes. Our policy is open adoptions—do you know what those are?"

"Yes, I'd get to meet the birth mother."

"Not only *meet*. In most cases, she'd choose you if you're the one. Our agency starts with a written set of autobiographies of you and your husband and a set of pictures. Then when we have a birth mother who's looking, we give her her pick. If she's interested in a meeting, we contact you and set it up. She gets to refuse after that if it doesn't feel right. And vice versa. We want people to be happy on both ends."

"This must be a large operation."

"There are seven of us, but four are part-time. Yep, things are hopping. Do you want me to send you an application form? I might as well."

Marina said yes. She knew what the next question would be. Something like stage fright came over her when she had to say the lines. For they were lines. A performance. "Marian Blessing. 323 Emerson Street, Pittsburgh, Pennsylvania. 15232." She gave the phone number.

Somewhere in the back of her mind, Marina thought, if she could be someone else in a matter of weeks, couldn't anyone? Who was Joe now? By what name was Emelia Rodriguez known these days?

"I'm putting this in the mail right now," the woman said before ringing off.

Marina made a note next to Sunlight Adoptions and its phone number on her legal pad: "agency, upbeat, seven employees, promotes open adoption." And an X in her "Not likely" column.

What she was looking for was something that felt more *private*, an organization with more that was hidden. While she knew she was repeating everything the FBI was already doing, and doing much better than she could do, while she knew she was spinning her wheels, she couldn't stop herself. Because she had time and patience. What if on the off-chance . . . ?

What else was she to do, sitting there all day? She would not be able to bear it much longer. Witnesses didn't stay hidden. Richard had let that slip. They usually gave up. She was as bad as the rest of them. Risk your life for five minutes of freedom? Yes. Life was outside the doors and inside you were no better off than a convict. Tomorrow or the next day or the next she would not be able to bear it and she would leave the house. In a blond wig or a strange hat or having cut off all her hair. Or just as herself. She didn't know. She only knew she was reaching the limit.

So, she was Marian, a woman asking for information and applications. She always said, "My husband and I are interested . . ." The words at first brought Michael back into the picture. Yet she was someone else, an imaginary Marian. She even had a different self-image. Someone more stolid and slower-moving than Marina. Each day the husband in her mind looked more and more like Richard.

There were times, when she'd been acting, that she'd had to wrestle one image away and let it be replaced by *reality*, by the actor playing the role. Now something similar was happening.

Sometimes she thought about Richard's children, the one pale, towheaded, the other dark. She had seen pictures of them and tried to imagine what they were really like. Richard wanted her to meet them. He was looking for a way, he said, an excuse. Sometimes, as if she were learning a new play, she would imagine a house and weekend visits, growing love between her and the two children. A day at Kennywood, with her going on wild rides, being whipped into circles, just to please them.

She tried not to leave too much information on the voice mail systems since she wanted the sound of a voice at the other end. It was voices she judged for their sound of truth. The people who took Justin—where were they listed, how could she find them?

She opened the door of her apartment and got a rush of fear as she remembered the other apartment, where she'd been caught by Vol. She hadn't been out, except with Richard, and once with an officer who delivered her to her doctor to have her sutures removed. She tiptoed down the stairs to the front hall where there were six mailboxes. She fumbled with the small key she'd been given. There were two pieces of mail for Marian Blessing. She got the wild idea that when she'd filled out the applications, she would walk out the front door to a mail-box. And tell no one. She went back up to the apartment, heart beating hard.

"You get every kind of thing on the Internet," one woman said irritably.

"I know that. But how do I sort it out?"

"Slowly. Do you know that some Web sites are nothing more than some jerk printing all the slimy ads he's found in the newspapers?"

Marina felt a thrill, which she tried to cover over. "Sets of newspaper ads. They're just buried in there with every-thing else?"

"They say something like, 'Adoption Advice,' or 'Legal Counsel,' or 'Are you pregnant?' and then they give a phone number." There was a long pause. "Don't fall for the junk, honey. This can be a sad business."

There were six hundred thousand entries on the Net. She'd been making calls to newspapers, large and small, in Ohio and West Virginia and other cities in Pennsylvania, only to be met with resistance when she asked them to search their files for her. But somewhere down the list—she only needed patience, entry three hundred thousand, per-haps—were newspaper ads.

When she wasn't working, she put all of her notes away in a sideboard drawer in the dining room. It would be no help to Richard to know how desperately she worked at something nobody wanted her to do in the first place. Her list probably amounted to nothing, and he might try to discourage her from continuing expensive, time-consuming work he would not be able to use.

The lab experts, poring over the contents of the buried garbage, well, that was real, that was useful. Garbage with the value of diamonds because there might be a good print in there somewhere or a strand of thread from Anton's clothing or a bit of a footprint from his shoe.

Finally she began to find the kind of entry she was looking for—attorneys working on their own, promising privacy, discretion. She tried to narrow the list to places a day's drive from Pittsburgh. Four, she had four she wanted to pursue.

She made an omelet, stood at the window, eating. The mailman sauntered down the street, took out a key, came in, went out. She tiptoed downstairs more easily than she had the day before, put two pieces of outgoing mail in the box, and gathered three pieces that had come in— more applications. She touched one of the small window panels at the side of the front door. Not today, not yet, she thought, as she looked out.

She knew about the Martindale Hubbell directory because she had helped Michael fill out his own application to be listed. When she got upstairs again, she typed in "Martindale.com" and the page assembled before her on the monitor.

Of the four names she searched: The man from Indiana was not listed. The two men from Pennsylvania had bare, complimentary listings, but at least she had addresses and phone numbers for them now. The attorney from Ohio had a formal listing. Born in Pittsburgh. Attended law school in Pittsburgh. Practiced in Ohio. Her stomach fluttered. She studied the entry as if it would yield something else.

The phone rang. She let the Internet connection terminate, and picked up the phone, thinking it was Richard.

"Checking in," Michael said. He had begun calling her several times a day with announcements—he planned to get some therapy, he thought he'd change law firms, he'd been thinking about shifting and working in business. Today he said, "I get my evaluation later today. If they're critical, I don't plan to stay here."

"Maybe it'll be all right."

She didn't want to encourage his dependence on her, but the question she had on her mind was one he could answer, and she spoke it before she could stop herself. "Is there anything—a CD, a book—that gives more detail than Martindale Hubbell? Biographies, work histories?"

"What's this for?"

"It's a little job I'm doing for someone. Research."

"We have an annotated list of area lawyers here at the office. . . . We don't deal with anyone without checking out everything—disbarments, black marks, whatever. You want me to see if I can find it?"

"Yes."

"And bring it?"

"Yes."

"When?"

"Your choice."

He suggested nine that evening. Good, she thought, he's having dinner with Kendall. She gave him the address.

The day stretched out, long and full of anxiety. Even a short phone call from Richard didn't help. He was busy and she told him it was all right, she was letting Michael visit. You can't hold out forever, he said. He wanted to know, did she think Michael's anger was under control? Yes, she said, she thought so.

At nine, she opened the door. Michael stood there, looking freshly scrubbed. And hurt. It broke her heart.

"What are you *doing*? What's this about?" he wanted to know, meaning everything, apparently. His arm swept the apartment.

After she closed the door and led him to the sofa, she said, "I'm reading about lawyers, just in case one was involved in the Graves case. I'm trying to figure things out."

He shook his head. "You can't."

She said, "I know. I know it's dumb, but I'm trying anyway. It seems to be necessary."

"Why?"

"I have time. If the fibers people spend eight days looking at a couple of hairs, I can read about lawyers, just in case."

He handed her a stapled sheaf of papers, showing her how it was organized, the crowded little symbols for number of years practicing, black circles for complaints. Leafing through the list, she asked, "What happened today?"

"They didn't fire me. It went okay."

"I'm glad. That's really wonderful."

"You look . . . better. You're feeling all right, huh?"

"Yes."

"Good."

She saw, soon enough, that the material he'd given her added little, if anything, to what she knew. There was nothing about the particular lawyer she was interested in. "You want a beer?"

He nodded.

When she brought it to him, he said, "I think you're doing whatever to keep from thinking about us."

"No, that's not it."

"There must be a way we can go to Caldwell again. Maybe she'd even come here."

She shook her head. "I've changed a lot. I'm somewhere else now." She looked at him steadily.

He swallowed hard. He didn't throw anything. His hand tightened around the bottle, that was all. "I don't know what to say except that I want to keep trying."

"Someday, you're going to have such a clear vision—of how I can like you, and love you, and know the marriage is over. It isn't anything I'm taking lightly. It's just what I know."

They were silent with each other for a while.

Michael stayed an hour altogether and it seemed more like three hours. He kissed her on the forehead as he stood to leave. She felt so much anguish for him, for their mistakes with each other, she put her arms around him. When he left, she let herself weep.

She lay awake for a long time.

After a few hours of fitful sleep, she got up again, wondering what work she would be able to do on the weekend. She looked at her list. She logged on to the white pages. If the home address and office address matched . . . a small operation, maybe a seedy operation.

She stopped, startled by what she saw. The attorney, who had been born in Pittsburgh and educated at Duquesne Law School, also lived in Pittsburgh, even now. Lived in Pittsburgh, practiced in Ohio.

On Monday, she called the Duquesne Law School and asked for the records department. She said she was calling from Picking, Martin, Reese, and Pule. When the woman who answered her call asked, "What was your name again?"—a phrase Marina hated, but which had assumed accuracy now that names were fluid, hers included—she froze, then answered, "Kendall," surprising herself.

The woman told her the man she was checking out was local all the way. "Home was 281 Wylie Avenue. High school was Fifth Avenue."

"Fifth Avenue? Is that a name or an address?"

"Name. Hill District. It doesn't exist anymore. High school. Belonged to a couple of clubs. Future Teachers. Business Club. Here at Duquesne, let's see. Business Club, again. Chess Club. Is this at all helpful?"

"Sure," Marina said. "Everything helps."

"Your bosses are awfully thorough."

"They really are. They're real sticklers."

She got on line and, after a few clicks, typed in "281 Wylie Avenue." A map appeared. The map showed Wylie Avenue and the streets that were near to it.

She started with a small grocery store. The owner had taken over the store only ten years ago, but he gave her some names to call, people who'd lived in the neighborhood, he said, forever.

She said she was working on a high-school reunion.

She said she was writing for *American Lawyer* magazine.

One man and two women remembered things. *Shy boy, smart in school. An ambitious kid, sold tickets to things, his own little business, I don't know where he got them, sports events, concerts, all kinds of things. Just a teenager. Smart and a good sense of humor. Overweight and he joked about it. They used to call him "Mountain." Didn't let anybody get him down. Took care of his little sister like a champ.*

She had a feeling, she had a feeling.

ON TUESDAY, SHE CALLED THE LAWYER FOR AN APPOINTMENT. She did not pretend she was doing an article on him. She pretended instead that she was trying to adopt a baby.

He said he'd be out of town all week, but he'd send an application, which she could get to work on, and he'd try to find a time to meet her and her husband. The coming Saturday was not out of the question, he said. He had a crushing schedule, but he might be able to meet her very early in the morning before he headed out on a dawn flight.

She told him Saturday was fine.

USUALLY, AT THREE O'CLOCK SHE BEGAN EXPECTING RICHARD'S call. He got there sometime after four, closer to five, most days. They were not calm together. He was inside out, she could see that. And she was not herself, locked up like a criminal. He kissed her eyebrows, her cheeks, her hair, her lips. He told her he loved her and thought about her all day long, through everything he did. He said it was like a joke, how he had resigned himself to the family life he had, and now this.

Would he one day sit his wife down and tell her about Marina? And she? Supposedly truthful. When was she going to tell Michael? And what would she tell him? Would she go through those motions she had heard about from friends, about friends, of filing for divorce, of watching things drag out, of choosing and changing lawyers, of finally getting a piece of paper in the mail, which then, no matter what, shook and depressed her? She wanted to speed up her life so she would know the answers to these things.

ON WEDNESDAY AT THE END OF JULY, A WEEK AFTER THE child's remains had been found, Marina decided it was time to tell Richard how she had spent her days and what she had set in motion.

"Let's order dinner in," he said before she could say anything. She stopped herself and closed the drawer in the dining room where she kept her legal pads full of notes.

"You can stay?"

"They're all going to the ball game tonight. Believe it or not."

"You aren't tempted to go?"

"I could go. For the kids. But I don't want to."

"Go," she said. "This is something I don't want to be responsible for."

"If I go, you know what it'll be like. The kids'll be jumping up and down, I'll forget to notice why. I'll be thinking about Karen and Ryan. I'll be somewhere between the stadium and here. I'll be the ghost at the Boulevard of the Allies exit."

"Wow. You're dramatic, too."

"Basically, I'll be here."

Sometimes she felt she was at his office with him, moving around the gray metal desks and cabinets, becoming at home in the slummy poverty of the Investigative Branch, checking the bulletin boards, the wanted photos, familiar with it all, interview rooms with their big steel squares on the floor for attaching leg shackles.

"I'm supposed to go on vacation next week," Richard said.

The announcement took her completely by surprise.

He took her hand and led her to the sofa.

"Not while the case is unsolved?"

"I had orders to go."

Marina felt she would not breathe. Time with him? Three days away somewhere? Was that possible?

"My family—we've had this apartment booked in Cape May for six months. Other years I've let them book and then at the last minute I haven't gone. I've worked. Maybe gone for two or three days. Two separate cars, that kind of thing."

"They must get really angry."

He nodded.

"But can anyone make you take a vacation while you're still heading up the case? If you don't want to."

"Yes. There are . . . politics involved. I really have no choice. Chief called me in about it."

"That seems crazy." She studied his face. He was drained. He was being pushed aside.

"There's pressure from the Feds to have their crack at the thing. They've been at me from the beginning."

"You told me Horner was a friend."

"Up to a point. Believe me, he'd like to make a big, flashy discovery."

"What if things begin to happen? What if it's time for things to happen?" What had she done, what had she started?

He sighed. He stood up and took off his coat, unstrapped his gun. When he sat again, he said, "Today, all day today, I thought maybe this time I ought to go. It would give me a chance to— You know."

"With your wife, make things better. . . ."

"No. Settle down. Think. Stare at the ocean and think."

"Oh."

"Not to mention, spend a few moments with the kids."

He had to go. Yes, she saw that.

4

MANNY HAS DREAMED, AWAKE AND ASLEEP, THAT ONE DAY HE will be ordering a bagel or putting gas in his car when someone comes up behind him, trench-coated, and suggests they have a little talk. In his daydreams (if they can be called anything so over-the-line of consciousness), he sometimes prevails with a condescending laugh, saying, "I know the law. I don't have to go in with you. You don't have anything better to do than bother private citizens like this?" At other times, he wins his freedom more subtly with, "Sure, if I can be of help . . ." And always to them, the shadowy figures who have come to ruin him, he's a large, sweating, innocent, beleaguered, cooperative, and completely unhelpful man.

At a little after four on the Saturday morning in August when Richard Christie began his vacation (up early, having black coffee, putting rafts and shopping bags full of provisions into the car), Manny passed through the basement and into the garage of his small house in Crafton, getting ready to make the drive to his office. In the still dark, as he backed his car out of the garage, two men came up to him. "We were just about to knock, but here you are," one said.

The two men spoke over each other. "Excuse our oddly timed visit," the one said, "but we're pretty backed up." The other was saying, "We have such a full plate these days, you're just the lucky one who gets the early-morning call."

One man was black, one was white, both were dressed in ties and sport coats. He saw them mostly shoulder to waist through his car window.

Had Anton sent them—not detectives at all, only pretenders—or were they the shadowy figures he had dreamed of these last fifteen years? In the rearview mirror, parked on the street, was a car he didn't recognize. By the time he looked back to the men, they had identity cards out. "FBI," the white man said. "Special Agent Terrence."

"Pittsburgh Police. Detective Dolan," the black man said. "Artie Dolan."

They asked if he would help them out by coming to the Investigative Branch in East Liberty and answering some questions about the Justin Graves case. Manny said he would. He had no choice. What if he refused and continued on his way, going to his office across the border in Ohio, where a couple of adoptive parents were supposed to meet him? These detectives might try to come along, or worse, tail him and get a look at the couple, maybe later follow *them*, and eventually talk to them. What if they went through his paperwork—there were no records on Manny's books about this couple, and that in itself would look bad. Manny had kept it down to two brief phone conversations. His only "record" was a phone number jotted into the yellow pages of the phone book, near "Churches." So, better he should go with the men and let the couple go to the Ohio office, look for him, try to get into the building, eventually leave. The couple would be upset, he knew, but he could call them later with some excuse.

And maybe he'd have to ditch the new clients if they took a certain tone of voice with him or if things were heating up on his end. The Blessings. Marian and Michael Blessing. Pretty names. He expected them to be pretty people.

But when these men, dressed in plainclothes, stopped him as he was pulling out of his garage, and showed their badges, Manny began to shake. They asked him to park

for a moment and get out of his car. He hated that he was
shaking.

"Taking a trip?"

"No, going to work."

"You keep the same hours we do. Saturday, to boot. We
knew that, though. Your secretary told us you were always
up at four, so we figured, go with the luck, go with the
need." Then they asked if he would give up a day to help
them, because they were at a crucial place in the investigation, and he said he would. "If you want to put your car
back in the garage, we'll drive you down to the station,"
Terrence said. "Bring you right back."

He told them he would rather have his car with him.

Detective Dolan said that was fine.

He was not under arrest, then.

He said he just needed to close up the garage. He could
do it from his car with the remote, but instead he went inside and used the wall button, ducking out under the
closing door. Maybe they'd be impressed that, big as he
was, he could manage such a move. He worked at saunter-
ing back to them. "What's this about?" he asked, as if they
had not already said.

"You're somebody we thought could help in a case
we're investigating. Pretty well-known case. Lots of media
coverage. The Graves baby."

Manny was aware of the sound of his own breathing.
Did they hear it? He had to admit he'd read about the
Graves baby. Who hadn't? "Don't see how I could be of
help on that one," he said. "That was kidnapping."

He let them usher him to his own car.

Dolan opened the driver's door for him and waited
while he got in. Manny felt Dolan's arm brush his shoulder as the detective reached around to unlock the rear
door. He could hear Dolan getting into the backseat.

"What kind of work you doing this morning?" Terrence
asked through the window.

He lied, said he'd agreed to meet a client at the client's
home before the guy started out early on a trip. "Problem

with a son in lots of trouble," he said. The detectives grunted absently. He hoped that meant they bought it, hoped they didn't have someone drive to the Ohio office and run into the Blessings banging at the doors.

"We could wait until you've seen your client."

"I'll give him a call in a couple of minutes," he said, looking at his watch. "His business with his boy can wait. He just got antsy." His plan was that when they got to someplace—a parking lot, the police station—where he could ask for privacy, he would dial Emelia's number and let it ring once. Dial it again and let it ring twice, cutting it off during the second ring. He would pretend all the while to be talking to some guy who was about to take a trip. Even while he was doing his act, if the system worked as it was supposed to, Emelia would be packing her bags.

"Good enough."

Keep your head, he told himself.

Now he sits in an interview room at the East Liberty office, waiting. It might be a cubicle in an army barracks, seven feet square, with gray steel tables, institutional chairs, windowless walls. It's cozy in its contained way, in its institutional, hardworking, schoolroomish way, except for the plate on the floor intended for leg shackles. Whew, that scares his heart rate up.

On the tabletop are the scratchings of the men who have waited here. Doodles in the form of triangles, mostly, some squares, some hexes, all angles—the angles of tension. With only a line or two, he could make clean triangles everywhere, isosceles, equilateral—the words for the shapes coming back to him. The tabletop is like a child's puzzle and he studies it, making imaginary lines with his finger. He has been waiting for a long time; it's now nearly six in the morning. The office seems under-manned and sleepy and not at all cranked up to do any hard business. Why question him, then, at this hour? He makes a goal to leave in two hours. In two hours a little anger would be in order and he can insist on getting out of there. He makes a vow that he will not mention Emelia's name no matter what.

The door opens. The compact black man enters, and extends a hand. "Artie Dolan. Did I say?" He smiles as if they will be friends.

Even back at the house, he liked this man with the sweet face, dreamy eyes.

"We never got to ask you if you had any breakfast before we asked you to come in and help us," Artie said. "We always order things in here. Our eight meals a day, we always say. What can we get you?"

"Will I be here long?"

"Might as well eat. How long, it's hard to say, but of course we'll be as efficient as we can be."

Detective Dolan was so muscular he seemed to be bursting out of his clothes, but he was only about five-seven. Manny guessed this was a man who had *developed* himself, taken frailty and changed it. He had good bones, or whatever it was that made a handsome face. His eyes were almost green, with thick lashes. He did not seem old or angry or rough. He was saying to Manny, "I still eat a high-protein, cholesterol breakfast myself, but most of the guys here"—he paused and leaned forward almost conspiratorially—"love their sweets, so we get every sort of thing in here. What'll it be, couple of donuts, or you want eggs and hash browns and bacon, like me?"

"I'll have what you're having," Manny said. "How much?" He reached into a pocket.

Artie Dolan waved the money back to where it came from. "Our greasy spoons around here are the best in the city," he said. "The real old-fashioned kind of place, where your whole breakfast comes to about three bucks. If that. I love that kind of place."

"Me, too," Manny said.

"Owned by Greeks. They're good with restaurants, for some reason. It's in their genes. You Greek?"

"Who knows if," Manny laughed, "there might be a *little* bit of Greek in me, too. We don't know for sure, except the Italian and Mexican and Hungarian are the biggest part of the mix."

"I have a little bit of Italian, I'm told," Artie says easily.

"My taste buds are Italian. I sure do like Italian food. Those spicy olives, everything."

Manny never knows who will be repulsed by his weight and who will embrace it. He has always been large. As a five-year-old boy he was obese, and he can't imagine what it would feel like to be thin, even though there's that saying about a thin person inside every fat person. "Are you the one I'm talking to?" he asks Dolan.

"Yeah. In two minutes. Let me just order the breakfast."

Artie leaves the door open when he goes out to give directions to one of the officers out there. The other guy nods and picks up a phone and consults a bulletin board. He can hear Artie saying something about knocking on their door as soon as it comes. So. Maybe they won't be slamming him up against any walls. Manny looks at his watch. It's now six in the morning. Artie will go off duty at eight, probably, which means the questioning should be finished by then. Surely they won't want somebody else to take over partway through. Leave at eight is his goal.

Artie Dolan comes back in, closes the door, and sits down. In hand is a file folder and a notebook he did not have before. "I usually start at eight, but I'm doing a double shift today. Or rather last night. Whatever."

Manny feels sweat running down his neck. "Okay," he says.

"You being a lawyer and that you've done some adoptions, we wanted to talk to you. Your name has come up in our computer. Probably not all you do, I know . . ."

"Hardly," Manny says. "That's a very small portion of my work."

"I understand. We need some help in how the routine private adoptions are done and how, if somebody were selling a baby, how that might be done. So you could be very helpful if you would just share with us the kind of information—well, you'll see. Simple questions. Like how do most people get your name, how do they contact you, what happens first, second, third. That kind of thing. Routines."

Manny said, "Every once in a while I put an ad in the paper. I don't overadvertise, because most people who are interested look for a long time and there aren't likely to be that many matches out there—well, that many *babies*."

"What's a match?"

"A couple looking and a woman—usually a single woman—wanting to give up a baby."

"The mothers must be hard to find."

"They are. Few and far between."

"How do you find them?"

"They . . . they see the ad."

"Okay. Makes sense. How would you say they make a choice? Why choose you rather than some agency or something. What is it, like Catholic Charities and those kind of places?"

"I'm private. Circumspect. Efficient."

"Good enough. You pay more than some of the others?"

"Pay isn't the right word."

"But there's more money for the mother?"

"Sometimes a little more."

"Do you get many African American mothers—I wouldn't think so, I'm just curious how this works," Dolan asks, his face taking on a sad expression.

Manny admits, "Most of the couples I get are asking for Caucasian babies."

Dolan nods thoughtfully. "So, okay, now tell me about the couples. Like, a typical case. When they come in, what they ask, what paperwork you do, how the court hearings go."

■   ■

AND NOW HIS WAS THE CAR WITH THE CHILDREN KNEELING on the backseat, waving at strangers, and being ordered to dip back down into their seat belts. His was the car with bicycles hanging off it, and coolers, swimsuits, boogie boards, and other brightly colored things creeping up toward the rear windows, advertising destination.

"You're thinking about work," she said. "I hope you're going to figure out a way to let that go."

"Daddy, tell him to quit shoving the shovel into my leg. My leg is all red."

"Shoving the shovel," Eric chanted.

Catherine turned around and said angrily, "Eric, those are for the beach. Stop it or you don't go to the beach."

"Ha. Where would I go, then?"

"We'll lock you in the room."

"I'd climb out."

"We'll tie you up."

"Oh, terrific," Christie said, regretting his words immediately, but Catherine's limp promises of violence always set his teeth on edge. He reached over and pushed the odometer button until the numbers came up all zeros.

A silence. Eric and Julia, with wide eyes and almost-held breaths, were watching, as children do, when they know the real battle is being waged by the parents.

"Do you have that blue bag with you, Eric?" Christie asked finally. He railroaded through the "What bag?" and "Do you mean the Gap bag?" and simply said, "Put everything back in there. Now. Right now."

He heard movement, and since there was no protest from Julia, he had to assume his son was putting away the neon pink weapons of torture. He knew Catherine was miffed that he was erasing her threats. He'd urged her many times to quit talking that way to the kids. She'd said he was the most serious self-righteous stiff she ever knew. Both things were true: She was hurting the kids with her anger; he was humorless, at least lately.

Marina had urged him not to call her during his two-week vacation. She had told him to spend the time with his family, see what could be repaired, try. Did that mean she didn't want him after all? The idea of being without her didn't seem possible. The idea of actually leaving his family didn't seem possible either. He tried on every day, every hour, the role of a man making a speech to his wife, packing a bag, walking out the door, but the thought of it still shocked him.

He looked over at Catherine, who was shifting around, trying to get comfortable. Her face was angry, as it almost always was. Wasn't it insanity to try to repair things with a woman he didn't love, now that he *felt* love again? And she, whatever she might say, she didn't love him anymore, that was clear. As he drove away from Pittsburgh, passing Donegal, Somerset, then Breezewood exits, he felt he was leaving his real emotional life behind him. A little death. A two-week vacation—unwanted. He felt his fists clench. He saw Catherine watching him.

"This morning," he said, grabbing at something he *could* talk about, and that full of tension, too, "they're pulling in this guy that I would have loved to question. I thought the Feds would want him all to themselves. But then Behavioral Science profiled the guy as somebody who would crumble better if we had a low-key, *local*, minority kind of guy question him, and well, there's Artie. Perfect. Since the guy, LaPaglia, grew up in the Hill District. If somebody had to take over, I'd rather it was Artie than anybody else." He couldn't tell if she was listening. "It was unlucky timing for me, though. Something is going to happen. Definitely. Today, tomorrow."

"Life is lousy." Catherine closed her eyes and seemed not to be interested in pursuing the conversation. But then with eyes closed, she asked, "How'd you find this guy?"

His stomach jumped. No escape. "It's wild," he said, his voice going wild as he said the word. He couldn't stop the manic energy rising in him and had no choice but to own it, assign it to the Graves case and not to love and guilt pulling at him. "The woman who tried to save the Graves baby? Well, she got involved again. She's been on her computer contacting all these adoption lawyers, very methodically, and then she started on newspaper ads, and she found one guy she thought might be the right kind of sleazy. She decided she needed to study him, what he was like. She found out where he grew up, called old neighbors. I mean, you wouldn't believe it. Unbelievable amount of work. Heard he had a little sister. Says she wasn't sure why she needed to call these neighbors again two days ago, but she got them talking and, bam, there it was. The sister has a similar name to one that keeps coming up in the case. Little girl who started out as Amelia with an 'A' and then it looks like got to changing the spelling over the years. The Feds had LaPaglia on their list of people they wanted to talk to, but she, the Benedict woman, put them to shame. She got the Amelia connection. Just wouldn't stop until she could hand us the whole package. Wanted something to . . . to give to the Graveses, I guess."

"She sounds kind of nuts."

Catherine's words deflated him. Had he done Marina a disservice, then, in the way he talked about her? He said carefully, "Obsessed, maybe. A natural detective, in a way. She actually made an appointment with the guy. We . . . instructed her not to go. Our idea was to flush him out of his house and pick him up. This morning. That was this morning." He looked at his watch. "It's hard being away from it."

Understatement of the year. It was almost laughable. The case was going to break and he would get no credit; it was some form of spiritual torture sent him, a task of putting aside ego.

He thought of Marina almost laughing when he asked her how she had done it. She told about a word game she used to play. Jotto. Won it every time, she said. Her opponents would be crossing out letters, they'd be scientific, logical, orderly, she said, getting down to five letters and rescrambling those letters, and she would simply go halfway and intuit the answer. It always astounded people, sometimes made them angry, the way she would look at an only partially crossed-out alphabet and guess the secret word. Some people could intuit things. He had no trouble believing that.

"Is that music bothering you?" Catherine asked.

He wasn't sure what he'd been hearing or if he had even heard anything at all. Now that he listened, he heard a man singing slowly and also some child's upbeat rhyming doo-de-doo kind of music. "Yeah."

"Use your earphones," she told the children. "We don't want to listen to two different pieces of music at the same time."

There. He had referred to Marina, more or less naturally, and that was done. It felt like honesty, bringing her up. Honesty, and maybe, too, he was trying to revise, rewrite her role in his life. She was part of the case, an ongoing part of the Graves case. If you took away all feeling, that's who she was. He waited as both of his children plugged themselves in, going the way of technologically induced autism—glazed expressions, slack jaws.

He'd wanted to engineer some kind of meeting between Marina and his kids, but there had been no time. He was prepared for the children to find her amazing but untouchable at first, and for them to come off as unhappy, whiny, uninteresting. At first. Then what? A laugh. A small connection. Stepmothers and split lives and three days here and three days there. He had sworn he would never, ever do that to his children. Did he know himself at all? Did anyone?

He felt Catherine sighing and sighing.

For a long moment, it seemed to him that if Marina were in the seat beside him, all would be well, his life would come together, the children would do as they were told, the car would fill with inventive, alive, playful games set in motion by her, he would be different.

No. She was too good for him. She was smart and artistic, quick, and he was— Oh, what good was he? A decent detective. But clunky, not in her league.

He grabbed again for what he *could* talk about, and told Catherine, "So right about now, they're talking to this lawyer. Big strange guy, apparently. If they can crack him . . ."

"You should have the glory," Catherine said. "You work hard enough for it." She smoothed her dress and dug in her purse for something.

Glory isn't the main thing, he wanted to say, but she was interested in finding a stick of gum, only playing that halfhearted tennis game of marital conversation, lobbing the what-she-thought-he-needed-to-hear ball.

Pennsylvania rolled by, beautiful and lushly green.

"So, if I'm irritable . . ." he said. "To bring a case so far and then have to leave it."

"I know."

HE WILL CALL INTO THE OFFICE AT THEIR FIRST REST STOP and see how Artie is doing. He could do it now, but that would bring work into the car, into their vacation, and he has it in his mind to somehow keep them separate.

He feels naked. He is not wearing his gun. He is not wearing his pager. Catherine took it off his hip and put it on the kitchen table. He didn't want to fight. He left it there until she was in the van and then he went back for it. He didn't have time to get the pack of batteries out of the police car, the Taurus, without her seeing. He turned off the pager and dropped it into his deep left pocket.

He has a persistent uninvited fantasy that intrigues and terrifies him: that while they are on vacation, he will make an excuse some morning to Catherine, early, even before she's fully awake, about some excursion he'd love to make, say down to the wetlands, then he will start out at six or seven in the morning and get to Pittsburgh by two, see Marina for two hours, and start back. Get to his family at midnight. Say something about the car, a muffler problem.

This is how insane he's become.

But now he examines the fantasy cold-bloodedly. The wildlife preserve is something he's been interested in, and he thinks he's mentioned it before, but what if Catherine says she and the children want to come along? What does it mean that he could think up such an elaborate lie?

He knows men who lie all the time and wonders how they do it.

A second image he can't get rid of frightens him, too, but it feels more right. He will tell Catherine. The truth.

And talk to the children in that way parents do in situations like this. Say, "I am moving out because I have to but I still love you very much," and "It's nothing you did, it's something between Mommy and Daddy," and all the rest of it. Things they will never really ever forgive him for. He knows how it goes and yet he imagines making these speeches sometime soon, even if Marina should decide she doesn't want him.

■   ■

THE EGGS HAVE COME AND BEEN EATEN AND EMELIA'S NAME has been mentioned, but not by Manny, no, he didn't break on that one.

By now her bags are packed, by now she is gone. She's fast, she's fast.

But. They knew her name. Manny is sweating even more heavily now, but reluctant to ask how they know so much about his life.

"She's your next of kin?" Dolan said, filling in a form. "If we ever needed to contact someone . . ."

"Why would you bother her?" Manny asked. "I'm not having a heart attack here."

"Let me put it another way. After today, say in six weeks, if you weren't around and we were looking for you, she'd be the person most likely to know you went to Malaysia or Alaska or Hawaii—wherever you vacation. I mean, you're alone. She's the closest relative, right?"

"Yeah, but I don't tell her every place I'm going."

"You're not close?"

"No, not really."

"You're what—forty-something?"

"Forty-eight."

"She's how much younger?"

"Ten years."

"That's a lot." Dolan appeared to dismiss the whole subject. He rubbed his head and said, "Let's get back to business. Like, how many people come to you in a year, would you say?"

But before he could answer, Dolan said, "My parents died when I was real young, too. You were like, what, fifteen. I was seventeen. Man, I was close to my little brother. Essentially I raised him. I was kind of like a father *and* a brother. So it's a no-brainer, I was close to him. Anyway, you were saying—?"

Manny tried to explain the larger numbers of people who called, maybe two hundred, the somewhat smaller numbers who actually sent in applications, maybe a hundred, the smaller number still whom he interviewed, those whose applications were completely filled out and serious, maybe twenty, thirty in a year. He said some years he placed no children, but some years made as many as a half-dozen matches. This his records would show. He did not include in his calculations the dozen or more a year that appeared on no records at all, nowhere except in coded entries in the phone book.

"Your practice floats? You make a good living?"

"Oh, yes." A little money under the floorboards, a substantial amount in the bank, and lots of it paid out to Emelia and her cohorts.

When Emelia found out he'd been called in for questioning, what would she say? What would she tell him to do next? He knows it's all upside down, the way she bosses, always has, even as a five-year-old. "The baby beats the nurse" is a line that comes to him from a play he saw once on one of the few dates he ever had in his life. He had liked the play, but not the woman. He has never liked any woman much in that way. And he knows it's because of Emelia, how close they were. But he has never met anyone else so determined, tough, beautiful. And the truth is, she prides herself on being determined in a way he could never hope to be. She says she is willing to grab whatever she needs when she needs it, and although she tells him she will one day teach him to grab as well, he knows his role is to be the solid one, to balance her selfishness. Always was his role, always was.

Dolan asks the dullest questions. Did he get into adoption because he had been a caretaker once in his life?

He would die for her. That's the truth and he always knew it. What right does Dolan have to feel important because he loved his little brother when he, Manny, raised Emelia, did everything for her, supported her, even put up with a joker like Anton for her. "That's an idea," Manny says, "maybe so."

"Of course, then they get to be teenagers and people must wonder why they wanted to have a kid. I mean, in my experience that's a hard phase. The kids take the reins. You know? Willful."

Yes, he knows. For when he bemoans, even now, his sister's attachment to Anton, she laughs and says they *use* each other, as needed, when needed. Emelia is utterly, utterly free.

He has not met his goal of getting out of there by eight in the morning.

Terrence taps on the door and says, "Can you take a call? I'll sit for a while."

Terrence is not at all friendly like Dolan is. He crosses one leg over another and tries to look comfortable. "You grew up around here?"

"In the Hill."

Terrence explains that he grew up locally, too, in Monessen, went to New York for a while, but what with an aging parent to see to, he thought he'd better come back to the Burgh. Terrence strikes Manny as a man who is constantly trying to be casual, even when Dolan comes back in and they exchange places. Manny is just glad to see Dolan again.

Now Dolan says, "I know it's nowhere near noon, but I'm going to start seeing about lunch. The Greek restaurant is good for tuna melt, a special they sometimes run called 'pastitsio,' and fried chicken. I could show you a whole menu, but those are their best things."

There have been other interruptions. Dolan has to keep taking calls, and several times he's left Manny alone.

At one point Dolan begged his indulgence and brought in a stack of magazines and today's newspaper. The Terrence fellow makes him nervous, but none of them seem to know anything, really. So he must just hold on.

Manny hesitates between pastitsio and fried chicken. Detective Dolan says, "Look, I'll order both and we can split them half and half." He hurries out into the squad room, leaving the door open. Manny can half hear the jokes the detectives make about one another's working habits, desk displays. They are like little kids in school, he thinks. He remembers school desks, the kind with the tops that lift up, secrets held within.

Dolan comes back with a photograph. "Remember anything about her?"

Manny's leg, propped on a chair, falls to the floor. He fumbles for his glasses. At first he thinks it's a photograph of his sister and that she's dead, wounded or dead, and he is almost crying when he gets on his glasses and sees they are photographs of the Benedict woman who got involved in the Baby Graves case.

Manny's body is out of control. His legs want to keep falling even though his feet are on the floor. His large chin quivers. He tries to hide that with a hand. "I'm sorry. I made a mistake. You were talking about my sister a while back and I thought—I got—She's all right, isn't she?"

Dolan seems to search his face. "We could get you a phone and let you call her to make sure. I . . . was trying to show you how one very courageous woman got herself in trouble over the Graves case. Well, you probably read about it in the paper. And I just wanted you to know you could probably make all of that right again if you know anything at all about how this baby was transferred. About where the baby is, anything."

"I don't know anything about it."

"If you know anything at all, even something small, or even if it's that the baby is dead, now would be the time to say it. I'm going to get a phone in here so you can call your sister."

But he's already done that, two times, one ring, then one and a half. And he will not call her on their phone.

■   ■

ANTON DROVE DOWN THE ALLEY A COUPLE OF DAYS AFTER HE got into town, studied the windows, the garage, and even, for a few moments, because no one was around, tried to look past the newspaper into the garage, but he didn't have any luck. He drove to the husband's place of work, wondering which man going into the building and leaving it was Marina's husband. He looked around for someone to ask, but thought better of it. He tried to imagine where the Benedicts might be if their house was closed down, which it seemed to be. It would take time to get that answer.

There were over a hundred motels to choose from. He decided he'd be more anonymous at a chain, so he chose the Best Western in the university area.

Bad news came then. Vol's body found. His picture and Joe's making it into the papers again, suspects, freshened in the minds of the police and the public. He froze up, watching the news. Joe alive, the bitch alive, and what was he to do? Leave town? Go back to Elise? Stay put? He knew what Emelia wanted, and he did, too, to get rid of Joe and the Benedict woman for good. He stayed put. The flap over Vol died down in two days. He wore his dark glasses, extended his stay at the motel, and mostly stayed inside his room for a week.

The second time he ventured down the alley, a neighbor saw him, a man, washing his car, and the man stopped him. "Excuse me, may I help you?"

Anton stopped the car reluctantly. "Just, uh, putting together some roofing estimates on a couple of houses."

The neighbor sputtered, "Well, you can skip me. I have a perfectly good roof."

Anton managed to drive away without saying anything more. And then he stayed away again, waiting to hear on the news that he'd been spotted, but there was nothing. He switched motels to a privately owned place on Ohio River Boulevard.

The next time he dared to drive through the alley, it was nearly midnight on a Friday. He stopped right behind Marina's house, feeling all jittery. This sitting tight was killing him. In town for two weeks and nothing to show for it but fear. A boy walked down the alley, but the kid seemed more nervous about his own safety than curious about Anton. From time to time, Anton checked his rearview mirror, but mostly he watched the house, thinking if he could break in, he could find information that would lead to her somehow. A phone number, an address, a parent.

Something caught his eye. He wasn't sure *what* he'd seen, but there was movement in there. Someone was inside! Not an empty house, after all. If only he could find her alone in there and do it, finally.

Something shifted at the window. He thought, Yeah, she is in there. Her time has come. Make sure the husband is out of the house and then . . . Two women came driving down the alley. He let his foot off the brake of his car, and started forward, leaning toward the passenger seat as if he were trying to keep something from slipping to the floor.

And when he came back at three in the morning he was gratified to see what he thought was a face near the window, just a sketch of a face. A man? Maybe the husband, he thought, up late at night, maybe the husband. And he tried to figure out what to do next. He backed up and tucked the car close to a parking space a couple of houses away.

Not long after that, the back door opened. A guy was coming out. Had he been seen, heard? He slid down in his seat, way down, invisible, his gun drawn. He heard no sounds, no footsteps, not even the gate closing. He did not hear the garage door opening or a car engine. He slid back up again, slowly, carefully, and saw the man heading down the alley on foot, in the other direction. Something about the walk of the man . . . He almost laughed. Could it be? He was almost hysterical with wanting to laugh. The man walked like *Joe*. The explanation came to him, a beat at a time. It was fantastic, perfect. The crazy logic of it! He started the car and followed. It was unmistakably Joe, with his loping walk. And he blessed his luck, his not always good luck, that he happened to be coming by as Joe left the house for—? Where?

What did it mean? Had Joe gotten in and done the job, after all? It looked for all the world as if Joe was making a middle-of-the-night foray to the market.

For a while, Anton ducked behind shelves at the Giant Eagle, watching Joe load up a cart with groceries. Then he thought, Better get out of here, and he went back to the parking lot where he'd kept the motor running in the Escort, Elise's car. Eventually, Joe came out, carrying several heavy bags, not looking around, and certainly paying no attention to the car, which was unfamiliar to him.

Clever Joe. Anton had tried to figure out where Joe would go when the news hit about Vol being dead, but he hadn't come up with this. Clever, stupid Joe.

Did he know where *she* was?

Joe walked fast with his grocery bags. Anton quickly parked the Escort on the street a block away from Marina's house and made his way silently down the alley behind Joe, not too close, until Joe opened the back gate to the house. Then Anton sprinted, got a hand over Joe's mouth, and shoved a gun into his rib cage. One of the bags dropped. Joe managed to hold on to the others. There was a rattle and clink of bottle in the bags in his hand.

Anton said, "Pick up the bag and keep going." He kept his body right up against Joe's while Joe gathered the groceries and used a key to let himself into the kitchen door.

Even after Joe closed the door, Anton kept hold of him, almost an embrace, and said, "You live here? How long?"

"Couple of weeks."

"Done nothing in that time, huh? The bitch is alive, right?"

Joe nodded.

Anton began to get accustomed to the dark. He let Joe go and took a step away and just looked at him for a while, shaking his head. Joe had gotten them all into deep trouble and now the idiot put a set of keys in his pocket as if he belonged here. He saw Joe look at the bags of food without moving toward them. "Why don't you put away your groceries?"

"I don't usually use the refrigerator."

"And why not?"

"Don't want anyone to come in and figure there is anyone here."

"Smart. I guess. You eat spoiled food?"

"I have a system."

"I'll bet you do. You don't turn on lights?"

"No. Never."

"I saw you from the window. A very faint light."

Joe nodded. "Microwave. I knew not to use it at night. I shouldn't have."

"Now you have me to feed."

Joe looked sadly toward the food.

"Just kidding. I'm not going to stay long. I want to know where the bitch is."

"I don't know."

"Don't know." He kept his gun on Joe, who sat down at the kitchen table, all defeat, finally.

"They've got the phone rigged. I know that. It rings twice, then stops, no message, so it must go to where she is. Because otherwise there'd be a backup of messages."

"Call forwarding."

Joe nodded. "I went through every piece of paper she has. I . . . I thought things, like pretending to be offering her an acting job, but I didn't think I could pull it off. And besides, where would I tell her to go that she would believe? I mean, I thought about it. She's not going to give out her address to somebody on the phone, no matter what the person says."

"You're right. I didn't know you could figure the angles like that."

"You never gave me half the credit—"

"You stole a kid from downtown. Broad daylight. Got us all in the newspapers. And you think you're a genius."

Joe sighed. "It was Emelia's idea."

"Yeah? I think it was your idea."

"The one kid died on us, right in the car."

"I know that."

"Emelia said there was a whole lot of money involved, you know, and she didn't want to make the people suspicious—the people who were buying the baby. She told me to do something."

"She didn't tell you to go downtown and take a famous kid!"

Anton knows perfectly well how Emelia gets, passionate and strange. Like a madwoman. She goes into rages. So she went ballistic that day and took it out on Joe. Surely she didn't really expect him to *do* anything. Not anything so risky. But Joe panicked. And then they were all in it. And no way to get out except dump the Graves baby, dump him or kill him. Which they had discussed, him and Emelia, at length, by phone, that afternoon. Until she persuaded him Manny would be able to pull it off, selling the kid.

Now Marina could identify the three men. Two. It's down to two.

"We've got to find your girlfriend," he said. Joe looked up, startled. "There must be some clue here."

Dumb Joe mumbled something or other.

"Or we trick her into coming home, then," Anton said vehemently. "There's got to be a way!"

Joe hung his head and asked, "Can I put these things away now?"

"This is weird, living in the dark."

"The sky will be light soon."

■   ■

RICHARD DOESN'T WANT HER TO, BUT SHE WILL ANYWAY. She's told him as much before he left. She'll visit her mother and sister. She will have a rental car brought to the door, the way Enterprise does it, with one car carrying another. The Enterprise driver will drive off. The slips of paper will say the charge is to Marian Blessing. What could be safer?

Richard will have time to think about his wife, his marriage. He won't have the familiar image of her in the little apartment, waiting for him. She feels lighter now that he is gone, the expectation of parting being the hard part.

"I've never seen you like this," Lizzie told her a week ago.

And it was true, the way she'd taken what she wanted without considering anyone else, it was unlike her. It had felt wonderful, but as soon as Richard announced he was going off with his family, the chink opened up and she didn't feel so much free and vital as she did uncertain.

The small suitcase is all she needs for two days, three if they are calm days, with her family. After that, she's not sure. A drive to Canada, Mexico, Arizona. Suddenly there is no doubt that she wants to be free, at any cost, any danger. She packs the small tweed bag with shorts, a nightgown, T-shirts, two light dresses, a sweater, a sweatshirt, and underwear, seeing at once that all the colors are khakis and greens. Jungle warfare colors. The car rental man will be here in seconds. When her phone rings, just as she puts the small makeup bag in the outer pocket of the suitcase, she assumes it is the Enterprise man saying he has pulled up, or is pulling up downstairs. The zipper sticks, delaying her getting to the phone, so when she does, and the voice on the other end says, "Uh-oh, just a minute, who do I? What number did I get?" She thinks it is certainly the Enterprise man downstairs, lost between his paperwork and the names on the buzzers. "Blessing," she answers, "Marian Blessing," a name she does not like nearly so much as her real name, but the buzzer, she explains, happens to say Amy Bissinger. There is a pause. "Is this Enterprise? Hello?"

"No, I thought I had . . . I'm sorry," the man says, "Amy?" and while he says, hurriedly, "I know it's been a long time but I thought she might still be . . ." she gets a funny feeling, and he adds, "Bissinger, did you say?" and she hangs up. The caller ID device shows the number the man is calling from. She doesn't recognize it. And it's ten numbers—long distance. She understands she has made a grave mistake.

When she hangs up, she is shaking. She tries to replay the voice in her mind to determine if she has heard it before. Her hand still shaking, she writes down the number of the phone from which the call originated, just as the phone rings again, and a voice says clearly, "Enterprise. I'm downstairs, white Ford Tempo."

This voice is different.

"I'll be right there," she says.

Richard warned her. No good. She was caught off guard, expecting the car rental agent. How could she explain it to him, the way her mind made the caller an old friend or lover of Amy Bissinger, the split-second decision she made not to get in the way of a reconnection. Now the memory of the voice makes her shake. She looks out the window. The white Tempo seems to be waiting, waiting. Consulting a small notebook, which she then slips into her purse, she dials the Investigative Branch and asks for Artie Dolan. "He's in conference," she's told.

She says, "Never mind, then." But when the woman asks for a message, she shifts and says, "I'd better talk to him."

In her mind, the man in the Tempo taps his foot with irritation. She should have told him she'd be ten minutes. When Dolan finally comes to the phone, she says, "I had a phone call. I said too much. I was caught off guard. If Commander Christie were around, he would insist on checking out the number. So I thought I'd better report it. I feel . . . really bad. It might be nothing, but—"

"Let's have it," Dolan says. "We'll check on it."

Her head throbs from allowing the fear in.

"You okay?" Dolan asks.

"I'm okay. Going to be okay."

She walks downstairs, carrying her bag. The stairs are unfamiliar. Everything is. The light that hits her when she opens the door and goes outside is an assault, a photographer catching someone in the dark.

The man in the Tempo laconically shows her the windshield wipers and the lights. He flips on the radio and flips it off again. He asks her to sign a piece of paper in four places, which she does, hardly reading a thing, only taking in something about filling the tank again, and calling the company for the return of the vehicle. When the man goes back to his towing vehicle, she sits in the rental car, unmoving. The Enterprise man rolls down his passenger window as he pulls out, and asks, "Everything all right?" Yes, she says. She continues to sit and then very slowly starts up the car and puts it in gear.

She pulls out, stops in the middle of the street to fasten the seat belt and put on the radio. She can hardly breathe.

By the time she reaches the corner, she is almost weeping. Now she sees she might live passably without love, if only she could rent a car, get out of the house, figure out which corner to turn, and when, and why, and go away where nobody can find her.

■   ■

THE CHILD SHE KISSES AT NIGHT IS NOT HERS, NOT YET, maybe never. It's a trick of the mind, isn't it? Sometimes she looks at the birth certificate, which arrived, as Attorney LaPaglia promised it would, a few weeks after the handing over of the child, and she touches the line that says a boy was born to her and her husband on March 14, 1998, in a hospital in New York City. She knows this is how it's done with "amended birth certificates" after adoptions are legalized by the courts. The hospital and the date are the originals, but the new parents' names are substituted for the biological parents' names. The child's new name appears as well. It's an odd process, an elaborate bureaucratic lie, the way the birth mother gets erased. There is supposed to be a hearing and a court process that formalize this erasure, but she and Stephen have been spared that.

She does not know how Attorney LaPaglia got her this birth certificate, with its raised seal and its signatures, but she is grateful, grateful that there was no court process, no triallike session in which her fitness was measured. An avoidance of failure, a side-stepping. Valerie takes off her reading glasses and looks out the window of the room her husband uses as a study. When she hears a small noise at the door, it makes her jump.

"Oh, sorry. You're doing something important?" Katie asks her.

"Nothing much. Going through my papers."

"You want me to take him for a walk?"

"Good idea. It's so hot, though. Don't put much on him."

"Okay."

Some people can have one baby after another, and she, after a million tries, nothing. Nothing, even the first adoption ending in tragedy, and things worse and worse in the marriage. And now this son, a baby, fixing things, pulling things together.

"You don't want to walk with us?"

"No."

"You should spend more time with him."

"What?"

Katie is leaning forward a little. She looks owly and earnest in spite of the wild hair. "I'm sorry to be pushy, but . . . I think he needs the attention."

"What makes you say that?"

"Just the way he keeps looking toward you. I'm sorry. And his cry. I guess you're busy. Mrs. Emmons?"

"Valerie. Didn't I tell you to call me Valerie? You look nice in that dress." Katie is wearing a dress that Valerie used to wear a lot, a seersucker sundress. She hopes Katie is grateful and is not going to be mouthy with her, telling her what to do.

"Valerie. It's not just me, either. Please don't hate me, but Mrs. Moziak, well, she ended up saying the same thing. She's been a mother and she said he cries too much. I think he needs more—more something."

"More what?" Valerie hears that her voice is small, tentative.

"More of a strong identity from you. More of a take-charge attitude. I know I'm being out of line. I know I could just be being very sentimental. I mean, I've read all about how in other periods, nannies and nursemaids did the whole job, but that's just how I feel, that a baby needs a very strong sense of who is the main person who loves him." Valerie feels her whole body harden against the words. She sees with alarm that Katie is almost crying.

"I'm sorry," Valerie says, but she doesn't know what sense that makes. Why is she apologizing? To Katie? After a while, she says, "We'll talk more."

Katie turns and goes toward the sound of the crying child.

"Thank you, Katie." Not a dismissal so much as a "thanks for caring."

She thinks for a moment she might open the door of her consciousness and allow in this little fact and that little fact. She might. But what would she do if the ideas she let in couldn't be looked at?

He's hers. Soon it will feel that way. It's too late now. She cannot turn back.

■   ■

"ARE WE HALFWAY THERE?"

"More than half." They would already be there if the kids didn't require a bathroom break what seems like every couple of minutes. No, Marina is wrong. He is a bad father, begrudges them their childhood. Even that. And calling, talking to Artie Dolan, it was clear to him that he would turn around in a second with an invitation to get back on the job. Give Catherine the car keys, hitch a ride to Pittsburgh. Something wild. He was only around the corner from it.

The lawyer, LaPaglia, is going to break sooner or later. Artie's got a feel for him, and when Artie gets that feeling, that not quite empathy, but some kind of understanding, he knows how to make a guy talk. Little sister named Amelia, with an "A." Unbelievable.

"What time will we get there?" Julia asks in a voice that covers an octave of suffering.

"So, aren't they, like, classic?" Catherine says. " 'Are we there yet?' "

"At least they know their lines," he says.

"At least they're normal," she says, "in spite of us."

"What's normal?" Julia asks, and decides to pronounce instead the truth she wants. "You're normal, too."

"I wasn't talking to you."

"If you weren't—" he begins, looking back at the kids. Julia had put her earphones back on. "What would you want to do with your life if we hadn't—? If things were different?"

"What? What things?"

"If we had time and money. If you didn't have the kids to worry about. Would you want to go to school? You used to talk about it all the time."

"Well, yeah, sure, but I can't, so why discuss it?"

"I'm going to help you do it."

"I . . . I don't know what you mean. You mean money? You're getting a raise or . . . ? What are you saying?"

"Only that we need to find a way. You haven't been happy for a long time."

"What is this?"

He tells her he doesn't know, shrugs off her question, but then ventures forward anyway. "Vacations, they say, make people see things, do things. I heard that. I heard that people staring at the ocean see inside themselves."

"We haven't hit the ocean yet. Two and a half more hours, you said."

"All right, never mind. You know what I meant. I was trying to help."

But why should she like what he's saying—that he wants to fix her, that she's been unpleasantly unhappy? Bitter. Bitterness is a poison, and most of the world has eaten it, too, because nothing ever is what you want it to be, always the ideal somewhere inside making you curse the way things have happened. He tries again. "So? If I could figure out the finances, the schedule, when I watched the kids, who we paid to watch them when I didn't, would you go to school?"

Catherine runs her fingers through her hair, pulls down the visor, and looks at herself, brushing the hair forward again with her fingers. "What's the matter with me as I am?"

He'd like to believe her voice is a little softer, even though she's angry, but he's not sure it's true. That's the way it goes.

"Julia! Eric! Do you want to hear some stories?" he calls.

Of course they do. He catches a glimpse of their wide eyes in the rearview mirror. Julia's sticky hand lands on his neck—red pop or licorice, one or the other. A little sugar chill goes through him. Eric competes by getting a stranglehold on his neck, which means he has somehow gotten out of his seat belt. Christie has to pull over until he's sure they're safely buckled in again.

Catherine nods to him when it's done.

As he gets back onto the highway, he tries to imagine leaving them—no, never, he is not that kind of person, no, they need him, depend on him. Soon he begins to conjure monsters and bad men to threaten the children in his made-up story. Even though he is inventing as he goes, inevitably the monsters (sometimes they have been from another planet, this time they are from another country) snatch two little children and keep them from their parents in a dark dungeon; but the children have each other, and they have their wits, and they have the wishing of the listeners to escape the horrors that seem inevitable.

■   ■

HER MOTHER HAS DRESSED UP FOR HER, A COOL COTTON pants outfit with a printed top. Her mother's hair has a huge dip in front that gives her a look of more daring than she had ever exhibited. Her mother's eyes are afraid.

That's the word, "afraid." But of what? Everything, everything.

Marina hugs her, trying to press out the tension. She looks around at the small, perfect living room, the metal coasters perfectly stacked, the single painting on the wall, the sliding cabinet door that hides the television and its magazine guide. Her mother looks uncertain, standing as if she doesn't own the place. "Come, sit with me," Marina says. "Let's just be together for a while."

Her mother obeys, following her to the sofa, where they sit, holding on to each other's hands. "When I try to think, to tell myself you've been shot, I can't stand it, I can't believe it."

Not to be believed. Any of it. That her father could get so angry, that he could upend tables, strike her mother. Not to be believed, violence and trouble, and so a sliding door around it, make it something on a screen that can't come into the living room. A story.

Marina says carefully, "I'll show you. I was very lucky. Both shots only grazed me. My head—"

"Still . . . but they shaved it."

"A little. Because of the hair getting in the way."

"It hurts?"

"No, hardly at all." She turns and lifts her shirt up. "My side. I always feel a little like Jesus when I show this."

Her mother studies the wound, now nicely healing over. "Like you had an operation."

"In an unusual place." What's there at the side, at the Jesus spot? "You can touch."

"No."

She wishes her mother would touch—hard to explain, but she wishes her mother was not afraid to soothe her. The job did not come naturally. Marina adjusts her position on the plump sofa cushions, feeling herself buoyed unnaturally by the overstuffing.

Her mother says, "I'm taking us out to dinner tonight. All three of us. At a nice place. But let's have something now. I have sandwich makings."

Her mother goes to the front door as if to confirm

something she thought she saw earlier through the window. "You have a new car."

"A rental."

"What about the old Tercel?"

"It died."

"And the Saturn?"

"Michael needed it."

"He couldn't come?"

"No." So this is the time to say it.

Her mother slips into the kitchen.

"It's turkey. You want lettuce and mayo on it?"

Her mother's name is Tamara; her sister's name is Delia. It's been her mother's only acting-out, the naming of her daughters. All else is meant not to attract attention.

"I'm coming. I'll help. You can't believe how much I want any kind of change of scene. I look at things I never looked at before. Road signs, furniture. Everything looks good to me."

Scooping crumbs from the butcher block after her mother cuts slices of bread, Marina says, "Not only is the car new, but I had to use my new name when I put it on the charge. Marian. Marian Blessing. I could have picked Samantha Jones, but I guess I needed my little joke." Her mother will only understand the initials are the same. Not the way "Benedict" equals "Blessing." "I look at the same little apartment eighteen hours a day—I tried to explain all that to you. It's hard. It's like some sort of spiritual exercise. . . ."

Her mother looks confused.

"Anyway, I'm alone almost all the time. What I'm saying here is, I have to tell you something. Michael isn't with me. Maybe you guessed?" Her mother looks puzzled. "We've separated."

Her mother is taking already cleaned lettuce from a small fold-up plastic bag. She stops midmove, holding the lettuce over the almost made sandwiches, which are beautiful, very appetizing.

It turns out her mother has wondered why Michael never answered the phone and has thought Marina didn't sound right when she asked about him. And it turns out Delia tried to tell her something was wrong. "He left you?"

"Not exactly."

These words appear to relieve her mother, who, if she behaves as she always has, will hope for a happy ending to this story of separation, and who is surely, even now, as she puts down the lettuce, reminding herself this daughter of hers was always different, always stirring things up.

Marina says, "It's a separation. My idea. It's been a long time coming." Her mother's face keeps changing as she speaks. "I'm sorry." Marina comes around the table where she can hug her mother. She holds on for a long time. "You're going to have to believe me. Things were very bad between us. I'm going to need your support."

"What did he do?"

"Threw things. Hit me once. He has a lot of violence in him." She takes a chance. "As you know, that's what I was running away from. That's what I thought I was safe from."

"It means something is wrong in his life."

"I know. That isn't a good enough reason. I didn't want to be hit again."

"What's wrong in his life?"

"Oh! Well! He hates his work. We still have debts. He can't father a child. There, you might as well know it. He can't have children. He can't accept it. Took it out on me. There *are* other ways to handle things, Ma. What's wrong is not the issue. Bad luck comes to everybody eventually and people have to face up."

"You think people are strong. You always pushed people to be strong. Not everybody can be like you."

Marina lets that go for a little while, crosses around the table again, and takes her seat. When the plate with the sandwich slides toward her, she says, "Thanks." And when her mother asks, "Something to drink?" she says, "Just water or iced tea, if there is any."

She wonders if it was Anton who called her at the apartment and if Dolan has found the time to trace the call yet, but she doesn't tell her mother about this new fear. She feels that things are happening, finally, and in a way, she's glad.

The kitchen clock says it is two. Her sister is on the shift that ends at three, but Delia will stay longer, for she always does, and Marina has always joked, used to joke, that if she were dying, she'd want her sister to be the attending nurse, the way Delia would put in extra hours.

The way she has said it to everyone is: The wounds she had weren't serious enough to call her sister to her side. But she had known her mother and sister would not come, so she didn't ask. If she'd been dying, maybe, Delia would have come to her.

Oh, she aches, aches for a family like Karen Graves'.

Her mother brings an iced tea to the table, saying, "Michael needed something from you."

"I tried everything. Talking, affection, waiting . . . It felt like whole years that he hardly talked to me. We went to a counselor. I tried everything." Here she begins to doubt herself. Was it enough, what she did?

If she stays, her mother will persuade her once more that Michael needs her.

She tried to explain all this to Richard and he had listened soberly. "You've never been loved, not in that good way," Richard had said.

"It's not that bad," she'd told him. "It's only like other people's lives."

"No," he said. "It's like some lives. It's like my life."

Well, if that's the case, people who haven't been loved in that good way—freely, confidently—are often sweeter than those who have. Why is that? Deprivation causes longing, longing causes understanding—well, she is seeing Richard's face. He feels for people.

"Are you going to eat? You're staring at the sandwich."

Marina picks it up and begins.

Her mother takes a small bite of her own sandwich, saying, "I waited until you got here to eat."

"Sweet. But you didn't have to."

"I did. I waited for you."

"Thanks."

"You'll never find anyone as good as Michael."

She is tempted to protect her mother, even now, from the truth, but surprisingly words come to her, rolling off her tongue. "Here's what I need. I need for you to accept what I tell you. When I say I couldn't take it anymore, I need for you to believe that." Her mother's face is like a child's face, about to give in to crying. Marina says, "I need for you to believe I tried hard, and that if I say I couldn't go on, I couldn't. I need for you to believe me. Not to doubt me."

"Okay."

"I love you. I'm not leaving you."

Her mother starts to cry.

Her mother's crying is so awful, so deep, Marina doesn't know if she can go on. Then she does. "The woman who lost her baby, Karen Graves, left a stroller unattended and her family came to be with her. . . . They love her. They . . . they see her as human."

This is Richard's word. "Human." All of the inexplicable horrible things that happen, he puts under this very large banner.

"That's all I want."

"Me, too," her mother says. "You seemed okay. I thought you were fine all that time."

Her problem in life is this seeming okay, and not being okay, this chaos within her and nobody can see it, nobody, not even the mother who wants to love her.

"I'm human," her mother says, her lip quivering.

To stay with her father? No, that's different. Marina struggles. Staying *hurt* her mother. It robbed her of life.

She touches her mother's arm, her forehead, smooths her hair. Putting up with. Allowing. Human, too.

■　■

"SO YOU'RE WILLING TO SHARE YOUR PAPERWORK WITH US? Phone logs, that sort of thing?"

"I have such a small practice. There isn't much to see."

"Phone bills?"

"I don't know. This is not what you said at the beginning. A few questions. An hour or so, you said. It's afternoon and I'm still here. I shouldn't have agreed to come in."

Dolan sighs. He closes his eyes.

Manny is not sure how to work Dolan. He's usually good with people, but Dolan puzzles him.

"You don't want to continue to cooperate?"

"I'm under suspicion?"

"Every adoption lawyer is. It's a kind of wide net."

"You never made this clear. I need to have my own lawyer if you're going to start asking for papers."

"But if you have nothing to hide—"

"I have nothing to hide, but I know an invasion of privacy when I see one."

Dolan laughs. "Funny. You're a funny guy. Look, I'm not as schooled as you are. You do what you have to do. I'll do my job. My job is to check you out. Look, it's the weekend. You want to just relax for a while?"

"I want to go. I've given you a whole day." And missed an appointment, he thought. And he needs to talk with Emelia, away from the police station. He also needs an Alka-Seltzer, between the nerves and the interrupted routine and the greasy food.

He knows, even as he gets up and shakes Dolan's hand, that he has lost the battle. Goal one, to get out of there. Lost. Leave Emelia out of the conversation. Lost that one. He bumps into the gray table on the way out and it scrapes over the floor. He bumps into a chair. "Damn," he spits out.

"Feet fell asleep," Dolan says.

He thinks maybe he shouldn't have pretended to call his sister from their phone, dialing incorrectly on purpose. But they know all about her. Surely if they know as much as they seem to, they could be at her doorstep in minutes. And maybe they already were. This makes him queasy with apprehension. But they had an arrangement: He promised her if he was ever picked up, he'd let her know right away and she would scatter, disappear, maybe even leave the country. She had plenty of good ID and she always kept cash on hand. "Thank you again," Dolan says, seeing him to the elevator, and pushing the button. "Here's my card. Call me if there's anything else you want to say. If you change your mind about the phone records. If your sister is at all involved with this Vradek guy—well, I already asked, but if you really want to take care of her, you'll tell us everything you know." Dolan lowers his voice. "He's the scum in this picture. That's what I see."

They know much more than he thought at first. His stomach burns, burns. Between the oppressive humidity of the day and the sweating he's done upstairs, his clothes are soaked and rumpled. If he were going to have a heart attack, today would be a good day to have one. His chest hurts.

In his car, the heat presses so hard against his forehead, he must leave the door open and wait until the vents cool off the car. Stretching with some difficulty, he opens the glove compartment and takes out a box of Tums and eats four of them. Then he takes the cell phone out of his glove compartment and turns it on. The caller ID function tells him she has tried to call him twice. He closes his eyes and imagines what he hopes were the events of the morning: Emelia's bags packed, ready for an emergency, as she used to brag, and her on her way somewhere. In a way, he prays for this.

He is halfway home when the phone rings.

"Did you get out?" he asks.

"I'm at the airport in Miami. Almost out. What happened?"

"Police took me in."

"You called me from the police station?"

"Parking lot. I used my phone." In the silence he is being blamed for something. "Did you keep to your end of it?"

"I closed up the place. The girls are on the street somewhere. Speaking Russian, for God's sake. I tried to separate them, break them up, but I didn't have much time. What a waste."

"Don't talk about waste. This is as serious as it gets."

"The timing! Damn it, Manny, three babies. We have three babies close to delivery. We could have quit after those three."

They could have quit after the first one or the second. She wouldn't quit, she's greedy, greedy, and likes the game of it, too. It's odd, but he can hear his sister laughing. Why would she be laughing? "What a fiasco," she says. "The three of them on the streets, jabbering."

They knew this would happen at some point. They knew. They'd talked about it a million times. Had broken up camp once before, years ago, when they were working out of Mexico. "You'll get away. That's the main thing."

"Oh, I'll make it."

"Is Anton with you?"

"Last I heard he was on his way to Pittsburgh to try to find the bitch who got his mug in the paper. And he's right, too. If he shuts her, we're all a million times safer."

"Oh, my God." He had never intended to get into it in this way, this deeply. One child at a time, he had made strangers happy and dug himself into this, this thing.

"It's got to be done, and soon. Anton is very logical about things like that. You keep your head. Joe is long gone. Nobody knows where he is. I'm not worried about Joe. He knows how to disappear, and as long as he's not found, he's not saying anything. If Anton gets rid of that woman, they can wonder all they want, but they won't *prove* anything. If he gets rid of her, we're absolutely in the clear."

She is dreaming. The girls will wander the streets, trying to find one another, they will speak and speak, cry and cry, tell the story in their language until someone listens and understands.

■   ■

THE LATE-AFTERNOON SUN CASTS LONG UMBRELLA SHADOWS on the sand. Catherine lies on her stomach, reading, under their Coca-Cola umbrella, with her legs sticking out.

It's possible she will have a jagged, uneven shadow of umbrella on her upper thighs, but she does not seem to care and shows no signs of irritation that back at the beach apartment they rented, there is unpacking to be done. They simply dropped everything on the living room and bedroom floors and ran to the beach, carrying what umbrellas, chairs, and towels they could readily grab.

The waves gather and swell from nothing, nothing visible, only the ordinary ripples of water moving, and by the time they reach Eric and Julia, they are hillsides of foam crashing over their shoulders, or if the children work them right, as they are learning to, the waves come underneath them and lift them up on their bellies, on their boogie boards, and deposit them closer to him. They look up each time to see if he sees them. He always raises a hand so they will know, with the sun in their eyes, that he is not glazed with fatigue or even asleep, but watching them. Julia wears a pink bathing suit from last year, now already a size too small for her. She keeps tugging at it. But the way she tugs at it, the way she walks into the ocean, when the undertow runs the waves in the other direction, is like flirtation—a small hesitation, a pose that shows off her body before she plunges forward. She is talking to the ocean.

Where did she learn that? Men and women, women and men, the subject that has always interested him most. The center of almost every murder case, after all. Eric, just the opposite, arguing with the waves before they've formed, arms thrashing as he forces himself forward toward what's coming, and always he gets there before Julia does. Up into the waves his son rises, bony rib cage, pale hair and upturned nose like his mother's. Up goes Julia, darker hair, which came from him, cut short for the summer in a bob that makes her look like a twenties actress. His own skin is dark, as if he's been in the sun all summer. Which he hasn't, not at all. They beckon him into the water. "Oh," he groans. "I was so comfortable." But he is up, shaking the kinks out, almost setting off.

"They want some roughhousing," she says blandly.

"Oh, boy. I wish they were over that phase."

"Scare them and thrill them. Nobody's ever over that phase."

DELIA HAS CHANGED OUT OF HER WHITES AT WORK AND NOW, sighing, plops into the only armchair in the living room. The love seat and sofa suggest too much togetherness for her. "So," she says, "you made it," as if Marina has been remiss in not getting there sooner instead of the other way around.

"Work was hard today?"

Delia's eyes catch a lampshade to her right and a window to her left but do not find Marina's eyes, quite. Her head tips back in the chair, chin to the ceiling, a long stretch, the sign of a trying day. "People dying all over the place."

"I'm glad to see you, finally."

Delia goes still.

"Your hair is cute." It's a 1960s cloud of hair, the same dark color as Marina's, but cut in a pouf.

"It's okay." Delia runs her hands through it, frowning.

If she must continue to disguise herself, Marina is thinking, she might as well cut her hair, too. "Your hair reminds me of those pictures of Mom in the sixties. It suits you."

"Eh."

"Why are you angry with me?"

Delia gets up and goes to the kitchen, saying, "Look, I had a hard day. Nothing you would understand."

Marina waits, hears water running, waits, listens for their mother in the bedroom, scraping hangers, letting shoes drop. Marina has already changed to a summery dress. Her hair is long and loose. She looks like the photo they used in the newspaper. She looks identifiable. She supposes life could be crazy and full of accident and that the restaurant they're going to for dinner might be one that Anton frequents. Or Joe. Maybe they're Virginia boys who happen to have guns tucked into waistbands. But the odds are like winning the lottery, so she will try not to be afraid.

Richard would say she should not go to restaurants at all, period, but she is free, free. Is he as bad as the rest, wanting to capture and contain her? Probably. It hardly matters, he is with his wife, wife and children, four and six, and the waves are glistening before them, a family, with ties to one another.

Delia comes back into the living room. "I'm just going to wear this." She gestures to the neat linen pants, the sporty cotton top with an orange band across the breast. Delia doesn't think she's pretty, but she has fine-looking features, and what's more, if she had any joy in her, she would pass up pretty and move toward beautiful. She wants to meet a man and has not been lucky in that.

"Maybe after dinner we can take a walk and talk, just the two of us."

"I'm kind of tired. Maybe just bring you back here—"

"Oh!" It's like sewing, trying to catch a fragile thread, a delicate piece of cloth falling apart. "I haven't been out for a walk in a long time. I try to exercise in the apartment. But to be able to swing my arms . . ."

"Hmmm. I hadn't thought of that. How long will this go on?"

Marina shrugs, all the while trying to hold on to her sister's eyes. She thinks of the phone call she received, how she wishes she could tell Delia, but Delia would automatically assume she was being overly dramatic. Yet if it was Anton or someone sent by him? Maybe it won't go on long at all.

It *was* Anton. She knows it.

"No leads, huh?"

"Some leads. Some good leads. No arrests. No baby." She would like to ask again about Delia's anger, but she already knows the answer and asking would seem like harassment. It's something like: Delia is on her feet all day and Marina doesn't have to work, Delia has a humdrum life and Marina was plastered all over the newspapers and getting cards from strangers, Delia has no one to care for her and Marina has a handsome husband. That Marina doesn't like idleness and isolation, that she wouldn't give twenty cents for the media fuss or the looks her husband was blessed with, is something Delia can't find the room to know. Marina is suddenly tired of trying so hard to win her sister's acceptance. She must give it up. Jealousy has its own rewards and Delia has decided to reap them.

"I'm taking a walk after dinner, with or without you."

Their mother comes into the room then, having added earrings and a bright yellow blazer. Her outfit bridges the difference between her daughters'. When she sees conversation is strained, she says, "You told her about Michael, I guess."

"No."

"What?"

"We've split up."

"I knew that. Didn't I say?"

DELIA, DRIVING, SLUMPS WHEN SHE COMES TO A STOPLIGHT and runs her hands over her face. "Here we go," she says. "It's always about Marina."

"If you did things, it might be about you."

"What?"

"If you acted on *something*." Marina is almost laughing, it feels so good to say it finally. "You slump. Collapse. Complain. It's all you do."

"I'm not going to dinner."

"Oh, yes you are," their mother says. "And no fighting. I made a reservation and we're going."

"If you *would* fight—I think your life would be better."

"Who am I supposed to fight?"

"People at work. Me. Probably a couple of guys who don't take you seriously."

"And you've got it all down. You're just so special. You're just lucky, that's all." Delia's agony is comic—the way her face scrunches up—the final insult.

"Right. I've got a hole in my head, I'm not allowed out of my apartment, I have no job, my marriage has fallen apart, and, well, let's just say I've figured out a way to get hurt all over again. . . ."

THEY ARE HALFWAY THROUGH DINNER AT THE RESTAURANT when Delia figures out what she thinks her sister means. "You left him for someone!"

"No."

"You did!"

"No. The someone came after."

Delia eats a bite of steak, staring at her. "While you were sick? You are some piece of work."

Their mother throws her hands in the air.

Marina is laughing and she doesn't know why. He's married, he has children, they are not at all alike, she doesn't know what she's doing, there's a contract out on her life, Richard is falling apart, he's off on vacation with his wife. "My affair is falling apart, too," she says.

"Why are you laughing, then?"

"I don't know."

Richard made love to her more in two weeks than Michael did in two years. And it was wonderful. She'd needed that so badly, touch, although her sister wouldn't understand she could be so lonely.

But the way she'd grabbed what she wanted, with very little guilt, maybe for the first time. It makes her laugh. "I guess I'm happy."

■   ■

THERE WAS NO AMY BISSINGER IN THE BACK OF THE PHONE book, where the friends and doctors were written in. But there was an Amy Bissinger in the white pages and that gave Anton an address. "She was there. It was her. I heard her voice," Anton told him. Anton paced the house studying what photos remained. "I saw this guy. Going in and out of work. Really. He has another chick. Found himself a better one. Wonder how Marina feels about that. We're going to go pay her a visit."

"Better to wait here for her," Joe told him. "There must be some way to get her over here. Our pictures . . ."

But Anton scoffed at him, saying he wasn't about to take advice from a retard. "We're going to chance it later on. People don't remember pictures."

The night is not very dark or very quiet, but at three in the morning, Anton orders Joe up from the living room floor where he has been lying down, pretending to sleep, while Anton has sat up on the couch, over him.

Joe has been careful, the way he lives here, inventing his elaborate system for being invisible, but now with Anton here, recklessly doing what he wants, it isn't safe anymore.

"If we're going, now is when we go," Anton orders.

Joe checks his pockets for every little card and screwdriver and file he is supposed to have with him. He has asked Anton for a plan, every hour or so, and Anton has said he will flush her out of her place with a phone call once her husband is at work, and if the phone call doesn't get her, they will get in and Joe will finish the job properly.

"Then . . . why are we going on a Sunday morning?"

"Just do what I say." Reckless, always reckless, and blaming everyone else.

So now he's back to taking orders again. This is the way it's been the last three or four years, once Emelia hooked him up with Anton and Vol. He liked his life better before all that, living wherever he could, taking whatever he needed, spending his time alone and safe.

"What's the matter with you? You liked her?" Anton asks, pushing Joe toward the kitchen door. "You owe me, you hear?" Joe quietly unlocks the door—he has figured out how to do this without making a sound at all—and he puts up a hand to keep Anton from moving right away. For a good minute, he just listens.

Every time he goes out, he figures, it's one more point off the odds that he will do it safely. He messed up once, walking right into Anton's arms.

They try to walk normally, as if they are an uncle and a nephew come to visit, and now are going out to—what? Who goes out at three in the morning? And for what?

The gate creaks because Anton does not know how to ease it open. Joe does not breathe. Hardly breathes while they walk down the alley and around the corner to where Anton's new car is parked.

Joe starts for the passenger door.

"You drive, you stupid son of a bitch," Anton spits at him.

He has been in this play before. The key going into the lock, the seat belt, all moves, interestingly, at the same time, both familiar and unfamiliar. He has not driven for a while. And yet he moves smoothly, starts up, does not rev the engine, does not put on the lights, drives slowly down the block and around the corner. Puts on the lights. He has chosen a path, a zigzag of small streets that is not in the camera eye, but he has done this without knowing there is a camera focused on the front of the house.

Marina's new place is easy to find. Anton has consulted a map along the way, tilting it toward streetlights. Fifth to College, turn, turn, and there is 323 Emerson Street, the address the telephone book lists for an Amy Bissinger. Joe sees Anton take out his cell phone and check that the phone number is still in the memory bank. Joe is frightened Anton will do something very stupid—make a call at four in the morning. Anton puts the phone away and folds the map and puts it into the glove compartment. Anton wears a white polo shirt and chino pants. He is handsome, and so he looks as if he might be a friend of somebody like Marina. Joe does not blend as well.

Maybe six apartments at the most in the building. Which is hers?

Anton gets out of the car and goes straight up to the entrance door, where he reads the names next to the buzzers. Joe, sitting in the darkened car, does not want to imagine what Anton will do next. He opens the driver door to get some air as Anton walks around the building to the back. For a moment, Joe imagines driving away and never going back to Marina's place at all, just driving, driving until he is far away from Anton. But he sits there. After five minutes, Anton returns.

When he gets into the car, he says, "There's a back entrance people use for the garbage. That's a possibility. Also, if I were just coming down the block when somebody was coming out the front door, I could have a set of keys in my hand and I could just speed up and catch the door."

"They would know you didn't belong."

"They wouldn't. I'd just say, 'I'm staying in Number Four with my sister.' Number Four is where she lives."

Good, then, let him do the job himself.

"You'd see I got in, and you'd go around back and I'd let you in. Then we'd have to get into her place."

"That simple," Joe says bitterly. "How will we know she's in there? Maybe she doesn't answer the door."

"She's not there, we get in, we wait."

"What do you do if she looks through the door or calls someone?"

"I'll get in. Don't worry."

In the end, it's simple.

■   ■

THEY ARE SLEEPING. HE TAKES HIS CELL PHONE FROM THE table in the living room, where the sofa bed is opened up to leave only a few feet on either side in which to move. The children are flung away from each other, each to a side of the bed. Arguing in their dreams. Their already tanned bodies are flushed with yesterday's intense beach sun. From a slicker hanging on a door hook, he retrieves his notebook. His pager is still in his pants pocket. He does not go back for it. He slips the phone into his sweats and lets himself out the kitchen door to a third-floor porch. Below him there are other porches, like his, with banners of T-shirts, towels, swimsuits. How alike people are, he thinks, in their unlikeness. The floorboards are wet with dew, slippery.

He holds the banister and goes down the steep steps slowly, like an old person. When he reaches the yard, he

stops to look at the herbs the owners have planted and offered to their tenants, a sweet gesture, but Catherine is
not likely to be cooking complex meals. Catherine said
she does not want to think about a pot or a pan for two
weeks. Fair enough. Out to breakfast, even, she said, and
he said okay. She has needed a break. She needs . . . *love*.
He tried to make love to her last night and couldn't do it.

Hardly slept again, an unquiet mind.

How he likes this time of day! The sun is just coming
up, everything is fresh and still. He turns out of the yard
and toward the ocean. He is not alone. A bicyclist here
and there. A car starting up. A runner and then another.
He's got the right shoes on and so he begins with a light
jog toward the ocean. By the time he reaches the boardwalk, he is running, too. An old man, a panting runner,
passes him, says, "Good morning."

How did it happen to him—the gray office every day,
the dregs of society, when there is this other world of
bright color, friendly breakfasts. . . . He has half a mind to
call up old Will and say, Send me a ticket to Australia.
"Still fighting the bad guys?" Will laughed last time they
talked.

How did you come to be a policeman? Marina had
asked him. I wanted to be special, he said. They were sitting in her living room. Her hand was on his knee. He was
looking at his watch. She was smiling about his admission that he wanted to be special. He was awash in guilt.
No time for his family and there he was, sitting with her,
watching her eyes close and open up, so full of everything.
A woman filled up with emotion, tons of it, kept in check.
Marina said her fault was that she, too, was always trying
to be special in some way, to everyone, even to strangers.
She said it was part of being an actress. A flaw that she
was working on. She shook her head at herself as if she
were the mother—the child self standing before her, right
at the coffee table, one knee knocking into the other, a
child trying to be special even then.

The waves are low rolling waves, but the way they catch

the sun is nothing short of spectacular. The light is brilliant. It hurts to look and yet he looks because it's better than a Christmas tree, better than prayer.

Darnell Flowers. He wants to be special and he might be good at it, too, he might be an Artie Dolan. Get there sometime soon, find him, talk to him.

Christie runs to one end of the boardwalk, where the Fisherman's Cove restaurant is, and considers going farther on the sand, to the lighthouse, but that will take a long time and the children will surely be awake and waiting for him. He turns and starts back, working up the beginning of a sweat because of the sun on his back. There are lots more people running now. About halfway back to the apartment, he stops dead, and sits on a bench. The panting man goes by again and says, "None of that, now." The old man's joke has cheered him like nothing else has for a long time, maybe because he's a reminder of a father, somebody's father, the one he didn't have, still alive, still panting.

The noise of the waves is like a static in the air. He dials the Branch and asks for Dolan, who sometimes comes in early. Dolan isn't there yet, so he talks to Coleson, who says Dolan had a big day yesterday, talked to that lawyer for a good six hours, and then, Coleson says, there were other things, so Dolan left a message in case Christie called in. His heart jumps. His whole chest tightens. Something is happening. Well, he knew it. What? What? he thinks. He can't get Coleson to go faster. He hears papers rustling. " 'Another big lead on the Graves case,' is what he wants me to tell you. You're supposed to call him at home to get the info."

He rings off impatiently and looks at his watch. Dolan will be up at six-forty, surely. If not, too bad. He goes into storage for the number, although he knows it by heart.

Two women jog past. A bicycle wobbles by.

"I knew it would be you," Dolan says. "Like you'd ever be able to forget all this."

"Fat chance."

The waves are noise in the air, but he manages to hear.

"Big news. All kinds of it. Are you ready? Manny is our man, for sure, but there are others involved, and Manny is very scared. We couldn't make sense of the number he called from the pay phone, so we got into his car and went to his cell phone while we held him. I know, I know. Let's just say he left the car open. We pushed redial and a number came up. We pushed the number 1 and the same number came up, a New York number. We traced the number. Took the next four hours to do it. Looked like the sister. Is this good or what?"

"It's good." Marina has done this. Everyone else will take the credit, but she checked out old family connections and all the rest of it as if she worked on the force.

"Then we had the Feds run it down, but the sister was long gone by the time the guys got there to take a look. They're printing the place. The neighbors say there were several pregnant girls living there along with the woman, but they were gone, too."

"Damn." He moves toward a simple brown-tile building that says REST ROOMS and goes into a stall so he can hear better. There is a high, open window, but the sound of the waves is muted a bit.

"Yeah. They call it a baby farm. Feds do."

"But the Graves baby—?"

"We're giving him a couple of hours to sweat while we get a search warrant. . . ."

"Good work."

"Yeah, but that isn't all. There's lots more. I knew you'd want to know about this other thing. . . ." Here Dolan sighs and slowly explains about the call from Marina. A feeling of alarm goes all through Richard's body even though Dolan is assuring him he went over and checked Marina's apartment. "She was gone," Dolan says, "but she told me she was going to her mother's place. I felt somewhat better about that." He explains how he left the interviews to call Enterprise, and the company assured him they'd delivered her a car.

"I'll check on her, then," Richard says. "The phone call . . . ?"

"Cell phone. Took a while, but we ran it down. Belongs to a woman in Michigan. We sent some agents to question her real late last night. She knows Anton, all right. He's been living there. She lent him her car. They got a make of the car and a license number. So that's on the APB. Turns out the other car we've been looking for was sitting in her garage the last five weeks! We had them impound it and they're going over it for evidence."

"He's in Pittsburgh, then?"

"You better believe it."

"You're sure Marina's place looked all right? No signs of—?"

"It looked good. Feds are ordering surveillance for it this morning, first thing."

"Thanks."

Dolan, in carefully measured tones, apologizes to Christie for not talking to Marina more before she left, but her call came in just as he was questioning Manny LaPaglia. "I never got to tell her the call was from Anton."

"I'll call. I'll tell her."

Dolan says, "Tell her to stay at her mother's house. Tell her if she leaves there, definitely *not* to go home or to the apartment, but to a motel. Don't give her a choice."

He blesses Dolan for not asking why he happens to have her mother's phone number with him on vacation. But he insisted on it and he's glad he did. To break the silence, he says, "I had to go away for things to happen."

"It's always that way. Call anytime. I'm okay with it. I can't believe the Feds let us have a piece of it at all."

He fumbles in his pocket for the notebook—a simple small schoolbook of a thing that he would be lost without—and then for the number. He begins walking fast back to the apartment, even as he begins to dial. "In case there's an emergency," he'd told her, but he hadn't actually expected one.

Her mother answers, sleepily. Who is this? Is this a friend? Why are the police bothering her again? If it can wait, it must wait. Marina is there, yes, she is safe, and no, she's not awake just yet. If he could call back . . .

"It's a very serious matter. Wake her, but don't scare her." He gauges the distance to the apartment, the time it will take him to gather his things. "Have her call me in half an hour."

"I don't have a pen and paper here."

"She knows the number. Tell her it's important."

How can he keep her safe? If he were Anton calling, Marina's mother would still say, Yes, she's here, she's safe, she's sleeping.

■   ■

ANTON AND JOE GOT INTO THE APARTMENT LONG BEFORE surveillance started—two hours before the team set up.

They looked through all the drawers and closets. No evidence of a husband's things.

"Perfect, perfect," said Anton, breathing heavily, "the guy has some sense, but where is the fucking bitch?"

Joe saw her pictures on the bookcases, the pictures that came from the house. And just hers, too, none of the husband's. He supposed Anton was right about the husband being gone. He found it curious, interesting.

"We're so close," Anton kept saying.

Joe was worried about the size of Anton's voice, but he knew from experience not to ruffle Anton when he was raging, because it always got worse. The Enterprise car rental number was on top of the desk. Joe was the one who found it, but Anton grabbed it from him, spewing, "Enterprise. Shit. This is what she meant." He dialed the number. When he got a recorded message about business hours, he cursed and slammed down the phone.

Joe tried to motion Anton to cool down. "You're the one's going to get us killed," Joe said. "Let's get out of here."

"We're waiting here for her. She'll come back some-time. You want to get in my good graces again, you can finish what you started."

They could muffle her sounds easily, the two of them against her, easily. Joe said, "This isn't where to do it. This isn't a safe place." He didn't know if it was true or not. "Your car's parked outside. People notice things like that. They have street cleaning. People move cars back and forth. They notice things. We can't just stay here."

Anton appeared to think about it. "Okay," he said. "We'll go and come back, then. We got in once, we can do it again. Leave the door unlocked. Let me figure some things first."

Anton sat down at Marina's tiny kitchen table, which was wedged between the refrigerator and the counter. As he tugged the chair in under him, his eye went to a small notepad that had some scratchings on it. Joe, too, tried to read it, but it seemed it was only about groceries. He was surprised that Anton looked away from him, even to study Marina's writing. Then, using his own phone, Anton dialed someone fast, while Joe stood at the refrigerator, sick with feelings, one of them the certainty that Anton was going to get them caught.

Joe squeezed around the table to read Anton's face. He could hear an answering machine click on and a woman's voice on it.

"Elise. Elise, where the fuck are you? I'll call again." When Anton hung up, he muttered, "It's Sunday morning, for God's sake. Where the hell could she be?"

"Sleeping."

"Maybe. I'm calling Manny, then Emelia." Anton fumbled for his wallet, then for a piece of paper in it, and punched in the numbers angrily. What did he want? What did he need?

Joe felt his eyes close, a sign like an old lady would make when she was fed up. But what he wanted was to slow something down. Anton was going very fast, like when he drove ninety miles an hour, and Joe could not stop him. Joe was afraid to feel in his pocket for his gun. He moved away from the table, out of Anton's line of vision. Nausea swelled up to his throat. He tried to think.

Did it matter, since he already had Vol as one count against him, what he did? Did it seem possible Anton planned to let him live after they finished off the girl? No. No, not possible.

Manny answers. Everything stops and races forward at the same time. Joe can hear the voice, tentative inside Anton's phone. Not words, only rhythm comes through. Then Anton saying, "What, what did you say? What did you tell them? You what?"

Trouble. Big trouble. A matter of time, then.

Joe sees only that he must get on a bus to Florida or Texas and live somewhere alone, making no contact at all with anyone he has ever known before. He gets up jerkily, opens the refrigerator door, which is just to the left of Anton, slams some food on the table, until Anton looks up in irritation at the sound. Anton says, "Who? How long?" Joe takes out turkey breast, mayonnaise, anything in a jar, any excuse to stand behind Anton while he talks; the food is the decoy, the food disarms. Anton curses and leans into his phone, but begins to turn around. Joe doesn't have time to take the gun out of his pocket. But it's perfect where it is. He pulls the trigger just as Anton pushes the OFF button on his phone. He feels it happen, right up against Anton's back, right under the heart, right through his own clothes, the little soybeanlike thing, without size or velocity, exploding nonetheless into a wide fireworks inside the white shirt. Anton tries to claw at him, saying, "Son of a bitch," then he collapses across the table, but that's only for a minute, until he slides to the floor. His hand reaches out. He tries to grab at Joe's pants leg. He's cursing. His face is pure hatred, even at the end.

Joe does not know how to clean up. He cannot tell how loud the sound was. He did it in a dream. So fast, so fast . . . For a while, he stands frozen, trying to think of a way to erase his presence here. He has touched the photograph frame, the jars, the cellophane on the container of strawberries. . . . It's self-defense, both cases, but who would believe it? He must get to a bus station and buy a ticket to somewhere.

■   ■

THE HIGHWAY IS STILL PRETTY CLEAR, THE WORST OF THE Sunday exodus not having begun yet. A lot of people want a last breakfast at the beach. "I have to go," he said. "It's too messy to leave it to twenty others. Even *I* probably can't catch all the parts of this in time."

"That isn't the whole story, is it?" she asked. She wore only a long T-shirt and underwear. Her legs were sunburned, her hair sticking up. "You're leaving me, aren't you?"

"Yes," he said. "Not without talking, not without figuring what we need to do, but yes."

"For her."

"Yes."

"Fine. I knew it."

"Now I have to go or something terrible will happen."

"Something terrible is happening."

He almost stopped himself so that the damage would not happen after all, not to her at least. But then he said, "Catherine, we're not good at all with each other, not for a long time. . . . We're both so unhappy."

She didn't deny it. She sat down on the red ladder-back kitchen chair, putting her face in her hands. It seemed very dramatic, that's all he could think of, something an actress might have to do in a play.

Something terrible is happening, it's true.

Families in cars all around him, some coming to the beach for the day, pale; some in the northward lanes, brown-skinned, exhausted, exhilarated; lots with rafts and bicycles hanging off their vans. Just like the family he'd seen when driving with Marina. That had started the conversation that had started everything, hadn't it?

Now he realizes he doesn't know what she will do. Or why she hasn't called him yet. If she doesn't call in an hour, he will call her again. He puts on the radio, shuts it

off. Takes out his phone and dials the office to tell Dolan
he's on his way.

Dolan is eating a donut. His voice is muffled with dough
and sugar when he says, "Surveillance team is on the way."

■   ■

ANTON'S BLOOD IS FLOWING ONTO THE KITCHEN FLOOR IN THE
apartment Marina has rented from Amy Bissinger.

Joe is carrying plastic bags full of food and a bedspread
as he leaves the building, because he has to take his fingerprints away and he has to hide the blood on his pants. He's
got the spread folded over his arm. He's trying to make it
look as if he's taking it to the cleaners or the beach, nothing more than a little unfancy picnic in the making.

■   ■

MARINA IS SLEEPING BETTER THAN SHE HAS SLEPT IN YEARS.
She doesn't know her mother is standing at the edge of
the bed, looking at her, thinking how beautiful she is,
how safe she looks, and not wanting to wake her to call
back that man, no matter how urgent it is.

Marina doesn't know how her mother frets that she
can't find a way to express herself to this daughter. She always intends to throw her arms around Marina, but something gets in the way. Today she's going to tell Delia to put
her jealousy away, like putting a toy in a toy box, put it
away, and love Marina just because, no other reason.

■   ■

MANNY IS WAITING FOR HIS SISTER TO SIGNAL HIM FROM
Brazil or wherever she has gotten to, so he will know she's
safe. He knows already, he sees the future, how he will *not*
implicate her, no matter what he is asked, because he is
strong when it comes to his sister. He understands if he
doesn't run or kill himself, he will go to jail. His picture will
be in the paper, he will lose his practice, be disbarred, he will

suffer shame. He knows he should run. Leave it all. He'd rather kill himself. He sits at his kitchen table trying to get down a cup of coffee and wondering what Anton will do, what Anton will say to save himself when they catch him, which they will surely do, because everything is coming apart now.

■   ■

KATIE IS PARKING HER CAR AT THE EMMONSES' HOUSE. SHE cannot continue with the job, that's clear to her. They've increased her salary once already (and it's only been three weeks!), when she said she thought she ought to go back to her old way of working at *In Pittsburgh*. On Wednesday Valerie begged her to stay. She relented for two days, but on Friday she realized she still wanted to leave. She will tell Valerie today. Before they go to Sunday brunch.

The Emmons depress her. They have a baby they don't know how to love. Adopted, Mrs. Moziak says. That explains it, but it doesn't *explain it*. Valerie is afraid of her baby, afraid to touch him. When she leaves, who will take care of the baby? Katie wonders. When she leaves and has a life again. Maybe Mrs. Moziak will step in.

Is she crazy giving all this up? The money? Fancy lunches. Free clothes. She passes the sculpted hedges, wondering how she will break the news to Valerie. As she gets to the front door, which the Emmons always leave open for her, she hears the baby crying.

■   ■

LAST NIGHT HE TOLD HER HE CAN'T FATHER A CHILD. SHE WAS quiet, clearly disturbed by the news. She tried to brush it off with a joking tone, asking why he let her use a diaphragm, which she always hated. Finally, she said, "Hmmmm. I'm thinking."

"About what?"

"Us. Our lives."

He has been admitting it little by little, every day a little, disorienting as the news is to him, that they are an item. But he doesn't want this, he doesn't love her.

"How sure are you?" Kendall asked this morning when he was starting to get up.

"The doctors are very sure."

"I'm not," she said. "And I never believe anybody except myself." She is all bravura, he understands that, but she does bravura fairly well. "I love to tempt fate," she said, beckoning him toward her. "Don't you? You know you do."

■   ■

KAREN AND RYAN GRAVES ARE LYING IN BED, LATER THAN usual. She understands he wants to touch her but doesn't know how to begin. She, too, is stuck, and realizes they may never be able to make love again. She is not asleep, not dreaming, but she drops over the edge of something, as people do in dreams. She is thinking, thinking, and then she is over the edge. She says, "When I left Justin, I was having certain feelings." She feels Ryan go still in the midst of adjusting his pillow under his neck. She's caught, too, both of them afraid to move. The stillness is like a white, unbroken landscape, winter forever. "I was thinking how our lives were always centered around you," she says, "your hopes, your career, and me with nothing to do but take care of the baby and be around when it was the right time to be around. I got disgusted. I thought, So I'm supposed to be the pretty wife. Well, let Justin just sit until I can find the damn stuff that puts the blond streaks in, if I have to be the pretty, blond wife, if that's who I am. . . ." She can't believe how clearly she remembers her thoughts. Her chest is tight. She falls the rest of the way, letting her eyes close, trying to hit the ground.

"Honey," Ryan says. "Honey?" Where did the tenderness in his voice come from? Why now?

He doesn't understand what she's trying to say. So she

turns toward him to tell him how it was hate in her heart that did it, but when she sees him, his face over hers, all concern, she can't remember hating him, even though she did, because she isn't the nice person everybody thinks she is, she doesn't know anything about love, she never really loved anyone, she's trying to tell him, but his face is so—There's something in his eyes like love, understanding, like nothing she's used to. She begins to sob. It's not uncontrollable sobbing, like before, but a river nonetheless, not uncontrollable but endless, more and more of it, the more he holds her.

■ ■

"I'M ON MY WAY BACK," HE TELLS HER FINALLY, AFTER ANother phone call to prompt her mother, after making sure she is all right. The signs say he is almost in Philadelphia. "Under five hours if I don't make any stops."

"What are you going to tell the chief?"

"I don't know." Not something he cares about right now. He'll get into significant trouble if he's anywhere near the case, but who cares? "I need for you to leave where you are. Find a hotel somewhere near your mother's. Or on the road back. Page me when you've done that so I have the number."

"I just got here."

He tells her what they've learned about the phone call. "It's Anton," he says. "Good news and bad news. You can't go back there now, no matter what. For as long as it takes."

"I don't want to hear that." She still sounds sleepy. "I can't leave right away. The sun is shining. I smell something cooking. Maybe ham or Canadian bacon. Things are very nice here this morning."

He gets her to promise she will leave. He will come find her, he says, when things are calm.

How could she give the anthropologist's name to a voice on the phone? He senses recklessness gathering in her. Impatience. Something he sees more clearly than before, a part of her personality. He understands now he doesn't know her at all. Why, she went ahead and called LaPaglia and made an appointment before she told him what she'd done! Not that he or any of the investigators can exactly blame her for the groundwork on Manny. Not that they weren't getting to Manny themselves, but she certainly bumped things along.

"Tell me what's happening," she says, more alert. "With the lawyer. Did Dolan find out anything about the baby?"

He can hear dishes being put on a table in the background.

He tells her everything because he always does. That it looks like LaPaglia is connected to several others, Anton included, the sister, Emelia, being the key, and that they work out of New York. Illegal adoptions. Black market babies. All kinds of names for it.

She wants to know everything, as usual, this time how they get babies for people, how the mothers who seem to be from Russia get here.

"Probably bring them in like visitors, ship them out . . ." That isn't his end of it. The Feds will be dealing with Immigration to see how it's done. He's not sure which way Manny and the others are working it. He would tell her any secret, just to stay on the phone with her.

She wants to know if LaPaglia told all of this to Dolan yesterday.

His shoulder aches from trying to balance the phone and get through the parkway traffic around Philadelphia. The phone slips and he has to catch it while he tries to retrieve her voice, which seems to be falling, too. "He tried to stay buttoned up. Protecting his sister. Dolan, who can get to almost anybody, came up way short of a confession."

"What about Justin, then?"

Everything is moving, traffic is moving, the case is moving, the phone is falling again, his relationship with Marina is shifting and seems like nothing but business now, but they have nothing on Justin. It comes back to that coin, the bright dime on the pavement that stops them in their tracks. ". . . how to get one of these people to talk," she is saying.

"LaPaglia is very, very, very scared. Dolan says he's like a man in a dream. Dolan's looking to figure out how to apply the pressure in just the right way. . . . LaPaglia is delicate, he says. Something about the sister would do it, maybe. He seems to be . . . almost in love with her."

There are long silences, which frighten him.

"I told Catherine I'm leaving," he says.

■   ■

MANNY IS WAITING, AGAIN WAITING. THIS TIME FOR EMELIA to call him. For Anton to call back. He packs a small bag and puts it at the back of his closet. He checks to see that his gun is loaded and puts it back in the drawer of the shelving unit in the dining room, under the dinner napkins. He waits near his phone, eating small bits of bread and drinking Alka-Seltzer. For a long time, the phone is absolutely silent.

JOE HAS TO DRIVE ANTON'S CAR AWAY FROM WHERE IT'S parked on Emerson Street because he has blood all over his pants and he is carrying a bedspread. He never killed anyone before, and now Vol and Anton, one after the other. His whole body is filled with nausea. He wishes he could hop a city bus to the Greyhound station, then run, run, run, but he will need to get cleaned up first.

■   ■

MARINA IS HAVING BUTTERED TOAST AND COFFEE WITH HER mother, talking about not losing faith in herself as an actress, and trying all the while to figure out how to get information about Karen Graves' baby from Manny LaPaglia before he kills himself. A big, overweight, lonely guy, Richard said. A strange man. He will not want to live. She feels the certainty of this in her chest.

"I have to get back," she tells her mother. "They need me to identify a suspect."

"Oh, I wanted you to stay. Maybe live here for a while till things settle down. Can you come back?"

"Yes. I'll just drive into Pittsburgh for the day and then I'll come back."

Relief floods her mother's face. "I like having you around. I like having someone in the house to take care of. I'm not too good alone."

Marina wonders who is, really.

■   ■

THE SURVEILLANCE TEAM SCOPES OUT THE NEIGHBORHOOD on Emerson, looking for an Escort sedan. They don't see one. It's been gone for twenty minutes.

■   ■

AFTER NOON ON SUNDAY, MARINA PASSES OVER THE BORDER into West Virginia and well before two o'clock over the border into Pennsylvania. In under half an hour, she could be at her old home, the one she shared with Michael. In under an hour, she could be at her new home, the apartment, the one she let Richard into. Both are dangerous. So they say.

"Take my old phone," Delia said. "It needs to be charged, but . . . better than nothing." It sits on the seat beside her, charging.

She ticks off motels along the road—Holiday Inn, Ramada. She knows what she is supposed to do.

Instead she drives to Crafton, a part of the city she has never seen before, passing large apartment buildings, small low-income housing, a few nice old houses. She pulls into a Gulf station, fills the tank of the Tempo, unable to fully enjoy the thrill of doing these ordinary things, because while she does, she is rehearsing what comes next. She goes inside to pay, plunking down a twenty, sliding a Coke across the counter. When she has her change in hand, she asks directions to Manor Street.

The clerk is a teenage girl with bad skin and bad attitude, but she knows her directions. She makes a map with her fingers on the counter, using her knuckles to show how many lights, how many turns. Under her chaotic armor she is delicate. She's Joan of Arc, just trying to manage the voices.

Soon Marina is in front of the house on Manor Street. The address is something she's had ever since she found it on the Net. She pauses for a moment in front of the house before driving off again. The phone beside her is only a whisper above dead. In a few blocks, she finds a Sheetz, where there is a pay phone. She puts in the quarter and nickel required and is halfway through dialing the number when she changes her mind. Too risky.

She gets back into the car, finishes the Coke, closes her eyes, calms herself, trying to find the role, the voice, the attitude she wants, then starts off again.

FOR A WHILE, SHE FEARS THERE IS NO ONE HOME. THE HOUSE is so still. The windows are all down. She can hear no television or radio. And she has rung the doorbell three times, three long times.

But finally she hears him shuffling toward the door.

The front door opens and he stands there behind the glass storm door, in sweatpants and a polo shirt, squinting against the light, for she is in silhouette. "My God," he says at first, and he almost opens the latch of the glass door. But then he squints. "No solicitations," he says, beginning to close the big door.

"My husband and I came to see you yesterday . . ." she begins, and then she does the rest of her act.

He looks at her for a long time, then opens the glass door.

AT FIRST HE THOUGHT IT WAS EMELIA, COME HERE INSTEAD of flying to Brazil or somewhere south as she'd promised, and his heart leapt with joy and fear all at once. But then the woman was saying, "We came to see you and you weren't there," and he couldn't see her very well because there was a small roof over the porch, which put her in shadow with the bright sunlight behind. She was saying, "You have no idea how we waited for that appointment with you. My husband, well, he's in terrible shape about it, and I thought I would just come to see why you didn't show up."

Still squinting into the light, he thought to open the door a crack, but he didn't. He asked, "How did you find this address?"

"We went to my cousin, who is a lawyer, and he did something on the Internet—he's the one who helped us find you to begin with—and he, I don't know how, but he found some listing that had your home address."

He cursed the Internet, the way it could bring someone to his door, breaking open his Sunday afternoon. He muttered, "Some old listing, then. I used to work out of the house."

"Please. Give me five minutes."

"Where's your husband?" He looked around her to the street, where he saw only an empty, unfamiliar white car.

"He doesn't know I'm here. Would you give me five minutes?" She looked down at his bedroom slippers, suede things with fleece inside, and waited. He saw her looking and felt embarrassed about the slippers, childish things. He pulled the polo shirt down over his sweatpants to make himself as presentable as possible. A large whirring sound came from the side of the house, where the air-conditioning system had switched on, and he wasn't sure he could always hear her completely. She reached for a tissue and wiped sweat from her forehead. Even then for a moment she looked like Emelia—the mass of hair, the dark eyes. But it was probably only that Emelia was on his mind.

He opened the door.

He was hit by a blast of hot air. Nineties outside, sixties

inside; it was quite a difference. "How delicious," she said, moving into the living room. "So cool. I'm parched."

HE CAN'T STOP LOOKING AT HER. HE DOESN'T OFFER HER anything because he wants to keep to the five minutes she asked for, but follows her into the room, noticing her trim legs in clunky sandals.

"Sit down for a minute," he says. "I'm not sure what the mix-up was, but I did get there to the office, only I had not one but three emergency phone calls that morning, and I was a little late. I guess you and your husband left. I missed you."

"We got nervous. We drove to a convenience store and tried to call. Then we came back. We . . . might have just missed you."

"I guess that's what happened." Now she's sitting and he can see her. He studies her face while he tells her, "I may not have a prospective birth mother for you for a while. The girl who was planning to give up her child seems to have changed her mind."

"Oh!" she says. "Oh, no!"

He finds her extraordinarily beautiful, the way the light catches her hair, and the way she looks down at her lap, like a painting.

"I'm sorry," he says, examining her.

"How long a wait do you think we'll have, then?"

"I can't say."

While he searches her face, a part of him is plugged into routine: how to find out, as Emelia would say, that she's a good bet to drive to some motel in the middle of the night on no notice at all with a bag full of money. There are routine things he says at this point with a prospective parent, various openings, but her beauty disturbs him. Besides, he doesn't know what he's doing, what he and Emelia are doing, after yesterday. We're running, Emelia said. She told him to get on a plane, too, and not look back. But that's easy for her to say. He's the one with a house, an office, money in the bank. To run is an admission of guilt and he isn't sure what he'd do after he ran.

She looks up and he gets a jolt again. It isn't only her beauty. He has seen her before.

He recognizes her.

Fear floods his system like an illness come over him. There must be others behind her, in another car. He feels as if his legs will not move, or his arms hoist him out of the chair. "I'm going to get myself something to drink," he says. His voice is frightened and raspy, which makes him furious with himself. "Would you like anything?" He looks toward the front windows while he moves, awkwardly he knows, to the bar cabinet, trying to keep her in sight the whole time.

She refuses, but changes her mind and asks for water. "Water," he mutters. "Water." He does not want to leave the room.

She sees his hand is shaking. He knows she sees that.

Still, he is afraid not to keep up the pretense. He takes out a glass and looks at her again and at the windows again, then wills himself to go into the kitchen. He turns the tap on and off again, that quickly, leaning his forearms heavily on the sink. In a moment he is hurrying back with a dripping and only quarter-full glass of tap water. She sees as he hands her the glass that he knows who she is. She looks as if she is about to cry. He looks out the front windows again.

"My husband isn't with me. Nobody is," she says.

A lie? His hand shook when he handed her the water. It's shaking still.

He knows she is watching him hurry to the dining room cabinet and reach into a drawer.

"Don't," she says. "Please, don't."

How can he not? He doesn't try to hide it. He lets her see his hand, see there's a gun in it.

"Please. I'm not here to hurt you," she says.

His eyes do not leave hers. "Why are you here, then?"

"Please don't hurt me."

"No more lies."

White noise and almost nothing else fills the air. The glass in her hand seems to bother her. She looks for a place to put it down and chooses the floor in front of her chair, looking up the whole time.

"You're from the police. . . . They sent you."

"They don't know I'm here."

A pained attempt at a laugh is all he can manage. He continues to stand at the cabinet, his right arm just behind his thigh, even though she's seen the gun.

She says, "Please don't hurt me. I'll do whatever I can to help you."

He scoffs, to let her know he will not believe anything she says.

"I lied about one thing. My husband and I are not together anymore. He's not in this at all. He doesn't know I called you or that I'm here. Nobody knows, not even the detective who . . . who heads up the case. I asked for applications from a hundred lawyers and agencies and I got a feeling about you."

Manny's eyes go to the windows again.

"Nobody's here."

"Why should I believe you? I don't."

"And I lied about something else. I didn't go to see you yesterday morning. When I told the detectives, one of them, what I'd done, he said they wanted to take you in for questioning."

So she was responsible for it, one lie upon another, responsible for the falling apart of everything. . . . She confuses him. He can't tell truth from beauty.

"And Anton? What happened to him?"

"I don't know," she answers. "You know him, then."

"Nobody is with you?"

She has said "they," and yet according to her, nobody is with her. If he shoots her here, he will have to hide her, and her car, and he will have to run, leave everything behind. His mind ticks off the jobs ahead of him, unfamiliar jobs, Anton's and Joe's kind of work.

"I know about things because I was involved at the beginning—"

"I recognized you."

"And then I fell in love with a detective, the detective who heads up the investigation."

"He doesn't know you're here?"

She shakes her head. "I had the idea you were capable of hurting yourself. I thought that maybe if you did, the whereabouts of the Graves baby would maybe never be known. It's a fault in me, my biggest fault, wanting to fix things, taking on things . . . I don't want to hurt you. I just want to find Justin."

The air conditioner whirs on again. She shivers. She sits forward, her upper body leaning forward toward him. In this position, she looks thin and sinewy, athletic, like a runner at the end of a marathon. "I thought if I could describe to you how their lives are ruined—Karen and Ryan Graves—I thought it might move you to help them get their child back. I thought if I told you their lives are worth nothing now, you might listen. I'm not a policewoman. I'm not turning you in. I'm interested in the baby. Is he alive?"

Manny purses his lips. Surely that guy Dolan sent her. The same sympathetic eyes, just like Dolan has. Long eyelashes, both of them, and eyes you find yourself falling into. And asking questions, the both of them, as if he is just sitting around, eager to spill all kinds of beans.

"If you've killed the child, there's no hope for any of us," she says. "If you've got that murder charge on you . . ."

Manny finds himself saying, "That baby had nothing to do with me. That was somebody else's idea. That half retard—"

And she cuts him off before he can assign further blame. "Joe's idea, I know. I could tell by how they treated him it was Joe's idea. It's not your fault, then, don't you see? Maybe not even Joe's if he's . . . what you say. I don't know. He seemed *different,* very lonely, all alone."

She must be pretending even now, is all he can figure. Because Joe is the one she followed, the one who shot her, and yet she speaks of him as if she knows him, an old friend, a strange relative.

"Did Joe hurt the baby?"

Manny hears Emelia telling him to button up. He is seventeen and she is seven, he is twenty-seven and she is seventeen, and always she has to remind him. Sometimes he can't think how to be quiet. His arm is tired and stiff. A pain snakes its way up his arm to his neck. His clothes are soaked.

Surely they will follow this woman who is trying to make him talk. Surely they are only a few steps behind her. He needs to grab his suitcase and go, to run like Emelia did. In a flash he imagines his office, his underworked secretary, and he feels something like embarrassment about leaving her to come in and find out he is missing. He shakes himself, like a dog. Surely, surely his house is being watched. He shakes himself partly to get out of the dream he's in.

"Do you know if the child is alive?"

". . . last time I heard," he hears himself saying.

She is weeping suddenly, saying how grateful she is for that news. Is she acting? He can't tell, that's for sure, but if she is, she is very, very good. The tears are big and luxurious. They linger, then splash aside. She's better than a movie.

All she wants, she says, all that stands between her and the door, is the name and address of the new parents.

He raises the gun. "Who's the policeman?" he asks. "Dolan?"

"No. His boss."

In the Sunday afternoon, with the sun and humidity topping the charts outside, they sit in the chill and wonder what to do with each other.

■   ■

WRONG, SHE WAS WRONG TO COME. HE WON'T LET GO OF THE gun. It's like the other time. She is pinned to a chair. How much time has gone by? She looks around and finds a small round clock on the bookshelves, up high. Two-fifty, it reads. Is Richard back in the city yet?

Manny sees her eyes go to the clock. He gets up and edges a step at a time forward. Marina closes her eyes and waits for pain and then blackness. How disappointed in her Richard will be. For not letting him protect her. For meddling as if she has a right. For not being able to believe in evil. This is a fault and she knows it. She thinks people will behave with kindness in the end, all the evidence to the contrary. Believes beasts can be tamed. Her eyes open to see Manny slowly making his way back to the chair opposite her. She watches with surprise and a flash of hope as he lowers himself into it. He sits with the gun still in his hand and his hand across his lap.

"I read about you in the paper. Everybody did."

"It seems that way." She reaches for the small purse at the foot of her chair, to the left, balanced by the water glass on her right. "I don't have a gun. I'm getting a notebook and a pen. You can watch me." There's little else but a wallet and some tissues in her bag, so she finds these things easily. She opens the notebook. "If you gave me a name and an address, I'd leave. You'd have time to think what you want to do next."

The surprise is, she can hardly believe it, he speaks a name and street. She looks up. The truth? It's twenty minutes away! Less. His face is a dog's face, large and hanging. It is impossible to read it. Is he lying? She writes the names down, not that she would ever forget them, but because she has the notebook before her and some motions are dictated, automatic.

Moments later, the notebook is back in the purse and she is at his front door.

She doesn't know if he's still sitting or if the gun is pointed at her. Her own movement scares her—opening the wooden door, finding the latch on the storm door. "Thank you," she murmurs, waiting for the bullet, waiting for the end. She would like to run to the car, but she walks instead. She would like to look at him again and ask him not to shoot himself, but she is too afraid to turn.

She is in the Tempo and driving away before she realizes her whole body is shaking. She pulls over to the side of the road. Other drivers blare their horns in frustration. Her sister's old cell phone registers a battery two-thirds full. She dials the Investigative Branch, leaves half a message for Dolan before the phone cuts out.

■   ■

THE BATHROOM, THE BEDROOM, THE OUTSIDE HALLWAY. NO, she is not there. Only the man in the pool of blood, not a shadow of a pulse.

Bit of a surprise in her kitchen, that's for sure. But as he knew, things were about to fall, one card hitting another. The blood is everywhere, a humid swampy puddle, with Vradek, or whatever name he was going by, in the middle of it, surprised and almost crisp in his light clothes. Good-looking guy, clearly a dandy, as Marina had pretty much said. He examines the door, looking for how Vradek or Vladic must have gotten in.

The two men from Surveillance watch him moving about. He has a hand out to still them. They are puzzled. Is he in charge again? Isn't he on vacation? How did he have a key? Shouldn't they be making a phone call?

He is losing the players, and no Baby Graves yet.

The doorbell rings. He buzzes in the paramedics.

His beeper goes off. He recognizes Dolan's number and displays it to the Feds, saying, "Dolan," before he dials back. "I was *just* going to call you," he says before he tells what's on the floor of the Emerson Street apartment.

"She wasn't there?" Dolan asks, no preface to the "she."

"No."

The two federal agents look at each other uncertainly. Christie nods to them to open the door for the paramedics.

In comes the stretcher. And noise.

"The guy was long dead?"

"Not long, but he's for sure dead as a log."

"Shame you had to be there . . ."

"Messy."

"Messy as shit, but we'll figure out something."

Anton's blood makes a large circle. Containing him, framing him.

Marina will have to move again. She won't want to live here. He doesn't want her to.

The anthropologist will have to be contacted, cleaning services called in. Messy, every which way he looks, messy.

The paramedics have broken the circle and are hard at work. The agents are upset. They like to know who is in charge. He is their commander, but he's officially on vacation, so what's—?

One of the agents moves forward, sweating. "This is awkward, Commander."

No hiding what is. He feared for her. He came back. He loves her. That's all there is to it.

Christie holds out his phone, his pager, his gun. "You want?"

The young agent shakes his head.

"Question me later. I'll give you all the time you want. For now—" He doesn't finish. He sees they will let him leave.

■   ■

"I KNOW I SHOULD HAVE CALLED FIRST," SHE SAYS TO THE girl behind the glass door, trying to override surprise and confusion. "I planned to. I was just driving by to see where you lived, and then I couldn't resist stopping and introducing myself." She watches the slightly knock-kneed girl, too young to be an adoptive mother, her hands reaching up to put her hair up in a rubber band.

Manny has lied to her. He has given her the wrong place. This is surely the college-going daughter of rich parents. She feels every part of her go heavy and drop in despair. She cannot pick herself up, she cannot find the heart to go on with—

Then she hears a baby cry. She feels her face go still and almost can't continue speaking. Perhaps this is the place after all, and before her is just a barefoot girl who stands in a large elegant foyer. The floor is tile, cool-looking. The girl wears a dress with straps that keep falling down over her upper arms no matter how many times she slides them up again.

"Is she expecting you?"

"Who?"

"Val?"

"I thought so. Are you a daughter?"

"I'm the nanny."

And now to say the things she has rehearsed, about a certain lawyer giving her the name of another person who might help her through some of her doubts, who might talk to her ... those things are less powerful without the surprise element. And all she wants, really, is to see the kid, to see if it's possibly the truth before she tells the police and the Graveses where the baby is. She will not break their hearts again.

"I'm supposed to interview—" Marina says, and stops. The girl is looking at her curiously, but words won't come. Her performance is not fully prepared, conviction is slipping, ideas won't stay put. Her story changes midsentence. Interview, she has just said. What would be better, a would-be adoptive mother or a journalist?

"For the job?"

Her breathing stops. She can't tell if the girl can see how difficult it is for her to catch a breath. So, another role, a different role—not asking, but being asked. She turns her head aside for a moment and switches scripts, trying to catch up. "Yes," she manages to say. She squints to get a glimpse of whatever is behind the girl, to see if there is movement in the large, beautiful room. Will she know this child when she sees him? A month, no, more. Children are sometimes indistinguishable from each other at those ages to anyone except a caregiver. What does she think she can accomplish here?

"Val's asleep."

"Oh."

"You were supposed to come?"

"Tomorrow."

"Oh, I wondered. She didn't say she'd called anybody. She'll need someone right away."

"It's all right." She is not sure what the job is. "What a beautiful home. It's sort of intimidating."

"I'm sorry, I have to go get him."

The girl does not ask her in. In fact, she leaves the door so fast, Marina wonders if she has gone to call the police. Which, in itself, is almost amusing.

She turns to see that the street, really a private road with only one other house on it, is quiet, not a child bicycling by. Her car in the long driveway is getting a haze of dew from the sprinkler system that mists the lawn. Not so much a noise, but a feeling of movement, draws her back to the doorway, where she sees through the glass door the girl putting a child in a stroller, and that's the part she wants to see, but in the foreground of that picture, a man is striding toward her. He is not very tall. He is angular, a bony-faced, aggressive-looking man. His head tilts forward and his brow is furrowed. His eyes take her in, and there is a change in his expression, confusion. He turns toward the girl. She can hear something like "to interview for my job" and she almost laughs at the absurdity of it, luck, luck on her side, a new role, the nanny, just like that. She stills herself. If she can only hold on long enough to see the child for a few seconds.

The door opens. ". . . can't just come by like this," he's saying angrily. But his eyes flinch when he looks at her as if she keeps being the wrong person, not the person he thinks she's going to be and is willing to yell at.

She cannot see the baby from where she is. She considers saying, "I was so eager . . ." But this will prejudice him against her. Reluctantly, she says, "I'm sorry. Of course, you're right. I'll come back tomorrow." She lingers, smiling an apology.

And still the girl has not wheeled the stroller around.

She has no choice but to turn and walk to her car and leave.

■   ■

THE BUS PULLS SUDDENLY TO THE RIGHT LANE, AND THEN AF-ter a pumping of brakes, pulls right again, into a service plaza. "Ten minutes," the driver says.

People move in slow motion, up and out of their seats, reaching low for garbage, purses, bags. He watches. He wears a baseball cap pulled low and dark glasses. This is a good choice of costume. Many others have the same look. He picks up the bag with the essentials in it, toothbrush and gun, and goes into the Sbarro for something to eat. He gets in line behind an overweight, ragged man in a dirty T-shirt. The man orders a couple of slices of broccoli pizza. When the clerk turns to him, he points at the same pizza, trying not to use his voice because he is afraid it will sound odd. "Broccoli?" the clerk asks irritably. He nods.

When he's slid the tray down the counter and paid, he looks for a table away from everyone else. A small table is empty, over next to the service door. He considers leaving everything behind, bag of clothes in the hold of the bus, unused portion of ticket, and heading off on foot, or hitching, after he's eaten his broccoli pizza. He has al-ready lost so much, it seems. Not that he had much more than a few shirts. Well, the car, of course. And he lost peo-ple. He has lost all the people he worked with; he's com-pletely without contacts, leads.

And he's lost Marina's house. That suddenly seems the main thing. The best place he ever stayed in his life, a whole month, and now he will never have that again. He pictures the clean shower curtain, with flowers on it, daisies. And a painting of daisies in the basement, un-framed, which maybe Marina did or maybe somebody gave her as a gift, not good enough for the upstairs. The one little red couch in the second-floor room that he liked to sit in and do nothing at ten in the evening. Now he will have to stay in fleabags again to make his money stretch. Depending. Depending on what he can *take*, for it's back to that now.

The car was worth a little money, but a red car is easier to trace than a man with a small tote bag and a baseball cap, so he let it go. When they find it in the garage, they will figure everything out and look for him. Maybe they have found it already and are looking now. He glances at his watch. It's after three in the afternoon. Perhaps they're at the house now, examining the car.

He holds up the large cup of iced tea and sees it's still half-full. Something about this determines that he will get back on the bus, carrying it with him. Don't get dehydrated, he thinks, trying to remember where he heard people talking about that. It'll be a while before they find him.

They. Men in crew cuts who carry briefcases, cops in uniform with fleshy frightened faces and guns drawn. All kinds of law enforcement people gathered or gathering to press him toward anonymity. Three-thirty. Worst-case scenario, someone has found the body and the car already and cops are posted at the bus stations. Best-case scenario, both car and man are sleeping peacefully where he left them.

A few more hours on the bus, he decides, then a stop for a few days in whatever town the bus ends up in at six-thirty, seven o'clock tonight. He's bought a ticket to Albuquerque, but he doesn't have to use it.

A number of the other passengers look like deadbeats, much worse than he looks. Sometimes he thinks of his aunt saying "scum of the earth." She hated scum, but they were scum. He thought that was interesting. "We're cleanup men," Vol used to say. "Society's janitors." One way to look at it.

Stealing the baby was different, the only really bad thing he ever did. And he only did that because Emelia had screamed at him and called him every name she could think of and told him he was responsible for the other one's death and he had to make good on it, get her a kid. The screaming was awful and he went to putty. Then Vol drove her back to New York, and he did something.

When he gets outside again, it's raining, only a bit, a drizzle. It makes the atmosphere feel soft and safe. He climbs on the bus in time to hear the man in the dirty T-shirt ask the driver what time they pull into Kansas City. "Close to four in the morning," the driver says. He wonders if he stayed on the bus all that time if he could maybe get some sleep and then have Kansas City to roam around in.

They will never find him.

Sometimes, lying in Marina's bed, it would be just a bit of sheet or a pillow, but for a moment he smelled the clean soapy smell of her and imagined her hand caressing his face.

■ ■

INSIDE THE TEMPO THE HEAT IS AWFUL. SHE TURNS ON THE ignition so the air-conditioning can crank up again. She is only a hundred yards or so from the house where Justin might be, but hopefully she is just far enough around the curve of the road that the man and his wife and the nanny can't see her car from their windows or hear it running. Ahead of her is a long curved driveway with sculpted hedges on either side, and at the end of the driveway is another house, the only other house on this road. It looks still. The owners are on a vacation, hopefully, or an afternoon excursion.

She cannot make herself go; she wants to be there in case the nanny takes her walk. She wants to see for herself.

She should have found a way, an excuse, to talk to the mother.

But if she's helped, if this is it . . . then she has done what she wanted.

She sits watching the house for movement.

She must not tempt him. If it happens, it must happen over time, with this case behind them, solved. If it's love, there must be no forcing, only the usual "hills and valleys," he would say, or "ups and downs," of a relationship. The way he talks. No embarrassment at summoning the well-used phrase.

They are un-like. Michael and she are more like. What will Richard do when he comes to see her in a play—*The White Devil* or some other Jacobean tragedy? Squint at the stage and wonder why?

All she had ever wanted was to avoid the violence. First running to Michael. And now. A trick the gods play. Just where you think there *isn't* violence, that's probably where it is. Her life is all violence now, everything about Richard is violence, the gun he carries only a reminder. There is a kind of violence in her chest.

She's stiff from the way she's turned in her seat to look at the house. No activity. Suddenly she feels dizzy.

She puts a hand to her head. Even though she feels feverish, she's probably not. It's only that it's so hot out. She must get something to drink, because the heat is making her light-headed. Reluctantly—and she examines her reluctance with dismay, with a disappointment in herself—she reaches for the cell phone. The battery registers full. She punches in the numbers of the Investigative Branch, wondering if the phone will hold.

"Commander Christie," she's told by the receptionist, "is on vacation. And Dolan's in the field."

"Take this number," she says. "Tell Detective Dolan to call. That it's important."

She hangs up and consults a small card in her wallet. Does she have a number for Dolan's pager? She doesn't have it. He will call her.

And why is she at the end of the block, sitting in the heat, he will want to know when he finally gets in touch.

She will answer, So they don't leave the house with the baby, so they don't leave town without anyone knowing, so I can do something. She is ridiculous. What could she do if that man she just met, Justin's new father, all hauteur, zoomed down the street in a Mercedes or whatever he drives, right past her; what could she do? Follow him? Even if she managed to glimpse a child in the car?

As if, just waiting there at the corner, she is helping.

Somebody has to keep watch.

She dials Richard's number. The phone rings for a long time with no answer.

A patch of red and purple and then the handle of a stroller, and then the nanny behind a large flowering bush. Breathing is impossible.

■ ■

THE FRONT DOOR STICKS FROM THE HEAT AND THE NEW DRIZzle. It smells closed-off, hot. He wants to call out to her, in case she's thrown out all advice and come here, but he knows not to make a sound. He draws his gun and looks carefully at the living room, backs up to slide into the kitchen. He doesn't know her. He doesn't know what she will do in any given situation. When he gets to the kitchen, Christie inadvertently lets out a sound.

Has she been here after all? Food. Crumbs, fresh. He opens the refrigerator. More. Something is wrong. Maybe not Marina, but Michael. That's it. The place doesn't have her care, the way packages are shoved into the refrigerator, the vegetables not in the bin.

Now he moves fast. Three-thirty in the afternoon and he is up the stairs, afraid of everything he might find. The shower is wet. The bed is made, the window-blinds down. Yet he smells something, soap or shampoo. He opens the toilet. The water level is full. There is not the yellow ring or the sour smell of the dried-out, unused toilet. He proceeds carefully to the attic, where the heat chokes him, to the spare room, where there is a desk with a folder of medical bills on top. It looks as if she's been working here.

He begins to understand. Cursing himself, he hurries to the basement, gun drawn, where he sees more of the puzzle. There is unevaporated water in the washing machine and on the floor of the laundry area. Another smell. Detergent or bleach. Someone has recently lived here.

He slowly marvels at the ways people find to live, slowly gathers conviction that it was either Michael or Joe here at the house, playing the bachelor role. By the time he reaches the garage, breaks in and sees the red car with its bad paint job, Christie has his answer and a kind of respect for the odd man who has been and gone, just trying to live.

■   ■

"WHAT NANNY?" VALERIE ASKS.

"The one who's supposed to come tomorrow?" her husband says.

Valerie does not know what he is talking about or why he is talking so fast or who the man is at the door, the man with the kind, beautiful eyes, who is asking about the baby.

The man shows a badge to her and tells her his name is Dolan.

Her husband turns to Dolan and says, "Let's get moving and find the girl, then."

"But she only went for a walk!" Valerie blurts. "Katie's okay. I don't have any idea who this other person is you're talking about."

"I'm getting real scared," her husband tells her, but his eyes are making some message different from the one he's speaking. "Someone was here an hour ago. She said she had an interview with you. She said she had an appointment for a nanny job. . . ."

"Maybe Katie told her to come," Valerie says. "Maybe Katie arranged it. Katie is going to quit."

Her husband is surprised, she can see that. She hasn't broken the news about Katie until now. She watches him working to separate one fact from another.

"Something is going on," he says. "Something's funny." He makes faces at her again and starts for the door. She can't tell what her husband's messages are, she can't read him, but she's glad finally that he's not so sure of everything.

Detective Dolan raises his hands to slow her husband down. He says, "Let me do what I have to do. This is serious." The detective looks to Val as if she's on his side and will help him.

"Steve. Wait," she says. Her husband is halfway out the door, but he turns to her, still anxious.

Dolan is asking, "Is there a usual place Katie goes for a walk?"

"Just around. It's all grounds around here. Like a park."

Dolan starts out the door. "All right, then. Can't be too hard."

"I'm coming with you," her husband announces to the detective.

Dolan does not tell Steve not to follow, but it's clear he doesn't want him around. He puts a hand up and goes to his car, once more appealing, with a quick look, to Val.

"What's it about?" she says, going outside after them and grabbing on to Steve's hand.

■ ■

WHEN HE TURNED ON HIS PHONE IN THE CAR, IT RANG IMMEdiately. It was Dolan saying, "You want a piece of this, you better get out to Sewickley quick." Christie drove away from Pine Street even before he heard the rest, the address. Dolan said, "I'm just right now making circles around the neighborhood. It's like a woodsy section. I think the kid is here somewhere."

"How—? How can that be?"

"Your Marina left an address for me. Said she got it from Manny LaPaglia. Do I argue with somebody at a time like that or do I run over here? I run," Dolan finishes. "I'll let the Feds have Manny."

"Marina's there?"

"Somewhere. I haven't seen her. There's a couple out here, supposedly parents—well, we're definitely going to be grilling them, but I figure that can wait. This might be the baby. *Might* be."

"Where are you exactly?" Christie asks. Dolan gives him the name of the lane he has turned onto.

Richard is driving the family van sixty, seventy miles an hour down Ohio River Boulevard and he doesn't have a set of flashers. What he understands is that everything is happening all at once. And it's as if he hears Marina's voice behind it, saying, All else can wait. Get the child first. Everything else can wait, everything.

"This is a good lead?"

"My best guess is—they say the nanny just went for a walk—I might be like a hundred yards from the Graves kid," Dolan tells his friend. "I'm looking around bushes. Where you been since you found what's-his-name?"

"I checked out her house, her original house, and the guy Joe's been there, a hundred to one, all along. Don't ask me how Surveillance missed it. He's gone now. You'll have to call Forensics in. What's happening?"

"Couple ran back for their car. They're following me now."

"I've got to be like two miles from you," Christie says. "Aren't cell phones great? I love cell phones."

He can hear Dolan's radio in the background, and Dolan say to Terrence, "I'm giving you an address. Get over to LaPaglia's house as fast as you can. Take enough men with you. Check the airport. Lawyer's either dead by now or he's long gone. He talked to Marina Benedict."

Terrence is cursing and it comes over the radio and through the cell phone and to Christie. "How did this happen without anybody telling us?" Dolan says, "Trust me. It happened so fast I couldn't tell you." And Christie can hear the Feds ask irritably, "Got any idea where Marina Benedict is now?"

"In fact, I know exactly where she is," Dolan is saying. "Exactly!" Then it's impossible to tell who Dolan is talking to: "Oh, baby, you're going to like how this is turning out!" he yelped. " 'Cause it's happening, finally. It's all coming together right now. Yeah, I see her. She's just standing talking to this other girl. Now she's stooping down and touching the kid in the stroller. I'm like ten feet away now. I'm telling you. It's coming out right. How do I know? How do I know? The way she's crying."

■ ■

FOR GOING AGAINST ORDERS, CHRISTIE IS SUSPENDED FOR three months and he has to see a counselor. Dolan gets quite a few honors. Dolan gets the newspaper interviews.

Manny LaPaglia tried to shoot himself, but he couldn't bring himself to do it, and so he was sitting in his house, still holding his gun, when the Feds came for him. He gave himself up but was unable to say where his sister was. He seemed truly not to know.

She is on the most-wanted list, the only woman on the list.

New York police found two of the three Russian girls. The girls did not want to say much about Emelia. When pressed, they said she was good to them in terms of food and daily comforts. They had no idea why she dumped the three of them on the street in three different places so suddenly one day.

Joe is on all the bulletins. Agents are hunting for him everywhere, filling in the blanks. They found Buddy Kinder after they discovered the red car. He told them he had put a guy up but he thought his name was something else, Dan Quayle or something close to it. He said he'd never seen the news, but Dan ... no, Henry, now he remembers, Henry, was a pretty nice guy so far as he could tell.

In Manny's confession, which fits except for the denials about his sister, he told them the kidnapping of the Graves kid was Joe's idea and that when he gave the baby up for adoption, he didn't know about the kidnapping. Nobody believes this part of Manny's statement, but he sticks by it so passionately, it captures Dolan's thoughtful attention.

Long before Richard is back on the force, the search for Joe Prowser and Emelia Rodriguez is firmly on the desks of the FBI. The task force is dissolved, and he has nothing to do with any of it anymore. Not officially.

He was the one who took the baby back to his parents. He and Marina. Dolan has a big heart and he let it be that way, which was the right way, after all. Christie got to see their faces. Marina, Justin, the parents. He'll never forget their faces. He figures he got the best part of the deal in the end.

■　　■

SHE HAS KNOWN IT WOULD COME TO THIS, ALL ALONG, ALmost from the beginning. No, from before the beginning. At another beginning, the beginning of a thought.

She is in her own house again, and it feels wrong, not like any place she ever lived. It's clean, very clean now, no evidence of Joe, but still, he hovers, his spirit hovers, as so much does here, and that's why she's moving sometime soon. Some of the boxes are packed already, but even the things in the boxes don't feel like hers anymore. As she can, she will replace pot holders, clothes, CDs, everything.

Another clean start, another role.

Stands, arms folded, looking at it all.

She hears a noise and her heart goes crazy.

She has known it would come to this moment all along, her standing at the front door, scared, him getting out of the car, scared and looking up at her, naked emotion on his face, then next, something like anger, something like, What have I let her do to me? Then he answers himself. To see him like that, with those thoughts arguing within him, moves her. Then him going to the back door of the car, letting out the two of them, and them, the way they clamber out, suspicious, sullen, and fearful. Expectant, too. Wondering. She is. They are. Violence being let in, invited in, life unraveling without plan, her ugly, selfish, terrible self using and being used. No explaining it to anyone. Who cares what they think? It makes no sense, except some sort of pure velocity. Wonderful.

ABOUT THE AUTHOR

KATHLEEN GEORGE, a director and theater professor at the University of Pittsburgh, is also
the author of *The Man in the Buick*, a collection
of stories. Her fiction has appeared in many
publications, including *North American Review*
and *Mademoiselle*. *Taken* is her first novel.